Praise for Kate Wilhelm

"Her carefully crafted approach to the legal thriller continues to separate Wilhelm from the competition."
—*Publishers Weekly* on *No Defense*

"Sensitive, thought-provoking, and involving, *Death Qualified* is an unqualified success."
—*Los Angeles Times Book Review*

"Wilhelm is a masterful storyteller whose novels have just the right blend of solid plot, compelling mystery, and great courtroom drama."
—*Library Journal*

"Brilliantly plotted, lyrically written, alluring and magical…Wilhelm's story is a wrenching masterpiece about love, loyalty, and lies."
—*Booklist* on *The Good Children*

"Wilhelm demonstrates once again her sure understanding of human nature and her ability to wring more suspense from emotional violence than the physical variety."
—*San Diego Union-Tribune* on *The Deepest Water*

"One of the masters of psychological fiction in America."
—*San Francisco Chronicle*

"Wilhelm's skill in spinning out endless complications while keeping every subplot perfectly clear makes this legal thriller her best in years."
—*Kirkus Reviews* on *Defense for the Devil*

KATE WILHELM

THE
UNBIDDEN
TRUTH

ISBN 0-7783-2204-1

THE UNBIDDEN TRUTH

Copyright © 2004 by Kate Wilhelm.

www.MIRABooks.com

Printed in U.S.A.

Call home the child, whose credulous
        first hours
Burn at the heart of living, and surprise
The better reason with unbidden truth.
                —David McCord
                    "A Bucket of Bees"

Part One

1

It was a lazy Friday afternoon, the kind of day that leads thoughts to hammocks and shade trees. Barbara Holloway stifled a yawn as she escorted her last client of the day at Martin's Restaurant to the door. August was always slow, and she had taken notes of four clients' complaints about neighbors, evil debt collectors, recalcitrant landlords. She had caught up with Internet news, had her terrorist anxiety renewed, answered e-mails and was wishing that she had a shade tree and a hammock. She was looking forward to a dinner with friends and then a movie.

Now it was time to take down her Barbara Is In sign. "Don't worry," she said. "Guys like that turn into pussycats when authority hits them in the head. Sometimes the law can carry more punch than a bat." Her client, a thin young woman of twenty-one, with a three-year-old child and a one-year-old, looked relieved.

When Barbara opened the door she was surprised to see another woman standing by the steps. And she was not the sort of client who usually turned up at Martin's. Her hair was gray and beautifully styled, short with a bit of wave; her skin was lovely and unwrinkled. About sixty, trim, and well-dressed in a cream-colored linen skirt and silk shirt, wearing a gold chain and small gold earrings, she looked as if she could be the owner of the black Saab parked at the curb. It was as out of place here as she was. Martin had renovated a simple house, had torn down interior walls to make a dining room with six tables and six booths, and he cooked some of the best food to be found in Eugene, but Barbara doubted that the woman on the doorstep had ever driven through this neighborhood, much less considered eating here.

"Ms. Holloway, may I have a few minutes?" the woman asked.

It was ten minutes before five, and at five-thirty Martin liked to have the restaurant empty, in order for him and his wife Binnie to set the tables.

"Of course," Barbara said, moving aside. She took down her sign and motioned toward her table where Martin was picking up the carafe and cups. He paused a moment.

"Can I bring you something? Coffee, wine?"

Martin was big enough to fill a doorway and as black as night. A white beret was striking in contrast; it seemed to glow. And he never offered wine to her clients. He had sized up this woman as rapidly as Barbara had done.

"No, thanks," the woman said, seating herself.

Then, as Martin walked back to the kitchen, she turned to Barbara. "I know it's late and I'll be as succinct as I can. My name is Louise Braniff. I'm in the music department at the

U of O, and I give private piano lessons to a few students. Also, I'm a member of a society of women. We call ourselves the Crones' Club, but officially we're the Benevolent Ladies Club. We sponsor various causes that we consider worthy. Sometimes surgery, sometimes a scholarship, or helping someone get a start in business, various things. All directed at girls or women. We want to retain you."

"To do what?"

"Defend Carol Frederick, who is accused of murdering Joe Wenzel."

Barbara studied her more closely. "Murder suspect comes under your definition of worthy cause? I think you'd better start a bit further back."

"Of course. How we choose our recipients is a starting place, I imagine. When one of us learns of a particular instance where a gift of cash would change a life, we meet and discuss it and investigate the person we're considering, and if we all agree, then one of us is chosen to make the proper arrangements. In this instance we decided that I should approach you since I was the one who proposed helping Carol Frederick originally."

She paused and gazed past Barbara as if gathering her thoughts, then continued. "One of my associates at the university told me about a young woman who was playing piano at a lounge here in town and insisted that I go hear her. Another member of our group and I went together. We had dinner in the adjoining restaurant and then sat in the lounge for most of one evening listening. She is a first-class pianist, gifted but untutored. She needs a bit of technical help. We took it up at our meeting and the other members arranged to go hear her play, and then we voted to assist her. What we proposed was to make it possible for her to go to Hamburg and study under the tutelage of Gustav Bremer. He is the master, and after a year under his guidance she could become a world-class pianist. I am convinced of that. I was chosen to make the arrangements, but before anything could be done, someone killed Joe Wenzel, and the following week, last week, she was arrested."

"Do you know her, anything about her? Or him? Wenzel?"

"No. None of us know her. Apparently she has been here in Eugene for no more than five or six weeks. I don't think any of our group ever met Joe Wenzel. I don't know whether she killed him, but that's beside the point. She needs the best defense possible and we agreed that you could provide it, not a public defender, who is overworked and understaffed. She, of course, has no money."

As Barbara continued to regard her thoughtfully, Louise Braniff opened her purse, withdrew a check and placed it on the table. "If you agree, there are certain conditions," she said.

"I thought there might be."

Louise Braniff nodded. "First, you won't try to find out who else is in our club. We prefer to remain anonymous. For tax purposes you are to give the Benevolent Ladies Club as the payer for your services. I am the only one you will ever contact, and then only if the retainer is not sufficient to cover your expenses and your fee. We understand that if she accepts a plea bargain, the expenses will be minimal, but if she continues to plead innocent and there is a full trial, the expenses will be much higher. In that case you will notify me and I will provide another cashier's check for whatever amount you name. And finally, Carol Frederick must never be told who her benefactors were, only that a group of people put together a defense fund for her."

"I see," Barbara said, although she didn't. "Why the secrecy? Why did you come here instead of using my real office? I assume you investigated me and know that I have an office."

"Yes, we know about your office. And some of us have followed your career for the past few years. We know about you. But my name is never to be associated with this any more than the names of any other members of our group. Not in your records, not in your files, nowhere. The only client you will have is Carol Frederick, and the Benevolent Ladies Club will be financially responsible. You won't report to me or anyone else except your client. We shall follow the case as it is reported in the newspapers, that's all."

Barbara glanced at the check then. Twenty-five thousand dollars. "I have to think about this," she said. "You must know how irregular it is, and for all I know you killed Joe Wenzel yourself, and in a fit of conscience you're trying to make amends to a wrongly accused woman." She spread her hands. "You do see my point."

"I do." Louise Braniff smiled. "And it's well taken. I have permission to give you one name for reference. Judge Barry Longner. But I warn you, that's all he will admit. We exist, and we help girls and women. You'll want my card, my address and phone number so you can verify my identity." She took a card from her purse and put it on the check.

"It will be her decision," Barbara said. "If she says no thanks, then what?"

"Send the check to that address, registered mail. That's all. If it isn't returned, we'll assume you've accepted our proposal and that you're working on this." She pushed back her chair. "But first, your word that you accept the conditions I outlined."

"No written receipt? No lawyer-client agreement? Not even made out to the Benevolent Ladies Club?"

"Just your word," Louise Braniff said. Her expression had remained almost bland, neutral, as if she were interested but not involved in the matter and now, for the first time, she leaned forward and watched Barbara intently.

After a moment Barbara nodded. "If she agrees and becomes my client, I'll honor your conditions."

Louise Braniff stood up, her expression once more that of an interested bystander. "Thank you, Ms. Holloway. Don't bother to see me out." She turned and walked to the door and left as Barbara remained by the table watching her.

Barbara sat down again wondering what Louise Braniff's stake in this case could possibly be when Martin came from the kitchen carrying two glasses of pale wine.

Barbara stirred herself. "Thanks, Martin, but she's gone."

"I know. I saw her leave. That's one classy lady. This is for you, and this one's for me. You look like you've walked into quicksand and haven't got a clue about how to get out."

Barbara took the glass he offered and sipped a very good chardonnay. "Martin, you're not only the world's greatest chef, you're also a very perceptive mind reader. That's exactly how I feel, as if I've blundered into quicksand."

"It's Dad's fault," she muttered later, sitting in her nice office, which Louise Braniff had bypassed. On returning to the office, she had learned that quite sensibly Shelley, her colleague, had left shortly after five, while Maria Velasquez, secretary to both of them, had pretended to be busy until Barbara got back. She seldom left until Barbara ordered her out.

After making notes about the clients who had consulted her

in Martin's Restaurant and putting the check in her safe, Barbara sat at her desk thinking about Louise Braniff. Backtracking, she found the cause for her unease: For a moment she had seen past the neutral exterior on Louise Braniff's face to the intensity of her gaze, an almost rigid stiffness in her posture.

She would research Braniff and Wenzel, of course, but later. Now she mused about her conclusion that her acceptance of a case she believed to be hopeless was her father's fault.

First, in March his book on the art of cross-examination, years in the making, had finally been published. And he had thrown a party to celebrate. She had been his hostess. She recalled the expression on his face when she took off her coat and revealed her costume for the event: a long black velvet skirt, silky white cashmere sweater and the lovely necklace he had given her for Christmas. Sapphires and amethysts, it had been her mother's. For a moment he had gazed at her saying nothing, then embraced her, and she murmured, "She would have been so proud." Drawing back, he had nodded. "She would have been," he agreed, and she understood that his book was not uppermost in his mind.

Then the guests had started arriving, and among them had been Darren Halvord. She stared at him. "What are you doing here?"

"Invited," he said with a grin. "I called to congratulate your dad, and he invited me to his party. Do I get to come in?"

All evening, every time she glanced around, he had been there, chatting with a judge, in conversation with an attorney, laughing with Alex and Shelley, uncorking more wine, bringing in more hors d'oeuvres, talking seriously with Frank in the kitchen.

For the next months it had seemed to her that every time

she turned around Darren was there, invited, coincidence, whatever, and she had realized with indignation that her father was scheming, playing matchmaker, for God's sake! And with Darren! He had set off her anger button the first time they met, and almost every time afterward. A more arrogant, self-satisfied man she could not imagine.

The last time, only two weeks ago, Darren and his son Todd had appeared for dinner at Frank's house on Sunday, the day Barbara always had dinner there. After the meal she and Darren volunteered to clean up the kitchen.

"What are you afraid of?" Darren asked.

"Cobras, black widow spiders, ravenous tigers, homicidal maniacs wielding axes."

"And?"

"That's it," she snapped.

"Ah," he said, handing her another plate to go into the dishwasher.

A day or two later Will Thaxton had called, inviting her to dinner and to hear a new sensational musician. Theirs had been a comfortable, easygoing relationship, no questions asked, no demands, good dancing, good sex, never an argument, her anger button untouched. Although she had decided that it was over, she had accepted. Why not pick up where they had left off? Make it more than clear that she had no interest in Darren Halvord?

Will was always up on any jazz group playing in town, any group touring, any new genius waiting to be discovered. She was surprised that Saturday night when he drove to a motel restaurant not far from the interstate, one of many motels on the strip along with fast-food eateries, gas stations, myriad brightly lighted tourist-oriented outlets.

This restaurant was called the Cascadia, and apparently it catered to first-class travelers. The restaurant had white table-cloths, waiters in black, an impressive menu, and the food was better than just passable. In the background, piano music played, the kind of easy-listening nostalgia-arousing melodies that tended to be soothing even when only vaguely recognizable. Throughout dinner Will talked about a new client in the mocking tone he occasionally used to describe his clients, and she half listened.

She didn't know when the music stopped, but it was not there when Will beckoned the waiter and murmured, "We have a table reserved in the lounge. We'll have coffee and cognac in there."

The waiter led them to a bistro table and a minute later brought coffee and oversize goblets with cognac. Barbara swirled hers and watched the way the liqueur crawled back down, expecting now to hear the phenomenal jazz discovery. Instead, she was jolted when the piano player started again, this time with the passionate, assertive opening of *Rhapsody In Blue*. She had not seen the pianist return, and her view of the woman playing was obscured by a fishbowl on the piano with a few bills in it. Without a pause the music changed, became sweet and dreamy, "The Blue Danube." Again a change without a transition, and it was "Dancing in the Dark." From there it dissolved into "Greensleeves," into something she did not recognize, then Mahler, Chopin, something she did not know. The lounge had gone silent, no murmuring voices, or clinking of glasses, just the music with one piece dissolving, flowing into another with apparently effortless ease. The poignant strains of "Where Have All the Flowers Gone?" a lilting and gay "Farmer in the Dell," Offenbach's "Barcarole," a bit of Mozart. She stopped trying to identify the pieces that came and went seamlessly, and then there were single notes, and she heard the words in her head that went with them. *When will they ever learn?*

There was silence for a minute when the last note sounded; someone began to applaud, and then everyone applauded wildly. The pianist stood up, bowed her head and swiftly walked away out of sight through a doorway behind the bar.

"My God!" Barbara whispered.

"Didn't I tell you? Phenomenal, isn't she?"

Her coffee had grown cold, and she no longer wanted the cognac. Will had finished his. "She'll be back in twenty minutes or so," he said. "But not like that. More easy-listening stuff. Want to leave now?"

Will had talked about the pianist all the way back to her apartment until she had wanted to gag him. "Probably an addict, those long sleeves are hiding needle marks, or maybe she's shacked up with a guy who beats her and she's hiding bruises. She could have become a concert pianist, but instead she's playing in a bar in a two-bit town. Probably a hooker. She'll rake in the tips, you bet she will. And move on."

At her door she had not asked him in, to their mutual surprise.

Now that woman was her client, although she had yet to meet her. And it was Frank's fault, she said to herself, getting back to her starting point. If he hadn't tried to push her into Darren's arms, she would not have gone out with Will, she would not have gone to that lounge and heard Carol Frederick play, and if she had not heard her play, she doubted that she would have taken the case. It appeared to be open and shut.

Carol Frederick was a drifter with no permanent address, no known family, no real friends in Eugene. According to the newspaper, and the leaks providentially dropped by the D.A.'s office, she had been pursued for weeks by Joe Wenzel, the owner of the motel and had avoided him, or lured him on, depending on how one looked at it. The night of his death she was seen talking with him in the parking lot after she quit work, arguing with him? Fighting with him? She had been seen entering his room.

The next day Joe Wenzel's body was discovered on the bedroom floor of his suite in the motel. He was wearing a lightweight summer robe, nothing else. Carol Frederick's hairs were on his coat, her fingerprints on a glass in the suite.

Tried and convicted by leaks, Barbara thought then. But any public defender, with a minimum of bargaining, would get her off with no more than involuntary manslaughter. And that would result in prison. Barbara shuddered to think of that magical piano player in prison, but she doubted very much if she or anyone else could do any better for her than that.

2

At eleven the next morning Barbara was in a small meeting room in the county jail waiting for Carol Frederick to be delivered to her. The room was dismal, with a metal table bolted to the floor, two wooden chairs and a harsh overhead fluorescent light that turned skin tones to a shade somewhere between yellow and avocado-green, and made any lipstick a garish purple. The door opened and a guard ushered Carol into the room.

"Hi, I'm Barbara Holloway," she said, standing by the table. "Can we talk a few minutes?"

Carol Frederick was not pretty in any conventional way, but striking looking. Long, straight black hair in a ponytail, dark blue eyes, heavy eyebrows straight across, and facial bones that suggested some Native American in her genealogy. She regarded Barbara with suspicion and remained standing by the door. "Why? I don't know you. How do you rate a private room?"

"I told them I'm your new defense attorney." She pointed to her briefcase, which had been searched. "My credentials," she said with a smile. "Of course, that can change if you kick me out, but as it stands now, that's why."

"What happened to the one they already gave me? Quit already?"

"Nope." Barbara pulled out a chair and sat down, motioning Carol toward the other chair. She approached it warily as if suspecting a trap. "It seems that you've become the cause for a group of people who donate money for various worthy causes. They want to pay for your defense. I'm not connected to the government in any way. I'm in private practice. They hired me to represent you if you'll have me."

Carol perched on her chair as upright as a person could be, and now drew back and crossed her arms over her chest, her suspicion even more pronounced in her expression of skepticism. "What's in it for them?"

"Not a damn thing that I can see," Barbara said. She repeated some of what Louise Braniff had told her, then spread her hands. "I'm sworn to secrecy concerning your benefactors. I have a cashier's check for a retainer, and I'm not to report back to them along the way, just get in touch with the spokeswoman if I need more money."

"I don't believe it," Carol said. "No one hands out money for a stranger."

"They apparently do, and they did. It's up to you if we go on from here. You don't have to decide this minute. Do you know anyone you can ask about me, confirm that at least I'm legitimate?"

Kate Wilhelm

Carol shook her head, then contradicted the gesture. "Yes, maybe I do. If I can trust the matron who brought me here. She said you're okay. I should grab you if I can. But you listen to me. If you're just going to try to talk me into taking what they're offering, the way Bill Asshole is, forget it. Spend the money on a cruise or something."

Barbara grinned, remembering the time she had called Bill Spassero the same thing, only to be rebuked by her father. "He's a pretty good attorney, actually, just overworked. What are they offering? What did they say when they questioned you?"

"At first, it was all sympathy. They said they understood. The creep dragged me into his room and locked the door and when the party got too rough, I shot him and took off. Self-defense, what any girl would have done, maybe get off altogether, or else involuntary manslaughter, minimum sentence. They said they were on my side, make it easier on everyone if I just admitted it up front and be done with it." She pushed back her chair, ready to stand. "I said I wanted a lawyer and they said what for, no problem with self-defense, no lawyer needed. Like that. Two, three hours like that. Only problem is that it's a lie, and I wouldn't admit to anything and I just quit talking. They charged me with second-degree murder. Some sympathy. So if that's your line, forget it."

"As I said, it's up to you. And that's not my line. I don't have a line since I haven't heard your side. Want me to leave now?"

"Wait," Carol said. "Why did you agree to do this?"

Barbara studied her for a moment, then said, "Because I heard you play."

Her words seemed to strip the tough veneer off Carol. She slumped in her chair, looking very young and vulnerable for a second, and very frightened. She straightened again and her expression tightened. "So what now? What do you do? What do I do?"

"This is just a preliminary, get-acquainted meeting. There are certain formalities I have to see to on Monday, and after that we'll be spending a lot of time together. I'm Barbara, by the way."

The young woman hesitated, then said, "Carrie. I go by Carrie."

"Okay. For now, just tell me what happened that night. Your side of it."

"I don't have a side," Carrie said almost sullenly. "I quit work at midnight and went out to my car, and the creep was waiting for me on the walk by his door. He grabbed my arm, and I shook him off and kept going. He was drunk, talking crazy. He followed me and when I got to my car he tried to hold the door open, but I closed and locked it and took off. I went to the apartment where I lived and went to bed. That's what I told the detectives, all I could tell them, because it's all I know about it."

"Okay," Barbara said. "Had you known him before? Ever been to his suite at the motel? Had drinks with him? Anything at all?"

"No. He was a slob, a fat and ugly slob. I didn't know who he was until I complained to Mark—he's the manager, Mark Ormsby—and he told me the creep owned the place and to try to get along with him. I never even saw him until a couple or three weeks before he was shot. He began hanging around at night, watching me, brushing me in passing, touching my hair, like that, and I complained to Mark. I told him I'd quit if the slob didn't lay off, and that's when he told me to cool it, that he'd talk to him."

"Did he?"

"I don't know. If he did, it didn't do any good."

"You could have filed a harassment complaint."

"Yeah, right. Against the owner. Sure I could."

"But you didn't quit. Why not?"

That strange vulnerable look crossed her face again as she gazed past Barbara and said softly, "I wanted to play the piano."

Whatever reasons Barbara might have assumed, good tips, or good hours, leaving her free during weekdays, to play the piano had not been among them.

"Okay," she said. "We have a few details to work out." She opened her briefcase and brought out a folder with the client-attorney agreement and a steno pad. "Don't bother with that right now," she said. "Read it overnight, and we'll sign it on Monday after I clear things with the Public Defenders' office. Also, make notes of anything that might be of help, anything at all that you noticed at the motel, tension between Wenzel and others, things of that sort. What he was saying to you that night. Even if it seems inconsequential, it might be something we can follow up on…." She finished with her instructions, leaned back and said, "Now, what do you want me to bring you, or send over?"

"Like what?"

"Personal items, books, your favorite slippers, things like that. Nothing expensive. You don't want to get robbed here."

"My sheet music from the lounge," Carrie said after a moment. "Can I have that?"

Surprised again, Barbara nodded. "Let's make a list. Where is your stuff, by the way? Your car, clothes?"

"In the apartment. The car's parked at the curb. I have a couple of boxes, two suitcases…. They took my keys."

"I'll get them back. I'll collect your belongings and keep them safe for you." She got the address of the apartment Carrie had shared with Delia Rosen.

"You'd better write a note to your friend," she said then. "Give me permission to pick up your things. And another one for the lounge."

"Delia isn't a friend. Just someone I met in Las Vegas. She might have tossed my stuff out already to make space for a new roommate. He, Bill Asshole, didn't offer to do anything about that."

"Well, as I said, he's overworked. He would have in time."

Carrie shook her head. "No. It's part of the pressure to make me take their offer. He thinks I did it."

Barbara did not argue the point. Carrie might even be right, she knew, recalling Will Thaxton's easy assessment of her: addict, abused, on the make. Besides, Bill Spassero had seen the evidence gathered by the investigators.

Delia Rosen's apartment was on the second floor of one of the fine residential houses that had been converted to apartments to accommodate the university students, in walking distance to the school and downtown, and dilapidated after many years of abuse and neglect. Delia had light-brown curly hair, eyes the color of milk chocolate and a dimple in her cheek. Her building was like an oven, and she was wearing shorts and a halter that hot day when she opened the door at Barbara's knock. She appeared to be as friendly as Carrie had been guarded. She hardly even glanced at the note Barbara handed her.

"Boy, am I glad someone's going to take her stuff. I didn't know what to do with anything. I guess my boyfriend will move in and share rent, and her stuff's in the way. Come on in, I'll show you."

The apartment had a living room with kitchenette, a bedroom and a bath. An ironing board was set up in the living room with several blouses on hangers on the end of it. Delia motioned toward some boxes and two suitcases against the wall. "That's her stuff. I packed up everything I could find." She picked up a can of diet soda and said, "You want a cold drink?"

Barbara, who hated carbonated drinks of any kind, and especially diet drinks, said, "I'd love it. I'm burning up."

"Yeah, me too, and I'm stuck with ironing on a day like this." She went to a small refrigerator and brought out another can, which she handed to Barbara.

"Had you worked with Carrie very long?" Barbara asked, opening the can.

"Not really. We didn't work together in Las Vegas, just in the same casino. She was in the dining room and I was a cocktail waitress. We saw each other now and then, that's about it." She motioned toward a rickety chair and pulled out another one for herself. "When she got fired I said how about going to Eugene with me, and she got this real funny look and said, who's he? See, like she thought I meant a guy. Maybe I was suggesting a ménage à trois or something." She laughed. "I went to the U of O here, and I knew I could get a job...." She rambled on, wanting to talk about herself, and now and then Barbara nudged her back to Carrie.

"I wanted to come up early enough to find an apartment and line up a part-time job. If you wait too long you can't find anything, not after the kids return. So she said sure, she'd drive us to Eugene and hang out a while."

"Why did she get fired?" Barbara asked during one of the infrequent pauses.

"I don't know firsthand, just the rumors and stories. Some gals said she slugged a customer, or else she just gave him a shove when he wouldn't keep his hands to himself, or something like that. Anyway, she got fired on the spot. She's a funny girl, you know. I never did hear her make on it. She doesn't talk about herself. You know, that's a long drive from Vegas to Eugene, and she hardly talked at all. She's just strange."

Barbara nodded. "Some people don't seem to have a lot to say."

"Not just that. We applied at the lounge the same day, and there were some others waiting for an interview. She spotted that grand piano, and it was like a magnet for her. First thing I knew she was over there playing like a pro. And she never even mentioned before that she knew how to play. Anyway, they hired her to play and she raked in the tips, believe me. They loved her. And every morning she'd go over there around nine and practice for a couple of hours. A magnet."

"What about Wenzel? Do you think the motel will change now that he's gone?"

"It wasn't his, you know. It's the property of Wenzel Corporation, the developers. He moved in after his house burned down. He was off at Vegas losing money and his place burned to the ground, I guess. We called him Joe Weasel. And he got after Carrie right away after he moved in. It was spooky the way he watched her, like an obsession, and she made it worse by the way she cold-shouldered him. Probably if she'd just kidded him along a little, he would have let it go. Or she could have said something like her boyfriend was a gun nut and jealous, or something. I mean, you can usually say something to make them back off, but she didn't."

"That's a good line, about the boyfriend," Barbara said. "I'll have to remember that. Does she have a boyfriend?"

"Not that I know of. Or girlfriend either, if you know what I mean. She's just funny. Sort of a loner."

When it appeared that Delia had confided all she knew about Carrie, Barbara stood. "Well, I'd better haul that stuff out of here. Thanks for the soda."

"And I'd better finish my ironing," Delia said.

Barbara carried the boxes and suitcases to her car, then sat for a minute. Where to take them was a problem. Not to her small apartment. They would just be in the way. Not the office, same problem. Her old room at Frank's house, she decided. Plenty of room up there, in no one's way, accessible. She would swing by the lounge and pick up the sheet music and then head for her father's house.

3

Barbara heard Frank's car when he arrived home that Saturday afternoon, but even if she had not heard it, the two coon cats would have alerted her. Keeping her company, jumping in and out of boxes while she sorted through Carrie's few possessions, they had both twitched their ears and abandoned her without a backward look when they heard him. Soon he called up the stairs, "Bobby? Are you up there?"

"Be down in a minute," she yelled back. She was holding a newspaper article, so worn and frayed that she feared it would fall apart in her hands. With a sigh she returned it to a clear plastic folder, then sat back regarding her efforts. One box of cool-to-cold weather garments; one box of warm-to-hot weather things. Underwear, gowns, slippers… A sleeping bag. A small box of books, poetry, paperbacks, dictionary… Some lotion, hairbrush, comb, face cream… Half a dozen papers of various kinds—birth certificate, her parents' death certificates, medical records, school report cards, bill of sale for a car that would be fourteen years old now, some sheet music for piano.

She was putting the documents together in a folder, then paused to regard the newspaper clipping once more. Marla and Ronald Frederick had been killed instantly in a fiery crash when their truck collided with a concrete barrier, and their daughter, Carol, had been critically injured. There was a poor photograph of Marla and Ronald; Carrie looked more like her father than her mother, the same straight eyebrows and black hair. Her mother apparently had been fair—it was hard to tell from the newspaper photograph—and very pretty, with a big smile that showed a lot of teeth. Carrie had been eight years old when it happened.

She added the folder to the documents she would take to the office to keep in her safe, then closed the overnight bag she planned to take to Carrie. She put the other things in her closet.

When she entered the kitchen a few minutes later, her father was sorting his own collection of items. Pots, packets of seeds, watering can… "Hi," he said. Then, eyeing the overnight bag, he asked, "Are you coming or going?"

"Going," she said. "What's all that stuff?"

"Look out back," he said, motioning toward the door. "I got the shade cloth on yesterday, and today I did a little shopping. Perlite, vermiculite, coconut pith, pots. I'm ready to set up shop."

Over the past two weeks he had had a lean-to greenhouse built onto the side of the garage, then found that it was too hot this time of the year to enter, much less do any work there. Now the structure was covered with a shade cloth.

Barbara glanced out the door and nodded.

"So, what's the bag for?" Frank asked, a bit annoyed that she showed so little interest in his new greenhouse.

Briefly she told him about Louise Braniff's visit, and her own visit to meet Carrie. "I think I'm going to like her," she said. "She reads T. S. Eliot and *Finnegan's Wake,* for one thing, and she plays the piano like an angel. Also, she called Bill Spassero Bill Asshole. Ring a bell? She says she didn't do it."

"Don't they all?" He thought a moment. "Barry Longner? I know him. Appellate court. Want me to make the call?"

"That would help, but I assume it will all check out. There really is a Benevolent Ladies Club and they do good deeds, period. Why do you suppose anyone would want sheet music if there's no instrument to go with it? She asked me to bring her music with the other stuff."

"Maybe she's like some people who can read cookbooks and taste the dishes. Maybe she can hear the music in her head."

"Taste the dishes? From reading a recipe? You're kidding."

He knew there was no point in arguing about it. "Ask her," he said. "I read about Wenzel's murder. Seems pretty cut and dried. Will she take a plea bargain?"

"No way. At least that's what she says now. I'll know more after I've talked longer with her. I've got to go. And you can go have fun in your playhouse."

"You don't look like a lawyer," Carrie said the next day, back in the conference room.

Barbara looked down at herself, jeans, T-shirt, walking shoes. "How am I supposed to look?"

"I don't know. Power suit, medium heels, discreet jewelry,

expensive makeup. Like someone who makes a mint and shows it in good taste that lets you know there's plenty more where that came from."

Barbara laughed. "What you see is what you get where I'm concerned. On the other hand you don't look like a jailbird."

"First time for me," Carrie said. "I'll grow into the role."

"You'll have to learn how to sneer," Barbara said.

This time Carrie laughed, and for a moment she looked more like her mother's photograph than her father's. The same big smile with a lot of shining teeth.

"What I'd like to do today," Barbara said, "is get some background to start working with. You know, past history, things like that. Okay?"

Carrie nodded, the smile gone as quickly as it had come. "Sure. But I have to tell you up front that I don't have any memories that go earlier than before age eight and a half. You saw the things in my box? The newspaper article, all that?"

"Yes. You don't recall the accident? Your parents' deaths?"

"No. And nothing before that. I was born around the age of eight and a few months." The words were spoken lightly, but the guarded look had returned, with a new tightness around her mouth.

"Well, let's start with what you do remember. The hospital where you were treated? Any of that?"

Carrie shook her head. "Flashes of memory, snapshots, drinking water with a straw, restraints in bed, a lot of pain, just things like that. A cast. Physical therapy. Nothing real, nothing in any kind of order, no first this then that."

"Where does your real memory begin?"

"A home for kids and being taken in an airplane to people who were to be my foster parents, in Terre Haute. Stuart and

Adrienne Colbert. I lived with them until I graduated from high school, and then I took off."

Whatever ease she had managed to achieve only moments earlier had vanished, and she looked strained. "What difference does any of that make? It's got nothing to do with me now."

"If you put up a fight, the prosecutor will dig out everything available about you, and I have to have the same information they'll gather." She paused a moment, then said, "So let's talk about the foster parents. Were they good to you?"

"They'll dig up my past that far back?"

"Probably."

Carrie looked away; then, keeping her gaze on the wall, she said, "What they'll learn is that I was considered crazy, maybe schizophrenic. And maybe I was."

"Because you had amnesia?"

"I don't know why."

Studying her, Barbara nodded slowly. Carrie knew something, and she was not going to talk about it, that was apparent. For now they would drop it, but they would have to come back to it as often as it took to get her to tell what the prosecutor would surely discover. "Okay," she said. "Back to the Colberts. Were they good people, decent to you?"

Carrie shrugged. "Stuart was okay, I guess, but he wasn't there a lot. You know, work, doing stuff around the house and yard, out fishing. Adrienne and I didn't get along."

"They gave you music lessons, didn't they?"

Carrie grimaced. "No. Adrienne liked country-western and accordion players. That's all she listened to. I can't recall that Stuart listened to any music. They didn't have a piano or guitar, anything like that in the house."

"You learned to play before the accident? Is that what you're saying?"

"I must have. But I don't remember."

Frustrated, Barbara dropped it. "You said you took off right after high school. Tell me about that."

This, at least, seemed to be a topic that Carrie was willing to talk about at length. Stuart Colbert had said there had been some insurance money for her education but, not interested in college, Carrie had bought a car and started an odyssey that wound through one state after another, one city after another, sometimes with a companion, most often alone. Boyfriends never lasted very long, she added. Barbara noted the various cities where she had stopped to work for a few months, six months, one time for a whole year, before moving on. The last city before arriving in Eugene had been Las Vegas.

She told Barbara about the incident that resulted in her being fired. "This slob, drunk as a skunk, wouldn't keep his hands off me when I served their table. When I took the check over, he tried to put his arms around me, and I gave him a shove. He staggered back a little bit and knocked some things off the table. The manager was there faster than lightning, apologizing to the jerk. That was it. I was out." She shrugged. "I probably wouldn't have stayed much longer anyway. Good excuse to hit the road again."

"Why Eugene after that?"

"I never even heard of Eugene before Delia mentioned it. I don't know why. I just felt as if that's where I had been heading, not here, just the northwest in general, and I might as well have help with the gas."

The shuttered look had returned. Barbara was learning to read her client's expressions, and that was what these preliminary conversations were for: to get acquainted, comfortable with each other, and become familiar with expressions, body language, learn where the land mines were, what territory was forbidden. Carrie could flash that big open grin, she could be candid and forthcoming, or as unyielding as a statue. Those off-limit areas were the ones Barbara intended to revisit often.

"Had you seen Joe Wenzel in Las Vegas? Run across him?"

"Never. You know how the casinos are set up with restaurants? A cafeteria with the world's worst food, a cheap dining room, family dinners for four-ninety-five, and the high-class dining rooms. I waited tables in el cheapo. From what I know about Wenzel he probably ate in the high-class joints. No crossing of paths."

Barbara stayed a while longer, then stood up. "Enough for today. But tell me something. Why did you want your music if there's nothing to play?"

That other expression appeared on Carrie's face: a softness, a vulnerability, a look of deep hurt perhaps. Her hands began to move on the table as if it were a keyboard. Her fingers were long and beautifully shaped, the nails short, well cared for. It was fascinating to watch those hands, and Barbara forced her gaze back to Carrie's face.

"I need practice," Carrie said in a low voice. "I'm so out of practice. I can hear the music when I read it, hear my mistakes, hear when it's right." Abruptly she clenched her fists and pushed herself away from the table. "Thanks for bringing my stuff." That closed, guarded look had returned.

It was a calm, cloudless day, temperature in the mid-eighties, the sky flawlessly blue, a perfect day for a long walk by the river, but Barbara knew that the park would be full of people on a nice Sunday afternoon like that, and she headed for Frank's house instead. Knowing she would find him out back, either on the porch in the shade, or in his new greenhouse, she didn't bother with the front entrance, but walked around the side of the house.

It was fitting, she thought, for him to have a new toy; a Depression kid, he had had very few toys in his childhood, and now in his second childhood he had a playhouse. She was grinning at the thought, and rephrasing it in her mind to tease him when she rounded the corner of the house, then stiffened in annoyance. Darren again. And Todd. Their bikes were leaning against the garage door, and Darren was lounging in the doorway to the greenhouse talking to Frank. Todd was on the back step reading a comic book.

"Hi," she said, drawing near.

Darren turned and grinned, and Frank stepped out of the greenhouse. "You're right," he said to Darren. "Simple screens over the bed will do it." He looked at Barbara. "Those fool cats think the raised bed in there is the world's finest litter box. I'll screen them out."

"It won't take much," Darren said. "One by ones, screen stapled on top. Three sections? Easier to manage that way, and to store."

"Now you're a master builder, on top of all else," Barbara said, not hiding the sarcasm a bit.

"Doesn't take much to outsmart a cat," Darren said. "Actually I'm here on a mission. You're both invited to a little gathering at the clinic next Sunday to celebrate the official opening of the foundation. They particularly want you to show up, Barbara. A lot of debts to pay, that sort of thing. You saved their skin, you know."

That was her cue to point out to Frank that Darren's interest in her was due to his gratitude. The previous year he and Annie McIvey had been prime suspects in the murder of Annie's husband, and the clinic that Darren actually ran was in danger of being taken over by outsiders who would have turned it into a for-profit facility as fast as possible. Barbara had pulled their chestnuts out of the fire and they were all grateful, Darren as well as all the others. But she couldn't go into that with Darren and his son at hand; it had to be a private conversation, a well-rehearsed off-the-cuff spontaneous remark. She had promised herself to find the proper place to make her "spontaneous" comment, and put it aside again.

Todd stood up. He was twelve, still enough of a child to be direct with his gaze and his questions, the flush of childhood still on his cheeks. He looked very much like his father, pale hair, pale blue eyes, wide shoulders. "You want to go on a bike ride with us?" he asked Barbara. "Dad fixed up your bike."

She glared at Darren, then at Frank, who looked as innocent as a newborn. "What do you mean, fixed it up?"

"Just some tires, a little oil," Darren said.

"I haven't ridden a bicycle in years," she said.

"Don't you know how to ride?" Todd asked in amazement.

"Sure she does," Darren said. "It's like swimming. Once you know how, you never lose it. Your body remembers."

"You kids go on," Frank said. "Think I'll mosey over to Jerry's, pick up a few pieces of wood and some screening. I wonder where I left my old stapler?"

He knew perfectly well where he left it, Barbara thought, watching him saunter toward the house. He never misplaced anything.

"You game to give it a try?" Darren asked.

She shrugged. "Sure. Why not. We'll see if my body remembers squat."

Darren led the way through side streets. The neighborhood they rode in was quiet, with little traffic on the streets, and it was pleasant pedaling from sunshine to shade to sunshine. Some patches of lawn, not irrigated, had already turned golden brown, but flowers and shrubs were in full bloom. The grass was summer-expendable, and also winter-reliable. It would be green again with the first fall rains and then stay green until the following year's summer drought. Soon she stopped admiring the yards and gardens, and was aware only of the increasing soreness of her bottom. She shifted her position again and again; it didn't help, and finally she slowed down, then stopped altogether and got off the bike.

Darren wheeled about and returned to her side. "Problem?"

"Sore butt," she said. "You guys go on, I'll walk back."

He swung off his bike. "I'll walk with you. Actually you were doing great for someone who hasn't ridden in twenty years. I was betting myself that you wouldn't last this long."

Todd joined them, looking disappointed. "That's it?"

"Todd, be kind to me," Barbara said. "I am an old woman, and my butt is sore."

He whooped with laughter and raced on ahead.

"Why did you decide to come along?" Darren asked after a minute or two of silence.

"I wanted to see if it was true that the body remembers. I remember how I struggled to learn in the first place. I kept falling over."

"Yeah, I know. It's an impossible task, keeping your balance, learning to steer and pedal at the same time. You have to learn it all together, but once it's there, it's always there."

"Do you think it would be like that for other things people learn? Like a foreign language, or playing an instrument? Once you learn it, you remember, or your body or hands remember?"

"Pretty much. You had a wobbly moment at first, then somatic memory took over. Your body responded to synapses your brain formed years ago. I had a patient once, a Hungarian woman in her fifties, brought over when she was five or six and never spoke or heard Hungarian again until she was forty. She said she heard Hungarian being spoken on a train in France, and at first it was like gibberish, her wobbly moment, but suddenly it was music to her ears."

"You think it would be like that with a musical instrument? A violin or guitar, or a piano?"

"I think so. Every bit of real learning involves synapse formation, and once there and reinforced through usage, they remain, ready to fire again given the proper cues. The younger you are when you learn, the stronger the synapse linkages are, the more ineradicable they are. That's what we work with all the time in physical therapy, forming new synapses, teaching an undamaged part of the brain to take over the functions that the previously trained part can't do any longer. Anything particular on your mind?"

"Maybe," she said. "I'm not sure."

They walked on in silence, and she was thinking about Carrie in her cell practicing on an imaginary piano, listening to imaginary music, correcting her wobbles as she went.

It took longer to walk back to Frank's house than she had anticipated; the ride had not seemed that long. Todd raced up the streets, back down, waited for them at the corners, then raced on again. Showing off for her, Darren said, when he came zooming by "no hands."

"Why me? Why not you?"

Darren just laughed.

At Frank's house, he didn't go in with her. "I told the brat we'd take our ride, then have pizza," he said in the driveway. "A soaking bath with Epsom salts is what you need."

She grimaced, then nodded. "Exactly."

Todd caught up with them again and grinned at her. "It won't hurt so much next time."

"Next week," Darren said, "after they toast you royally, will you bring Frank over to my place? I'll grill some steaks or something."

She hesitated, then nodded. "Okay."

"Great," Darren said and got on his bike again; he and Todd headed toward the park. She understood that he had led before to avoid the crowded path there, to let her practice without an audience.

"I don't know, Dad," she said later in the kitchen. "It looks like I'll have to find the foster parents eventually and see what they can tell me. I hate that amnesia thing. She learned to play the piano before she was eight, and evidently didn't touch one again until she spotted the grand piano in the lounge. You'd think she would have come across a piano somewhere along the line before that."

He paused in slicing tomatoes. "Maybe it took a grand piano to stir up her memory if that's what she learned on. Maybe just any keyboard wouldn't have done it."

"And just how many houses have grand pianos hanging around?"

"Good point. So come up with a better explanation." He resumed slicing.

She sipped her wine, watching him do his thing with dinner. While she could admire his skill, she had absolutely no desire to emulate it. Or try to.

"You want to set the table?" he asked. "Maybe out on the porch. Nice out there this time of day."

Or any time of day, she thought and stood up. She groaned. It hurt to stand up, and it hurt more when she first sat down. Frank chuckled and tried to disguise it with a cough.

She didn't linger long after dinner; her mind was on a soaking bath with Epsom salts, and the things she had to do the following day. First, formalize her arrangement with Carrie, then arrange for bail. Before, it had not been an option; now it was. Consult with Shelley and Bailey, get them started. But first a good soak.

That night Carrie was too restless to go to sleep. All those questions, and there would be more and more with no end. Questions she couldn't answer. Then one of the snapshot memories that tormented her rushed in.

She saw herself lying in bed, her eyes closed hard, hands over her ears, but there was no way she could block the voices, or stop the images. They were yelling again, Stuart and Adrienne, in the living room. She crept down the hall and listened.

"For God's sake, I can't stand much more of this! She's been telling Wanda's kids her fantasies like they're real. A house with a thousand rooms! Her father and that goddamn king. Uncle Silly and Aunt Loony. She's the loony one! They didn't tell us that she's a mental case. I want to send her back."

"Adrienne, give her time. You know what they said. Post-traumatic stress, that's all it is. The poor kid lost her parents, she nearly died. She just needs a little time."

"Time isn't going to cure her! You heard that caseworker. Schizophrenia. She can't tell the difference between fantasy and reality, dreams and being awake. It's all the same to her, and it just gets worse. She's crazy! She might even become dangerous. She belongs in an institution, a mental hospital."

She was crawling backward, faster, faster, then rose and ran to the bathroom and threw up into the toilet. Hospital and pain, send her back there. She washed her face and studied herself in the mirror, looking for craziness. Her hair was still short from where they shaved it off. It stuck out like a porcupine or something. Ugly. She'll never cut it again, and she won't talk about the house with the thousand rooms and Uncle Silly and Aunt Loony. They weren't real, nothing she remembered was real. That's what crazy meant. You couldn't tell what's real and what wasn't.

A train whistle jolted her and the memory was gone as swiftly as it had come. Sometimes it sounded as if the trains were coming through the jail, they were so close. That was real, she thought. Down the corridor someone was sobbing. That was real. She was in jail, charged with murder. And that was real, too.

4

By late Monday afternoon Barbara had finished most of the tasks on her list. She entered her office, waved to Maria, who was on the phone, and looked in on Shelley, who was at her computer.

"When you have a minute, come on back," Barbara said, and headed to her own office.

"Coffee?" Maria asked, hanging up the phone. "I just made it."

"You're an angel, you know that?" Barbara said. In her office, she put her briefcase on the round table with its lovely inlaid semiprecious stones, sat down and put her feet on the table next to the briefcase.

Shelley came after her and held the door for Maria, who was bringing a tray and the coffee service. "What's up?" Shelley asked, seating herself across from Barbara.

"Your father called and asked me to give him a ring when you got here," Maria said. "Okay?"

"Sure, call him. Send him on back when he gets here. Anything else cooking?"

"Not a thing." She left again. Not only did she have an uncanny sense of when to expect Barbara to return, she also knew when to bring up inconsequential matters and when to pretend they didn't exist.

Shelley poured coffee, then settled back waiting.

Barbara told her about Louise Braniff's visit and her follow-up, and was still at it when Frank tapped on the door and came in.

"So there it is," Barbara said, including him now. "I posted her bail bond, and we retrieved her car and picked up her belongings from the house, and got her a motel room, where she said she intended to take two or three baths. She can't stay in a motel room more than a few days. We'll need to help her find an apartment, and that won't be easy. No references and awaiting trial. Not a great recommendation."

She didn't add the comments Bill Spassero had made: that Carrie would have realized exactly what prison meant in a couple of weeks and then copped a plea for any sentence less than what faced her for conviction for murder, which was a sure bet. He had not yet looked at all the material the investigators had collected, and he wouldn't have done so until closer to the trial, she well knew. Overworked was hardly the word for the caseload he had.

And there was no reason to add his comment about Shelley, that he had been seeing her around, and she looked terrific, but different. And she was different. She was keeping her golden hair cut short, but more than that, she had matured in the past year and was no longer simply Valley-girl pretty, but rather beautiful, with a radiance she had not shown before. No longer floating in her bubble of happiness, with her feet firmly attached to the ground now, she still could not conceal her contentment.

"I'll find her an apartment," Shelley said. "What else?"

"See if you can track down the Colberts. Last known address was in Terre Haute, but that was fourteen years ago. God knows where they are now." She got out her notes with the address and gave it to Shelley, then handed her a copy of the newspaper clipping about Ronald and Marla Frederick. "This will be harder, to find out anything about them, and I might have to sic Bailey on to it, but see if there's anything readily available. They died twenty-four years ago, death certificates issued in Boston. Can do?"

"Sure."

If she failed to find them, Barbara knew that Bailey would dig until he did. He was the best detective in the business.

"I called Barry Longner," Frank said. "There most certainly is a Benevolent Ladies Club, and they do good works, and hasn't the weather been fine recently."

Barbara grinned. "And Louise Braniff has been with the university for twenty-some years, does volunteer work here and there, and has not a single blemish. Way it goes." She stretched. "Well, I'll read the material Bill gave me, have Bailey in in the morning to get him digging, and Carrie's coming in at ten and we'll go over all that stuff together. I want you to meet her, Shelley."

"When you're done here drop by the house and I'll give you some dinner," Frank said, rising.

"And I'll get started with the Colberts," Shelley added.

After they left together, Barbara pulled her briefcase around and withdrew the folder Bill Spassero had handed her.

"Okay," she said to Bailey the next morning. "That's the basic story." He was actually sitting upright with a notebook out, coffee at hand. He was dressed in chinos and a sport shirt open at the neck, with a lightweight jacket draped over his chair back. He carried the jacket, but never wore it. She suspected he believed it made him look respectable, and he was wrong. He would never look respectable. He looked like a bum who bought every stitch of clothing he owned at Goodwill.

"Apparently no one heard a gunshot. It was Wenzel's gun. His only brother, Larry Wenzel, and Larry's son, Luther, were at Bellingham from Saturday morning until they were notified on Sunday that Joe had been killed. The other son, Gregory, was home with his mother until about eleven, when he left to join friends who had been to a movie. He was with them until two, and left with a woman. They were together in her apartment about an hour or so. Time of death between twelve and two. Larry's wife was home on the telephone talking to her daughter-in-law—Luther's wife—and her daughter-in-law's mother from about eleven until twenty minutes later, her car in a garage being serviced." Bailey raised his eyebrows, and she added, "Larry had taken his car to the airport and left it there. Moving on, two different couples saw Joe and Carrie outside the motel." She gave him their names. "One couple said Carrie was walking and he was tagging along toward the rear of the parking lot. The other two said she was at his open door, apparently talking to him, and she entered and closed the door.

"There's a Web site for the company, but I want more than

the puff piece there. Dig into them a bit, and check them all out." She gave him the manager's name, and that of the bartender. "Shelley found the Colberts, but not a thing about Ronald and Marla Frederick. Here's a copy of their death certificates, and the article about their deaths." She studied the copy of the article one more time, then drew in her breath and handed it to Bailey. "What's wrong with that?"

He read it, glanced at her and read it again, then grunted. "Where's it from? What town or city? What's the date? Frontage Road. Jeez, every town in America has a Frontage Road."

"And where did the newspaper get the photograph?" she said. "It says there that all their possessions were destroyed in the fire after the crash. Where did the photo come from?"

He nodded, put the article down and made another note.

"Just a little more," she said then. "Apparently Joe went to the bank on Friday, visited his safe-deposit box, deposited a check for five thousand and withdrew a thousand. It was missing when they found his body." She told him which bank.

"I sure hope your client didn't turn up with a thousand bucks in her pocket when they nabbed her," he said.

"Almost that bad. She put two new tires on her car the next week."

"And they let her out on bail? Incredible."

"Okay, that's it for now." He was hardly out the door before she was at the phone dialing the number for Stuart Colbert. She reached Adrienne Colbert and made an appointment to talk with them both on Friday afternoon. Adrienne had a shrill voice and asked many questions before agreeing to see her. Barbara walked to the outer office and asked Maria to get her a seat on a flight to Phoenix. Carrie arrived then.

She was still in the outer office after introducing Carrie to

Shelley and Maria, when to her surprise Frank turned up. "Good morning," he said. "I was on the way to my office and thought I'd drop in to meet our new client."

He looked very much the successful attorney in his pale gray summer suit and white shirt and tie. Barbara made the introduction, then added, "Dad often works on my cases with us."

"How do you do, Ms. Frederick," Frank said, taking her hand. "I won't stay this morning, but I hope to see more of you as we work on your behalf. Are you comfortable enough in your motel room?"

Although Carrie had appeared measurably more relaxed when she arrived, she looked puzzled and a touch apprehensive as they shook hands. "My room is a lot more comfortable than the one I just left," she said. "It's fine."

"Good. Well, I'll be on my way."

And what was that all about? Barbara wondered, shook her head and took Carrie on back to her office.

"What we'll do is sit over here," Barbara said, motioning to the sofa and chairs by the coffee table. "Coffee, tea, soda, anything like that for you?" Carrie said no. "Okay, maybe a little later. Just get comfortable and we'll talk. I want to go over the statements the police collected, tell you what they have and ask questions. If you get tired, or want to use the rest room, or decide you want something to drink, just holler. Okay?"

"Sure." Carrie looked around at the office, then said, "This looks good. Impressive."

"Shelley's father and mine outfitted it," Barbara said. "Proud daddies, I guess. On my budget it would have been secondhand stuff, crates, cushions on the floor."

Carrie flashed her big toothy smile, not believing a word of it apparently.

"What I want to start with is the night Wenzel was killed. Tell me what you did when you finished playing."

"I told you. I got up and left. Out to my car—"

"Hold it. I mean a step-by-step playback. You finished playing, then what?"

"I got up and walked around the bar, through the door to the office behind the bar." She paused. "Like that?"

"Exactly. Did you take your glass with you?"

"No. I never did. Or the bowl with tips either. Mickey always waited a few minutes for customers to toss tips into the bowl and then brought the bowl back to the office for me. Anyway, next to the office there's a dressing room with lockers, and I went there for my purse. I washed my face. I get sweaty playing that long. And tied my hair up off my neck. Mark told me to let it down when I play, more glamorous that way, he said. So I tied it up, went back to the office and put the tips in my purse, and gave Mickey a five. He's the bartender. And I left. Wenzel was by his door when I passed and grabbed my arm. I pulled away and walked faster. The employees had to park in the back. He followed me and I just kept walking. At the car he tried to hold the door open. I already told you all this."

"Right. Let's backtrack a little. Did you always tip the bartender?"

"Yes. The first night I played he brought me a mixed drink and I told him I don't drink. I do, a little, but only wine and only with food. Hard liquor makes me sick. He said a customer ordered it, and if I didn't have something there, someone else probably would order another one. I asked him to bring me water, and he did. After that he always brought a glass of ice water."

"You just left it on the piano when you were finished?"

Carrie looked shocked. "I never had it on the piano. He started to put it there the first time, and I told him not to do that. You don't put a glass on the piano. He brought a little table over, and that's where the water was."

"You always left it there after playing?"

She nodded. "Yes."

"What did you do on your breaks? Where did you go then?"

"Back to the dressing room to hang out. Like I said, I get sweaty. I wash my face and put on fresh makeup usually. Probably I did that night. I don't remember."

"You didn't walk outside for some fresh air, anything like that?"

"No. I usually did some stretches maybe, just relaxed."

Barbara nodded. "You had seven hundred dollars when they arrested you, and you had put two new tires on your car that last week. Where did that money come from?"

"My tips. I was making more money than I'd ever made before. I need two more tires. I was going to get them the next week, and still have enough for my share of the rent and food."

Impressed, Barbara asked, "How much were you making in tips?"

"About a hundred or hundred fifty a night. Once it was two hundred. I worked three nights a week. My car needs a tune-up. I figured a few more weeks and the tires would be good, and I'd get a tune-up, a few clothes and then move on probably."

"Why, Carrie? You were doing so well, why move on?"

She had been open, talking freely without hesitation, now she closed, and that tightness appeared around her mouth.

After a moment, she shrugged. "I don't know why. I just don't like to stay in one place long. I like to keep moving."

"Maybe we'll have coffee now," Barbara said, rising. "Would you rather have something else?"

"Coffee's okay."

Later, talking about her life as a wanderer, Carrie said, "I slept in the car pretty often, sometimes at the rest stops on the interstates. No one bugs you if you look like a tourist, and I guess I did. And when I got a job, I usually could find a pretty cheap room somewhere. It wasn't too bad."

"Were you ever in trouble in any of those cities? You know the district attorney will probe, just in case, and if you were there's a record of it."

Carrie shook her head. "I was told to move on a few times, that's about it. No speeding tickets, nothing. I wasn't looking for trouble."

"What were you looking for?"

She drained her coffee cup and set it down. "Nothing. I wasn't looking for anything."

"Okay. Did you remember what Wenzel said to you that last night? You said he was talking crazy."

"He called me a bitch and a slut, and said I'd find out it didn't pay to try to play games with him, to fuck him over." She shrugged. "Crazy talk. I wasn't trying to play games with him. I was trying to keep out of his way."

Soon after that Barbara stood up. "It's after twelve. I've kept you long enough. Thanks, Carrie."

"Just one thing," Carrie said. "You told me some people said they saw me going into his room. It's a lie. Why would they lie about it? What for?"

"I don't know. We're looking into them."

Carrie got up then, but still hesitated. "It looks bad for me, doesn't it? I don't even have a character witness."

"It usually looks bad at this stage," Barbara said. "Remember, I haven't even started to poke around in Joe Wenzel's past. He might have had a hundred enemies. If he did, we'll find them and go on from there."

As if she had not heard Barbara's words, Carrie said, "They charged me with murder to scare me, didn't they? They said it could be ten years to life. So I'd agree to something less, like self-defense or something. Is that how they play their game?"

"Maybe. You understand that you can plea bargain anytime, from now until it goes to trial? What you can't do is take off in your car for parts unknown. You understand that?"

"Sure. They'd really bag me then. But I won't say I did it, no matter what. Because I didn't. But I'm scared, Barbara. Real scared."

She could go from street-smart tough to vulnerable and hurt to frightened, and each had an entirely different effect on her expression. Her eyes widened now and she blinked several times. Barbara wondered if she wept when she was alone.

After Carrie left, she turned to Maria. "And you go to lunch. Why do you always wait to be told?"

"I was busy," Maria said. She smiled. "I'm afraid you'll have to go to Phoenix on Thursday to keep your date on Friday. I have the schedule here, and a map, plane reservations, room reservations, a car reserved. All set."

"It's hard to hate you," Barbara said, taking the folder Maria held out. "Thanks. Now beat it."

"Shelley's on the track of an apartment," Maria said, picking up her purse. "She said she'll check in this afternoon."

* * *

At that moment Frank and Shelley were standing in the middle of an apartment over Darren's garage. It was unfurnished except for the usual kitchen appliances. Darren lounged in the doorway watching them.

"What do you think?" Frank asked Shelley.

"It's perfect. Do you want to help me pick out furniture?" she asked Darren.

"No way. I haven't even finished my own place yet. Get whatever you'd get if you were moving in."

Frank cleared his throat. He suspected that Darren had no idea just how rich a young woman Shelley was. Her father built yachts, her mother was an heiress in her own right and Shelley had come into a big trust fund when she turned twenty-one. She probably never looked at a price tag. "Maybe you should keep things in the price range you think Barbara would go for. You understand. Pick out things that she might have chosen for herself."

Shelley dimpled and nodded. "Gotcha. Why don't you both go on down and eat your sandwiches while I start a list?" She already had her notebook out, making a sketch of the apartment.

Frank had called Darren as soon as he entered his office that morning and made the date for lunch, with a business proposition, he had said. He had picked up deli sandwiches on the way to the clinic to collect Darren. In the car, he had explained what he had in mind. It was a simple deal. They would furnish the apartment for Carrie in lieu of rent for a couple of months, if that was agreeable.

"She'll blow her stack when she finds out," Darren had warned, without defining whom he meant by "she."

Frank had smiled and explained the difficulties Carrie would face trying to find a furnished apartment in her predicament. Then Darren had grinned and said it sounded like a great deal.

The two men left Shelley to do her list, and went down to eat lunch. Frank knew "she" would blow her stack, but he also knew that as she became more and more involved in her case, Darren would be put on hold for a long time, and he did not intend for that to happen. "She" would be out of town Thursday, Friday and most of Saturday, and with any luck, Carrie would be settled in by then. Fait accompli.

5

The Arizona desert was the most desolate country Barbara had ever seen. White sand and rocks on both sides of the road glared heat waves, and the barrenness of the landscape made the Oregon desert seem lush in comparison. Here, only a few, widely spaced cactus plants were visible. Ahead, a water mirage on the road receded as she approached, formed farther away, only to vanish again. Frank had admonished her more than once to carry plenty of water, Shelley had warned her to make sure she had water, and even the agent at the car rental counter had told her to load up on water. She had bought a six-pack, and began to think she should have bought two of them. Two bottles were already empty, and she intended to pull over and open a third one. The temperature was 112 degrees; her eyes burned, her lips felt cracked and she was developing an itch from dry skin.

Here and there wind-blown sand covered the highway. She shuddered to think how it would abrade unprotected skin and flesh if one had to walk out there. She had gone fifty-eight miles, four to go before her turnoff onto a county road that apparently wound up into the mountains. It would get cooler, she consoled herself and slowed down, then pulled over and opened another bottle of water.

The county road was narrow and did wind up and around, and there were pine trees, scant at first, but soon almost a real forest. She slowed down more, watching for the Mercer Lake community, where the Colberts now lived. It was a retirement development, Shelley had written in her notes.

She began to pass driveways and caught glimpses of houses set back among the pine trees, then passed a large church and revised her first estimate of the size of the community, for the most part hidden on the surrounding hillsides. She came to a village with a few shops, a supermarket, a café… On the other side of it, she spotted the development sign: Mercer Lake Retirement Village.

She had seen such developments before: six basic house plans with cosmetic differences. The Colberts' house was ocher-colored with brick-red trim, a cactus garden out front, gravel spray-painted green in place of lawn. Low maintenance. The good life.

When she got out of the car, she nodded. It was cooler, all the way down to ninety-five, she thought derisively, and went to the door and rang the bell.

Adrienne Colbert admitted her. She was a tall angular woman with such a dark tan she looked scorched. The sun and aridity were taking a toll—her skin was leathery and deeply lined. She was wearing Bermuda shorts and a tank top, her elbows and knees bony and sharp. Everything about her looked sharp, the bones of her face, her hands, her wrists. Her hair was dyed strawberry-blond.

Stuart Colbert was standing in the living room behind her, and he was twenty or twenty-five pounds overweight, nearly bald with a fringe of sparse gray hair, and red-faced. But where Adrienne's expression was one of built-in disapproval, he was smiling in a genial way.

"That's a long hot drive. How about an iced tea? Ms. Holloway? That's the name, isn't it?"

"Barbara Holloway," she said. "I'd love a cold drink."

The house was built on an open plan with the kitchen and dining space separated from the living room by a counter. Everything in it was white, beige, or black. A ceramic black-and-white cat was stationed at a sliding glass door to a patio with a tiny swimming pool. The good life, Barbara repeated to herself, and not even cat hair to clean up.

They sat in the living room, the Colberts on a black sofa, Barbara in a low-slung beige chair. A fluffy rug was snow-white. She was almost afraid to put her feet on it.

She thanked Stuart Colbert for the iced tea and then said, "And thanks for letting me barge in on you this way."

"Couldn't very well say no to anyone willing to leave Oregon for this hellhole," Stuart said. "All those trees up there. Never saw—"

"You said you had questions about Carol," Adrienne said. "She's in trouble, isn't she? I knew she would be, it was just a matter of when. What's she done?"

Adrienne was leaning forward watching Barbara intently. Stuart had leaned back and was regarding the ceiling with a little smile on his face.

"Actually," Barbara said, "I'm trying to fill in her past. You know she has amnesia for the early years of her life—"

"She's in trouble. Amnesia! Ha! She didn't want to talk about her mother and father, that's what that amounted to. She made up a fairy tale and pretended it was true."

"Why do you say that?" Barbara asked.

"Her father was a no-good, out-of-work housepainter. They lived out of his truck most of the time, moving from place to place, probably one step ahead of the sheriff, scamming old people. Like gypsies. They were like gypsies. He probably molested her and her mother let him, and she wanted to pretend they didn't exist, just to get away from her past."

"Do you know about them? Did the caseworker tell you their history, or give you documentation?"

"She hinted, that's all. Just hinted. They swallowed the story about amnesia. I had my name, our names, down for a regular little girl, eight to ten years old, no bed wetter, no alcohol syndrome, no mental case, just an ordinary little girl, and they brought me Carol. She was a liar and a sneak from the first day. She said she lived in a palace with a thousand rooms! And her father was going to bring home a king for the queen! I made her stop that nonsense, all right. I told her she was crazy, and crazy people belonged in the hospital. She was afraid of the hospital, afraid of loud noises, afraid of fire, just afraid. And scrawny, with her hair sticking out like spikes all over her head."

"Mrs. Colbert, do you have the name of the caseworker, or the agency that handled the foster-care arrangements?"

"Just the children's service people. I don't remember their names. It was twenty-four years ago. But I remember that child sneaking around, prying into things, telling her lies.

Autism, that's what she had. I didn't have a name for it then, but now I know. She was autistic. I made her stop that, too."

"What do you mean?"

"Slow. She was slow in school, slow to develop, slow to catch on to things. She missed only a couple of months of school. The accident happened in June and we got her in October, so she didn't miss much, but she didn't know anything other kids her age should know, and it took her years to catch up. She'd move her hands the way they say autistic kids do, in some kind of compulsive, repetitive action, over and over and over. I slapped her hands and made her stop that. You can cure them if you're firm. And she cried a lot. I could hear her at night, crying. For nothing. We gave her a good home. We couldn't help it if her parents had mistreated her. We gave her a good home."

"What kind of motions did she make with her hands?" Barbara asked when Adrienne paused for breath.

She began to move her bony fingers as if on a keyboard.

"Was she evaluated psychologically?" Barbara asked. "Did you get any reports regarding her mental health?"

"No. Just the caseworker. She agreed that she was crazy, but she said she'd outgrow it. Childhood schizophrenia, she said. Caused by some kind of stress syndrome. She said she'd outgrow it, but she didn't. She just stopped talking. But she was still crazy, I could tell. It was in her eyes. I knew she'd be in trouble sooner or later. I was afraid of her when she got older. You don't know what crazy kids will do next. You read all the time about those shootings, things like that. I was glad when she packed up and left."

"You bought her a car when she graduated from high school, didn't you?"

"We never did. The caseworker said there was insurance due when she turned eighteen. Enough for her to go to a technical school or something and get training to support herself. But she wouldn't do that. Not her. She had to have a car and take to the road, just like her father. Gypsies, that's what they were."

Barbara asked her a few more questions and found the answers to be meaningless, filtered through a layer of hatred. "Mr. Colbert, was that your opinion of Carrie, also?"

His wife answered before he even had a chance to turn his gaze from the ceiling to Barbara. "He always said to give her time, she'd been through a lot for a little girl. He always took her side like that. He wasn't with her day in and day out like I was."

When Barbara decided there was little point in listening to any more of this vitriolic blather, she stood up. "Well, I'll be on my way. Thanks again for talking to me."

"You still haven't told us what kind of trouble she's in," Adrienne said. "What has she done? I have a right to know."

Barbara regarded her for a moment, then shook her head. "I don't think so, Mrs. Colbert."

Stuart Colbert roused and got to his feet. Adrienne's face had turned to a shade of purple-brown. "I'll see you out, Ms. Holloway," Stuart Colbert said, and walked to the door with her. He stood on the stoop and said in a low voice, "If you go down to the café and have another iced tea or something, I'll join you in a few minutes and try to fill in a few more details." He didn't wait for her response as he turned and reentered the house.

If she had left a chicken on the seat it would have been done to a crisp, she thought when she got into her car again. She opened windows and turned on the air conditioner full blast, but it had not been effective yet when she stopped at the café in the village, and by then she felt roasted to medium rare. The café was cool and dim, with blinds on the windows against the glare. She drew in a breath of relief. Fifteen minutes later Stuart Colbert joined her.

He sat opposite her in the booth, ordered a draft beer and wiped his face with the napkin. "I won't apologize for Adrienne," he said. "Pointless for one adult to apologize for another one. She's what she is. Life didn't turn out the way she expected, and our retirement isn't what she expected. We lost a lot of money these last two years, and there went our plans to travel, see more of the world. Anyway, she's what she is."

The waitress brought his draft beer and replenished Barbara's tea. After she left, Stuart Colbert took a long drink, then said, "We were on lists for over two years before they called and said they had a child for us. Adrienne had a room ready, all pink and frills. I guess she had an idealized child in her mind, and when Carol was brought, it was a letdown. I doubt that any human child would have measured up, and Carol was pale and thin, scarred from surgeries, and fearful. Whatever they had told her she had interpreted as going home, and instead she ended up at our place, and she let out a howl like a wounded cat. She wanted her mommy and daddy." He drank again, then shook his head. "Not a good beginning. We explained that she would live with us now, and she clung to the social worker, yelling that she wanted to go home."

After Carol settled down, he said, the social worker had told them about the amnesia, that it often happened to trauma victims, and very often involved a loss of memory. Post-traumatic stress syndrome, she said. She might recover her memories, or possibly never would. In any event she had made up a past to account for the first eight years of her life, and it was more real to her than any reality, but she would drop that as she matured. Think of it as something like schizophrenia, she had said, where the person could not distinguish reality from fantasy. Children often invented playmates, other realities that they believed in absolutely, but they gave them up eventually, and she would also.

"She never said the child was schizophrenic, only that her condition resembled it. A huge blank had to be filled in, and she had done the best she could in filling it.

"She had beautiful table manners," he said, "and she was well-spoken, polite. Someone had taught her well. Her father really was a housepainter, apparently, who followed the work south in the winter, north in the summer. They had nothing against him or the mother. No sign of any abuse on the child, no old bruises or broken bones, no sexual abuse. They were just poor people getting along as best they could. He had been working in Virginia, on his way to the Boston area when he crashed the truck."

He finished his beer and wiped his mouth. "Carol began baby-sitting when she was twelve, and she saved almost every cent she made. Then, all through high school, she had an after-school job at a diner, and she saved that money, too. I think she had already decided she had to hit the road as soon as she got out of school and collected the insurance. She knew it was coming, or I imagine she would have taken off sooner. I took her to buy the car, and gave her the rest of the money in traveler's checks. Four thousand, plus whatever she had saved. I thought then, and I guess I still think she was trying to track down her family." He shook his head. "And there wasn't any family to track. Dead, no relatives. I felt sorry for her. That poor kid had been through hell and was coping one way or another."

"She stopped talking about her imaginary family, her aunt and uncle?"

He nodded. "She stopped talking altogether for a long time, and never said anything meaningful after that. Adrienne scared her with talk of sending her back to the hospital. She had a real phobia about hospitals, explosions, sudden loud noises, fires. She talked about frying once, when she was coming out of a nightmare, babbling. She had been terribly burned, and they tell me physical therapy for burn cases is excruciating. She was terrified of going back there."

"Was she mentally retarded?" Barbara asked when he paused.

"No. Traumatized, that's all. She forgot a lot of her schooling apparently, but after a year or two she caught up and after that she stayed in the top five percentile of her class. She could have had a scholarship if she had chosen that route."

He told Barbara the name of the social agency and the caseworker, then spread his hands. "I don't know if any of this will prove helpful to you. Same incidents, same kid, different slant, that's what it amounts to. I hope she isn't in serious trouble. No one should have to go through hell twice in one lifetime." He eased himself out of the booth.

"You've been very helpful," Barbara said. "I'm grateful. Thank you."

Deeply frustrated, she started the drive back to her motel in Phoenix. The heat was as intense as it had been earlier, the glare as bright, and it didn't help her mood a bit when she saw dust devils spinning across the white sand in the distance. An itinerant housepainter who lived in his truck with his family, migrating like swallows to follow the work, did not seem a likely person to have taught Carrie to read music and play the piano.

6

"All I want to do is walk and breathe," Barbara told Frank on the phone when she got home Saturday. "Just breathe and take in the cool air."

"Hot, was it? Well, August in Arizona," he said.

"Not too bad. It got down to ninety."

"Oh?"

"At two in the morning."

"Oh. Well, don't forget we have a date at the clinic tomorrow. Want to come around and pick me up? The reception's from four until six. I reckon if we make our appearance near five-thirty, that will be plenty of time for both of us."

She had forgotten entirely. Now she remembered that they were to go to Darren's afterward. "Okay. I'll come earlier and fill you in on the Colberts. See you tomorrow."

This was one of her favorite places on Earth, she thought

a few minutes later on the bike path by the river. Temperature about seventy-eight, a light breeze, sparkling water flashing brilliantly at little rapids, egrets and herons, blackberries ripening on the side of the path... Two kayaks in the river. Kids on bikes, other walkers, perfect. She had made her notes in the motel, had caught up with her e-mail and phone messages—Bailey would check in first thing Monday morning, and Shelley had settled Carrie into an apartment—and now she could relax. Except, she thought, she couldn't. Instead, she brooded about Carrie's lost childhood and what Stuart Colbert had said: she had left Indiana to track down her family. An endless exercise in futility.

Barbara thought with regret that if she had played her hand just a little better, she would have taken her trip a day later, arrived home on Sunday with a perfect excuse not to attend the reception. And then Darren's place. She had agreed only because she had sensed that he wanted to show off his new house now that he had moved in, and she owed him something for giving her an insight into somatic memory. She had remembered how to ride, and obviously Carrie remembered how to play the piano. That was something. But when the devil had she learned?

The reception was easier than she had thought it would be, and over quicker than she had hoped. It was good to see them all happy and excited about the foundation, and they very clearly had been grateful to her for getting them out of a jam. But when she caught Frank's eye after their obligatory half hour, he had nodded ever so slightly toward the door, and they had made their exit. He enjoyed cocktail parties just about as much as she did.

"Done our duty," Frank said in the car. "Darren's going to be delayed a bit, and Todd will be our host until he gets home."

It was only a five-minute drive to Darren's house, and already it looked like a home. A basketball hoop over the garage door was a dead giveaway. Todd proved to be a gracious host, ushering them with aplomb to the back patio where a table was set up with a covered tray of cheese and crackers, to which he added a decanter of wine. His cat Nappy circled the table, then sat as if watching for a chance to make a leap. The last time Barbara had seen Nappy he had been little more than a kitten. Now he was a full-grown, handsome tiger-striped cat with ideas.

"Dad said I should offer to show you the house," Todd said. "You want to see my posters?"

Frank nodded. "I'd like very much to see them." He glanced at Barbara, who had her head cocked in a listening attitude. Then he heard it, too. Piano music. He suspected that Darren's plan was to have her discover Carrie before he got home, get the fireworks over without him.

"Who's playing?" Barbara asked, but she knew. She turned a cold eye on her father. "Do you know who's playing?"

"It's Carrie," Todd said. "She moved in yesterday. She's cool."

"She moved in yesterday," Barbara said in a carefully measured way. "I see." She continued to regard her father. "Why are you not surprised as much as I am?"

"Well, it seemed an ideal solution to her problem, and Darren was agreeable."

"I bet he was. I think I'm getting a headache."

The music stopped, and a moment later Carrie hurried around the side of the house. "Barbara, how can I thank you? It's perfect! The apartment, even a piano!" She stopped her forward momentum just short of Barbara, as if restraining herself from throwing her arms around her. "Just thank you, more than I can say."

Another new expression, Barbara realized, and this one made her look beautiful. Her eyes were shining and high color fired her cheeks.

"Thank Dad," Barbara said. "He's responsible. And I imagine Shelley was his accomplice."

Carrie drew back slightly and said to Frank, "Mr. Holloway, thank you very much. How did you know about the piano?"

He nodded toward Barbara. "Why don't you two go inspect the apartment, make sure everything's there that should be? I'll have a look at Todd's posters. Should we cover the cheese?" he asked the boy.

Todd took the cheese plate inside with Frank following closely behind him. Barbara nodded to Carrie. "I'd like to see the apartment. All right with you?"

"Oh, yes. I want you to. It's the nicest place I've had in years, maybe ever."

It was nice, Barbara had to admit, and furnished better than her own apartment, with a velour-covered sofa in a deep red, a comfortable brocade-covered chair with a good lamp, end tables, a small bookcase, television and an upright piano. A Scandinavian rug in a geometric pattern of gold and deep blue finished the room. A folding screen separated the living room from the kitchen space. The bedroom was smaller, and crowded with the bed, a dresser and a bureau. A quilted comforter with forest-green trees covered the bed that even had a tailored dust ruffle.

Shelley had done it all, Barbara knew. Good taste, everything harmonious, in scale with the size of the apartment.

Carrie said it didn't need a thing. The piano was a rental,

and the television was from Shelley's house. She hadn't used it in months, Shelley had said, and it was good that someone would get some use out of it.

After she had shown it all to Barbara, Carrie said, with a touch of shyness, "Last night, when I was getting ready for bed, I cried. I mean it just hit me, what trouble I'm in, and that you guys are there for me. I haven't cried in years. I can't remember the last time. I think I needed that."

Helplessly Barbara felt her icy fury melt away in the face of Carrie's gratitude. But she would get him, she told herself; she would fix that old fox one of these days.

When Barbara returned to the patio Frank and Todd were having a discussion about training cats. "I doubt that you can," Frank said. "I didn't teach those monsters at the house to retrieve. It was their game from the start. It might help if you keep a little catnip handy, and the first time Nappy brings something back to you, reward him. I'll bring you a start of catnip. I grow mine in a cage, to keep the brutes from eating it down to the ground and digging up the roots. Anything that makes it above the cage is fair game."

He glanced at Barbara, then hurriedly away. "Everything all right up there?"

"It's fine," she said.

"What kind of cage?" Todd asked.

Frank described his wire cage, and Barbara sipped Darren's wine. Carrie had started to play. It was faint, not intrusive, and very pleasant.

When Darren joined them, he started the grill, apologized for his delay, then said, "Would you object to having Carrie come eat with us?"

No one objected and he went to invite her. Ah, Barbara thought then, maybe that was the solution to the Darren problem. Darren and Carrie. She could not account for the unexpected twinge of unease the idea brought her.

Through dinner Frank and Darren carried the conversation; Carrie said practically nothing, and Barbara was polite. Then, eating ice cream with raspberries, Todd asked Carrie, "Why do you keep playing the same thing over and over?"

"Does it bother you?" she asked.

He shook his head. "I just wondered."

"She's doing classical scales and key progressions," Darren said. "Even concert pianists practice more hours than they perform. Isn't that right?" he asked Carrie.

"I don't know," she said. "I didn't know there was a name for that kind of practice."

"Practice before theory," Darren said approvingly. "That's the best way to learn anything. It's how we learn language. I'd bet that you started by three or four, and practiced several hours a day. Also, I'd bet that your rostromedial prefrontal cortex is ten to fifteen percent bigger than the average person's. That's the part that recognizes harmonic relationships and can pick out a sour note in a flash."

Carrie was watching him intently. "I don't have any memory of learning and practicing. It just seemed like what I should do now. I hear my mistakes, all right."

Barbara was watching him also, and he caught her gaze and spread his hands. "No, I'm not an expert in music. Can't play a note. But neural bridges and synapses fall into my domain, after all."

He had made the connection, she realized; he knew she had been talking about Carrie when they took the bicycle ride. She suspected that he had done some research in the meantime.

"No matter what the subject is," she said, "you seem to have some basic information at hand."

"Jack-of-all-trades. I know a smidgen about a lot of things, nothing except my own field in depth. I suspect it's very much like that with the law."

Frank nodded. "Very much so. You learn what you need to know in each individual case, and too often forget it again when the case is concluded. Ongoing process."

Later, when Barbara drove Frank home, he said, "Mad at me?"

"Conflicted, Dad. Isn't that a good word? Conflicted. Good night."

7

"What do you have?" she asked Bailey on Monday morning.

"A lot, but you won't like it," he said. "Just starting, you understand, but still, it doesn't look great for your client."

He slouched into a chair as she left her desk to sit on the sofa. Shelley was in the other chair with her notebook out.

"Okeydokey," Bailey said. "First, all those Wenzel alibis check out so far. Can't find a crack. The cops looked there first and did a good job."

Barbara was scowling at him. He shrugged. "Just reporting. The bartender, Mickey Truelove, took Carrie's glass and tips to the office just as she was coming from the dressing room about ten after twelve. When she left, he took the glass to the kitchen. Mickey said the younger Wenzel boy, Gregory, has a key to one of the rooms, one he keeps, and now and then he takes a girl there, but not that night. Confirmed by the maid. Gregory still lives at home, and he's still playing the field. Older son Luther is married, stable, starting a family, churchgoer, the whole virtuous works. He's never been known to have used that room."

He consulted his notes, then continued. "The couple who saw her walking toward the rear of the parking lot, nothing there. He's a computer geek out at Symantec. She's a medical technician at Sacred Heart Hospital. They saw her walking, Wenzel following, got in their car and left. The other couple, married five years, with a two-year-old son. He's a sound engineer at a radio station, she's a stay-at-home mom. They saw her at Wenzel's door, talking to him, then saw her go in and close the door."

He glanced at Barbara and said, "If your face freezes like that, you'll be sorry."

"I don't worry about eyewitnesses," she muttered.

"She's pretty distinctive. Black skirt, white blouse, that long black hair. They seem pretty positive."

"What about the company? Another blank?"

"Just about. Larry and Joe Wenzel started from scratch down in California, saved, worked hard and made good. Joe took a leave of absence to go to business school in 1972, and in '75 they moved the business to Eugene, where they've done fine. Their motto is 'We Do It All,' and they do, from buying the land to finishing whatever. They built this complex you're in, in fact. Good work, no complaints. It's a respected company, they've always had a lot of work lined up until the downturn in the economy. Strip malls, apartments, office buildings, a church or two, but mostly commercial projects. Featured in national magazines a couple of times for innovative design, and so on."

He grinned at the expression on her face. "It gets a little more interesting."

"It better, or you can take a hike for all the good you're doing."

"The brothers are as different as bottled water and pond murk. Larry's stable, married forever to one woman, two sons, pillar of the community type. Joe's a case," he said. "Or was, I should say. Three-time loser in the marriage game. No kids. Three exes. He had two passions, gambling and music."

Barbara sat up straighter. "What about music?"

"Rock. He followed bands around and taped them. One of the biggest tape collections known before the house burned. And he was a real horse nut, Hialeah, Churchill Downs, Pimlico, even England, Epsom Downs."

"What do you mean? Bet on races?"

"Not just that. Followed them to Miami, Kentucky, New York. Three, four, five times a year he took off for weeks at a time. Horse races or else Vegas, even Monte Carlo. It raises an interesting question."

"When did he work?"

"That's the question. The company built the new headquarters back in '92, and although wife Nora has an office, curiously they forgot to put in an office for brother Joe."

"Where did he get money?"

"He was on full salary until the day he died."

Barbara leaned back and drew in a breath. "Now that is interesting," she said. "How long did that go on?"

"Don't know yet. Working on it."

She thought a moment, then said, "The ex-wives. They'll know something. Do you have their names, addresses?"

"Nope. Give me a day or two. They've probably all remarried by now. Want me to go after them?"

She shook her head. "I think that's a job for Shelley and me. Anything else?"

"The fire roused some suspicion, but it died down. Electrical wire went sour, they say. No one home. It got out of hand before anyone reported it. And Joe's signature at the safe-deposit box raised some suspicion, but it turns out that he was wearing a wrist brace and that accounts for it. Nothing there. The teller and the safe-deposit attendant made positive IDs."

"No enemy list, anything like that?"

"Nothing real. He paid his debts when due and was a good tipper. I guess he figured easy come, easy go. He was a drunk, but he didn't cause trouble with it, except for women, and they just shied away from him for the most part, except those he paid. I think the cops figure the missing thousand bucks was to buy himself a new girlfriend."

"Keep digging into the family, company, finances, house help, whoever you can get to talk about them." She told him what little she had learned from Stuart Colbert. "So last we know, Frederick was in Virginia heading for Boston. See if you can dig out anything from the agency and the caseworker. Just a last name for her, Bergstrom, in Terre Haute, twenty-four years ago. She may be dead by now, and the case may be gone from the files."

"Virginia," he said. Now he was scowling. "Better than before. Then it was just back east somewhere. Barbara, tell me something. What difference does it make?"

"I wish I knew," she said. "I don't like blanks in my cases, and that's a big one. No hospital record of her birth, just a home delivery by a midwife, who also could be dead by now, or has had three name changes."

There were a few more details, then Bailey saluted and ambled out.

"What do you want me to do?" Shelley asked after Bailey left.

Barbara's first thought was: *You've done quite enough,* but she did not voice it. Anyone who had heard her father argue a case would know that Shelley hadn't had a chance against him once he had decided to place Carrie in Darren's apartment. "Not much to do yet, not until we get more information," Barbara said. "I received a new packet from the D.A.'s office this morning. I'll go over that and see if there's anything worth following up on. When we get the ex-wives' addresses, I'd like you to tackle the last two, and I'll go after wife number one. Meanwhile, if you could go to Martin's today, that would be helpful."

"No problem," Shelley said. "I know it's early, but it does look bad, doesn't it? I hate that. I like her."

"It's early," Barbara agreed. She also agreed that it continued to look as bad as her first assessment had been. "Dad always advised that an attorney shouldn't become attached to a client. One can break your heart."

On Wednesday they had the names of the ex-wives, one in Seattle, one in Portland and one, Inez Carnero, in El Cajon, California. Barbara had to look it up on a map.

"I'll take her, if you don't want to," Shelley said, regarding the map with Barbara. El Cajon was in the San Diego area and sure to be as hot as Arizona had been.

"Nope. A deal's a deal. I'll manage. Are you sure Alex won't mind if you're gone a couple of days?"

Shelley looked surprised and a little indignant at the question. "He knows what I do, and that I might be gone from time to time.

He'd never interfere with my work. I think it might be easier for me to drive than fly. Labor Day on Monday, you know."

Barbara was in a foul mood by the time she checked into a motel that Friday evening. She had been searched at the Eugene airport, again in San Francisco, had a bumpy airplane ride, and endured gridlock on the interstate from the San Diego terminal to El Cajon. An all-day trip from hell, she thought irritably. On Saturday she would talk to Inez Carnero, and on Sunday reverse her trip, and no doubt face the same kind of journey. Her room smelled of chemicals, and the air conditioner either blasted icy air or let the room get overheated.

She stripped off her clothes, showered, put on her swimsuit and went out to the pool. It was crowded and so heavily chlorinated that she lasted only a minute or two. Life in the fast lane, she told herself, heading back in for another shower.

Inez Carnero's house was a neat little stucco hacienda with a wide overhang, two palm trees in the front yard and on the edge of a golf course that was miraculously green. Nothing else visible was green. Even the palm fronds were a dusky olive color.

Inez was a pretty woman not an inch over five feet tall, and to all appearances perfectly round. It was hard to tell because she was wearing a loose cotton print garment, splashed with red poppies, that reached her ankles. Her black hair was streaked with gray, done up in an elaborate coil with combs.

"Ms. Holloway? Come in. Come in," she said. "You must be so hot, not used to our weather. And so overdressed."

Barbara was wearing cotton pants and a short-sleeved shirt neatly tucked in. But she felt overdressed.

"I have a cold drink waiting for you," Inez said, leading the way through a living room to a room at the back of the house. There was no air conditioning, but the room had a wall of windows all wide open, and a faint breeze wafted in bringing desert smells of heat and sand. The room was furnished with wicker chairs and a glider, a glass-topped table and a television. A big ceiling fan whirred and helped stir the air. A pitcher and two glasses were on the table, along with a cigar box.

Inez talked as she poured drinks for them both. "After you called, I got to thinking about Joe and the old days. I haven't thought of that time in years. Like another life." She handed Barbara a glass. "Try that, see if it doesn't help."

It did. It was pale green and frothy, with fruit juices that she could not identify, and it was delicious. "That's good," she said. "Thank you. And thank you for seeing me."

"I read about his murder. Done by a woman. I always thought that some day a woman would finish him, and now…" She sighed. "What can I tell you?"

"I'm trying to fill in Joe's past," Barbara said. "How the brothers got started in business, things like that. You know they became very successful developers?"

"Yes. They were bound to, they were so hardworking, both of them, and smart. We all went to the same high school, sort of grew up together. Larry was older, and when he got out he went right to work, learning to be a carpenter. Then Joe graduated and joined him. We got married when he was twenty, and I was nineteen. Too young. That's way too young. My girls did the same thing, married too young, but what can you do?"

Barbara sipped her drink and did not interrupt as Inez rambled on. Joe's mother drowned in a boating accident when he was still in high school and his father took to drink, and a few years later drank himself to death. "I always thought that was what happened to him, being left so young, but I don't know. Anyway, we had some good times, the four of us, Larry and Nora, Joe and me. We were poor, but it didn't seem to matter so much then. And they were ambitious."

They fixed up a house or two and sold them, and they met a man, H. L. Blount, who had a big pickup truck and helped them buy a piece of land to build a gas station and motel. "That was the start of the real business," she said. "They worked on the truck, put in seats and a canopy, and even side covers that could be let down, against the sand, you know, and they'd go down across the border and bring back workers. Those Mexican men worked like slaves, and they did good work and were glad to get it. And that left Larry and Joe free to go look for other places to build on, and that's how they began to get the business going. H.L. told them they were crazy to do the work themselves, they should hire it out and work as developers, and they did.

"I used to go down to Mexico with Joe once in a while. We'd park the truck and spend a day shopping and eating and then drive back the next day with the workers. Nora always went with Larry when it was his turn. She was a hustler, more than Larry even, right from the start. Her and H.L. did most of the planning, what to buy next, what to put on it, like that. After I talked with you, just remembering those days, the good times we had after it cooled off at night, drinking a little beer, singing, danccing, it seems like a dream. I found a box of pictures. You want to see them?" She opened the cigar box.

They spent the next hour looking at the pictures, with Inez talking about them. "That's the first big job they did, the gas station and motel, out on Highway 79." The buildings looked to be in a vast rocky desert.

"Out in the middle of nowhere?" Barbara asked.

"It was all desert back then," Inez said, waving her hand to take in everything. "You'd never know from the way it's built up now, but this, all of this was desert, with little tiny villages where there's towns now, or maybe just a gas station, or not even that much, just a crossroad. Just desert and more desert, but they knew it would grow. H.L. knew it would all grow."

She turned over another picture. "That's the first truck they fixed up to haul workers. See—seats, a canopy. Here's the four of us by the next truck they fixed up."

She had been tiny, slender and delicate-looking and very pretty. Nora was a lot taller, with fair hair, also pretty. And the brothers were handsome and very alike, muscular, with dark wavy hair, big smiles. They were both armed. Larry had a rifle and Joe had a gun belt with a handgun.

"Did they always carry weapons?" Barbara asked.

"Always out on the desert and going down to Mexico. Banditos, rattlesnakes, gila monsters. No one ever bothered any of us, but you never knew, it was always a chance. You needed a gun out there. We all could shoot." Then she said, "I don't know if Joe would of shot anything, but he could shoot a target real good."

"What do you mean? He wouldn't have shot a snake or bandito?"

"He threw rocks at a rattler once and everyone was yelling to shoot it, but he wouldn't. He drove it off. And he'd never watch movies with a lot of blood, anything like that. He was real gentle in those days. Strong as an ox, and gentle." She turned over another picture.

There were many pictures of the four of them and their

truck. Barbara held one of them. "Would you mind if I take one? Or I could get a copy made and return the original."

"No. No. Just take it. I got plenty more. Here's a big apartment they did. Isn't it nice?"

She talked about some of the other jobs, then said dreamily, "Those early days, they were good. We'd sit around with the crew at night sometimes, and they'd play their guitars and sing, and Joe taped them and played it back. They liked that."

"Who was managing the business end of it all?" Barbara asked when she paused.

"That was Nora and H.L. They got the permits and all that. He taught her a lot, I guess. He'd get the plans drawn up, and they'd go for the permits, and then he'd be gone for days or even weeks at a time. Scouting other jobs, I guess. Joe and Larry were going back and forth from one job to another to make sure things were going right. And we were going down for workers a lot, then taking them back. Sometimes they'd have three or four jobs going at once."

When they finished the pictures, Barbara said, "No picture of H. L. Blount?"

Inez laughed. "He said he was camera shy. The camera would steal his soul. Isn't that silly for an old man?"

"How old was he?"

"Then I thought he was old, now I'd say maybe forty-five. But I was young and he looked old to me."

"What happened? Why did they give up a business that seemed to be doing so well?"

"I don't know. One day Joe went to the job to wait for the workers. Larry and Nora went for them that time, and they said H.L. messed up. He always made the deals with the workers. But no one showed up at the pickup place that day, and they came back without anyone to do the work, and then they all got into a big fight. Joe wouldn't tell me what it was about. Maybe not finishing the job on time, something like that. I just don't know. The first real fight they ever had. We all quarreled sometimes—people do—but that was different. Then he said he wanted to go to school, to study business, and we went up to Los Angeles. It all happened so fast. One day everything was fine, then they fought, and the next week we were in Los Angeles."

She gave one of her big sighs. "It didn't work out. Joe began to drink a lot. We all drank beer before, down here most people do. But he began to drink a lot and he began to go after girls. He never did that before. We started to fight a lot, too, and we never did that before. Everything changed. And he went to rock concerts all over the state, hardly stayed at home, and when he was home he was studying or fooling around with his tapes. He wanted me to talk dirty. In bed, you know? Talk dirty." She looked embarrassed. "I wasn't brought up like that. I said what am I here for and came back home. I told him he knew where to find me if he straightened out, but he never came back. So I got a divorce, and met Juan and we got married and it worked out after all. Three beautiful daughters, four grandchildren. You never know what's going to work out, do you?"

"I don't think so," Barbara said. "What about Larry? Did he continue the business down here after Joe went to school?"

She shook her head. "H.L. took off, too, after the big fight, and I guess Larry just finished the things he already started. And a couple of years later, they were all out of here."

She emptied the pitcher into Barbara's glass. "Do you want more? It won't take a minute to mix up some more."

Barbara glanced at her watch. Four o'clock. She had been with Inez for three hours. "Thanks, but no. I've already taken up too much of your time. You've been very kind and generous to talk to me. I appreciate it."

"I liked it," Inez said with a smile. "I haven't thought of those years in a long time, and never talked to anyone about Joe. You don't talk about your first husband with the second husband."

Barbara had parked in the shade of a palm tree, but the shade had moved and the car was an inferno. She turned the fan on full blast and opened windows, then moved to another patch of shade and considered her next step. The thought of the motel for the evening was disheartening. Instead, she found a convenience store, bought a six-pack of water and headed east, out to the desert. She wanted to see what kind of country Joe and Larry had braved to become developers.

An hour later, she pulled over to the side of the road, contemplating the vista before her. Rocky, rough ground, mountainous, dun-colored, so hot and dry that not even cactus could grow more than a few inches high. It looked like rocks. Nothing moved out there, not a tree was in sight, not a building nor a person. The car had an outdoor thermometer; the needle was off the dial that stopped at 120 degrees. Enough, she told herself, and turned around to start back to the motel.

8

She walked to Frank's house on Monday, breathing deeply in the rose garden with its intoxicating perfume. Pools of cool shade, pools of hot sunlight and green everywhere that flowers were not. Then she breathed even more deeply on the river trail, fragrant with river smells and blackberries. She wondered how anyone could choose to live in a place where the only green thing visible was a golf course that was probably toxic with pesticides, fungicides and herbicides.

Frank was not home when she arrived. She let herself in and walked straight through to the back porch, shaded and cool, with myriad flowers and shrubs to gaze at. There she stretched out on a lawn chair, content.

Waiting for Frank, she began to wonder if her trip to Southern California had been worth the strain of air travel. All in all, she brooded, the telephone would have been easier and probably yielded as much. Then she remembered the snap-shot Inez had given her, and she got it from her purse. The truck was dirty, dust-covered, with an alteration that looked home-made, and had a few dents. The idea of traveling in that hellish country in such a truck made her shudder. But it was good to have a clear image of the Wenzel brothers when they were young and starting out. Despite the two years' difference in their ages, they were enough alike to be twins, she thought, then put the picture down on the table at her side when she heard a car in the driveway.

Frank came around the corner with Darren. They were carrying a big plastic can of some sort, and she remembered that Frank had said he would put in a water barrel. Frank saw her and waved, and after putting the barrel down, Darren waved. He walked out of sight around the house again, and Frank joined her on the porch.

"Hi. Darren's getting some concrete blocks out of the truck. I'll set that barrel on them and let gravity do its thing when the barrel fills with water."

Carefully she said, "I just dropped in to say hello. I won't be staying long."

Frank looked at her in surprise. "Is dinner off?" Then he said, "Oh. He isn't staying. We used his truck to haul things."

Darren was back with a garden cart and the concrete blocks. After unloading them near the side of the greenhouse, he came to the porch. "Hello, again," he said to Barbara. "A drink of water and I'll be out of here. Todd's waiting for me at the house. Today's planting day, rain or no rain."

"Help yourself," Frank said. "I'll get that catnip start for Todd. It has good roots. Just tell him to keep it watered and weeded, and keep it caged."

Darren went inside for water, and Frank went out for the catnip. Barbara felt churlish and mean, but helpless. Darren was doing her father a favor, that was all it amounted to.

Darren returned with his water and glanced at the snapshot she had put on the table. Slowly he set down the glass and picked up the picture. He studied it a long time before he replaced it.

"I haven't seen one of those in many years," he said. "It brings back memories." His voice had changed. This was how he had talked about his internment in the juvenile detention camp in the California desert when he was a teenager, after the gang he had run with had been busted on drug charges. He sounded lazy and detached, almost dreamy.

"What do you mean? You know about trucks like that?" she asked.

"Sure do. We used to see them now and then, hauling illegals to work and back. Some of the guys told me they hauled more than human cargo." He picked up the snapshot again and, pointing, held it out for her to see. "Look at the floor and the benches for the human cargo. It's a unit, detachable with little effort, but when it's bolted in place over the bed of the truck you have something like a bus. Take the benches out with the floor, and you have another cargo space. They hauled a lot more than workers."

Frank came back with the potted catnip, and Darren put the snapshot on the table and took the plant. He gave Barbara a searching look, then said, "You don't want to tangle much with folks who used those trucks. See you later."

Frank walked around the house with him, and Barbara picked up the snapshot and studied it again. There were no markings on the truck, and now that it had been pointed out to her, she could see that the wood floor was too high.

When Frank returned, he picked up the snapshot and examined it closely. "He told me they used that space for drugs. Guns in, drugs out. It has nothing to do with Carrie and the here and now. Leave it alone, Bobby."

"That was thirty years ago," she said. "I doubt there's much anyone can do about it now. It's just another interesting datum." She put the snapshot back in her purse. "Actually, I wanted a snapshot to show the kind of countryside they were working in. Hot as hell, nothing alive as far as you can see." Then she thought of Darren living out on that same desert for seven years from the age of fourteen until he was twenty-one. She didn't know how anyone could endure it.

A little later, while Frank was preparing dinner, she told him about her visit with Inez. "And that was the end of marriage number one. Inez doesn't know what happened, and I guess neither Larry Wenzel nor his wife is going to tell us."

"Well, if they were into smuggling, that's cause for blackmail," Frank said, dicing potatoes.

"Not if Larry and Joe were both involved," she said. "And apparently they were both in up to their necks. At least until 1972 when Joe skedaddled."

They ate on the back porch and lingered as daylight faded and the colorful garden turned into shades of violet-gray and black. Then Frank drove her home. He wouldn't think of allowing her to walk home in the dark, he said emphatically when she protested.

At her apartment building, he put his hand on her arm when she opened the car door. "Hang on a second. Tell me what you have against Darren. I like him quite a lot."

"I know you do. And I'm coming to think of him as a pal,

sort of a brother, someone you can turn to for a favor now and then. Okay?"

He grunted and put the car in gear. "Good night. I'll see you in the morning." He didn't believe a word she had said, he thought, driving home again. But, by God, he added to himself, she was stubborn.

Inside her apartment Barbara cursed briefly. That had been a perfect chance to recite her spontaneous remark about Darren and gratitude, and she had forgotten.

The next morning Barbara told Shelley and Bailey about her conversation with Inez. "H. L. Blount is a mystery man who wouldn't have his picture taken, and who likely made whatever drug deals were being made, as well as lining up the workers. Your job, Bailey. See if there's a shred of information about him in the universe. He was about forty-five then, and may well be dead and forgotten. Also, I want an enlargement of the truck and the Wenzel group." She handed the snapshot to Bailey, then turned to Shelley. "Your turn."

"Right," Shelley said. "I'll do the last wife first because she was a dud, and I didn't get a thing from her. She's Tiffany Olstead, up in Seattle. Joe promised her that she'd see the world, travel to exotic places. She said all she ever saw were airplanes, hotel rooms, horses and roulette wheels. She lasted eighteen months, late 1988 to 1990. He never worked a day that they were together. Then I stopped to see Alexis O'Reilly in Portland, wife number two."

She drew in a long breath. "They got married in late 1975, and they built the house that burned down. He was still working for the company. She said he drank, but not a whole lot. He was very much into rock music. Buying tapes, fooling around with them, making his own selections to retape to play in the car. I had the feeling that they had a decent marriage for the first couple of years.

"Then, things changed. Just like with Inez," she added. "She doesn't know why, or what happened, but he began to drink a lot, and he became abusive. Not physically, but hurtful things he would say began to rankle. And he stopped going to work. He didn't explain, just said he was through working. He began going to a lot of concerts, taping them. And he began gambling a lot more. She had a job—she's a dietician at a Portland hospital now, back then she worked at Sacred Heart—and she couldn't leave all the time, and he went to the track, or Las Vegas, wherever without her. In 1979 she found out that he had been sleeping with Nora," Shelley said in a hushed voice.

When no one in the office stirred, she continued. "Alexis said when she found out, she packed up and left and took a lot of his things with her. She was really furious and wanted to make him sorry. She took a box full of his music tapes, racing forms, other racing stuff. He kept notebooks about horses, who sired which colt, track records, things like that, and she took all she could lay her hands on. When she filed for divorce he begged her to give it all back, and she told him she had burned everything, but she hadn't. She still had the box of his belongings, and she gave it to me. She just wanted to get rid of everything of his now, but couldn't bring herself to dump anything or destroy the tapes."

This time when Shelley paused, Barbara exhaled softly. "Jackpot," she said. She thought a moment. "Even if there was an ongoing affair between Joe and Nora, how could that lead to his blackmailing Larry?"

"Maybe he was blackmailing Nora," Shelley said. "If she is as much a part of the company as Larry is, that might work."

Barbara nodded. "It could be. Anything in that line apparent, Bailey?"

He shook his head. "I haven't found a soul who knows much about them. No live-in help, just a day cleaner who shows up while they're both gone, and takes off before they get home. They eat out a lot, order food in, or else Nora cooks. If she has close friends, they're closemouthed. I'm still digging."

"Well, we have two dates to work with," Barbara said. "In 1972 Joe took off after a big fight and never went back to the desert again. Then in 1978 or '79 he stopped working, but never missed a payday."

Frank, who had been listening intently, now cleared his throat. Barbara turned to him and waited.

"It seems to me," Frank said, "that the Wenzels have a lot of secrets in their past. Most families do. And it also appears that unless one of them writes a memoir, you'll never learn what those secrets are. Smuggling? Probably. Affairs? Not unlikely. But what good that will do your client in the here and now is problematic. How good are those alibis, Bailey?"

Bailey shrugged and shook his head. "Cast iron, as far as I can tell."

Frank turned his gaze back to Barbara. "So, no matter what you can dig up about smuggling, blackmail or anything illegal in their past, it won't matter in Carrie's trial."

"But it's connected. I feel it in my bones." She eyed Bailey speculatively. "If Nora has no close friends to confide in, maybe we should introduce her to someone. What's Sylvia up to these days?"

Sylvia Fenton at sixty-plus years was the most outrageously flamboyant woman in the whole Willamette Valley, happily married to one of its richest men. No one ever knew if she would appear with hair canary-yellow, jet-black, or fire-engine red, and her clothes were equally garish. A former off-Broadway actress, she had captivated Joseph Fenton when he was visiting New York on a diamond-buying mission for his family's jewelry business many years before. Once accepted, Sylvia had established herself as a trendsetter, one who could galvanize any committee she served on to produce results. She just incidentally liked to play cops and robbers on Bailey's behalf now and then.

Bailey complained sometimes that she bugged him endlessly when she became bored, wanting a new assignment, a new thrill. He regarded Barbara with narrowed eyes, then nodded. "I think Nora would be excited to be included in Sylvia's inner circle."

"Nothing too fast," Barbara said. "Tell her to take it easy, let Nora think she's taking the lead. Can do?"

"I'll see," Bailey said.

Frank recalled the first time he had met Sylvia, whose maid had suspected that her mother had died of neglect in a nursing home. No one had been able to find out a thing until Sylvia had gone in as a cleaning woman, scrubbed toilets, mopped, did whatever she had to do, and got the goods on the place. She was first and foremost an actress, no matter how big her bank account was. She would do fine, he thought, nodding.

Bailey had not yet found out anything about Carrie's parents. "I ruled out about a dozen guys named Frederick. That's progress, I guess. Just a couple hundred to go."

"Okay, so it's just more of the same for now," Barbara

said. "I have an appointment with the motel manager this afternoon. And I have a list of the motel guests for the night of the murder, all accounted for, respectable, etcetera." She handed the list to Bailey. "We'll want that verified eventually." She spread her hands. "And that's it."

After the others had left, she sat behind her desk considering the coming weeks and months. If nothing developed, there was little she could do, she reflected, just wait for the trial and go in empty-handed. Eventually, she might have to talk seriously with Carrie about the possibility of a plea bargain.

9

Mark Ormsby was tall, over six feet, and so thin he looked
starved, with a sallow complexion and lank sand-colored hair.
He had deep vertical frown lines and crow's-feet, although he
was no more than forty.

"Mr. Wenzel said I don't have to talk to anyone about that
night," he said.

"And he's absolutely right," Barbara said. "You don't, but
I hope you will. I have to try to fill in background in order to
defend Carrie Frederick."

He looked over her shoulder, around the empty lobby with
a nervous darting glance. "Come on in," he said. "This way."

He moved quickly, and she followed him to the office behind the check-in counter. "If anyone comes, you understand
I'll have to go out to the desk," he said. "No one else is on
duty right now." He left the door ajar and seated himself at a
cluttered desk, motioning toward a chair for her.

"I understand," she said gravely, accepting his responsibility with the same concern he showed. "What I'm interested in is why you hired her and how she worked out. Things like that."

"Yes. I see. I needed two cocktail waitresses and six or seven showed up that day," he said. He spoke fast in a high-pitched voice that would quickly start to grate. "I was interviewing one of them when I heard the piano. We hadn't had a player for over a year. I mean, with the business climate the way it's been, it didn't seem worth the cost, and he wasn't very good. So it was a surprise. I started to go out and say knock it off, but it didn't sound bad, so I didn't. Then it got better. I interviewed another woman, and by then I was thinking that whoever was playing might be a draw. Business was already down these past two years, and with the smoking ban, it got worse. It wasn't my fault. Nothing I could do about it, but we couldn't keep waitresses. The tips were down, you see. And I just wanted part-timers. I left her for last, and by then I was sort of liking what she was doing, mixing things up like she does. And I hired her. Business was almost double within a month. Word of mouth, the best advertisement, you see."

"She said she complained to you that Joe Wenzel was harassing her. Do you recall that?"

"Oh, yes. Two weeks after she started, and I could already see that she was helping business. But he was part owner. It was a real dilemma. I didn't know what to do. Rock and hard place, you see."

"I understand," Barbara said, mustering some faux sympathy. "What did you do? Did you talk to him?"

"No. No. Not him. I mean, he already knew what he was doing, and he didn't care about business, or anything else that I could see. I mean, he took the executive suite and ordered things at odd hours from the kitchen, and his whole attitude said he didn't care what anyone thought. I talked to the other Mr. Wenzel, his brother. I thought he should know, and speak to him."

"Did he?"

"I don't know. He came out with Mrs. Wenzel to hear her play, and he looked at the books and saw how things had improved and all. And the sons came out to hear her, and they looked at the books, and I supposed they would have a family meeting or something, but no one told me anything—they never do—and Joe Wenzel didn't change, so I just don't know."

"What did you mean by his attitude? Was he abusive?"

"No. No. I didn't mean to imply anything like that. But, you see, he didn't care about anyone here. I mean, he'd come in late in the day, dirty. I don't mean road mussed like the travelers or anything like that. Dirty. Dirty hands, dirty clothes, like he'd been rooting through the ashes at his old house or something. I guess his clothes all got burned up and he only had what was in his suitcase when he came here, and he didn't get around to buying much new. So he'd come back from wherever he'd been, dirty, not shaved, with the same clothes on day after day, getting dirtier and dirtier, and he'd go through the lobby to the bar and get a bottle of Jack Daniel's and carry it back, no matter who was in the lobby. It made a bad impression. And he didn't care."

He sounded anguished, as if personally to blame for such reprehensible behavior. Barbara resisted an urge to either pat his head or belt him. She nodded. "Was he like that when he hung out watching Carrie play?"

"No. He cleaned himself up by evening. He'd eat in the dining room or else in his room. He wanted a table waiting for him whether he was going to show up or not. There had to be a table for him every night, no matter how busy the dining room got. And sometimes, in spite of the business climate, it did get busy, you know, but not like before. Sometimes when she practiced, he'd come to the bar and watch her. He didn't usually stay long because the cleaning people were around, and we'd be stocking the bar and doing things of that sort. She did that every day, after the continental breakfast was over at nine-thirty, she would practice. The nights she played, he'd sit at the bar watching her and drinking. She told me, and then Mickey told me the same thing. I wasn't usually here at night, you understand."

"Of course. They say no one heard the shot that night. Isn't that a little strange? With so many people in the bar, leaving, probably standing around and talking a little."

He shook his head. "Not really. I'll show you." He stood up, his movements as jerky as his speech had been. She followed him from the office through the lobby. It was spacious with comfortable chairs, a few tables, the usual tourist brochures, the check-in counter. "See, here are the rest rooms, women's, men's, and next is the elevator and then the stairs. Across the corridor, two meeting rooms, empty that night, of course, although they used to be filled, but then… Anyway, next, the housekeeping supplies room. His suite, the executive suite, is opposite. And on the upper floor it's the same layout, meeting rooms and the executive suite, unoccupied that weekend. Most weekends, in fact. Sixty-five-percent occupancy on good nights. So no one was very close, and the rooms are pretty much soundproof. Did you want to see the executive suite?"

She said yes, and he opened the rooms for her. There was

a large bedroom first, next to the inside stairwell, then a larger living room, and beyond it a tiny kitchen. The suite was very handsome, richly furnished. There were doors to the hall and doors to the outside in both the living room and bedroom.

"I suppose it had a lot of his things in it when he was killed," Barbara said.

"Not as much as you would think," Ormsby said. "Racing forms and newspapers, a few magazines. A lot of house plan sketches. Personal things in the bathroom, a few clothes. He had a CD player and disks, and a tape recorder and player. He had earphones that plugged into the tape player. Heaven knows why. There weren't any tapes. I've been told people could hear his music late at night sometimes, but I don't see how. If they complained, what could I do? He was part owner."

"What happened to his things?"

"The police took some. I made them give me an inventory, of course. Then Mr. Larry Wenzel came over and finished clearing stuff out. I gave him the inventory. I didn't want any problem to come up about something missing, you understand."

"That was wise," she said. "Did Joe Wenzel ever have a woman here?"

His mouth pursed and he nodded. "I believe he did now and then, but not that night." They left the suite and she asked which room Gregory used sometimes.

Obligingly Ormsby showed her the room reserved for Gregory Wenzel, next to the supplies room. It was a predictable motel room, with an outside door and the door to the hall, better furnished than most motel rooms, but not as luxurious as the suite.

"You're certain it wasn't used that night?" she asked, looking it over.

"Absolutely," he said. "The maid would have known. They can tell, you know."

When Barbara returned to her office, she found Carrie in the reception room talking to Maria. "Hi," she said.

"Do you have a minute?" Carrie asked. She looked as woebegone as a stray.

"Sure. Come on back." She led the way to her office. "What's up?" she asked, taking a seat on the sofa, motioning for Carrie to join her.

Carrie slumped into a chair. "I'm trying to find a job," she said. "I was going to register with a temp agency, but one of the questions asked if I had ever been arrested. I told the woman I wasn't feeling very well and I left. It will be like that, won't it?"

"Maybe," Barbara said. "What were you registering for?"

"Anything. Housecleaning, clean stores, wait on tables." She drew in a breath. "If I lie about it, would it hurt my chances? I mean if they found out."

"They probably would find out," Barbara said. "Eugene's a small town in a lot of ways. Hold it a sec, will you? Be right back." She went to the reception room again, where she was not at all surprised to find Maria measuring coffee into the coffeemaker so that all Barbara would have to do was push the start button. "Maria, will you ask Mama to poke around for a job for Carrie, no questions asked. She can say I recommend her, if that would help." Maria's mother knew everyone in the neighborhood. If there was a job available, she would know about it.

Back in her own office again she said, "Try to be patient. We'll see if we can round up something for you. Meanwhile, do you want to take a walk?"

* * *

Barbara drove them to the end of the parking area at Skinner Butte Park and headed toward the Rose Garden. Aromatherapy, she thought. No one could stay depressed after wandering among the roses for half an hour or so.

"Have you thought of any incidents from the lounge that might help?" she asked as they walked.

"Nothing specific. No one liked him, but no one hated him that I could see."

The river sparkled and foamed over rocks newly revealed by low water. Barbara could have named the month just by noting which rocks were visible.

"Are the berries edible?" Carrie asked when they began passing them.

"Sure. And clean. No sprays. Help yourself, if you can find any ripe ones left. They get pretty much picked over."

Carrie started picking blackberries and eating them. "Darren told me what you did for him," she said, wiping her hands on her jeans and grimacing. "That one was sour. Darren thinks you're terrific."

"He wouldn't say anything like that," Barbara said with a laugh.

"He didn't have to say it," Carrie said, hunting for another ripe berry. "I could tell." She jerked her hand back and put her finger in her mouth.

"Thorns," Barbara said. "I thought you knew."

Carrie shook her head. "I never was out in the country much, just cities. This is the first one I've ever seen that has blackberries growing in it."

"They're called noxious weeds in these parts," Barbara said. "There's a mother plant under Eugene, all of the county probably, and she sends her daughters up everywhere, overnight it seems. You can't get rid of them. What did you do in all those cities you kept visiting?"

"Got a job and a place to sleep, then walked around or drove around looking at things. I spent a lot of time in the libraries. Darren loaned me his card so I don't have to stay there to read. First time since I left Terre Haute that I could actually take books out with me. My God! Look!"

She stopped moving, gazing at the river, where a great gray heron was skimming inches above the water. They watched it out of sight. "I never knew they were this far north," Carrie said. "I used to see them in Florida."

"When you were driving around, do you think you would have recognized anything from your past?"

"Barbara, believe me, I wasn't looking for anything in particular. Just looking. Every city was new to me. Like Eugene is new."

"Okay. Pretty soon we'll leave the bike path. I want to show you one of my favorite places." They walked on in silence. But she had been searching, Barbara thought. She had been looking for a lost childhood.

They left the path, went up some steps and to the entrance to the garden, where Carrie stopped moving again and drew in a long breath. "It's beautiful," she whispered.

Then Barbara felt as if she had been forgotten, as Carrie walked along the path bordered with tidy little tea roses, on to the exuberant shrub roses with ten-foot-long branches heavy with blossoms, on to the ramblers, the reds so dark they looked black until highlighted by sun when they glowed bloodred. She had drawn ahead of Carrie, feeling the intoxication the fragrance always brought. When she turned to glance back, Carrie had frozen in place, staring at a rose blossom. Her face had gone white.

Carrie saw herself as a small child with her nose almost in a pink rose. Ramon drew her back and said, "Don't touch. That's a honeybee and she's working hard. Watch."

"How do you know it's a girl bee?"

"The workers are all girls. Look at her legs, all yellow and thick with pollen. She's collecting it to take back to the hive and feed the queen. Watch. Her legs are so heavy she's staggering."

The bee wobbled when it started to fly. She watched its unsteady flight. "That's what they eat? The king too?"

"There's no king, just the queen and the lady workers and babies."

"Carrie? Are you ill?" Barbara asked at her side. She saw a bee on the rose and looked closer at Carrie. Had she been stung? Was she having a reaction?

Barbara's voice jolted Carrie, banished the memory. Her lips felt stiff, and she shivered as if with a chill. "I'm okay," she said. Again, she thought. They kept coming back, snapshots of a forbidden past. It wasn't real, she told herself. Barbara was real, and the roses all around them, the perfumed air, the heron on the river. That was all real. She clung to them as if to a lifesaver, those things that she knew were real. "I'm fine," she said then. "I felt dizzy for a second. Too much perfume."

Barbara stayed at her side as they wandered through the garden for a few more minutes. Was that another phobia to add to the list, she wondered: hospitals, explosions, fire and now bees? Carrie had looked deathly pale and terrified.

Walking back, Carrie was withdrawn, yet at the same time

strangely alert, examining the river, the trees, other strollers and cyclists, everything before her eyes as if committing it all to memory. They returned to Barbara's car and she drove to the office, where they separated, Carrie to retrieve her old Datsun and go back to the apartment, Barbara to go back to work.

"If Mama comes up with something for you, I'll give you a call. Do you have a telephone in the apartment yet?"

"Yes. Darren put in an extension. It's his number. Do you have it?" Barbara shook her head, and Carrie told her the number, got in her car and left.

She could still see the little girl, Carrie thought fearfully, and the bee heavy with pollen. It was not like the flashes of fantasy; this was a memory lodged in her head like a regular memory, one she could revisit, a part of her. Carrie was shaking too hard to continue to drive. She pulled over and rested her forehead on the steering wheel, willing the false memory to leave, remembering snatches from the many articles she had read about schizophrenia. If the fantasy life became too real, it could replace the reality of the here and now. The voices could become too powerful to resist, the visions could overwhelm the actual world. You were lost in madness.

10

The stack of discovery papers grew day by day. Bailey's reports came in. Barbara asked for the inventory from Wenzel's suite, and days later received it. Bailey said morosely that Sylvia had made contact with the target. Her words, he had added, and Sylvia was as happy as a kid at Christmas to be playing cops and robbers again. Mama had found a part-time job for Carrie, making tamales. Carrie was delighted with it. That's part of the recordless, paperless underground economy, Barbara murmured to Shelley. Shelley had the whole crew out at her house for an end-of-season swimming and cookout party. Darren, Todd and Carrie joined them, and it was a good day, Barbara had to admit later.

"But," she said to Frank in late September, "a lot of stuff is piling up, and I can't see a way to make the puzzle pieces fit together. Blank walls everywhere I turn."

They were waiting for Bailey, who had called to say he had something.

"I've got some numbers to play with," Frank said. "It will keep until Bailey gets here."

He had been looking into the finances of the Wenzel Corporation, a job his law firm could handle even better than Bailey could. Now and then, he sometimes said, he liked to use the resources at his disposal just to remind his partner, Sam Bixby, that he was still in the game. Frank understood perfectly well that some of the junior partners lusted after his sumptuous office, and he had no intention of relinquishing it until some indefinite future date when his threatened retirement became an actuality.

Bailey and Shelley entered together, and he headed straight to the bar and mixed himself a drink. Barbara watched without comment. If he hadn't earned it, the next time he showed up he would find nothing but orange juice there.

He slouched into a chair, took a long drink and gave her a mean look. "You sent me on a wild-goose chase," he said. "I found Frederick in spite of everything you told me, not because of."

"What did you find?"

"Born in 1928, in Wheeling, West Virginia, died 1978. Fifty years old, Barbara. Light brown hair, nearly two hundred pounds. I don't know who the guy in your picture was, but he sure wasn't Ronald Frederick."

She drew in a breath. "Are you sure?"

"Barbara, come on. I narrowed it down to three guys and then sicced an agency back in Roanoke on it. They got it down to one, and found an old buddy who's still around and who kept in touch once in a while. He gave them a picture, and a copy of the old school book with pictures. Before and after years, and a paunch happened." He rooted around in his duffel bag, brought out a folder and handed it to her. Then he emptied his glass and held it up in an inquiring way. He always did that. The first drink was his for the taking, but additional drinks were by consent. Bailey lived by his own set of rules.

She nodded and examined the pictures from his folder while he returned to the bar. This Frederick had been blond as a boy; the later snapshot showed his hair darker, but still fair. And he was overweight. He was not the trim black-haired man in the newspaper picture who was almost certainly Carrie's father. A copy of that clipping was in the folder also. She passed them over to Frank.

"He was a housepainter who migrated with the birds," Bailey said, sitting again. "Sometimes he got back to Wheeling for a visit. Then, along about 1978 he dropped off the planet, as far as the buddy knew. No more cards, no more visits, nothing. His wife was his age, and I don't have a picture of her. The old buddy didn't know a thing about a daughter."

Frank was frowning as he handed the set of pictures to Shelley. She studied the clipping, then the other two pictures. "Someone faked the article," she said then.

"And the death certificates and her birth certificate," Barbara said. "Her whole history is a fake." She stood up and walked to her desk, trying to think through it all, then came back. "Let's leave it for a few minutes. Anything else?" she asked Bailey.

"On a more cheerful note," he said, "Sylvia is making progress. She's organizing a committee to hold an annual benefit to raise money for the homeless. The steering committee will be no more than eight people, and the qualifications include starting out dirt poor and making it big through hard work and a bit of luck. She invited Nora and Larry Wenzel to join. Larry said nope, no time for anything like that, but Nora walked right in. Sylvia had her out to lunch to discuss the event they'll put on. She's thinking of a masquerade party for Halloween, charge a hundred bucks a head, have a costume judging contest, the whole works, at her place. Nora's all atwitter. She got a peek at Sylvia's little place out in the country." He took another long drink, then, grinning, said, "Sylvia's going to go as Medusa. Bet she'll use live snakes in her hairdo."

Frank laughed, thinking how Sylvia must have handled this. She would have dragged out pictures of her cold-water flat in New York, and some publicity pictures of her early work on the stage, and she would have had Nora talking about her early work within minutes. He could imagine the conversations: Oh, I had it a lot worse than that. I was poorer than you were. Worked day and night… All that against the background of one of the biggest estates around, cluttered with expensive art, with semiprecious and precious stones strewn about, a staff of a dozen or so.

"Anything yet on H. L. Blount?" Barbara asked.

Bailey shook his head. "Nada. Probably a pseudonym. If you're going for a funny name, why choose Blount? Why not Green or Smith? I don't even know what the *H* and *L* stood for. Hector? Horatio? Lancelot? Lucifer?" He shrugged. "It's a wash, Barbara."

She turned to Frank. "You said you have some numbers or something?"

He knew she was as distracted by the mystery of Carrie's parents as he was, and he kept it short. "Yep. The Wenzels arrived in Eugene with more than two million, it appears. For the first five years or so they were shelling out more than they were taking in. Buying up parcels of land here and there, building on spec, building their own two big houses and offices. I have all their projects listed, how much they cost, how much they brought in eventually, and so on. For the past two years or so things have been tough, lost contracts, canceled jobs, things of that sort. It's reading material when there's nothing else around."

"I'll get in touch with Janey Lipscomb," Barbara said, veering off the subject, confirming his suspicion that she was paying little attention to his report.

Janey Lipscomb was a psychologist who looked like a pixie with a snub nose, curly red hair, freckles and an infectious smile. She was the least threatening psychologist imaginable, and it was impossible to think of her activating anyone's phobia of doctors and hospitals. Also, she was one of the best. She had worked on cases for Barbara in the past. If anyone could break through Carrie's wall of amnesia, it was Janey, if Carrie would talk to her, and if Janey had time to take this on. She worked for the Children's Services Agency, and those people were driven hard by a supervisor, who, Janey said, was a fire-breathing dragon. A children's psychologist was exactly what Barbara thought was called for. She wanted to get in touch with the child locked inside Carrie.

There were a few more matters to discuss, then the others wandered out, and Barbara sat behind her desk considering the best way to approach Janey. Over the years they had become friends who met for lunch once in a while, or had dinner or saw a movie together. They had a lot in common: two single, professional women who couldn't keep a flame going long enough to get warmed all the way through, was how Janey had put it. She was not supposed to take outside cases, but she was underpaid, working for an underfunded agency, and she was constantly running short of money. That was a starting point. This would have to be another bit of the record-less, paperless economy. She dialed Janey's number and left a message on her voice mail to call back, and while she waited, she planned her strategy, first to interest Janey, and second to make Carrie agree to talk to her.

She met Janey that evening at the Electric Station. With live music it was noisy and crowded in the bar and lounge, but very quiet in the back booth in the restaurant proper.

The waiter was at the table the instant they sat down.

"Are you really paying?" Janey asked. "If you are, I want a daiquiri, if you're not, I'll stick with water."

Barbara ordered two daiquiris.

"So let's clear the decks," Janey said as soon as the waiter left. "What do you want from me?" She grinned her big elfish grin. "I've noticed over the past few years that when you offer to pay, it's because you want to drain my brain. Drain away."

Barbara laughed and forgot the strategy she had planned. "Damn, you're on to me. Okay. Here goes." She began to describe Carrie and was still at it when their drinks were served. The food waiter came and they ordered, then Barbara picked up where she had left off.

She ended her recital as they were eating. Janey's grin had faded, and she shook her head when Barbara became silent.

"Amnesia's a tough one," she said. "After this many years, it could be intractable, and it isn't something you can get around if you find the right question to ask. No doubt, they had good psychologists in the hospital where she was treated, and her amnesia was new then, but apparently they got nowhere. I think you're talking about months of therapy with no good prognosis."

"What about recovered memories through hypnosis?"

"Hogwash for the most part. Read the transcripts. Answers are fed in along with the questions. Under hypnosis most subjects really want to please the hypnotist and, God, can they pick up clues, nuances, subtle influences. Usually they know in advance what the hypnotist is fishing for, and they try to satisfy." She sipped her drink, took another bite, then said, "Tell me again about the Rose Garden incident."

Barbara described it again. "I'm sure it wasn't the flower itself, but the configuration of the bee on the flower that set her off. She turned white and looked panic-stricken. I think she remembers things and then loses them again."

"And her foster parents said she made up stories out of fairy tales," Janey murmured. She pushed her plate back and drew in a breath. "I'm stuffed to the gills. Let's look at the dessert tray."

Barbara gave her an incredulous look and she said, "I'm eating for two. Two days, that is. Tomorrow I'll fast."

Barbara had coffee and watched Janey tuck away cheesecake piled high with raspberries and whipped cream. "You'll have to fast for three days," she said.

"Worth it. It all evens out," Janey said and poured coffee for herself. "Look, if Carrie will talk to me, I'll have a go at it. I have an idea or two I want to think about first. And it has to be over the weekend. I'm working overtime these days, and I'm beat by the end of the day."

"Cash," Barbara said. "Whatever the going fee is for private consultations."

"Make that singular," Janey said. "If it doesn't work, there's little point in continuing. I don't have time, and I don't think it would be worthwhile. Are you going to tell her what Bailey found out?"

Barbara shook her head. "Not yet. Not until I know more than I do now. I'm afraid it would send her spinning out of control to learn that her parents weren't killed in that crash. If that wasn't them, where are they?"

"Exactly," Janey said. "And who arranged for her to be brainwashed into accepting that story? And maybe more important, why?" She regarded Barbara very seriously then. "Have you thought through what you're doing? That you might be prying open Pandora's box?"

11

Barbara was too edgy to sit still that Sunday afternoon. She paced in and out of Frank's house, up and down the stairs, to the living room, back to the kitchen. She had talked Carrie into seeing Janey, had introduced them at two that day, and now was waiting for Janey. She would be no later than five, Janey had said. She had a date at six.

"You have to collect the seeds as soon as they get ripe," Frank said, coming in from his greenhouse. "I swiped seeds from Frazier's hellebore and planted them. The prettiest pink you ever saw when they bloom."

Barbara looked at her watch again, then stood up and walked out to the back porch. He had known she was paying no attention, and her restless wandering was making him nearly as edgy as she was. He washed his hands and thought about dinner.

* * *

In Carrie's apartment Janey was saying, "I imagine almost every child has an imaginary playmate at one time or another. Why don't you play the piano and tell me about yours."

They had been chatting for more than an hour although Carrie had been apprehensive at first. But Janey didn't look like a doctor, and she didn't talk like one. Carrie didn't even know what all they had been talking about. It was more like girl-friends confiding in each other, going from one subject to another, than like doctor-patient talk. Carrie had told her about the only psychologist she could remember. "He asked me if anyone ever touched me in a way that made me uncomfortable, and I told him yes, a lot of them had, and he got all excited. I told him about the doctors, and the people who made me do exercises and things—now I know they were therapists, but I didn't know who they were then—and he looked mad. Not that way, he said. I didn't know what he was talking about."

But play the piano and talk at the same time? She hesitated.

"I'd really like to hear you play," Janey said.

Carrie went to the piano. "It isn't concert-ready. The sound's off."

Janey laughed. "I'm not a musician. If you hadn't told me, I probably wouldn't have noticed."

Carrie began to play and Janey sat nearby listening. "The imaginary playmate," she said.

"I don't think I had one."

"Okay. What about the happiest day of your life as a child?"

Carrie played something fast and shook her head. "I didn't have that, either."

"Make up a story about an imaginary playmate and tell me what the happiest day of *her* life would have been like. You can tell a story, a fib, a fairy tale, anything."

"It's just a story, a made-up story," Carrie said after a few moments. "Like you said, a fairy tale. Is that okay?"

"Sure."

"She's little, smaller than me, but she sort of looks like me," Carrie said hesitantly. She glanced at Janey. At her nod, she continued. "She likes to run outside, then back in, then out again, just because she can. She's in a big house. She thinks it must have a thousand rooms, and she can go in them all if she wants to. Sometimes she likes to smell her mother's clothes in the closet. They smell like flowers. Daddy's clothes don't smell like that. They're like the woods."

She was speaking in a low voice and her hands moved effortlessly over the keys playing Chopin softly as she talked on and on, her voice becoming dreamier as she continued.

"Her Aunt Loony has a big tummy, and she lets the little girl feel the baby moving. It's like magic. She wants Mommy to get a baby too and Mommy laughs, then Aunt Loony and Gramma laugh. And Mommy says when Daddy comes back we'll tell you a secret. She loves secrets. She plays the piano and Gramma comes to sit by me and she plays too, and then she starts to cry and I think I did something wrong, but she says she's crying because she's so happy. I didn't know people cried when they got happy. When Daddy comes home, Daddy and Mommy go to her bedroom and read to her, and Mommy says that when Daddy is done with his work, we'll move to a real house with a garden like Gramma's and we'll have a baby. And I start to cry, and Mommy says I shouldn't be unhappy about it, and I tell her I'm crying because I'm so happy. We'll have a house and I can go in and out as much as I want to, and I'll have a little sister. So I cry."

Her voice trailed off and Janey asked softly, "What's the name of the little girl?"

"Carolyn. I like that name better than Carol. So I called her Carolyn. I used to dream about her."

"But not now?"

"No. I guess imaginary playmates fade out when you grow up. I made up a song for her. It's called, *Please don't cry, Carolyn Frye.*" She played a merry little tune, then abruptly stopped and stood up. "So there's your fairy tale," she said brusquely. "I have to go to the bathroom." She hurried from the room.

Janey moved away from the piano and was looking over the library books on a table when Carrie returned. "You offered me coffee awhile ago. I wonder if we could have some now."

Carrie looked relieved. "Sure. Isn't this a wonderful apartment? It has the neatest coffeemaker. Come on, I'll make some. Did you ever make tamales? I had no idea they were so complicated."

"Bobby, for heaven's sake, light somewhere," Frank said in his kitchen. "If eye power could make the watch hands move faster, you'd be in tomorrow by now."

She looked at him. "That doesn't make a bit of sense."

"Just sit down. She'll be here any minute."

It was ten minutes in real time, hours in Barbara's time frame, before Janey arrived. Frank went to open the door with Barbara close on his heels.

"Come in. Come in," Frank said. "It's good to see you again. Did you talk to Carrie?"

Janey shook her head. "No. I talked to Carolyn Frye."

Then, sitting in Frank's living room, Janey told them about her talk with Carrie. "You have to separate out the background gestalt from the pertinent recalled facts," she said. "First, going in and out freely suggests that wherever she had lived before, that was not possible. An apartment, a truck life, trailer court? Whatever. Then, not that her grandmother played the piano with her, which she seemed to accept as normal, but that her grandmother cried out of happiness. Her parents went to her bedroom to read to her, and told her to expect a new baby in the family. Again, the implication is not that they read to her, or that there was a bedroom, only that there was a secret that they revealed. And so on. If I hadn't known ahead of time that the memories of a nomadic life were imposed, I would have agreed that her stories were a fantasy."

She shook her head sadly. "Carrie really has amnesia for a large part of her childhood. Everyone does. We don't form long-term memories before three or even four, and then for another year or so they are sporadic, and usually concern events that disrupt an everyday routine. A birthday party, or a special Christmas gift, something unusual. Between six and seven the memories are firm for most people, but she doesn't have any until she was nearly eight and half years old. The fragmented memories she does have were labeled fantasies, and intellectually she had to accept that and attribute them to her imaginary friend, Carolyn Frye."

"If we can get her to talk about Carolyn Frye, we might learn what happened to her," Barbara said when Janey paused.

Janey shook her head. "She needs to be in the care of a professional. Do you know what abreaction means?"

"Reliving an incident, something like that," Barbara said.

"Something like that," Janey agreed. "Whatever happened to her wiped out more than a year of her life, not a trace left. That's real, Barbara. If she relives whatever happened, it could be worse this time around without professional help at hand. You can't provide that kind of help, and neither can I. I couldn't take her case and provide the intensive psychological support she needs. Psychologically, she's at risk. Don't push her. You don't batter down a wall unless you have a clear idea of what's on the other side and you're ready to stand by your client and face whatever it is with her."

Chastened, Barbara asked, "What do you suggest?"

"Normally I'd say she should be under the care of a full-time counselor, but she would have to agree, and I don't think she would. For now, I'd say leave her alone. She's built a strong wall around herself. Just hope it continues to hold until she's out from under the charge she faces, then deal with it."

Dinner was a quiet affair. Barbara was morose and the beef stroganoff was wasted on her, Frank knew. She didn't linger after helping clear the table and accepting her share of leftovers for another day. After she was gone, Frank sat in his study at his ancient desk and strained to hear voices that he well knew were not there. He felt as if there were whispers just out of earshot, and if he tried hard enough he could catch the words. Carolyn Frye, he thought. It was something about Carolyn Frye.

Carrie had been through hell, yet the self she showed the world now was a resilient, self-sufficient young woman. He admired her quite a bit. Carrie. Carol. Carolyn. Who was she?

He worked at the crossword puzzle the way he did most Sunday nights, but his mind kept wandering, and he kept straining to hear the nonexistent voices, and finally gave it up and got ready for bed. The coon cats settled at his feet like bookends, purring. He drifted, then slept, and suddenly he could hear the words clearly, and he sat up. Carolyn Frye. Robert Frye. It was six-thirty in the morning.

By seven-thirty he was in his office and by eight-thirty he had two file folders on his desk. When his secretary arrived at nine-thirty, she was indignant when she saw him. She never got there earlier than that, since he never showed up until ten or later, but there he was at his desk. After one look at his expression, fixed in a ferocious scowl, she held her tongue and went on to her own office to open the mail. She was even more surprised a few minutes later to see Barbara hurry past her door and go into Frank's office.

"What happened?" Barbara demanded. "Are you all right?" He had had a minor heart attack a few years before, and any call out of the ordinary from him made her own heart race. That morning he had left a message on her office phone to meet him at his office as soon as she could.

"Sit down and read this," he said, pushing a folder across his desk.

She sat in one of his clients' chairs and started to read, then stopped and looked at him. "My God," she whispered. She turned back to the newspaper article she had begun. It was in a Eugene newspaper, dated June 20, 1978. The headline said Two Killed in Car Bomb Incident. "Robert Frye and his wife Judith Frye were killed instantly when a car bomb exploded Saturday, June 19. Their daughter Carolyn, aged seven, was critically injured and was airlifted to a critical burn unit in Portland where she is in intensive care...."

She skimmed the article and read the next one. It said that

Carolyn Frye had succumbed to her injuries and died in the Portland hospital where she had been flown. Surviving the tragedy were Judith Frye's mother, Laura Hazlett, and her sister, Louise Braniff, who was also injured. The article went on to mention members of Robert Frye's family in California.

There were many more articles. She skimmed another two or three, then slammed them on his desk. "I want to talk to Louise Braniff," she said, as grim as Frank was. "Now."

"I called her. She was at a meeting at the university. I told her we have to see her immediately. She'll go home directly the meeting's over, and meet us there at ten-thirty."

"Was it solved?" she asked, pointing to the folder.

"No. It was in my unsolved cases files. I remembered the name overnight. But I missed the connection until I read those. I forgot that Louise Braniff's name was listed."

"That damn bitch," Barbara muttered, remembering that she had suspected that Louise Braniff had a personal interest in Carrie Frederick.

"Exactly," Frank said.

Barbara jumped up and walked across the office furiously. She wanted to kick something. No, she thought, not something. She wanted to kick Louise Braniff. She returned to Frank's desk. "That says Carolyn died. How did she end up in Boston hospital with a different name?"

"Let's ask Louise Braniff," Frank said, as angry as she was.

12

Barbara drove slowly down the broad, tree-lined street searching out house numbers, then stopped looking at them when she spotted the black Saab in a driveway. She pulled in behind it. The house before them was a stately three-storied mansion, with meticulously maintained landscaping of shrubs and evergreen trees. Neither she nor Frank spoke when she pulled on the hand brake and they left the car and went to the front door. It was opened almost instantly at her ring.

Louise Braniff was as carefully groomed as she had been the first time Barbara saw her, today in a simple rose-colored linen skirt suit with touches of gold at her throat and in earrings.

"Ms. Holloway, come in. I just arrived myself." She looked past Barbara at Frank and nodded. "You called?"

"My father and colleague," Barbara said brusquely. Frank nodded and they stepped into the house.

"Has anything happened? Is Car—Ms. Frederick all right?"

"Use her name," Barbara said. "Carolyn."

Louise paled and held on to the doorknob with a white-knuckled grip. "You know?" she whispered.

"We know. We have to talk," Barbara said.

Louise nodded, released the doorknob and walked ahead of them down a wide hallway, motioning for them to follow. The house appeared to be as well maintained as the front yard, with gleaming white woodwork, wide-plank polished floors, scattered Oriental rugs, good art on the walls. They walked past two or three open doors to other rooms, past a broad, carpeted staircase, and entered a room with wide windows and walls of filled bookshelves.

Louise motioned to matching tapestry-covered chairs, and seated herself on a love seat. When she faced Barbara she looked as if she had aged ten years since opening the door for them. "How did you find out?"

"What difference does it make?" Barbara said. "The question is why the charade, the hocus-pocus, the lies you told?"

Louise closed her eyes for a moment, then, with her head bowed, she said, "I had to. Does she know?"

"No. She thinks her name is Carol Frederick. What's going on, Ms. Braniff? What are you up to?"

"I'm trying to protect her," Louise said in a low voice. She drew in a breath. "Much of what I told you is true. I really did go to hear her play and encouraged others to hear her. We really did intend to send her to Hamburg. Then she was arrested. I knew the others would back out, and I didn't even approach them after that."

"You're paying for her defense yourself? Is that what you're saying?"

She nodded.

"Jesus," Barbara muttered. "If you recognized her, knew she was your niece, why didn't you acknowledge that, take her in, tell her the truth? What game are you playing?"

"I was afraid to, for her sake," Louise said. "She mustn't know the truth, ever. I'll pay whatever it costs to free her, and then I'll send her to Hamburg myself. But she can't know the truth!"

"You blindfolded my daughter, put her in a straitjacket and put her in harm's way," Frank said roughly. "We deserve an explanation."

"You would have done the same thing," Louise cried. "I would do anything to protect her, and so would you for your child. She's all I have left," she said, then fell silent.

Frank stood up and walked to a window across the room and stood with his back to them. "I think you'd better start back at the beginning," he said. He swung around. "What happened here back in 1978?"

Louise moistened her lips. She was still very pale, visibly shaken, and her voice was unsteady when she spoke again. "Judith and I grew up in this house," she said. "She married Robert and moved to the Washington area with him, but every summer they came for a visit." With her head lowered, she went on. "They came that summer, just Judith and Carolyn. Robert was working for Senator Atherton, on a fact-finding mission in California. He planned to come for just a few days later on. Carolyn was a magical child," she said softly. "Like a beautiful bird flying all over the house, to the garden, upstairs, down, laughing. She was so precocious. Judith and I were playing the piano, a Chopin and Liszt dialogue in music, and we kept getting our hands tangled, and broke up laughing. In just a few minutes we heard Carolyn playing, trying to do both parts. She could play anything she heard once. Then Mother sat with her and they played it together. She was so gifted, truly magical. She had just turned seven, an exquisite, rare prodigy."

Her voice had thickened, and Barbara realized that she was weeping, oblivious of the tears. Frank started to say something, and Barbara motioned for him to wait. In a moment Louise started talking again.

"Robert came on Thursday that week, excited about what he had learned. I don't know what it was. All Judith had said was that it was a fact-finding mission. They were planning on moving back to the West Coast. She was pregnant, and didn't want another child in a high-rise apartment building. We were all so happy." She sniffed, then stood up. "Please, excuse me." She hurried from the room.

Frank reseated himself, and he and Barbara waited in silence for Louise to return. She was composed when she got back, but her eyes were red-rimmed, and she had a box of tissues with her.

"On Saturday morning," she said, "they had packed a rental car and were ready to leave for Senator Atherton's ranch out by Pendleton. Robert was behind the wheel and Judith was at the door. She had opened the back door for Carolyn when Carolyn remembered Tookey. That was her stuffed elephant." Her voice became fainter now. "She said, 'I have to get Tookey,' and she started to run. I thought I remembered that it was in the breakfast room, and I had started back to the house when Robert turned on the ignition and the car exploded. I was knocked down, unconscious. I woke up in the hospital and Cyrus, my husband, told me that Judith and

Robert were dead and Carolyn was critically injured in a Portland hospital. I lost my baby that day, six months pregnant, and I was in the hospital for another ten days. Cyrus told me that Carolyn had died. Someone had delivered her ashes and a death certificate. He had Robert and Judith cremated, and later we had a memorial service for them all."

No one spoke when she became silent again.

"You recognized her when you went to hear her play?" Barbara said after a few moments.

"Not at first. It was pleasant, but not…not spectacular. It was when she started the medley. She did that by the time she was five, played phrases of one thing then another along with bits she improvised. I stood up to get a better look at her." She closed her eyes again and cleared her throat. "I thought briefly that I could see Robert on one side of her and Judith on the other, merging into her, fading into her, and I knew. I nearly fainted, and fell back into my chair and couldn't move again until she finished and walked out. I started to run after her, but I realized what it meant, and I didn't move."

"What do you mean, what it meant?"

"Who has the power to falsify a death certificate?" she cried in anguish. "To provide ashes? To make a hospital, the doctors, others go along with such a monstrous lie? And for what reason? They must have thought she knew something, that she had overheard a conversation, had seen something. Someone meant to kill them all with that car bomb. They might still be out there, the people who wanted her dead. She can't know the truth! She is Carol Frederick and she has to remain Carol Frederick!" She was weeping again. "It would be better for her to go to prison than to learn the truth and put herself in jeopardy."

Frank's tight-lipped anger had dissipated, and now he said in a very gentle voice, "You don't plan to enter her life at all?"

"I can't," she whispered. "I told my attorney to change my will. Everything is for her, and I'll set up a trust fund for her immediate use following the trial, but she can't know who it's from or why. I can't let her know me or even see me. She might remember."

Frank stood up. "Ms. Braniff, we have a lot of things to discuss. I wonder if it's too impolite to ask for coffee now, take a little break."

She jumped up, obviously relieved to be asked to do something. They all went out to her kitchen.

Later, sitting in a lovely green-and-white breakfast room with jalousie windows overlooking the garden, they continued to talk. Louise had recovered her composure, and even smiled when she said that Carolyn had started to call her Aunt Loony by the age of two. "They didn't come the summer she was five," she said. "She had chicken pox that summer, but they came for Christmas and she met Cyrus for the first time. He said he was sorry he had missed her birthday because she had stayed home with chicken poops, and she was so delighted. She called him silly, and he said, 'Child, show some respect, I am your uncle.' She said, 'Uncle Silly' and that was his name from then on. Aunt Loony and Uncle Silly." She gazed past Frank out the window and added, "I prayed that my child would be exactly like her."

"Did you speak with Senator Atherton?" Barbara asked.

"Not right away. We were paralyzed with grief. Mother collapsed and never really recovered. She died four years later. And I was injured, in the hospital, and was told there would never be another pregnancy...." She sighed. "Later, we learned that Robert had called the senator from here on that Thursday night, but that was several months later when Cyrus was going over the bills and found the record. Then I called Atherton. He had told the police there was no mission, that he had understood that Robert was simply visiting his family in California. When I called, he repeated that. The investigators decided it was a case of mistaken identity, that Robert had not been the target, and they didn't know who had been. The whole thing was shelved and forgotten."

They talked for a long time. Cyrus had been transferred to New York City, and she had not been able to go with him. She couldn't leave her mother, who had become ill and clung to her the way a child might, fearful when Louise left the house, afraid of cars, afraid of strangers. Cyrus had come back on visits a few times, but they had drifted apart and ended up divorced. Mostly she talked about the child Carolyn had been, and when Barbara and Frank prepared to leave, she asked almost timidly, "Will you tell me about her life, what she has been doing, where she has lived?"

Barbara told most of it, leaving out Adrienne Colbert's role almost entirely. Then she said, "She's very strong, Ms. Braniff. She has survived what few others could, and she'll continue to survive and grow."

"It's a wonder she isn't stark raving mad," Frank said. "They stole a year and three or four months out of her life, and convinced her that she couldn't remember that period because she had amnesia, and that all her other memories were fantasies." He patted Louise's hand on the table. "She's levelheaded, intelligent and self-reliant. You should be proud of her," he said. "She's a remarkable young woman."

A few minutes later, driving, Barbara cursed bitterly, and Frank did not say a word, did not clear his throat, but simply stared grimly out the windshield.

13

When they entered Barbara's office, she stopped by Shelley's open door and said, "Come on back." Shelley looked from Barbara to Frank and nodded. Maria started to hand Barbara a note of messages, withdrew it and put it down. "Get Bailey, and hold any calls," Barbara said to her, and continued on to her office.

"Order up some sandwiches," Frank said to Maria. "For you, too. Hang around. We might need you." He followed Barbara, and Shelley hurried in after him.

"Dad, will you fill her in?" Barbara said. "I have to think." She sat behind her desk and Frank and Shelley took the comfortable chairs across the room. As Frank began to talk in a low voice, she swiveled to face the wall behind her. Frank's voice became no more than a distant rumble as she thought furiously about the turn the case had taken.

When the rumble ceased, she swiveled back and stood up to join them at the round table. "We have a whole new ball game on our hands. We have a client who doesn't know who she is, and we can't tell her. I don't think Carrie can put the pieces together. She might not even know the name of her aunt. She had just turned seven, and how many families use last names around children? So I don't think she can make the connection now even if she regains her memory. But she might have seen or heard something that made her a danger to whoever placed that bomb, and whoever hid her away knows who she is, and might be watching her and us."

"It had to be the government," Shelley said in a hushed voice. "A witness protection plan, something like that."

Barbara nodded. "I think that's it. But it's still speculation. And I don't want her to vanish again. So we play it really close. What I want now is a complete rundown on Senator Atherton. What he was up to in the seventies, and especially where he is now, if he's alive. He had a ranch over by Pendleton in 1978, and he may still be there."

"You can't go after him," Frank said heavily. "That would be a giveaway."

"I want information, and I'll think what to do with it later," she said. She turned to Shelley again. "I hate to ask this, but you're the one for the job. You had a year of doing title searches down in California, and you know how to go about it. I can't ask for outside help. I want a list of the construction jobs the Wenzels did in California from 1970 to 1975. How much they paid out, how much they took in, and whose names are on permits and things like that. They arrived here in 1975 with at least two million, and I doubt they made that much building isolated motels and gas stations."

Shelley nodded. "I can do that. It's on record."

"We don't even know exactly where they did most of their work. Apparently through Southern California, down to the border, maybe all the way across to Arizona. I just don't know, and at this point I don't want to ask more questions of anyone down there. But I do want the locations of their projects, what they involved, how much they cost and so on. Maybe on a topo map. Do you have court cases coming up?"

"A few. I can work around them." She thought a moment, then said, "You know my mother hasn't been feeling well recently. I might have to take off a few days a week and visit her. You know, fly down, stay a few days, fly back. I think she'll be much better in three or four weeks."

"Give her my regards," Barbara said. "Okay, Atherton first."

After Shelley left, Frank regarded Barbara with a bleak expression. "You realize it's a stretch trying to connect early California to here and now."

"I know. But it's connected. You know it as well as I do. It *is* connected."

He didn't dispute her. "I know the Earth and moon are connected by gravity, but I sure can't get there from here."

Bailey and Maria entered bearing sandwiches and coffee. "Shelley helped herself as we passed her door," Bailey said.

"Anything else for me to do now?" Maria asked at the door.

"One thing," Barbara said. "I need a topo map or several, whatever it takes to cover Southern California from around San Diego south, and over to Arizona. Want to go shopping after you eat?"

Maria nodded and left them. As they ate the sandwiches, Barbara told Bailey what they had learned from Louise Braniff, then said, "So forget Frederick. Dead issue."

"Who?" Bailey said. "Now what?"

"I want a transcript of Joe Wenzel's college days at UCLA. He went for three years. That's for starters."

He eyed her morosely and reached for another sandwich. "Here it comes," he muttered.

"Right." She told him what Shelley would be doing, then said, "Coordinate it with her. Concentrate on late spring and early summer of 1972. As she locates their jobs, scour surrounding towns for newspaper stories about anything out of the ordinary. Bombs. Arsons. Killings. Like that. I don't know what you'll be looking for, but something that might have sent Joe Wenzel out of there in a hurry. Something that might eventually have led to blackmail. Whatever it was might have sent H. L. Blount running, too. I suspect it made newspapers. You might have to widen the search as you go, but start there. And don't leave tracks."

He regarded her with amazement and even awe. "You want me to find a grain of sand in the desert," he said. "Jeez, Barbara, why not give me a hard one? How many of those burgs do you think still have copies from the seventies?"

"Most of them," she said. "On microfiche, archived one way or another, and our event might have made a major newspaper. Give it a try, and come up with a good cover story. Not a hint of what you're looking for."

"That part will be easy," he said. "Since I don't have a clue myself what it is."

"You'll know it when you see it," she said.

"You don't think an affair between Joe and his brother's wife was the cause of the breakup?"

She shook her head. "It just doesn't add up. From what Inez told me, she and Joe were happy. I think she would have known if he was playing around. She certainly knew it later in Los Angeles. Picture it. Larry and Nora went to collect the workers, stayed overnight and returned the next day with no workers. Joe was waiting at the job site, and up to that point everything was normal. Then they fought. Something happened to set them off. I want to know what it was, if anyone can find out at this late date."

"Anyone," Bailey muttered. "You mean me." He pulled a folder from his duffel bag and put it on the table. "More reading material. The fire investigation report, insurance report, stuff like that. The company collected three hundred thousand. Joe was meeting the architect almost every day planning a new million-dollar shack. They might have needed that insurance money if Joe was splurging."

Barbara frowned. "Aren't you putting the cart before the horse? Was he splurging more than usual before the fire?"

"Maybe brother Larry uses fortune cookies to see into the future." He stood up. "Anything else? Want me to find a particular drop of water in the ocean? Something easy like that?"

She waved him away. "Beat it. Keep after Blount."

He saluted and ambled out.

"Dad, there's something I want to bring up," Barbara said then.

"That makes two of us. You first."

"You know I'll have to talk to Atherton, and I'm worried about Carrie's safety. Robert Frye called Atherton on a Thursday night, and the bomb was probably placed during the night on Friday. I see two possibilities. Someone followed him all the way to the house and waited for a chance. But I don't like that one. How would anyone know the whole family would leave on Saturday morning? The other possibility is that there was a leak from Atherton's office. One of his staff members got in touch with someone after Robert Frye called. They'd know he planned to drive over on Saturday morning. Or what if Atherton himself alerted someone? In either event, as soon as I show up, if that same staff member is still around, or if Atherton was responsible, Carrie could be at risk. They'll know we've made a connection to the bomb, Robert Frye, all of it. I think as Carol Frederick she was safe enough, but as Carolyn Frye?" She spread her hands. "I'm worried."

He was worried, too. "Don't make a move toward Atherton until we decide how to handle it. We might have to bring in some security for her. And damned if I can see how to manage that without telling her about it and why."

She nodded. "We might have to move her. It isn't fair to put Darren and Todd at risk. And they could be."

He suspected she was thinking of John Mureau, her former lover who had walked out when he thought his children were endangered. "Back burner for now," he said after a moment. "Let's think about it."

"Right. Your turn."

"Different aspect of the same subject," he said. "This is going to get ticklish. You'll be going to court misrepresenting the identity of your client, and a judge could get pissed off if he found out."

"How could he find out? I was hired to represent Carol Frederick. My client says her name is Carol Frederick, and she has a birth certificate and other documents to prove it."

"And that means that no matter what you dig up about the bomb or any of that matter, it won't be relevant to your case. It may be a wiser course to leave Atherton alone, leave that whole issue alone."

She shook her head. "I can't do that. The timetable won't let me. Something happened in 1972 that sent Joe out of there. He rejoined the company when it moved to Eugene. Then in 1978 he flew the coop again and never went back, but lived on company money until the end. And in 1978 Robert Frye investigated something in California and was killed. You know that Earth-moon connection? It wasn't easy, but we did get there."

14

Two weeks later Barbara stood by the greenhouse door watching Frank, who was doing something mysterious with tiny green plants and pots.

"See, you get the seeds started in a little flat," he said. "Then, after they begin to develop real leaves and roots, you move them to individual pots and let them grow on. These will keep growing most of the winter in the greenhouse here, and come spring out in the ground with them."

"All of them? You must have dozens."

"Some of them. I'll give away a lot."

She looked at her watch—fifteen minutes before two. "Bailey's due any time. I'll go listen for him. He flew in last night, and he'll leave again Monday morning. He's grouchy. He says Hannah's starting to bitch about an absentee husband."

"Darren's coming later," Frank said, lifting another small

plant. "I told him to plan to stay for dinner. Todd's at his mother's this weekend. Ah, look at those roots. Good job."

God, she thought, walking away, he was talking to them. She knew Darren would come by, they had to tell him they planned to move Carrie, and she had not wanted to go to his house to do it. Carrie would be sure to know they were there and wonder why they were talking to him and not her. But it couldn't be put off any longer. She had to go see Atherton.

When Bailey arrived, he marched past her to the kitchen, yanked a folder from his duffel bag and slammed it on the table. "More light reading," he all but snarled.

"Anything different?"

"More of the same. Cattle rustling, a school fire, a mom-and-pop store holdup, a shoot-out at the OK corral. I'm putting my eyes out, and my skin's turning to leather."

That last part looked right. He had burned to a dark brown and his nose was peeling, creating a strange pink-and-brown mosaic. He was posing as a writer correlating the violence in the cities and campuses swirling around anti-Vietnam War protesters with a spike in crime in more rural areas.

"Shelley came up with two more sites," she said. "I think that's the end of them."

"I haven't finished with the ones she already turned in. Those two better be the last. I'm thinking of retiring, taking up pearl diving."

Frank came in, nodded to Bailey, went to the sink and washed his hands, then got out two glasses and put ice cubes in them. One he filled with water, the other he half filled with bourbon, then passed it briefly under the faucet. He crossed the kitchen and handed that one to Bailey. "Let's go to the study," he said.

In the study he sat behind his desk and Bailey took the old brown chair that seriously needed attention. It was his favorite chair in the house, and Frank's too. That was where he sat to do real reading, and from the looks of the stack of books on the table by it, he had been doing a lot of reading lately.

"What do you hear from Alan?" Barbara asked.

"He and the architect are getting pretty chummy. The kid was doing doors and windows for more than a year, then he got the big job, Joe Wenzel's million-dollar house. When Joe kicked, he was back to doors and windows, and he's sore. He's looking for another job."

Alan MacCagno was posing as a philosophy major looking for work, with a lot of free time on his hands and a little money in his pocket. A good pal for a disgruntled junior architect.

"About Carrie," Frank said. "Any ideas?"

Bailey shook his head. "I don't see how you can guard her without telling her something. She might get suspicious if a strange dude started sleeping on her sofa. Or you could chain her to a water pipe in the basement."

"That's about where I keep coming out," Frank said. The doorbell chimed and he stood up. "I'll get it."

Barbara and Bailey scowled at each other while they waited for him to return. Bailey swished ice cubes around and drank the water they left. He would never dream of mooching a second drink from Frank. Then Frank returned with Darren.

Darren paused at the door. "Oh, I'm interrupting something. I'll come back later."

Frank waved him in. "Come on, have a seat. It concerns you."

Darren nodded to Barbara and Bailey and took a chair near the window.

"We will probably have to find Carrie a different apartment," Frank said. "Barbara and I agreed that we should bring it up with you before we make plans to do so."

"Am I allowed to ask why?" Darren asked. "She's more relaxed than she was when I met her, and she's getting better day by day. Does she want to move?"

Frank looked at Barbara and leaned back as if to say, "Your show."

Choosing her words with care, she said, "For reasons we can't reveal to you or to her, we think that Carrie may need more security than we can provide for that apartment."

"Would she be any safer in a different apartment?"

"We also believe that the people who may want to harm her would not hesitate to hurt others in their way."

Darren nodded, then stood up and faced the window. With the strong light behind him, he was an unmoving silhouette for what seemed a long time. He turned back and said lazily, "You know what I've been thinking? Todd needs a dog. A boy should have a dog, maybe one trained to guard, sort of a watchdog."

"There'd have to be someone to back it up if there's an alarm," Bailey said. "And she's alone most of the time over there." He straightened in his chair. "Your house need painting, anything like that?"

"Herbert!" Barbara said.

"Yeah. Your wandering long-lost cousin. He's the best security man I know." To Darren he said, "And he can paint, or do odd jobs, a little building. Whatever needs doing while he hangs out."

Herbert, the Texas lone ranger, as Barbara thought of him, had provided security for Frank in the past. "Is he free?" she asked.

"I can find out. Use your phone?"

"I was thinking of putting in a rec room in the basement," Darren said. "Ran out of time. It could take quite a while."

Frank motioned toward the phone on his desk, but Bailey said he'd use the kitchen phone and ambled out.

"Why are you willing to go along with this?" Barbara asked. "You certainly don't have to."

Darren sat down again. "I know what she's been through," he said. "I've treated people who've been through the same kind of therapy. She needs friends who care. Besides," he added with a grin, "she's giving Todd piano lessons, and he's teaching her to play chess. The best way to learn anything is by teaching it. I won't be able to hold my own with Todd much longer. And I may have to keep the piano after she leaves."

Bailey came back and stood in the doorway. "I left him a message to call back at my house."

"She goes out alone every day to the restaurant where she works," Darren said then.

Almost cheerfully Bailey said, "She won't if her car's disabled. Old cars like hers, sometimes it takes months to find spare parts. I'll mention it to Herbert when he calls. He'll be on hand if he can take the job, and he'll give her a ride when she needs it. It might delay the remodel work, but Herbert's not one to rush things. Give me your address. If he can do it, he should go straight there, not make any contact with the rest of us."

Darren pulled out a notebook and jotted down his address and phone number. He tore out the page and handed it to Bailey.

"I'm out of here," Bailey said. "I'll call when I hear from Herbert." He saluted and left.

Frank stood up and motioned to Barbara and Darren. "Come on out to the kitchen and I'll fill you in on Herbert."

In the kitchen he rummaged in the freezer, saying, "He was in Special Forces, army for a time, had FBI training, studied meditation in India and he painted my house a while back. Good job, too." He brought out a package and put it on the counter. "If he offers to cook for you, let him. He's a world-class gourmet cook." Then in an offhand way, he added, "And according to Bailey, he can shoot the fleas off a dog at fifty yards." His voice had been light and easy, but he turned to Darren and said in a very serious tone, "As Barbara said, you don't have to do this. You're under no obligation to take on a burden not of your choosing."

Darren nodded, as serious as Frank, and said, "I figure I can take care of my son and myself, and I have chosen. Did you get that rain barrel in place?"

Frank regarded him for a moment, then said, "Yes. Go have a look, see what you think."

As soon as Darren was out the door, Barbara said, "I'll call Atherton when I know Herbert is on the job, and make an appointment as early as Atherton's willing."

"You can't fly out there," Frank said. "That would be a dead giveaway if anyone's keeping an eye on you. Even if Atherton doesn't have a staff or anyone from the old days hanging around, others know he was behind Frye."

"I know. I'll drive. Leave on Friday maybe, see him on Saturday, come back Sunday. A snap."

"Not alone. Take Bailey."

"Show up with a detective escort? Not on your life. Someone might think it strange. And Bailey has his own chores to attend to at the moment."

"Then I'll go with you."

She shook her head. "Dad, it's about three hundred

miles. But aside from that, if anyone's paying attention and we both take off for Pendleton, it's the same thing, a dead giveaway."

"Three hundred miles of empty desert country," he said. "We can hire someone to go with you. Bailey will send someone."

She shook her head impatiently. "You're being childish. I won't mention where I'm heading, just take off for a weekend to relax, and I'll go alone."

"You won't," he said. "I'll follow on your tailgate every inch of the way. For all you know Atherton's the source of the leak, and he might not want questions popping up at this late date. You leave, and within two miles of Eugene you could have someone trailing after you just to see where you're off to."

"I'm in and out all the time without anyone noticing."

"After you make that call things could change," he said sharply. "You can't go alone."

From the doorway Darren said, "I'm on his side. You can't go alone."

Barbara whirled to face him and snapped, "Didn't anyone ever teach you not to eavesdrop? It's considered bad manners."

"I got a glimpse of a special truck," he said, entering the kitchen. "I know the kind of people who used those trucks, and I know they have long memories. You have special security coming along for Carrie, and you have to see someone on the sly as soon as you know she's safe. You can't go alone."

"For God's sake, stop it, both of you! Butt out, Darren. This is none of your business."

"I'm making it my business," he said. "What I suggest is that we take a little camping trip, just the two of us. My truck is outfitted for camping, and I can guarantee that no one will follow us."

For a time no one moved or spoke, then Frank said, "Do you have a gun?"

"A rifle," Darren said. "Some of the places Todd and I visit, a rifle might come in handy. Grizzlies, cougars, you never can tell. And I know which end shoots." He kept his gaze on Barbara.

She turned away as Frank slowly nodded. He said, "It's that, Barbara, or else Bailey's man, or me riding on your bumper. I'm going out to pick some dinner." He took a colander from the cabinet and walked out the back door to the garden.

He meant it, she knew. And he was perfectly capable of following her to Pendleton and back. She faced Darren again and said, "He's being childish and stubborn. I'm going to talk to a perfectly respectable old man, and absolutely nothing is going to happen."

"Then I'll simply be the chauffeur and camp cook. I'll demonstrate a skill you'd never suspect I had. I'll yodel for you."

"If you do, I'll turn your own rifle on you, and I know which end shoots, too."

He drew his finger across his lips, zipping them. "Rematch of our chess game?"

"Sure."

Frank came in with green beans and a few tomatoes. "Pickings are getting slim," he said after glancing at the chessboard. "It will have to do." He busied himself at the sink.

Soon he heard Darren say, "Check. I think your mind's on something else."

"You're probably right," she agreed.

Then Darren said, "Yipes! I walked right into it."

"Maybe your mind's on something else."

"I didn't think you'd sacrifice your queen," he said. "I concede. Best two out of three?"

"Later. My brain's had all the exercise it can take for one day. What will you do about Todd, if next weekend works out?"

"He's negotiating with his mother this weekend. He wants to be home for Halloween, and he'll trade next weekend for that one. He has it all planned. I'll do the planning for a weekend camping trip, by the way."

At the sink Frank grinned as he layered vegetables and lamb riblets in a casserole.

Bailey called midway through dinner and Frank left the table to take the call. When he returned, he said, "Herbert will show up at your place Monday night sometime. He'll bring a dog, and he says he's a longtime buddy of yours from California, down and out on his luck, looking for a place to crash for a spell."

Darren nodded. "I almost remember him. His room will be ready."

Barbara drew in her breath. "I'll make that call Tuesday," she said, "and try to get an appointment on Saturday."

She and Darren left at the same time. Heading for her car in the driveway, she felt his hand on her arm and stopped.

"You have no intention of taking me up on my offer, do you?"

She stiffened and drew back. "I thought that was agreed," she said.

"You didn't say so back then, and you caved in too easily. Anyone who sacrifices a queen doesn't yield an argument like that."

"I told you Dad's being childish and stubborn. Of course, he can't make that trip with me, and I certainly don't need a baby-sitter."

"Maybe you're both being childish and stubborn." His face was too shadowed to make out his features, but his voice was low and easy, the way he talked when he was angry or upset.

"I told you to butt out. I mean it."

"He's stressed out already by whatever is involved in this case," Darren said. "He'll know you've gone alone, and at his age he doesn't need that additional stress. Consider him before you go tearing off across the desert by yourself. I'll give you a call on Monday after the Marines have landed and before you make your appointment."

He walked back to the house where he had parked his bike, got on and left without a backward glance. She watched his receding lights vanish when he turned the corner.

15

Darren called on Monday night at nine. "I have company," he said. "An old pal and his dog. Do you want to take off a few days this weekend?"

She closed her eyes, then said, "That sounds good. I'll know tomorrow. If I can't make it, I'll give you a call. What time do you suggest we leave if it's a go?"

"I plan to get off at four. Your place by four-fifteen. Do you have a sleeping bag?"

"Yes."

"Give me a hint about our destination, I'll route us and we'll be all set."

"A ranch near Pendleton."

"Good. See you on Friday."

After a moment she opened her eyes, then said under her breath, "Okay, I concede." He had been right. Frank would

have come racing after her if she had gone alone, or, if it was
too late for that, he would have worried himself sick until she
got home again.

On Tuesday morning she called Atherton's number. His
daughter-in-law, Wanda Atherton, answered.

"I'm afraid that's impossible," she said pleasantly when
Barbara asked for the senator. "If you can tell me the nature
of your call, perhaps he can call back later."

"Give him this message," Barbara said. "I'm an attorney
in Eugene, and I'm calling about an incident that happened
in 1978 concerning one of his former staff members. I have
to speak with him directly. And," she added, "give him the
message now, not later. Let him decide if he will speak with
me. I'll wait."

After a pause, in a decidedly less pleasant voice, Wanda
Atherton said, "I'll tell him."

Several minutes later a man's voice came over the phone.
"Jerome Atherton here. Who are you and what do you want?"

She told him her name. "I have to talk to you on Saturday,
Senator. It's about a car bomb."

There was another pause. "I'm retired, Ms. Holloway. I
have nothing to say to you."

"Senator, I'll speak with you or else hold a news conference on Saturday and let reporters ask the question I much
prefer to ask in person."

There was another pause, longer this time. Then he said,
"I'll be here all day on Saturday." He hung up.

She drew in a breath, thinking *arrogant bastard*. She went
to Shelley's office. "It's on for Saturday," she said.

Shelley had been placing stick pins in a large map, the locations of the various work sites of the Wenzel brothers in California. Two of the pins were red, the others all yellow. There were a lot of pins.

"What are the red pins for?" Barbara asked.

"Those are the last two they did together. They both came in way over the cost estimate, and they were late." She stepped away from the map, then swiveled the easel it was on. The back side held a big print of a Georgia O'Keeffe poppy.

In the apartment above Darren's garage the alarm clock jolted Carrie out of the reverie she drifted into when she practiced. It was not really a reverie, she had decided, but an altered state of awareness, one that did not keep track of time. She stood up and stretched, picked up her purse and a kerchief to cover her hair, prepared for two to three hours of making tamales.

Outside, she was surprised to see a ladder against the front of the house, more surprised when Herbert called, "Howdy!" and climbed down the ladder. When he arrived on Monday evening, Darren had brought him up to her apartment and introduced them. Herbert was a big man with a big potbelly. He had been dressed in cowboy boots, jeans, a plaid shirt and a Stetson hat. And he had been grinning a big friendly smile.

"He'll be hanging out for a while," Darren had said. "And I didn't want you to get alarmed seeing him around the place."

Herbert motioned and a big shaggy dog came forward. "This here's Morgan," Herbert said. "Morgan, say hello to the lady."

Carrie drew back a little as the dog came to her and sniffed her feet, up her legs, her hand and then stuck his nose into her crotch. Embarrassed, she drew back farther, and Herbert said, "I can't teach him better. Morgan, cut that out." He looked embarrassed, too. He looked past her at the window in the living room and gestured to Darren. "See, it's like I told you, a pack of wild four-year-olds could walk right in." He looked at Carrie and said, "He needs some security here, and I'm the guy to do it. Worked for a firm down in Houston awhile back, putting in security. You ever been to Houston? Don't bother. Even two-room shacks have security down there and need it. Doesn't cost much, the money's in the labor, and I can provide all that."

Carrie and Darren exchanged looks and he shrugged. "He says he'll fix up a few things while he's hanging out."

"Lots here to fix up," Herbert said. "That fence out back, windows need caulk. I'll look at the paint tomorrow. Come on, Morgan, let's see what else."

He went down the stairs with the shaggy dog at his side. Then Carrie asked in a low voice, "Who is he?"

"An old pal who needs a place to stay for a while. Last I heard from him he was in India studying meditation. If he bugs you, tell him to beat it. On the other hand, if you need anything done, tell him. He has to earn his keep if he plans to stay."

Now Herbert was climbing down the ladder grinning at her. "Like I said, all them windows can use some work. But the paint looks okay. You off somewhere?"

"To work. I'll see you later." She walked around the house and got into her car, shaking her head. Herbert acted as if he intended to become a permanent fixture. When she turned on her ignition, the engine made a grinding noise, then stopped. She frowned and tried again. Nothing, not even the grinding noise.

Herbert came around to her side window. "That don't sound too good."

She tried it once more, pulled the key out and opened the door. "It isn't the battery. I know what that sounds like. I never heard that before." She looked at her watch. "I'd better call a taxi." And there would go her day's pay, she thought in exasperation. She liked working for Lupe and Carlos Juarez in their restaurant Tacos Y Mas, but she wasn't doing it out of enjoyment. She knew her car needed a major tune-up. She had been saving to get it done, but a repair bill on top of that was bad news.

"Hey," Herbert said. "Don't go calling no cab. I'll give you a lift." He pointed to his pickup truck that had rust spots and needed washing. "Come on, hop in. I have to get some wire, caulk and stuff. No big deal. Like Darren said, I got to earn my keep."

She hesitated briefly, then walked to his truck, and he spoke sternly to Morgan. "You, you listen to me, you dog, you. Stay here and guard. You understand what I'm telling you?" Morgan trotted to the front of the house and sat on the stoop there.

She laughed. "Morgan doesn't understand a word. You use hand signals, don't you?"

"Well, I figure he understands a few words, but he sure digs signals. I'll teach you some, and you can boss him around."

She told him how to get to the restaurant. "Did you really study meditation in India?"

"Yep. Teach you that, too. See, you got a worry, and you meditate a spell and your mind goes into some other kind of place where worry's not allowed. Makes you feel real good."

That was what happened to her when she played, she mused. She wished she could stay there.

To her surprise, when they reached the restaurant, he went in with her. She introduced Lupe and Carlos, then left to wash her hands and put on her kerchief. When she returned to the kitchen, the three of them were in an animated conversation in rapid Spanish. She had never had a real conversation with them. They were hesitant in English, and her Spanish was too limited.

Herbert grinned at her and said in English, "They say you have fast hands, do good work. The customers like the tamales and business is up when they offer them."

She got busy, listening to the music of their voices, and then her thoughts drifted. Since Janey had given her permission to think about her imaginary friend and even to talk about her, she had visualized her more and more often. She wanted to make up stories about her, but for whatever reason she never could. It was as if only the memories of the stories she once had made up had survived the years, and as an adult it was no longer possible to add to them.

She placed the soaked, pliant corn husks on her work surface and spread the cooled masa harina, added the filling and wrapped them, then tied off the ends with strips of the husks, one after another, and thought about Carolyn, who had lived in an apartment building with an elevator.

Carlos laughed and when Carrie glanced at the other side of the kitchen, Lupe, smiling, was waving Herbert away. She was dicing vegetables, and a big pot of beans was simmering on the stove. Another pot was simmering with a sauce that smelled of garlic and chili peppers. Carlos was shredding a large cooked pork roast. He was thick, not very tall, powerful looking. Like Ramon, Carrie thought. Ramon had taught her a few words of Spanish. Las flores, Tia Loony… For a moment Carrie felt faint, light-headed. Not her, Carolyn. He had taught Carolyn.

"I'm negotiating a deal here," Herbert said. "I'll caulk their windows if they'll teach me how to make a real molé. They think I'm kidding."

Carrie laughed. "You have a real fixation about windows, don't you? Sweeten the deal. Offer to put in a security system, keep out those wild four-year-olds."

"Hey, that's a good idea." He turned back to Carlos and there was another exchange that Carrie could not follow. She filled another tamale. Then, surprised again, she realized that Herbert was wandering about studying windows. Obviously he had made his deal.

She went back to considering a problem that thinking of Ramon had introduced. If he was just a figment of her imagination and had taught Carolyn a few Spanish words, how had she learned them?

On the way back to her apartment later, she asked, "Does *tia* mean aunt?"

"Sure does. And *tio* is uncle."

"Does *abuela* mean grandmother?"

"Right again. You picked up a little Spanish here and there?"

She nodded and turned to gaze out the side window, unable to account for the rush of fear that made her heart pound.

16

Darren arrived promptly at four-fifteen on Friday. Barbara was watching for him with her backpack ready. Her sleeping bag was strapped to it, and she carried a hooded jacket over her arm, ready for whatever weather the desert had to offer.

"Off to see the wizard," he said after stowing her things in the back of the truck and they were both belted in.

"I'm afraid part of the trip won't be a yellow brick road," she said. "Probably a yellow dust road for the last ten miles or so."

"We'll have a breath-holding contest for the last leg," he said and started to drive.

They didn't speak again until they were on Highway 126 east of Springfield, beginning the ascent over the Cascades. She loved the mountains all seasons, but especially now when the sumac and poison oak had turned red, and the cottonwood trees glowed like yellow torches here and there, vivid against the fir trees so dark-green they looked black. Now she could spot the giveaway red foliage of the mountain huckleberries and blueberries.

She glanced at Darren and caught his glance toward her. "You were smiling," he said.

"I like this drive."

"Me too."

"How's Herbert working out?"

He laughed. "Yesterday when I got home he was teaching Todd rope tricks and Carrie was playing Frisbee with Morgan. The cat was sulking on the roof."

"Who's Morgan?"

"Hard to tell. Part sheep, not sheep dog, but sheep, all gray-and-black curly hair and shaggy. Part goat, according to Herbert, taking into consideration what the brute eats. Part bloodhound, because of a superkeen nose. Herbert is a remarkable man. First thing he did was put in a security system at my place, wired to a camera and infrared light, and then to a bright light. First the picture, then the scare, he said. He's wiring the restaurant, too, and caulking their windows, putting in the same hours Carrie does."

"They're letting him do that?"

"He said they have to consider the harm a bunch of wild four-year-old kids could do if they wandered in. He mentioned to Lupe and Carlos that one four-year-old and one match could burn down a forest. That sold them. All he wants in return is a lesson making an authentic molé." He glanced at her again. "He said Lupe makes the best chili relleno burrito he ever ate. Are you sure about his qualifications?"

"I'm not," she said. "But Bailey is."

"Good enough, I guess. What we'll do is head for Redmond, then out past Prineville to John Day. A few miles beyond that there's a little campground where we'll haul it in tonight. Primitive campground, but with good water, and even a privy. Tomorrow we'll be at your ranch by early afternoon. Okay?"

"Sounds good," she said. "I went fossil hunting with some pals out by John Day once. Have you seen the painted hills there, the petroglyphs?"

"Yes. Todd and I collected fossils one year."

He was planning a long drive, she knew, and it would be dark when they made camp. But it couldn't be helped, that's how distances were out here.

"I'd like to do some of the driving," she said, fully expecting him to object, thinking of something her father had said a long time ago: don't get between a boy and his dog, or a man and his truck.

"Okay," Darren said. "Tomorrow, after we clear the mountains. The truck is a little tricky until you get used to it."

They went over the pass and headed down the other side to the high plateau of the Oregon desert. The luxuriant growth of the fir forest changed to scattered pine trees, their trunks glowing red in the late sunlight, then juniper trees with a scant understory of sage, and then even the juniper trees yielded and there was only a solitary sage plant here and there, and clumps of tough desert grasses. The plateau stretched as far as she could see until encircling mountains formed a fringe against the sky.

Near Redmond he pulled into a campground. "Break time. I have some sandwiches and a thermos of coffee. It's going to be a while before we have a real dinner."

"You don't think we were followed, do you?".

He shook his head. "I doubt it. I'll know for sure when we start again."

They used the bathrooms, ate sandwiches and had coffee, and then he drove on through the campgrounds, to a red lava-rock road and emerged on the highway some miles farther along.

The first time she had gone into Prineville she had been amazed at the sudden, steep downgrade in a land that had appeared perfectly flat. It still was startling to realize how the land fell here, down to a valley with many trees and houses, a river and a reservoir. The eastern sky was showing streaks of cerise and avocado-green against clear blue as they left Prineville. Darkness fell swiftly in the desert she knew, watching the cerulean blue of the sky darken to navy blue, then purple with bands of brilliant colors: red and yellow, a glowing orange, peach. The bands of clouds began to fade and turn black against the deep sky, and finally all merged to darkness.

Headlights appeared now and then, drew near, passed and vanished. No headlights had been visible behind them for a long time.

Darren slowed at the small town of John Day. "Practically there. Ten more miles."

The camp was as primitive as he had warned, and the temperature had nosedived after the sun went down. They sat huddled near a small fire and ate hamburgers and spicy black beans prepared on a camp stove.

"We'll stop before dark going back," Darren said. "I'll do a little better than this in the way of food."

"You couldn't," she said. "It's delicious." Her teeth were chattering.

Darren crawled into the truck and came back with thick, woolen ponchos for both of them. "You might want to put that over your sleeping bag tonight," he said. "The truck is going to be like a refrigerator by morning." He put a blackened kettle over the fire to heat water for their dishes.

When they were finished eating she was yawning.

"You get the bench with a foam pad and your sleeping bag," he said. "I'll take the pad on the floor. About ready?"

"I'm afraid so. It's been a long day."

"That and the desert air and cold night. I'll get our beds set up."

The canopy of the truck had been expanded to allow another eight or ten inches of head space, but it was still too low to stand in. He entered, crouching, and she could hear him moving about. When he backed out again, he turned the lantern to low and set it inside. "Whenever you're ready. I'll douse the fire and do some housekeeping. Yell when you're tucked in."

Inside, she took off her boots and stowed them under the bench, pulled off the poncho and her jacket and tossed them to the foot of the sleeping bag, then wormed her way into the bag and zipped it. "Ready," she called.

When he turned off the lantern the blackness was intense. She had forgotten how dark the countryside was at night. She could hear him moving about, then his own zipper being pulled up.

"Are you warm enough?" he asked.

"Getting there." Her feet were like lumps of ice.

When he spoke again it was like hearing a disembodied voice from a void. "I said some things a while back that need a little explaining," he said. "I called you stubborn without looking at the other side to see that you're reasonable along with it. Unstoppable, but for a cause. That's not bad. Arrogant, but you have a right to be. You know what you have to do and let nothing interfere. See? I've been thinking about that night."

"Please, Darren. I'm too tired for this. I don't want to quarrel with you."

"No quarrel. What I'm saying is that I was wrong on most counts, except for one. I said you were dangerous, and that one's right. I think I recognized that the first time I saw you in action."

"Darren, stop!"

"Not yet. This is about me now, not you. See, well you can't see, but understand. My life was in order. I had my work at the clinic. My boy was coming to live with me. I had my bridge club and chess buddies. An occasional date. Stable, that was my life. I was content to be in a stable life, and I knew that you threatened it. Except for Todd and the clinic, I was filling in the hours, that's all. Just filling in the hours."

She closed her eyes hard, but it was no darker inside her eyelids than with her eyes wide open. She had thought more than once that his was the most seductive voice she had ever heard, that, strangely, the more upset he became, the easier the cadences he uttered, and now his voice was almost musical as he continued.

"And it's not good enough," he said. "There's more to life than just twiddling your thumbs waiting for tomorrow. I asked you once what you were afraid of. I won't ask it again. Another question instead. Why was it that every time we were together more than a few minutes you got so mad at me?" He became silent for a moment, then said, "Good night, Barbara."

She was almost rigid in her sleeping bag, staring into darkness until her eyes burned. It was true, she had become angry with him repeatedly and now couldn't think why. Because he was arrogant? Self-satisfied? Because he knew who he was, he knew who lived under his skin. She realized that it was not a question. She had known so few people who knew that, and she did not count herself as one.

When threatened, the first two instinctive reactions were to flee or to fight, she thought suddenly, and she had chosen to fight. She closed her eyes and drew in a breath. After their first conversation she had thought him a dangerous man, she remembered, and now understood that at an unexamined level, even then, she had sensed that he posed a danger to her, no one else. She didn't want a new entanglement, a relationship that was certain to end in heartbreak or disillusionment. She knew more than enough about both, and she was through with all that. A relationship with Darren would not be a lighthearted affair, one easily started, easily ended, she also sensed, thinking of Will Thaxton and her dates with him, how easy they had been. How meaningless. Twiddling her thumbs waiting for tomorrow.

"Not now," she told herself under her breath. She was too tired to think this through. She would think about it tomorrow. But she couldn't stop her thoughts, and it was a long time before she drifted into sleep.

She awakened smelling coffee and bacon. The poncho was spread over her sleeping bag, and she was warm enough not to want to get up, but the breakfast smells were stronger than the pull of comfort and warmth.

She was lacing her boot when Darren opened the back of the truck. "Good morning. I thought I heard a stirring of life. Breakfast is ready."

When she stepped outside, frost glistened in the shadow of the truck and the long shadows cast by rocks. He had not made a fire that morning, but the sun was up and it was a beautiful clear day. The frost vanished before they finished the bacon and eggs. He scrubbed the dishes, filled the thermos and the water can, and they were ready to start again.

"I'm feeling pretty useless," she said climbing into the passenger seat.

"After we reach 395 you can take over the driving for a while," he said. "We have about a hundred fifty or sixty miles to go."

"I should show you my map, where the turnoff is." She drew it from her purse and they studied it together. "It's the Atherton ranch, about ten miles down that dirt road," she said, "or else we have to go up to the interstate, then over and back down what looks like a real road. That way is almost fifty miles farther, but might be easier driving."

"We'll have a look at the ranch road and decide then. Okay?"

"Yep."

He started to drive.

The day before they had talked very little, but now Darren began to talk about the different kinds of deserts he had visited, how cruelly this land was being punished by a continuing drought, and the difference between deserts that had given up hope and this land that was waiting.

Everything was dun-colored and dust-covered. Where there was any water seepage, juniper trees struggled for life, but fields that might have grown wheat had been left fallow, waiting for the rain to return. To the right, the Blue Mountains rose, forested where the high altitude caught moisture from drifting clouds that had been wrung nearly dry by the time they got this far inland. To the left, the desert spread out to the Ochoco Mountains, dry and scrub covered.

At U.S. 395, with the highway devoid of traffic for the most part, she drove for a time. She was used to everything automatic, she realized quickly. And, even when uncontested for road space, this truck needed more handling than she would have guessed from the ease with which Darren drove. Empty country, she thought, recalling Frank's words, hundreds of miles of empty country, with no farm in sight, no buildings, no towns, just the endless high, barren desert and an occasional dirt road that vanished quickly as it twisted and wound around rocks.

The day became warmer, hot in the sunlight, although still cold in shade cast by escarpments and an occasional rocky hill. As the sun climbed higher in a cloudless sky, the shade disappeared. They stopped for lunch several miles before the turnoff, then stopped again to consider the dirt road.

"Passable," Darren said. "I've driven worse roads."

"It could get worse," she said.

"Oh, it will. Let's give it a go."

The road became much worse as soon as they rounded a big boulder. He slowed down, shifted gears and kept moving forward over rocks and rutted tracks, so badly eroded in places that the road was indistinguishable from the surrounding country. Jouncing, lurching, followed by a cloud of dust that caught up with them now and again, they kept going. He slowed to a crawl when they came to a dry streambed, then headed downward and up the other side. The truck tilted, straightened, tilted again as they inched their way over more rocky ground, steadily climbing now. Finally, he came to a stop.

"There it is," he said.

Below, in a verdant valley, was a ranch house shaded by golden cottonwood trees, several manufactured homes in a cluster beneath another copse, cars and a truck, and a corral with horses grazing.

"Paradise in hell," Darren said, shifting gears again to begin the descent into the valley.

17

Barbara knew that Atherton and his wife, both eighty years old, lived here with their son Craig and his wife, Wanda, and their three grown children, all in college. Wanda opened the door at her knock. She was round-faced, with blond hair drawn back in a French twist, and she was dressed in jeans, boots and a Western shirt. Her expression was not friendly.

Barbara introduced herself, then said, "I have an appointment with the senator."

A tall, lean man stepped into a wide hall behind Wanda and beckoned Barbara. "Atherton," he said. To his daughter-in-law he said, "I'll speak with Ms. Holloway in my study." He looked past her. "Your friend is welcome to come in and wait."

"He said he'll wait out there."

"As you please. This way."

He took a few steps toward another door and waited as she

passed Wanda and entered the room. It was handsome with bookshelves lining two walls and windows overlooking the porch beyond. A massive desk, easy chairs covered with worn leather, and a rich-looking Navajo rug furnished the room. He indicated a chair and waited for her to sit down, then sat opposite her with his hands on his knees.

"As I told you on the phone, I have nothing to add to the story I told the investigators years ago. You have traveled far over bad roads for nothing."

"I was hoping that by making an appointment several days in advance you would have had time to refresh your memory."

"My memory is fine," he said.

In fact, there was little about him to suggest that he was eighty years old. He looked healthy, with deeply tanned skin, thick white eyebrows and bright blue eyes. His silver hair was trimmed and his hands were steady, although prominent dark veins indicated advanced years.

"I believe that," she said. "Let me tell you a story. In 1978 Robert Frye was doing a job for you, one that cost him his life, that killed his wife and injured her sister, who then lost her child. Carolyn Frye was critically injured and removed to a distant hospital. She didn't die, although the surviving members of her family were told otherwise. Months later, when she came out of the fog of anesthetics and painkillers, she was told she had a different name, a different birth date making her more than a year older than she was, and different parents who had died in an accident. When she persisted in remembering a forbidden past, she was punished."

He did not move as she spoke. Now he stood up and walked to his desk and seated himself behind it. She understood perfectly what that meant, since it was what she often

did when she had to take control of a situation. She followed
him and stood before the desk and leaned forward with both
hands on it.

He swiveled and gazed out the windows. "I told the investigators all I know about that," he said. "As far as I was aware,
Robert was visiting his family in California."

"Senator," she said, "you will tell me today in the privacy
of your study what I need to know, or I will subpoena you and
you will make that statement under oath before a judge and
jury. And, Senator, I will refute it and impeach you."

She left the desk, walked to the bookshelves and examined
the titles in the silence that followed. One wall held many of
the same law books that filled Frank's shelves. The other held
histories and biographies, archaeology, some philosophy,
books of exploration: Lewis and Clark blazing the Oregon
Trail, Byrd's march to the North Pole, Thor Heyerdahl's ad-
ventures on the *Kon-Tiki*... Not superheroes in red capes, but
ordinary, fallible men undertaking extraordinary tasks.

When she heard movement she turned to see him rising.
He stood with his back to her, still looking out. "Over there,"
he said, "beyond that knob a few miles, scientists are digging
up dinosaur bones. Nothing stays buried, does it? Eventually,
time, weather, possibly the indifferent hand of fate, stirs the
past and it all rises again."

He turned toward her then. "May I look inside your purse?"

She picked it up and put it on his desk. His examination
was cursory.

"Thank you," he said. "Please, excuse me, I forgot my
manners. I'll ask Wanda to bring coffee and have some refreshment taken out to your friend." He inclined his head in
a slight bow and left the room.

* * *

Minutes later, once again seated in the leather-covered chairs, with coffee at hand, he regarded her levelly and said, "May I ask what your interest in that affair is?"

"Carolyn Frye is my client," she said. "I have to know to what extent her life is threatened."

"I see. I had never heard of you, Ms. Holloway, before you called. Since then, of course, I have done a little research. Criminal law. With an exemplary record. Also said to be discreet."

She shook her head. "I can't promise discretion. I can try to keep confidential anything you tell me, but I can't guarantee silence."

"I understand," he said after a moment. "Of course, one's client must take precedence. I also studied law once."

"I know you did."

"We've both done a little research," he said with a wry smile. He continued to study her as if to gauge how much she had learned about Robert Frye as well as about himself.

Impatiently she said, "Senator, as you mentioned before, that's a long drive from Eugene, and it will be no shorter returning. Can we get on with it? I know Robert Frye was working for you, I know he was murdered following a phone call to you, and I can surmise a great deal from other clues. Smuggling is involved, both into and out of Mexico and points beyond, no doubt. The only thing we have that might be of interest to illicit buyers in Central America are weapons, and the only thing to such buyers in the States would be drugs."

He nodded. "Yes. You must understand that little mail received in a senator's office is ever seen by him. Various gatekeepers screen it, and it is diverted to the proper staff member to be dealt with. In the year we're discussing Robert brought a letter to my attention, and I must tell you that I honestly can't recall what it said. It was written by a Mexican girl or young woman in stilted schoolgirl English, and it mentioned slave labor and proof that it existed. I asked Robert to look into it. I was on the committee with oversight of INS at the time, and the letter was of some interest. I never saw that letter again, and that is all I can recall about it."

He sipped his coffee and put the cup on the table at his elbow. "I'm allowed three cups a day," he said. "I try to make it last as long as I can. But, please, help yourself to more if you like." As she did so, he continued. "Accordingly, Robert did look into it. He flew to California and from there on to Mexico to interview the girl. He was fluent in Spanish. When he returned, he said slave labor was not the issue, but he believed it was something much bigger—smuggling that involved guns and drugs. I blame myself for allowing him to proceed after that. It called for trained investigators." He paused again, this time gazing past her at the windows, as if thinking again about the bones being exhumed.

He pulled his gaze back to her and continued. "In June, his vacation time was coming, and he planned to spend it following leads he had uncovered. He called me late on that Thursday. I was due to fly home the following day, and we agreed to meet here on Saturday. He said, during that call, that he had unearthed facts that would incriminate people in high places, that he had enough to deliver the kingpin, that he would bring it all over here and we could decide our next move."

"Did he give you details, names?"

"No. As I said, it was quite late in Washington. He knew he would find me in the office as I was finishing a great deal of work before I left. In the middle of our conversation he excused himself, and I could hear him tell his child to go back to bed. She had overheard part of our conversation, and he cut it short soon after that."

"That's why you spirited her away," Barbara said. "She might have known too much."

He nodded. "Exactly. I knew no more than I have told you, but she might have known more. Robert was not a trained investigator for criminal matters. He was indiscreet on the telephone and might have been more indiscreet in the privacy of his home."

"There was a leak in your office," Barbara said.

"There must have been," he said heavily.

"And you denied everything."

"Yes. On Saturday, the day of the car bomb, I received a letter here at the ranch. No warning, no concrete threat, just a picture of Craig and Wanda and their three-month-old infant, my grandson, pasted over a picture of an explosion. That's when I called the FBI to protect Carolyn, and I denied everything."

He picked up his coffee cup and drained it, hesitated, then refilled it. "I returned to Washington and personally searched Robert's files and found nothing concerning this. I also went with the police to Robert's apartment to recover files that he might have taken home, and again there was nothing relating to this matter. If he had had anything there, someone else had gotten to the material first, or else he had it all with him and it was destroyed in the blast and fire. In either case, there was nothing tangible."

"Then you retired from the Senate," she said. "Washed your hands of the whole affair."

He nodded. "I brought dishonor to my office, to the memory of a fine young man, to everything I had held dear or even holy. I served out my term and did not run again." He drank more coffee, keeping his blue eyes focused on her in an unblinking gaze. "A few years later the entire Iran-Contra scandal was exposed, and I felt almost vindicated. If what Robert had learned had been a precursor to that matter, fate had arranged to reveal it without his aid, without my aid. I argued with myself that I could have offered nothing. The argument was hollow. In the end we all behave according to our personal inherent selfish needs. I valued my family over my ideals and beliefs."

She stood up and walked to the window but saw nothing of the scene before her. "Back to my original question," she said, turning to face him. "Is Carolyn Frye in danger today?"

"I think not. Those involved in the Iran-Contra affair were investigated, put on trial, sentenced. Even though some of them have risen to the top once more, much the way pond scum always rises, that chapter in their lives is now history of no interest to anyone. If I may offer advice, I would say leave it alone, Ms. Holloway. That path will take you nowhere. I never knew the fate of Carolyn Frye. It was understood from the start that I would not be told of her new identity or her destiny. When I read of her death, I did not know if it was true or fabricated. I see no possibility for anyone else to have learned more than I knew about that or, at this date, for any of them to care."

"Except," Barbara said, "someone was responsible for the bomb that killed her parents, and that person could have a vital, selfish interest in knowing if she survived. As you and I both know, there is no statute of limitations on murder."

18

Darren was leaning against the truck when she left Atherton's house. He opened the passenger door as she approached and she climbed in.

"I thought I'd take a different route home," he said when he got behind the wheel. "Okay with you?"

She nodded. He waved to someone, and a man lounging on the wide porch waved back. Darren began to drive. "They were keeping an eye on me," he said. "No horse rustling allowed, something like that. Also, a boy brought me coffee and offered beer. Not bad treatment for a suspicious character."

He headed out a gravel road for Pendleton. "We'll take the interstate over to 97, head south. There's a state park over there where we can pack it in for the day. Are you all right?"

She roused. "Sorry. Thinking. I'm fine." Then she lapsed into silence again, and he said nothing more.

Wishing she had her laptop along, she began to compose mental notes, although she knew she was not likely to forget a thing the senator had said. How much truth, how many lies? She stared out her side window and admitted she could not say with any assurance that anything he had said had been truthful. He had been a skilled politician, an attorney, trained to reveal no more than he wanted to. A little later she was startled to see the broad blue Columbia River on her right. The thirty or more miles they had covered already had passed unnoticed.

The river appeared to be placid, static, like a landscape painting, not a moving body of water. "When we get time travel," she said, "my first trip will be to a time when the Columbia was wild, untamed, when it crashed and foamed and made geysers of white water here and there, with waterfalls and pools of deep blue water where giant fish swam."

"Yeah," Darren said. "Or when the ice dam broke and that great inland sea roared out with a wall of water fifty feet high, scouring everything in its path."

"And met the Pacific tidal bore coming in," she said, seeing it in her mind's eye, "and the two bodies crashed together with thunder you could hear for a hundred miles."

Now they had reached the interstate, and the giants were trucks thundering past. Modern behemoths. What man hath wrought. She fell into silence again, once more absorbed in her own thoughts.

Darren made his exit from the interstate at Highway 97, and the high Cascades were off to the right, and desert and fields of irrigated winter wheat on the left. The newly sprouted wheat was deceptively tender-looking but hardy enough to withstand the cruel winter coming soon. Where no irrigation reached, the desert asserted itself. Soon they left the wheat fields and there was only the high desert scrub.

A little before five Darren pulled into the state park and wound through it to a spot with a few juniper trees and a picnic table. There were several other campers in the park, even a tent. He selected a site well separated from them all.

After they climbed from the truck, she moved restlessly about the campsite as he began to take out the propane stove, pots, the water can.

"Is there anything you want me to do?" she asked.

"Nope."

"I think I'll take a walk," she said.

He looked at the sky. It was not dark, but the shadows were lengthening, and the sun had gone behind the mountains.

"I won't go far," she said, and started up the road that meandered through the park. It wasn't cold, but probably would get cold again overnight, although not as frigid as the previous night. Here, closer to the river, the temperature would be moderated. She wished she could see the river and realized she wanted to be home, to make certain Frank was all right, that Carrie was all right. She walked faster, then abruptly turned and retraced her steps. What if someone had followed them? She chided herself for becoming spooked but continued back to their campsite, and was relieved to see Darren alone there. He had made a fire in the fire pit.

"Potatoes roasting in foil," he said. "Steak with mushrooms and onions coming up, and deli slaw. What more could a person want?"

"A glass of wine," she said.

"Right. But we'll call it Kool-Aid." He busied himself in the back of the truck, brought out a plastic glass and handed it to her. "I think they frown on alcohol in the state parks," he said, taking out a second glass.

She sat on a log near the fire and watched the flames for a time. "How long before it's soup?"

"Half an hour to forty minutes." He turned the potatoes with a long fork.

"I have to tell you what this is all about," she said.

He sat on another log, and she told him everything she knew about Carrie. "I don't know if I can trust Atherton. I don't know if he lied when he said he didn't know her identity. And I don't know if any of that has anything to do with the murder of Joe Wenzel."

"But you think it's connected."

"Yes. The point is she's at risk, and my actions might have increased that risk. I could have left her in the county jail, or I could have chosen not to have Janey talk to her. I could have chosen not to talk to Atherton. Everything I've done might have put her in more jeopardy. Now I don't dare do anything that might cause her to remember her past. I can't ask if she overheard anything, or saw anything that might be dangerous."

She sipped wine. "I can't change any of that. It's done and she's at risk, but you don't have to be. Before, it was simply an unspecified danger, but now you know how serious it could be. People who plant bombs don't care how many they injure or kill. You and Todd have nothing to do with this, and it isn't fair to involve you."

"All right," he said. He stood up and took her glass from her, went to the truck, poured more wine and handed it back.

"What do you mean 'all right'?"

"I mean you've told me. You're absolved of any responsibility on my behalf or Todd's. I asked you before if she would be at less risk somewhere else and the answer was no. That hasn't changed." He picked up the fork and turned the potatoes again, then turned on the camp stove and set a skillet over the burner. "Ten minutes."

"Darren, you have to consider Todd."

"Oh, I do." The skillet began to smoke and he put a large steak in it, drew back when a larger cloud of smoke rose, then faced her. "Last year when he turned twelve I told him about my past history, my sojourn in the desert, all of it. Afterward, he looked me in the eye and he said, 'It's okay, Dad.' He trusts me, Barbara, and the gravest risk I see for him is the loss of that trust. If he ever suspected that I turned my back on a friend in trouble, that trust would vanish, and I value it too much to let that happen. Now, do you like your steak moderately well done, rare, what? Don't say really well done or I'll hang up my chef's hat."

They ate at the picnic table and by the time they were finished and the coffee was ready, night had fallen. Sitting again on the logs by the fire, Darren said, "I think I'll suggest ghost towns for our next collecting expedition. This country is thick with them. Of course, there's not much to see."

"Oh, Todd will repopulate every one of them with ghosts and goblins, specters and monsters lurking in every shadow. He'll love it." She stretched her legs to get her feet closer to the fire. The air had grown much colder.

Darren stood up and went to the truck, returned with the ponchos. "You'll toast your toes and your backside will freeze," he said behind her.

She felt his hands on her shoulders and stiffened.

He began to massage her shoulders. "It's a heavy world, Barbara. You don't have to carry it twenty-four hours of the day. Put it down. We'll be home in the afternoon tomorrow, and you can pick it up again then."

She remembered what they had told her about him at the clinic, that he had magic in his hands. True, she thought, as second by second she felt the weight lifting.

"That's better," he said a few minutes later. He draped a poncho over her shoulders and back and returned to his log.

He began to talk about the different trips he and Todd had made over the years. "We take pictures and have posters made from them. He's accumulating quite a collection. When we get the rec room finished, he intends to paper the walls with them. I think you're right. He'll love ghost towns."

"I'd think you would hate the desert," she said. In the firelight his face looked almost ruddy against the blackness behind him.

"The first two years were pretty hellish," he said. "But you sort of get the rhythm of it. You begin to understand that today will be like yesterday, and tomorrow will be like today. Cooler in the winter, but still the same. So you learn to stay out of the sun from around ten until five or six, do the heavy lifting around dawn or after dark, and draw a lot of mental pictures of trees and brooks. I didn't mind it after the first couple of years. This desert isn't like that. Up here you don't know from day to day if it will rain, snow, be blazing hot or freezing. And sometimes you get the perfect day, like today. Like now."

She ducked her head.

"Barbara," he said softly. "I know you have a trial coming up. I won't get in your face while you prepare for it. But no promises for afterward. Fair enough?"

After a moment she said, "I just can't think of afterward right now."

"Okay. Listen." From far away a coyote was calling.

"Another beautiful day," Darren said when she stepped down from the truck the next morning.

It was. The sun was bright but not glaring yet, and the air had a hint of moisture. That would vanish soon, but it felt good at the moment. After breakfast Darren tidied up the truck, secured everything in its proper place and they both rolled up their sleeping bags. She strapped hers to her backpack and they were ready.

"Let's stop at Sisters for soup and salad," he said, fastening his seat belt. "And we'll be home by three-thirty or so. Tired?"

"Not really. What I am is gritty, down to the bone gritty. What I desperately need is a shower."

"I wasn't going to mention that," he said.

"Some free legal advice," she said. "The pot should be very careful in making remarks about the kettle."

"Noted." Laughing, he began to drive.

They pulled to a stop before her apartment complex at twenty minutes after three. Darren got out with her, retrieved her backpack from the truck and carried it to the door. "I'll take it up for you," he said.

She shook her head. "It isn't heavy." Then, feeling a strange awkwardness, she said, "Thank you, Darren."

He nodded, suddenly as formal and stiff as she was. "You're welcome. It was my pleasure." He returned to his truck and she entered her building.

She had a list of to-do things lined up: first call her father and reassure him that she was home safe and sound and would be by later, a very long hot shower, look over her e-mail, go to Frank's, eat and pick up the reports she had asked Bailey to leave with him, come back home and read…

Across the river Carrie had been startled that afternoon by Herbert's bellow from the backyard, asking if she wanted to go shopping with him. He said he never climbed stairs when he didn't have to. "You have just so many units of energy you start the day with," he had explained. "Say it's ten. You use up one just getting ready for whatever's going to happen. You know, shower, shave—well not you, but some of us—make a bite to eat, like that. Use two or three doing little things, straightening up, fixing this or that, if you're working you use a lot more, and later making dinner or just driving around. See what it begins to add up to? It all takes its toll. And if you need a lot of energy when the tigers come marauding, you just plain don't have it. I believe in conservation of energy, yes, ma'am, I do."

They had gone shopping. He had money, she suspected, since she had seen what kinds of things he had put in his cart—expensive wines, a large brick of imported cheese, a larger prime rib roast… He called the wine selection piss-poor and began to talk about the sherry bars in Madrid rhapsodically. "That's all they offer to drink," he had said. "Sherry. A hundred, two hundred different kinds of sherry, some brick red, some as pale as water, and they keep bringing these little dishes with tapas, so you got to keep on drinking, trying them all. Wouldn't do to miss out on the best one. Tapas, that's the way. Little shrimp, breaded fried mushrooms, great big smoked oysters, deep-fried octopus…"

That day in his truck going home with her meager supplies and his big bags of groceries, she had said, "What are you running away from? Don't tell me you aren't. You keep a good eye on your backside."

He looked sheepish. "Well, now. It's like this. I had this job down in California, fixing up a few things, and a pretty little lady comes sashaying along and she says, 'Whatcha doing?' And I say, 'Since you can't get no reliable help no more, I decided to do this myself.' And she looks sort of interested and first one thing, then another, and somehow she gets the impression that I sort of own that estate. Mighty fine estate it was, tennis courts, stable, the works. A man would be right proud to own an estate like that. Anyways, one of the other guys working around says that someone tipped her off and she's looking for me with a baseball bat, and I figure it's about time to look up my old pal Darren. And here I am."

"I don't believe a word of that," Carrie said through her laughter. "You know what I think? I think you're a two-bit four-flusher."

He looked deeply hurt. "Carrie, honest, cross my heart, Boy-Scout honor, semper fi, hope to die, I ain't never flushed a four in my life."

After putting her groceries away Carrie wandered back downstairs and Herbert yelled for her to come on in. "Making quiche," he said. "You'd think as good as they can cook, the French would take up spelling, but they don't. Anyways, I figure that Darren will come in hungry after a weekend of camp food with his lady friend, and I know Todd will be hungry. Boys that age have an appetite. So we'll have quiche ready and the roast in the oven…"

He was working butter into flour as he rambled on. He

sprinkled water on it and stirred with a fork, and soon had a ball of dough on the counter, rolling it out, talking all the time. She watched his hands and suddenly she was seeing a different kitchen.

"What are you making, Gramma?"

"Cherry pie. The first cherries of the season are the best."

"Can I help?"

"Yes. Bring your stool and wash your hands."

Gramma gave her a lump of dough and a tiny rolling pin. "Your mother used that when she was your age," she said.

"It's like Play-Doh," Carolyn said, making a snowman.

Gramma brought out a tiny pie pan and put it on the table. Carolyn had never seen one like it before. "It's a tart pan," Gramma said.

"Like the Queen of hearts made some tarts," Carolyn said. Gramma smiled and they recited together: "All on a summer's day. The knave of hearts he stole the tarts and took them quite away."

Carolyn knew what a knave was. Daddy told her, but she never knew that a tart was just a little pie. She loved the shiny tart pan.

"You'll spread butter on it, and a little sugar and cinnamon, and a spoon of jam in the middle," Gramma said. "Then we'll have a tea party, just you and I, out on the terrace." She had a tiny teapot and cups, blue and pink with yellow flowers.

"And in the oven it goes," Herbert said.

Carrie shook herself, cold all over, and without a word walked from the kitchen, up the stairs to her own apartment.

She went into the bedroom and sat on the side of the bed, hugging her arms around herself.

She whispered, "Raspberry jam."

19

On Monday morning when Barbara entered her reception room Bailey and Shelley were moving the big easel with the red poppy on one side and topo maps on the other into Barbara's office. She greeted Maria and followed the easel with Frank right behind her.

The four of them were still getting seated when Maria brought in the coffee, glanced around and left again. Barbara turned to Bailey. He never looked happy, but that morning he was more dour than usual.

"I read your reports," she said. "What else?"

"I thought you'd want a good night's sleep, and left something out," he said. "Maybe it's the jackpot. Maybe not." He went to the topo map and studied it a moment, then placed a black stickpin in the desert. Almost tonelessly he went on. "On July 30, 1972, a couple of tourists in a big camper were heading up State 2." He pointed to it on the map. "Something came loose on top of the camper, and the guy stopped and climbed up to fasten it down again. From up there he took a look around and saw something funny, and went out on the desert to see if it was what he thought. It was. The body of a man, about a hundred yards from the road. He hightailed it back down to Ocotillo and reported it. The sheriff went up to have a look. Then the state police came in, and they found fifteen more bodies, spread out for about four miles." He pointed to the black pin. "Around there, middle of nowhere."

"Dead from what?" Barbara asked when he paused.

"Exposure, dehydration, heat exhaustion. They figured they had been dead for three to four weeks, and they were pretty well picked over. Buzzards, coyotes, you name it. Not a scrap of paper on them, no way to identify any of them, just a bunch of sun-bleached bones, burned skin and rags."

There was a long silence. Frank stood up and went to the map to study it. Ocotillo had the red stickpins indicating the two Wenzel jobs that had come in late with cost overruns.

"Is there more?" Barbara asked.

"Nothing real," Bailey said. "The usual investigation. No one in Mexico wanted to talk about the illegals who went north to find work and bring home gringo dollars. Border guards didn't know anything. They could have walked in, or could have been driven in and dumped. It made a few local papers, even a paragraph in the San Diego papers, but attention was on Vietnam, Nixon—who knows what else?—and that kind of thing happened before, and it's happened since. And there it still sits. Just a bunch of illegals who had no business being where they were to begin with. Move on. One guy almost made it to the road, but what good that would have done him is anybody's guess. Not much traffic out there today and less then. The next nearest one was two miles in."

Barbara got up and walked to her desk, banged her fist on it. "Someone must have seen them crossing the border. You can't hide a truckload of people."

"Sure they saw them. A few bucks cross hands, turn your head, the truck passes and memory slips a cog. Make sure the gringo border patrol is somewhere else, home free." He slouched lower in his chair.

"How it worked, and maybe still does, is you need workers to pick cotton or strawberries, work in the chicken processing plant, construction, whatever, and you get in touch with a guy who gets in touch with a guy in Mexico. Set up a date and place for pickup. The Mexican guy collects workers from the countryside and gets them to the pickup place. A lot of them follow the work wherever it takes them and send money home to the family. Some work a few weeks or months and head for home. Some are never heard from again. In most cases the truck never crosses the border. But now and then someone goes down with an empty truck to a village or town near the border, turns the truck over to the local helper for safekeeping and spends the day sightseeing. Next morning, there's a bunch of workers waiting, and the other cargo space has been emptied and repacked with something else overnight. Let the workers off somewhere near the border when you're done with them and drive an empty truck down again. It's a big border, a long stretch of not much."

"Shelley, are you all right?" Frank asked, still standing by the map.

Shelley looked deathly pale. She moistened her lips. "Nineteen seventy-two, that's the summer Joe Wenzel went to Los Angeles, and H. L. Blount left."

"That's when Larry and Nora Wenzel went down to pick up their workers and came back with an empty truck," Barbara said harshly, standing by her desk.

"Is that what Robert Frye was investigating?" Shelley asked.

"Senator Atherton got a letter six years later, in the spring of 1978," Barbara said. She repeated what she had already told Frank about her conversation with Atherton. "The girl who wrote the letter thought it was about slave labor, but Robert Frye said it was guns and dope. The Wenzels had been in Eugene for three years by then."

"Leave it alone, Barbara," Frank said, moving away from the map. He sat down again. "It's thirty years old, and you can't let yourself be distracted by it until after Carrie's trial."

After a moment she nodded and went back to her own chair. "Then I'll go after them," she muttered.

"Then we'll go after them," Frank said.

"Anything else for me?" Bailey asked. "And don't tell me to go looking for the girl who wrote that letter. No name, no address, not even a town. Zilch."

She shook her head. "What I want is a full account of the accident that killed Joe and Larry's mother, and when their father fell apart, their home life, school records. Everything."

He groaned.

"And, Shelley, I'd like you to go talk to wife number two again, Alexis O'Reilly. Get a formal statement about when Joe retired, anything she can recall from that time. Get it notarized, the works. And after that?" She spread her hands. "I don't know."

"It doesn't seem reasonable for Joe to have been blackmailing his brother over the dead men, does it?" Shelley said. "I mean, why wait until six years later to start?"

"A good question," Barbara said. "I wish to God I knew the answer."

Shelley and Bailey moved toward the easel a few minutes later. She told them to leave it. When they went out together, Frank didn't stir from his chair.

Barbara went to stand at the map, seeing again that desolate country without a tree, a shrub, an outcropping to offer shade. Ninety at two in the morning and, as soon as the sun rose, the temperature would start to climb and be over 120 at four-thirty or five in the afternoon. She remembered the dust devils swirling in Arizona, abrading whatever they encountered. And the water mirages, just ahead out of reach, always out of reach.

"How long would it take?" she asked in a low voice.

"I don't know. Not long, an hour, less." He cleared his throat. "You can't use any of this, Bobby. You know that."

"I know they stranded those workers, abandoned them in hell. I know Joe was frightened, or simply couldn't stomach it. He ran and escaped with girls, drink, school, music, and didn't go back until the company was well out of California. And he got spooked again when the Frye family was wiped out, and that time he didn't go back." She turned to face Frank. "I know it's all connected."

"No," he said. "You intuit it. Three people knew what happened. Two of them aren't going to tell you, and the third one took to his grave whatever he knew. Intuition's a powerful tool. You couldn't do your job without it, but you can't present it as evidence, and even if you had proof, you couldn't use it. Larry and Nora Wenzel aren't on trial, Carrie Frederick is. That's the reality you have to deal with first and foremost. You have to put this aside and walk in the prosecutor's shoes for now. Build the case they're building and see if you have anything to counter it, and if you don't, you have to think about a plea bargain. You have to keep your focus on Carrie or you'll lose her. What happened that Saturday night last July in that motel room? That's where the prosecution will start and where they'll fight every inch of the way to keep you."

"It started on Friday when he went to the bank, visited his safe-deposit box and left with a thousand dollars. That was the beginning of the end."

After Frank left, Barbara sat at her desk for a long time, unable to erase the images of the brutal desert from her mind. She stirred finally and began to look through the folders until she found the snapshot of the Wenzel brothers and their wives with their truck. The original was too small to see their features well, and they were shadowed by the vehicle. She put that one down and picked up the enlargement. Tweedledee and Tweedledum, she thought, comparing the two young men. But now she could see that their faces were not just shadowed, they also were darkened with emerging beards as if both of them needed frequent shaves. They were smiling.

She remembered what the motel manager had told her, how scandalized he had been with Joe's appearance when he returned in the late afternoons—dirty and unshaved. He cleaned himself up before dinner, and before he lingered in the bar to listen to Carrie play. But by afternoon he probably had looked like a bum.

After a few minutes she realized that she had been gazing at the topo map again. She got up, crossed her office and turned it to face the wall with the O'Keeffe poppy showing, then sat down once more to read the newest reports from Sylvia, which she had skipped the night before.

Sylvia reported that Nora and Larry both had had affairs. She was crazy about her sons, and her two-year-old grandson. Larry would be gone for a week in November after the first good rain. He went down to the Rogue River with pals every year for steelhead fishing, Nora had confided. She had said wistfully that maybe he would fall into the river and not come out again, then she had laughed and said just joking. But she had not been joking, Sylvia had added. Sylvia planned to have a professional photographer for her Halloween party, and she would tell him to get a lot of shots of Nora and Larry.

And what does that have to do with Joe's murder? Barbara asked herself. She had no answer. Instead, she looked at the chair where Frank had been sitting when he lectured her, and she realized that she thought of it as a lecture. "See, Dad," she said softly, "I also *know* that Larry and Nora somehow managed to kill him even if I don't know yet how they pulled it off."

After a few minutes she went to Shelley's door and said, "Bailey's coming by at around four. Sit in if you'd like. I have a long shopping list for him. And something for you. When you see Alexis on Friday, find out where Joe kept his safe-deposit box key, and if he had a safe at home. It doesn't have to be in her signed statement, I just want to know."

Bailey arrived promptly at four and helped himself to a drink. He scowled at the O'Keeffe poppy and shook his head. "That's indecent."

"So much for art," Barbara said. "What do you have?"

"Wenzel family. Long or short?"

"You know better. Keep it short." His detailed report would be in the folder he put on the round table. It could wait for later.

"Right. Good people, upright and poor. The old man worked for a department store, delivery job, minimum. The mom cleaned a couple of neighborhood stores three nights a week. Larry got out of high school, moved out and went right to work as a carpenter's helper for a company building new docks or warehouses. Joe was still in school when Mom and Pop went on a church picnic. It was on a lake up in the mountains. There was a boating accident and she couldn't swim. Bingo. Two years later Joe got out of school and Larry and Nora got married. The construction company moved its operations out in the boonies somewhere and Larry and Nora followed, and before long Joe moved in with them. The old man took to drink about then. A couple of D.U.I.'s and he lost his job, then lost the rental house, and got in a couple of fights. Four years after his wife died, he was found more dead than alive and he kicked in the hospital a couple of days later. His head busted in, beaten up, like that."

There was a little more, but that was the gist of it. The boys had never been in trouble, they both had been pretty good students and had after-school jobs as soon as they were old enough.

Bailey shrugged. "The all-American-family success story."

"Okay," Barbara said. "Is Herbert still hanging out at the restaurant with Carrie?"

"Nope. After he got the place wired, there was no good excuse for hanging around. I've got another guy keeping an eye out while she's in there. You know, this is starting to add up to big bucks."

"Right. A few more things for you. When and how did Joe hurt his wrist?" She paused as Bailey got out a notebook and began to write. She had a long list of questions and went down her notes, checking off items, then said, "This might be a little harder. I want a fairly recent photograph of Joe, not as a corpse. I have that one. Wife number three, Tiffany Olstead, might have one that's ten years old and if that's all to be found, it will have to do. I don't know how to suggest you get it if it exists."

"Easy. I break into her place at three in the morning and search."

"If that's what it takes," she said. "Also, what's it like when guys go to a fishing camp for a week at a time? What do they do besides fish?"

"Drink, play cards, look at dirty movies. Have girls on call. Depends on who they are. Maybe they beat drums in the forest and chant. Or have prayer meetings."

"Larry goes to the Rogue every year for steelhead right after the rains start. I want pictures of him during the first three days, several for each day. Sylvia probably knows where the camp is, or she'll find out for you."

He made a note, then regarded her with a brooding expression. He held up his glass and she nodded. After ambling to the bar and replenishing his drink, he said, "I guess we've come to a hit-man theory. The Wenzels have good alibis. You're keeping that in mind?"

"You bet."

"And still trying to pin it on their tails," he said morosely.

"You're damn right I am."

20

That weekend the first real rain of the season moved in with blustery winds that stripped the trees of leaves and flattened flower gardens. Barbara stood at the back sliding door at Frank's house on Sunday watching asters sway and bend, then spring upright over and over. End of summer, end of daylight saving time, she was thinking without regret. She loved the rain and the misty days that would come.

"I should have pulled out the petunias before now," Frank said. "They're done for."

"You say that every year, and every year you can't bear to do it until they turn into black slimy mush." She looked at her watch. Frank had invited Darren and Carrie for dinner, and they would arrive any minute. It had been her idea this time. No one wanted Carrie to be at home on Halloween when masked people would likely be coming around, and Morgan would have to be restrained or else bark and growl at little kids and parents. Todd was at a party with school friends that evening, not due home until ten. And Herbert would be in the dark house on guard.

The doorbell chimed and she went to open the door. Before Carrie and Darren got inside a second car pulled into the driveway. Alan MacCagno had arrived, the other invited guest, and Bailey's most reliable operative. Everyone hung coats and jackets on an old-fashioned coatrack in the foyer with a drip pan under it. Barbara introduced Alan to Carrie, and they started to go into the living room when the bell chimed again. Alan opened the door. There was a man with a large black umbrella and three small children on the stoop.

"Trick or treat!" they yelled.

Barbara ushered Carrie ahead of her into the living room as Alan began to hand out candy. He would be the only one to open that door again until the dinner party was over and they all headed home, Darren's truck in the lead and Alan close behind all the way. As Bailey had said, it was adding up to big bucks.

It was a good dinner party. Alan and Darren compared tricks they had done as kids, and Frank began to talk about case law. "It's been on my mind a long time," he said, carving a leg of lamb. "I always said I had two books in me, and that's the second one, good old case law."

"Is that what we call common law?" Darren asked.

"Yep. The best known one is the oldie, that if a man finds his wife in another man's arms, and he shoots one or both of them, he's justified. Case closed. Same if a guy finds a rustler after his cattle. Hang the guy, be done with it. Case closed. It's law set by community standards, not legislated, but accepted by everyone in the area."

He mentioned another one or two, and was telling about one that involved sitting on the porch on a Sunday drinking lemonade. "Got you a fine every time," he said. "Case closed. But down the road in the next town they sat out all day Sunday and drank whatever they wanted to. Different standards."

As he talked, Barbara realized how strained Carrie was, how she reacted every time the doorbell rang. She smiled and laughed at the appropriate times, but she started as if in alarm when the bell rang.

It chimed again, Alan excused himself and went to the door, and Carrie said, "Is he an old friend?"

"We've known him a long time," Frank said. "I think he just wants to be helpful."

"He's a philosophy major looking for a job," Barbara added. Alan certainly looked more like an unemployed recent graduate than a private detective. "Not many calls for philosophy around here."

"Or anywhere else, I imagine," Carrie said.

When Alan sat down again he said, "The little ones are done for the night. Now the bigger kids are out getting soaked."

He looked at Carrie. "You ever go trick-or-treating?"

Barbara could have kicked herself. No one had thought to mention to him that they were not asking Carrie any questions about her childhood.

Carrie nodded. "A couple of times. In Indiana. I didn't like it. I thought it was scary, all those masks, kids jumping out at you and scaring you."

She picked up her wine and took a sip, remembering. Boys had jumped out from behind bushes, shooting cap guns and yelling, and she had started to scream and had run down the street screaming, and then she had tripped and fallen and had become hysterical. The mothers chaperoning the girls had taken her to a hospital. And afterward she had thought: screaming, running, falling meant crazy and hospital. She had refused to go out trick-or-treating again. Adrienne had been furious, she remembered.

She looked at Alan and asked, "What does a philosophy major do for a living?"

He grinned. "Not much. I might end up flipping hamburgers and talking about Spinoza to the customers."

She laughed. "The great watchmaker in the sky."

"You studied philosophy?" Alan asked a bit cautiously. He looked relieved when she said no.

"I just read Will Durant's *Story of Philosophy*. I skimmed the surface. I found a lot of it tough going. Kant, for example."

"Most people find him tough," Alan said.

Before she could say anything else or ask a question, Frank said, "Nine o'clock. Time to turn off the lights and let the little beggars get their candy from their moms."

"And I get the leftover candy," Barbara said. "I'll divvy it with you guys." To her relief they didn't return to the subject of philosophy again.

Frank said no when Darren offered to help with dishes. "You have to get home before ten, and Barbara will help me later. Now, warm gingerbread with applesauce and coffee."

Barbara smiled. That was one of her favorite desserts, and had always been made on Halloween, just as pumpkin pie came with Thanksgiving, and sinfully rich Sachertorte with Christmas. He never forgot a thing.

When Darren said it was time to leave, Alan jumped up. "Me too," he said. "In fact, I think I've got you blocked. I'll go move my car out of the way." He thanked Frank, waved to Barbara and left before Darren and Carrie had retrieved their coats. Barbara suspected that he had left so hurriedly to check Darren's truck, to make certain no one had tampered with it.

After they were all gone, she helped Frank clear the table. As she was rinsing dishes to load the dishwasher, he said, "Carrie's remembering things. Did you see?"

She nodded.

"God," he said, "I'll be glad when this trial is over."

She looked at him then. "No more than I will be." He was so troubled, she thought, so worried, and there wasn't a thing she could do about it.

"Bobby, stay the night," he said. "No reason, just uneasy, I guess, with spooks and haunts on the prowl."

"Sure, Dad. In fact, it's too nasty out there to go anywhere."

In her apartment, Carrie locked the door, remembering when Herbert had looked at the previous lock in disgust. "That piece of crap ain't worth shit," he had said, and he had installed a dead bolt.

"That will keep out the pack of wild four-year-olds," she had said gravely.

"You bet your sweet patootie it will." He had nodded approval at his handiwork. "That'll do the trick."

She was not laughing as she sat on her sofa and recalled her own private fright show of long ago. Why had she reacted like that? She had known the boys were there teasing the girls. They all had known that, and although Becky and Ruth, her two companions, had shrieked and screamed, it had been mock fright. Girls that age liked to shriek and scream. But she had been terrified, panicked, and she could not think why. Unless she had been crazy. It was the fire, she thought then. She had been so afraid of the fire. She shook her head. They had been shooting cap guns. There had been no fire, just cap guns.

She was freezing, chilled by the rain, she told herself. Then she said under her breath, "Do you really outgrow childhood insanity? Once crazy, always crazy?"

21

It always happened like this, Barbara thought, eyeing a new folder of material from Bailey. First you got all the material the district attorney's office released, and the preliminary statements you collected personally or through your investigator, and then everything stalled. And it stayed static for what seemed like forever while you searched for a direction. She knew the destination, and had known for weeks now, but too many tangled paths kept showing up in the wilderness of data. Which one to follow became the question. Then a trickle of new information, a stream, and with luck an avalanche. The avalanche had yet to happen. But the trickle was wider and deeper than it had been and might even be called a stream.

She opened a folder and started to read and was still at it when Maria tapped on her door and entered, closing it behind her.

"Mr. and Mrs. Wenzel are here to see you," she said in a hushed voice.

"Larry and Nora Wenzel? Isn't that interesting? Show them in, by all means." She glanced around the office, at stacks of papers on the round table, more on her desk, the poppy on the easel, then said, "Hold it. Let's move that easel over here."

After they moved it behind her desk, she waved Maria out and waited to greet her visitors. They were both impeccably dressed, he in a charcoal-gray fine wool suit and a discreet pale-blue necktie, and she in a powder-blue cashmere suit with a dark-red blouse. His hair was uniformly gray and well trimmed. He looked freshly shaved, and he appeared to be powerful, with big hands and thick wrists, a thick neck, and a bit jowly. And she had on too much makeup. To Barbara's eye any noticeable makeup was too much for day hours, and hers was very noticeable. Eyeliner, eye shadow the color of her suit, blush. Every blemish, if her face had any, was well hidden. No doubt it was very good makeup, expensive and expertly applied, but still it was a Wednesday afternoon, and she looked ready for the opera. Her hair was as blond as it ever had been, although the color now came from the outside.

Barbara motioned toward the two clients' chairs and took her own chair behind her desk. "What can I do for you?" she asked when they were all seated.

"Please excuse this intrusion," Larry said. "We should have called for an appointment, but our decision to come here arose quite spontaneously at lunch and we said let's do it." He smiled. It was a very good smile, warm and sincere looking.

Barbara closed the folder before her and said, "Well, as you can see I am quite busy."

"Of course. I'll be brief. I happened to meet Alexis O'Reilly in Portland a day or two ago, and she mentioned that you had sent your colleague to talk with her. I always cared for Alexis and never felt she was in any way to blame for the unfortunate marriage she and my brother had. During our chat she mentioned that she had taken some of his possessions when she left him and, further, that she had given them to your colleague. Ms. Holloway, this is an awkward and even delicate situation, but I don't feel that we are necessarily adversaries. I have no doubt that your client did what she had to do. I have no illusions about my brother. However, he was my brother, and we shared many, many happy years. When his house burned to the ground, everything he owned burned with it, and at his death I realized how little I had of his as keepsakes, mementos. My wife and I have come today to ask you humbly for his possessions. Something for me to keep and cherish, for our children to keep to honor his memory. They were both very fond of him. I understand that Alexis took racing forms with his notes and, tawdry as it might appear, I would cherish them, as well as his favorite music. We shared so many evenings listening to music with him, all of us singing along, and those are the memories that I want to hold on to. The good times we had together."

"I see," Barbara said, and glanced at the folders on her desk. "As soon as this trial is over and I'm no longer so rushed for time, I'll see what I can do for you."

"Ms. Holloway," Nora said then, "those things have no monetary value, of course, but we are prepared to pay for your time. I've found so often that in the crush of work things get misplaced, lost, and it would be a shame to let that happen. Would ten thousand dollars be a just compensation for a few minutes of your time?"

Larry's voice was good, he had come a long way from being a carpenter's helper working minimum, but her voice was astonishing. She was downright sultry. Barbara shook her head impatiently and stood up.

"Mr. Wenzel, Mrs. Wenzel, I really can't be distracted by matters that are extraneous to my case at the present. I'll be in touch after the trial. I'm sorry, but that's all I can offer now."

They both stood up, and there was steel in Larry's voice when he spoke. "Ms. Holloway, Alexis stole that material. I am my brother's legal heir, and that material belongs to me. I believe it's a felony to be knowingly in possession of stolen goods. I wanted to handle this in a civilized, amicable manner. It doesn't end here."

He took Nora's arm, in what Barbara suspected, from the look on Nora's face, was not a tender grip, and they walked out.

She sat down hard as soon as her door closed. "Idiot!" she muttered. "It's the tapes!" She waited for Maria to ring and tell her they were gone. It didn't take long. She hurried from her office, and said in passing Maria, "Get Bailey on the phone. Keep at it until you reach him." She went to the outside door and locked it, then to Shelley's door, knocked and entered.

"Where's the box Alexis O'Reilly gave you?"

Startled, Shelley stood up and started to move toward her closet.

"Don't touch it," Barbara said, opening the closet door. "Is that it?" She pointed to a cardboard box closed with tape. Shelley nodded. "Exactly what did you do with it after she gave it to you?"

"I brought it up here and put it in the closet."

"Did you open it?"

Shelley shook her head. "I haven't touched it since then."

"Remember that," Barbara said, picking up the box. "You

brought it up and put it away and haven't touched it since. That's all you have to say about it. Come on."

In her own office, she set the box on a chair, swept up the papers on the table and dumped them on her desk. So much for all the sorting she had done earlier, she thought angrily, getting out her letter opener. She returned to the box, cut the tape and dumped the contents onto the table. Racing forms, racing newspapers, notebooks and music tapes, forty or fifty cassettes. The phone rang. Maria had tracked down Bailey.

"Don't touch them yet," she said to Shelley as she picked up the phone. "We have a situation," she said to Bailey. "I need as many old music tapes as you can round up in the next hour. Old, before 1980. I don't care what music, but rock if you can find it."

"I have a few at home," Shelley said. "From my school days."

Barbara repeated that to Bailey. "Shelley will call Alex and have them waiting, but I need more than that. At least twenty, more would be better. Put them in your duffel bag, no boxes or shopping bags. And pronto."

Shelley hurried out to call Alex, and Barbara eyed the tapes, went to the washroom and dumped crumpled and crushed paper towels out of a small wastebasket, took the basket back to her office and swept all the tapes into it. She replaced it in the washroom, added the used towels, crumpled up a few more and tossed them in.

She was scanning one of the racing forms when Shelley returned.

"Are we in trouble?" Shelley asked.

"Depends," Barbara said. "Considering that we've probably been sitting on a powder keg for the past few weeks, and so far no explosion, not too bad. Now it hangs on who gets

here first, Bailey, or the sheriff of Nottingham with his hench-
men and a search warrant." She told Shelley about the Wenzels. "What I want to do is check out all this racing junk, just
to make sure there's nothing here, but it's the tapes. It's been
staring me in the face from the start, and I kept looking somewhere else." She glanced at her watch; twenty-five minutes
before three. It would take time to get the warrant, get a judge
to sign off on it, get back here, she told herself, but not a lot
of time.

The racing forms had margin notations, but they were all
about horses. The notebooks had the same kind of notes, and
one of them seemed to have several methods for beating the
roulette wheel. Each one had a black cross through it.

They were both looking at their watches more and more
often as the minutes dragged by until at ten minutes before
four, Bailey arrived. His apparent amble was as deceptive as
everything else about him, Barbara had learned long ago. He
could cover the ground faster than most people, and never
seemed to hurry. Now he seemed to move almost in slow motion as he opened his duffel and pointed.

"Twenty-six tapes. Now what?"

"In the box," she said, motioning toward it on the chair. He
began emptying the duffel, and she went to the washroom to
collect the wastebasket. She didn't bother taking out the paper
towels, but simply dumped everything into his bag after he
had removed the tapes he had collected. "Okay. Guard them,
and I'll want a couple of tape players with headsets."

"Three," Shelley said.

Barbara nodded. "Three. I'll leave here around five and
head for Dad's house. Meet me there."

After putting his own gear back in the bag, he said, "You

think your old man's going to sit around watching us listen to music?"

"Make it four," Barbara said. "Now, git!" He had not reached the door by the time she had tossed all the racing forms, newspapers and notebooks on top of the music tapes. She taped the box the way it had been before and carried it back to Shelley's closet. "Done," she said with relief. "Take off as usual at five, and if no one shows up by five-thirty, I'll leave. See you later."

Back in her own office she spread papers on the round table again, then sat at her desk with an open folder, not seeing a word in it. At ten minutes after four Maria buzzed her to say that a Mr. Kenmore and a detective wanted to see her.

"Bring them back," Barbara said. Kenmore himself, she thought in surprise. He headed the law firm that represented the Wenzel Corporation. He entered with the detective a moment later.

"Ms. Holloway," Kenmore said. "I regret this intrusion, however my client found it expedient to recover his possessions now rather than wait until later. This is Detective Mac-Clure. He has a search warrant, I'm afraid."

She held out her hand and the detective handed her the warrant. "A box of tapes and papers," she muttered. "I told Mr. Wenzel I'd get to it when I had time. Come with me." She walked past them, down the hallway to Shelley's office. She knocked, opened the door and entered, with the attorney and the detective pressing in behind her. Shelley looked up from her computer, put a notebook down and hit her screen saver key.

"Did Alexis O'Reilly give you a box of stuff a few weeks ago?" Barbara asked.

Shelley nodded. "Yes. I brought it back with me."

"Where is it now?"

Shelley stood up and went to her closet, opened the door and pointed to the box.

"Did you open it?" Barbara asked.

"No. I haven't touched it since I brought it up here. What's wrong?"

"Not a thing," Barbara said. She picked up the box and led the way out of Shelley's office. In the reception room when the detective reached for it, she said, "Hold it. Let's make sure it's what you're looking for. Tapes and papers." She didn't bother cutting the tape this time, but yanked the box open, ripping tape and box alike. She shook things around in it, reached in and stirred the tapes, lifted one to read the label and tossed it back. "Tapes and papers," she said, shoving the box toward the detective. She turned to Maria. "When these gentlemen leave, lock the door and don't let anyone else in here today. No more interruptions." She looked at Kenmore. "Is there anything else?"

"I'm sure there isn't," he said. "Thank you, Ms. Holloway." He bowed his head slightly and walked out with the detective.

"And that's where we stand," Barbara said in Frank's kitchen later. "We have to listen to those tapes tonight. The Wenzels might know exactly what tape they're looking for and if they don't find it, they might send someone else to find it. If there is such a tape in that pile, I want it put in a safe-deposit box first thing in the morning. Inez told me Joe was always taping everything. Alexis told Shelley the same thing. And there was a tape recorder and player with a headset in his motel room, but no tapes. They're looking for something and haven't found it yet."

"It could have burned up in the house fire," Frank said. "But you're right. We have to find out. I suggest the living room. At least we can be comfortable."

Bailey showed them how to work the tape players. They had variable speed, he said, real time, then faster and faster forward. "You'll find the speed that lets you know if it's just music or something else," he said gloomily.

Frank put the paper towels on the fire in the fireplace, brought in coffee and cups, and they started. It was an eerie party, Barbara thought, listening to The Doors scream about their mother, adjusting the speed faster until the words were lost and there was only noise. The others were doing the same thing, adjusting the tape players, sitting without a sound, sipping coffee.

Thing One and Thing Two tried to get on Frank's lap, but that never worked. They were too big to share a lap, and one of them stepped down and went to Barbara and stepped up onto her lap. They didn't have to jump, they could simply step up without a break in stride. Automatically she began to stroke the cat, and it purred. Bailey finished his tape first, tossed it into the box Frank had brought in and reached for another one. His expression was sour.

Soon Frank added his tape to the box. He moved Thing One aside, stood up and walked out with both cats at his heels. Barbara started a second tape. When Frank returned he had a tray with wine and glasses, cheeses and crackers, a bottle of Jack Daniel's whiskey, ice and water.

Barbara had just poured herself a glass of wine and was reaching for cheese when Shelley pulled off her headset. "I've got something," she said in a choked voice.

They all pulled off the headsets. Shelley adjusted the speed and the volume and they listened to a woman's voice. "Great balls of fire and a red-hot poker, up the asshole and grind me down, lover... Deeper. Deeper. Ah, a little shit makes the cream sweeter." Barbara closed her eyes hard and gritted her teeth as it got more and more lascivious. After another moment or two, she said, "Turn it off, Shelley."

In the silence that followed, Frank muttered, "Christ on a mountain, he was into audio pornography."

"We don't all have to listen," Barbara said. "There may be a lot more of that filth, but we don't all have to listen to it. Now we know what to be on the lookout for. Start with music, something else, go back to music."

Bailey had gone from gloomy to sour, and now he looked outraged. He probably was the most puritanical among them, Barbara thought, but she felt deeply embarrassed. You don't share pornography with your father. She avoided looking directly at Frank. "If we run into that kind of thing, let's just fast-forward it enough to make sure that's all there is to it, then put that tape aside," she said. She remembered what Inez had told her, that Joe wanted her to talk dirty in bed.

Before they resumed listening, Frank said, "I ordered some dinner from West Brothers. It should be here soon." He eyed the jumble of tapes on the coffee table and added grimly, "It looks like it's going to be a long night."

When the bell chimed, Bailey waved Frank down and went to receive the food himself. They had a silent dinner, and afterward Barbara couldn't have said what it was.

It was a few minutes past ten when Bailey held up his hand and took his headset off. Three tapes had been added to the one that Shelley had set aside earlier, but he made no motion to add his to that growing stack. "I think this is it," he said. He adjusted the speed on his tape player and turned up the volume and they listened.

Nora's voice came in too low to make out her words. He adjusted the volume again.

"Do you always have conferences in the bedroom?" Nora asked. Her voice was not yet the sultry one she had since cultivated, but it was throaty and suggestive.

"Best place for heart-to-heart talks," a man said. "Nice bedroom, isn't it?"

"Lovely. Joe, when are you going to stop pouting and come back to work? We miss you. I miss you."

"Nora, darling, I told you and big brother. I'm officially retired. That's it. A life of leisure, that's for me. Have a seat here beside me."

There was silence, a faint rustling noise, then a door opening and closing. "Bathroom," Joe said. "And that's a closet. I told you Lexy won't be back for a couple of hours. We have plenty of time." He sounded amused.

Her voice was faint, almost inaudible when she spoke again, as if she was moving about the room, or had her back to him. "Remember when you moved in with Larry and me? You were so young, just a kid. I could feel you watching me all the time, like burning holes in my skin. Sometimes I'd look at you and wonder if I should have waited, maybe I got the wrong brother. You were so sweet."

"And now?"

"Maybe I should have waited," she said huskily. "Larry's... He's not like you. For days and days he doesn't even see me. You wouldn't be like that."

More silence, more rustling sounds, then Joe's voice was

there. "I always said you were built like a brick outhouse. You haven't lost a thing, have you?"

"We could have fun, Joe. You and me. Larry wouldn't even notice. A week at Vegas now and then, or Hawaii. Have you been to Hawaii? The two of us in a beach cabana... Don't do that. Don't mark me like that."

"Why? Dogs and men like to mark their territory."

"Stop it, Joe. Later… You're so overdressed. Let me help you get rid of some things."

Silence and sounds of movement. Then, "Isn't that better? Now we're even. I always thought yours might be bigger than Larry's. I was right."

"Tell me something, Nora, darling. I've always wanted to know. What did you do with their hats? Those great big sheltering sombreros?"

"That isn't funny!" The huskiness was gone, her tone sharp.

"I guess not. But I was curious. Did big brother hold a gun on them while you patted them down? Remember how they always pulled off their hats when you got near? How respectful they were? Did they pull off their hats when you patted them down?"

"Shut up! Don't start that."

"It's just pillow talk, sweetheart. Just pillow talk. Something else I wondered back then. Were you putting out for H.L.? He always came back looking like the cat that had been at the cream."

More rustling, then, "Hey, you aren't leaving already are you? We've just begun."

"You can't do this to us, Joe. You measly little coward. We saved your ass and you turned tail and ran, and we covered for you. Not again. No cover this time. You're in or you're out, but no games. Understand that? No fucking games! You get your ass back to work or you're out. Not another cent. Larry will gun you down before he'll pay blackmail, and I'll load his gun."

He laughed. "You're so wrong, baby. That day when you guys came back with the empty truck, you know what I'd been doing, waiting for you? Playing with my tape recorder, mixing one tape with another. Remember how Larry used to yell at me for wasting all my dough on music and tape recorders, junk like that? I was buying an annuity, sweetheart, and it's come due. I turned it on that day, Nora. Can't tell you how many times I've listened to you explaining what you did, how you had to do it." His voice became falsetto, mimicking her. "They found the stuff. We couldn't buy them all off, one or two maybe, but not all of them.'" In his own voice he said, "And then you barfed. Remember? That's not a pretty sound, you barfing. Who cleaned it up, Nora? You or big brother?"

"You pile of shit, you asshole! You think you can bluff us? If we go down, so do you."

"Wrong. See, what I figure is if I don't get my monthly annuity check, I'll just go to the Feds and tell all. I'll be born again and repent and make the best witness they ever put on the stand. How big brother always liked to play with fireworks, how good he was at blowing up things, how H.L. called and big brother got busy in the garage playing with things that go boom in the night. I'm still taping stuff, you know. That's on tape, too, Nora, baby. Those little recorders come in smaller and smaller sizes, you'd never know a guy had one up his sleeve these days. And I do like to play with my toys. Multiple copies, that's my style. Stash one here, one there." He laughed again. "Insurance and annuities, that's what I learned in school. And I have insurance. Tell big brother I made sure that there's insurance just in case something bad happens."

"We won't let you get away with this," she said in a harsh voice.

"But you will. Oh, and tell big brother that every time he gives himself a raise, I want one, too. I'll come by and check the books now and then. I learned how to do that in school, too."

She cursed, and he laughed over it.

"I'll send him a copy of my tape of our little heart-to-heart pillow talk," he said. "Just so he'll know you really tried. Don't forget your garter belt."

A door slammed, and after a second or two Jerry Garcia was strumming a guitar.

22

There was a prolonged silence after Bailey turned off his tape player. Shelley stood up, sat down again, and Frank got up and went to the fireplace, added another stick to the low fire and remained there facing the flames.

He spoke first. "There's too much to ignore and not enough to take to the police."

Barbara shook herself. "Finish listening to it, Bailey. I'll transcribe it when you're done. I want to read their words in black-and-white. Tomorrow it goes to a safe-deposit box."

"Make two printouts," Frank said, turning. His expression was bleak and hard.

Bailey put his headset back on and adjusted the controls of his tape player, and after a moment Shelley returned to the one she had been listening to. Frank motioned to Barbara and walked out with her.

In the kitchen he said, "I'll tell Bailey to get Alan or some-one to follow Shelley home, and tomorrow have him arrange for a groundskeeper out at her place."

"Someone with a big dog," Barbara said. "Seventy acres to keep an eye on."

"A big dog," he agreed. "And you and Bailey spend the night here. We'll go on from there after we think about this."

She did not argue with him.

"We'll finish listening to the rest of them while you're tran-scribing that tape." He picked up the carafe, found it empty and put it down. "I'll make coffee. You'll want it before this night is over."

It was midnight before they were finished with the tapes and the transcription was done. Alan arrived, and he and Bai-ley went out to have a look around, and do something to the cars in the driveway so they could tell at a glance if they had been tampered with.

"I don't know what you can tell Alex," Barbara said to Shelley as she was putting on her coat.

"Nothing," Shelley said. "He knew what he was getting into, what I do. He won't ask questions."

Frank walked to the door with her and kissed her cheek. The little pink-and-gold fairy princess with a spine of steel, he thought, watching her drive away with Alan close behind her.

Barbara was in the living room gazing at three bubble-lined mailing envelopes, one oversized with the innocent tapes in it, a middle-sized one with eight pornographic tapes and a small one with a single tape. Like Papa Bear, Mama Bear, Baby Bear waiting for the intruder. When Frank and Bailey returned she said, "We don't even know if they were looking for that particular one, or just trying to make sure they had collected all of them."

Frank sat down heavily. "We have to assume they know and act accordingly."

"Wenzel's going on that fishing trip on Saturday, and he'll be gone five or six days," she said. "I'll breathe easier once I know he's out of town." She looked at Bailey. "Is your guy going to be in place at Shelley's by Saturday?"

Bailey said he'd be there. He was drinking coffee, she realized, and in fact his glass still had over an inch of bourbon in it, untouched for the past couple of hours. When Shelley had said that Alan could use a guest room at her house, Bailey had said Alan wouldn't be there to sleep, and apparently he didn't intend to sleep either that night.

"We know Joe had two or more copies of various tapes," she said. "He had a home safe and the safe-deposit box. I wonder if he had tapes like that—" she motioned toward the smallest envelope "—scattered in among others on his shelves. They say he had hundreds, an extensive collection."

"Purloined letter," Frank said. "Hidden in plain sight. Bailey, would tapes like that survive in a home safe with a fire hot enough to burn down the house?"

"Depends," Bailey said. "You said he had a safe key?" he asked Barbara. She nodded. "So the house was built in the mid-seventies, and probably the safe was put in then, an old model, not computer operated or even with a combination lock, just an old-fashioned key. They probably would have melted down, fused together, something like that. Might even have burst into flames if they got hot enough."

"And that would leave the ones he had stashed in his bank safe-deposit box," Barbara said, frowning.

"Maybe that's what he went after that Friday, to get them out and make new copies," Bailey said.

"And leave them in plain sight in the motel room, and then invite the killer in," Barbara said scathingly.

"Remember they all had alibis," Bailey said.

"Not Nora."

He shrugged. "After listening to that tape I think she'd be the last person he'd ask in. If you can get her there in the first place. I can't."

She ignored that. "I said before that I thought it started with his visit to the bank. Wrong. It started with the house fire. I think they had a plan that started with destroying the tapes in the house." She gave Bailey a cold look. "Nora had a car hidden away in the shrubbery and used that."

He shook his head. "They live in the Crescent Estates neighborhood, houses in the five hundred grand range and up, with their own private security patrols. No unknown car had a chance to stay hidden. A patrol saw the kid get home at three-ten. I talked to him. He's sure."

"She rode her broomstick," Barbara muttered.

Frank stood up. "I don't care what you two do, stay up and bicker all night, but keep it down. I'm going to bed."

He went to bed, but not to sleep. He heard Barbara when she went upstairs, and he heard Bailey prowling around. The cats were unsettled, displeased having people up and about at all hours, no doubt, and they wanted in and out of the bedroom frequently. Usually they settled at his feet, and they all went to sleep and stayed there until morning.

Too much and too little, he thought again and again. He kept seeing those hot desert wastelands and desperate men without shelter, without water, without hope.

* * *

In her upstairs room Barbara tossed and turned, unable to stop the flood of images that flashed before her eyes: swirling dust devils, sand blowing over the road, ankle-high scrub that looked more like rocks than plants; a six-pack of water that she had emptied; the temperature gauge of the outside air with the needle off the dial at 120; men staggering, falling, praying; the child Carolyn running away from an exploding car, hit by debris, falling, catching on fire; Joe Wenzel dead in his motel room; the Wenzels in their expensive finery in her office, at ease, comfortable.

One down, two to go, she thought.

Pale light was seeping in around the drapes before she drifted into sleep.

"Guys who play with bombs and light fires like to work at night, between two and four in the morning," Bailey said at breakfast. "You're spread out too much. Carrie in one place, Shelley in another, you over there, your dad over here. We can't do them all. Yours especially," he said to Barbara.

He didn't look any worse for wear after a sleepless night, but Frank looked tired, and she was bone tired.

"She'll stay here," Frank said. "Alan can be a house guest for the next few weeks."

Barbara started to object, but remained silent. Her apartment and her car at the curb couldn't be watched all night. Bailey had made phone calls already, and a man and a dog were on their way to Shelley's house. She had instructions to stay there until they arrived in order to meet them both.

"I'll follow you to the bank, and then I'll take off and get some sleep," Bailey said. "Sylvia has the pictures from the

party. I'll pick them up and see you at the office around four."
He gave her a sharp look. "And how about you knock off
working late at the office for the next few weeks. Bring it
home with you."

"I have to swing by my apartment and get my safe-deposit
key," she said. She turned to Frank. "Where do you keep
yours?"

"Desk drawer. Why?"

"Curious. Joe's key wasn't on his ring, and if it was in his
desk when his house burned, when did he get another one?"

An hour later, entering her office, she thought, and this is
how it's going to be until the damn trial is history and Carrie
is safe somewhere out of range.

At her desk she resumed reading where she had left off the
day before when her drop-in guests had arrived. She was still
at it when Bailey entered at four.

"Pictures," he said, tossing a folder on the table. "And
more dope about the Wenzel sons. Alan's at your old man's
house getting some sleep, and the guy's in place at Shelley's
house." He poured himself a drink and slouched into a chair.
"Tell me something," he said. "Why can't you hand that junk
over to the D.A., have that pack of Wenzels hauled in and be
done with it?"

He never would have dreamed of asking her father a question like that, she well knew, a little irritated that he didn't hesitate to ask her.

"It's corroborative evidence, not conclusive," she said.
"Like Dad said, too much and too little. You need all the
background that goes with it for it to be meaningful, and we
can't fill them in. We can't even hint of a connection between

the Wenzels and the Frye family, not until Carrie's out of the picture. With that tape the D.A. would have to conclude that Joe was blackmailing Larry, but that it's a separate issue, since as you keep reminding me, they all have alibis."

He scowled. "And when you do fork it over they slap a charge of withholding evidence on you. And me."

"So you hire a good lawyer to keep you out of the pokey," she said. "Any more questions?"

He shook his head. "If I do, I don't want to hear the answers. Larry's fishing trip is still on, bright and early Saturday morning. Sylvia's having lunch with Nora Saturday afternoon."

After he left, Barbara spread the party pictures on her desk. Each person had a small number, and there was a corresponding list of names, identifying them all. Some Barbara knew, some she had seen around, but they were mostly unrecognizable in their costumes and makeup. Little Bo Peep, Madam Pompadour, an anorexic woman dressed as Peter Pan... And Nora as Cleopatra. Her eye makeup was heavy, more like Elizabeth Taylor's than Cleopatra's possibly; she was wearing a tiara with twined serpents with emeralds for eyes and a beautiful, vaguely Egyptian necklace. There were tight little spit curls on her forehead, jet-black. Barbara sifted through the pictures until she found one showing Nora's back. The black hair was coiled intricately, with one long curling loop.

She studied the pictures for several minutes, then she dialed Sylvia's number. She had to go through a maid and wait for Sylvia to be found.

"Barbara, I can't tell you how grateful I am," Sylvia said in a low conspiratorial tone. "This is so exciting. What's cooking?"

Barbara grinned and shook her head. "Are you alone? Can you talk?"

"Yes, of course." But she didn't raise her voice.

"I got the pictures, and they're wonderful. Thanks. What can you tell me about Nora's hairdo? Her wig?"

"Wasn't it stunning! Absolutely stunning. It's real hair. Asian girls let it get long and sell it, a really valuable commodity for them. It probably cost two thousand or even more. What else do you want to know?"

"Bailey says you're having lunch with Nora on Saturday. If you can find a way to bring the conversation to the party and her outfit, find out when and where she got that wig. Was it arranged where she bought it? And who her hairdresser was if it was done somewhere else."

"That will fit right in," Sylvia said. "We're going to look at the pictures, and do a postmortem on the party and begin plans for next year. She wants it at her place next time."

"Sounds good," Barbara said. "Give me a call after you see her, will you? At Dad's house. You have his number?"

"Do I ever! Give that beautiful hunk a big smacking kiss and tell him it's from me."

After she hung up, Barbara found a picture that had Sylvia in it and her grin became broader. Medusa to a T, she thought, and hardly different from her day-by-day appearance. It would not surprise her at all to see Sylvia with snakes on her head.

23

When Frank bought his house, it was with a vague hope that Barbara would be willing to move in with him, and even as he recognized his never-voiced hope, he had chided himself as a foolish old man. He had known it wasn't going to happen, but still he had hoped. On the few occasions when circumstances made it necessary that she come and stay for a few days, or weeks in this case, he had to remind himself repeatedly to give her room, not ask questions, and above all not to give her any orders. He knew that she would take off if he crossed the line. What he wanted to do that Saturday afternoon was to tell her to light somewhere and relax.

She wanted, or more likely needed, a long walk, but intermittent rain had fallen all morning, and now she was waiting for Sylvia to call, and after that it might be getting dark, or the rain might return. She was upstairs and down repeatedly, and when up he could hear her pacing in the hall, and when down, she wandered into the living room, dining room, kitchen, around and around.

He heard the doorbell chime and left his study in time to see Alan admitting Darren.

"Hi," Darren said. "You're still job hunting?"

Alan grinned. "Times are tough."

"Afternoon," Frank said, stepping forward into the hall. "Come on in."

Barbara came downstairs and stopped at the bottom when she saw Darren.

His gaze on her was as searching as it had been when he saw Alan. "Hello again. I'm on a mission," he said.

He turned to Frank. "Herbert has Carrie and Todd working with him on the basement rec room, and I'm an errand boy. Herbert says you have a big steamer pan of some sort, and he'd like to borrow it. He plans to make molé tomorrow and Carrie's going to make tamales, and you're both invited to share the feast. The steamer is for her to use. You're welcome, too," he said to Alan.

Alan shook his head. "No, thanks. I have a lot of reading to do."

Frank glanced at Barbara. She shrugged. "Sure." She looked at her watch.

"Now I'm off to shop," Darren said. "I have a long list, and I don't even know what most of the things on it are. Herbert said I have to go to the Kiva for them. He also said my kitchen is piss-poor in the way of ingredients."

"I'll go with you," Frank said, glad to have an excuse to get out and leave Barbara to her pacing. "Maybe we can figure it out together. In fact, I'll buy salad makings and add to the feast."

Belatedly Barbara realized she should make a contribution. "I'll bring a dessert," she said.

After they left together, Barbara resumed her pacing. "Why doesn't she call?" Barbara muttered to herself, looking at her watch again. "How long does it take to eat lunch?" She went back upstairs.

It was ten minutes after four when the call came. Sylvia's voice was as hushed as it had been before. "Reporting," she said. "Pamela Costello was there. I couldn't get away. But I have what you need." She kept her voice almost inaudible and she referred to Nora by initials. The only thing she had not been able to find out was when Nora bought the wig. "She was either evasive or trying to remember," Sylvia said. "I don't think she suspected anything, though, and then Pamela changed the subject and I thought it wise not to go back there."

After hanging up, Barbara drew a deep breath. At least she could relax a bit now, since Larry had left early that morning for his fishing trip and he would not be back until the coming Friday. On the other hand, the wig shop was in San Francisco and that was a nuisance.

Dinner that Sunday was extraordinary, everyone agreed. Herbert had made duck molé, not turkey, and explained that any time turkey would be good, duck would be better. He went into a long description of how he had cooked two ducks the day before in order to cool them and skim the fat from the broth. "It's the broth that makes it," he said complacently.

Carrie listened and nodded now and then. Her tamales were equally good, they all said, and she smiled and nodded again. But she kept thinking how weird this dinner was, as if everyone at the table except her and Todd shared secrets. Darren kept his gaze on Barbara and Barbara's mind was somewhere else much of the time, and when it came back now and then, she said something that might or might not be on the subject. Or on a subject already over with.

Carrie had a feeling that Mr. Holloway and Herbert had already been acquainted when they both pretended to meet for the first time.

And halfway through dinner Morgan began to bark, and Herbert was on his feet and halfway to the door before anyone else even moved. When he came back, he said, "That dang dog, I can't teach him a thing. He's got a brain as big as a flea. Just a car turning in the driveway."

Carrie laughed derisively. She had watched Herbert make hand signals, and Morgan respond instantly. When she tried the same signals, Morgan simply looked at her with his tongue hanging out and an idiotic dog grin on his face. The way he was trained, it was almost as if Morgan was less a pet than a watchdog. But she had always believed watchdogs were big and fierce, Doberman pinschers or mastiffs or even pit bulls, and Morgan looked like a Raggedy Ann kind of dog. But no one could come onto the property without setting him off.

She saw the quick exchange of glances that passed between Mr. Holloway and Herbert when he came in, and she thought this was how it was when her parents and other adults had shared a secret. There had been strong undercurrents that she had sensed and had not been able to unravel. *When?* She caught in her breath and held it, but the moment was already gone, the memory too fleeting to grasp. Todd began to talk with enthusiasm about ghost towns, and she lost even the feeling that she had almost captured something from her childhood.

Barbara did not want to linger and socialize after they finished a bakery cake she had picked up on the way to Darren's house. "I know it's rude to eat and run," she said. "It's just that I have some things to get done tonight." It was less an apology than a statement of fact.

"Let's fix a plate for Alan," Darren said. "There's a lot left over."

"The philosopher?" Carrie asked. "He's staying with you?"

"At Dad's house. Out of work, out of luck," Barbara said. "It's temporary."

Carrie frowned, glanced at Herbert, then away. Two men crashing with friends? She felt a strange stirring in her stomach and might have asked more, but Herbert was gathering things from the table and talking to Todd, and she remained silent.

"I can reach you at Frank's house?" Darren asked, holding Barbara's coat a few minutes later.

"Yes, for now, at least. It's simpler that way." And that was less an explanation than a dodge, she knew, but there it was. She did not elaborate, and he did not ask any further questions.

Carrie had channel-hopped for a short time, then turned off the TV. She had never had her own television before, and it was now more of a curiosity than a necessity. She rarely found anything of interest on it. She picked up a book, put it down when she realized that nothing she was reading was leaving any impression. She missed her car, she thought then. She wasn't used to being cooped up, having to rely on others to take her shopping, take her to work, to the library. Every time she called about her car it was the same story, they were trying to track down a couple of parts, an alternator and a differential something or other.

Thank heavens, she thought, that Herbert had showed up when he did, or she would really be stuck, imprisoned here in this lovely apartment. Her eyes widened, and she gazed about as if seeing her apartment for the first time. Why on earth had Darren furnished it before he finished his own house? Everything up here was brand-new except the piano. She had not considered before how improbable it was for Darren to furnish the apartment so completely. He wanted the rent money, she told herself. She had no idea how much the rent was for the apartment. Her benefactors were covering it, Barbara had said. But why? Why pay for an apartment for a stranger? They should have picked a local girl or woman to help, not a stranger passing through.

And Morgan. The more she considered the dog the more convinced she was that he was really a watchdog, superbly trained to do a job. And Herbert was a puzzle. He could do everything apparently, and the first thing he had done here was put in a security system, and then another one at the restaurant. He hadn't needed any cooking lessons in molé. He was a true master chef. How had he known Mr. Holloway had a steamer?

The vague disquietude she had felt at dinner had returned, and it had grown to an undeniable worry, even a fear. Too many coincidences. Herbert appeared and her car died. Whenever she wanted to go out for anything, he was there to take her. If Morgan barked, he was out like a shot. She had thought it was to make Morgan stop barking. Now she considered another alternative. He was checking on whoever or whatever had roused Morgan. Like a prison guard.

Was Barbara distrustful, afraid she would run away? Carrie shook her head after a moment. She was certain Barbara had not known about the apartment until she returned from a trip and Carrie showed her around. If not to keep her in, then to keep someone else out? Guard her?

She shook her head harder. From what? From whom? She had never seen a criminal run off with the loot. Never witnessed any criminal act of any sort. Petty stuff, yes, but nothing big, nothing major. Nothing to require a bodyguard. She knew nothing about Joe Wenzel's murder. There was no reason anyone on earth would come looking for her.

Unless, she thought, there was something from her forgotten childhood. A chill raced through her, and she jumped up and went to the kitchen to make a cup of tea. She wanted something hot, something sweet. She stood waiting for the kettle to reach a boil. If she had no memories of her own, only those of that other little girl, Carolyn, so be it. She was through running away from them. Always before when those other memories surfaced, there had been a way to escape, to run to another state, another city, another job. No more.

The kettle whistled, startling her. She put a tea bag into a cup and poured in some boiled water. Then, sitting at her table waiting for the tea to steep, she recalled an article she had read about how to train your memory. She had rejected the whole notion at the time, not wanting to remember, afraid of being crazy. She was still terrified of the idea of insanity, but she couldn't run anywhere now. She was imprisoned, and Herbert was either her guard or her protector.

She was surprised by how much of the article she had retained, as if she had put it aside intact until she was ready to use it. If you have a snapshot of something, hold it, examine it, question it. Where were you? Who was with you? Were you warm, cold? Write it down with every detail you can recall immediately, then work to expand it. What were you wearing? What is beyond your point of view…?

When she started to lift her cup, her hand was shaking, and she said under her breath, "Cut it out! You're a big girl now. Adrienne isn't going to smack you, and you aren't going to the hospital. Get a grip."

A moment later when she started to pick up her cup, her hand was still shaking. Resolutely she held the cup in both hands, welcoming the warmth, and sipped the tea.

24

On Monday morning Barbara told her crew what Sylvia had learned about the wig, and then she said to Bailey. "Mattie Thorne, Gregory Wenzel's date for the night of the murder. I want you to drive from her house to the Wenzel house at between two-thirty and three in the morning on a Saturday night. Two trips, one sticking to the speed limit, one the way a young man might drive at that time of night. Next Saturday would work. Also, how long it would take to get from her place to the motel that late, and finally time from the motel to the Wenzel house in the middle of the night."

Bailey's scowl was set as he made more notes. "It won't work," he said. "Time of death before two. They can pin that down pretty close these days."

"Just curious," Barbara said. "Tomorrow I'm off to San Francisco to buy a wig, and it probably will be late when I get back. So you have plenty of time to get stuff for me."

His look was baleful, but he made no comment.

"You shouldn't be the one to go after the wig," Shelley said.

"What do you mean?"

"You don't fit the part. No offense, Barbara, but you really don't look like the kind of woman who would spend a couple thousand dollars for a wig. I should do it. And it will take two days at least. There has to be a fitting."

Barbara shook her head. "You went out and bought a wig in the afternoon less than a year ago. What do you mean a fitting, two days?"

"That was a cheap wig, and you're talking about human hair. Each hair is sewn or tied in place, and then a lining is made, and the whole thing is fitted to you, shrunken down or stretched, whatever it needs. It takes time. I can do it. Put on a couple of rings, earrings—you know, dress the part—and demand that it be ready within a day."

After a moment Barbara nodded, recognizing that she was out of her depth here. "Okay. I have a timetable. Carrie started to work at the lounge on July fifth and Wenzel was killed on August tenth. I want to know if Nora bought a wig within that period. I intended to ask for one exactly like hers, and get someone to refer to the books to make certain. I don't want any suspicion raised. I'll have to get a deposition and a copy of a receipt, but not yet and I don't want any paperwork to vanish mysteriously. Once I turn over my witness list the prosecution will know I'm going after the Wenzel pack, but I'll put that off until the last possible day."

"If she bought it before or after that time frame, do you still want a black wig of human hair?" Shelley asked.

"Absolutely."

"They might not have an exact match in stock and have to order one. I'll take care of it."

Barbara nodded. Shelley would deck herself out as the rich little playgirl, a real Valley Girl, and she knew exactly how to behave as such. She would do fine.

"You can say you will be Sacagawea in a play," Bailey said, deadpan. "A novelty, a blue-eyed Indian."

Shelley gave him a puzzled look. "I don't have to explain a thing. I just want it."

Well, well, Frank thought, admiring how the little pink-and-gold fairy princess had put down both Barbara and Bailey without hesitation. He suppressed a smile and did not say a word for fear she would add him to her hit list for the morning.

When the others had left and Barbara stood up to return to her desk, her gaze fell upon the red poppy, but she felt as if she were looking through it to the map on the opposite side. "Later," she promised under her breath, as if speaking to the ghosts of those men who had struggled and died in the desert. "First the trial, and then your turn."

It always happened like this, she thought days later. Time stalled for weeks, and then each day blurred and melted into the next too fast to track. Always a surprise, even if expected, time did its trick as the trial date approached.

On Thanksgiving, Herbert invited everyone to Darren's for a feast. Shelley, Alex, Dr. Minnick, even Alan, who had someone lined up to take his place for the day. On the phone Herbert had said, "And don't nobody bring nothing. I got it all planned out."

Dr. Minnick, who had been mentor to Alex during his tempestuous adolescence and into adulthood, was greeted as an old friend by both Frank and Barbara. Carrie had met him only once, during the swimming party Shelley had given at the end of summer, and she was surprised by the warmth he extended to her. Alex had been lucky to have him, she had decided months earlier, and she thought again that evening.

Todd explained to everyone how he and Herbert had brought down the table from Carrie's apartment, and also dishes, because his dad didn't have enough. And Darren was mildly apologetic about the mismatched dinnerware.

"Don't pay it no nevermind," Herbert said. "It ain't what the food goes on that matters, it's what goes on the plates that counts. Dig in, folks."

He had made broiled mushroom cups stuffed with tiny pink shrimp for starters. Then he brought out a mammoth whole steelhead stuffed with crab and lobster, covered with paper-thin slices of lemon that he had glazed in the oven; a casserole of baked squash topped with pine nuts; asparagus in a wonderful sauce that he had invented. "You start with a really good white wine," he said, serving it, "and go on from there. A little this, a little that." Potato puffs were crisp and brown on the outside, and melt-in-the-mouth tender inside.

The talk revolved around food. The best meal he had eaten before today, Dr. Minnick said, was in Paris, but that meal had to move to second place from now on. Frank remembered a pie his mother used to make with squash. Shelley said her favorite after-school food had been a hamburger drowning under ketchup, mayonnaise and mustard. Everyone at the table groaned except Todd, who nodded.

Herbert beamed. "I always say when folks are eating and talking about other food it means they're liking what's on their plates," he said a bit smugly. "If they start talking politics, you better see to what went wrong in the kitchen."

When they could eat no more, Herbert started to clear the table. "Now you folks just set still and enjoy your wine and start digesting, and me and these here volunteers will take care of this, and then we'll have us some dessert." Todd and Carrie were already up, starting to carry plates to the kitchen.

Soon Carrie and Todd began to place dessert plates, saucers, even shallow bowls on the table. Darren groaned. "Next week, I'll buy some dishes," he said.

"You'll forget," Carrie said, smiling at him. "You won't give it another thought until the next time you want them."

Herbert brought in the dessert. "It's sort of a hybrid something or other," he said. "Not quite a torte, not quite a bombay, not quite a baked Alaska. I'll get around to naming it one of these days." It was a beautiful spiral of white ice cream or whipped cream on top of a very dark chocolate base. Sugar cubes followed the curves of the spiral from base to top.

"He melted ice cream and mixed it with whipped cream and froze it again," Todd said. "I watched him."

"Hush, boy. You don't give away the cook's secrets." Herbert picked up a tiny saucepan and felt it, then slowly dribbled hot liqueur along the sugar cubes. He held a match to it and it flared with a blue flame.

Carrie screamed and leaped up, knocking over her chair as she backed away from the table. She was the same color as the white cream. She ran from the room. Barbara was on her feet instantly and caught up with her at the back door before Carrie could open it. She pulled Carrie away from the door and held her.

"It's all right, Carrie. You're safe. It's all right."

Carrie was shaking convulsively in her arms, and then Dr. Minnick was at her side. "I'll see to her," he said. "You go on back to the table. We'll go into the living room for a minute or two. Come along, Carrie. Come with me." He put his arm about her shoulders and gently led her toward the living room.

Barbara followed them to the door and watched as they sat on the sofa, Dr. Minnick's arm still about Carrie. And she was whispering. "I'm sorry. I'm sorry. It's my fault. I'm sorry."

Dr. Minnick looked up and motioned Barbara away, and she returned to the dining room where everyone was standing up as if in a tableau.

"Lordy, I'm sorry," Herbert said. "Lordy, I wouldn't hurt that girl for anything, and look what I did."

"You couldn't have known," Frank said. "No one could have known."

He looked at Barbara. "Is she all right?"

"Dr. Minnick's taking care of her," Barbara said. "They'll come back in a minute or two."

"Well, let's have dessert," Frank said. He didn't look as if he wanted another bite of anything, and no one else seemed inclined to resume eating.

Barbara gazed at the hybrid dessert Herbert had created. The sugar cubes had turned a rich brown, caramelized. "Stairway to heaven," she said.

"That's what I'll call it from now on," Herbert said, sitting down. "Except I'll never make that danged thing again."

In the living room Carrie's shaking had subsided. Dr. Minnick was speaking in a low voice, and only gradually did his words start to register with her. "You're remembering terrible things, child, but they all happened long ago and they can't hurt you now."

"I can't remember," she whispered. "I try, but I can't remember. I'm sorry." She could feel tears burning her eyes, but they didn't fall. There was no relief from unshed tears, they just burned and burned.

"Carrie, I'm going to teach you a trick to keep you safe from memory's pain. Put your hands out, child, like a viewfinder in a camera shot. Both hands, Carrie, straight out before you. Like this." He withdrew his arm from her shoulders and held out his hands, his thumbs together, forming three sides of a rectangle. "You, too, Carrie. Just like this."

She put out her hands. They were shaking.

"Good, that's just right," he said. "When you have a memory that hurts, that's where you'll put it. Right out there where you can look at it, but it can't reach you." Very gently he took her hands and placed them in her lap. "And it's still going to be out there, where it can't reach you."

He continued to talk to her in a quiet voice and gradually her hands stopped shaking, and she even felt peaceful.

In the dining room Todd said, "The ice cream is melting." He looked at Darren, then at Herbert. "Are you going to cut it?"

Herbert shook himself and nodded. "You bet I am, and you get the first piece."

Everyone had been served, and Todd had his half eaten before Carrie and Dr. Minnick returned. She went to her chair and said, "I'm terribly embarrassed. I'm so sorry. It was the fire. I seem to have a fear of sudden fire. Please forgive me." She was still a little pale, but otherwise she looked completely normal. Dr. Minnick held her chair and she sat down. "Oh," she said, "it's melting. Have you named it yet?" She took a bite.

"Barbara named it," Herbert said. "Stairway to heaven. Reckon that's as good a name as you can hope for."

Dr. Minnick returned to his chair, sat down and took a bite, then closed his eyes and said, "Superb! Kahlua! The secret ingredient. That's exactly the right name. Herbert, you're a genius. This would win prizes."

Herbert's big grin spread across his face and they all began to eat and talk again.

In the foyer at Frank's house later, taking off her coat, Barbara said, "What if she breaks like that in court?" She was thinking of what Janey Lipscomb had said about abreaction. If Carrie began to relieve whatever nightmares haunted her, there was no way to predict the outcome.

That Frank's expression reflected her anxiety was not reassuring.

Carrie's table and chair had been restored to their proper places in her apartment, and she had finished putting away her dishes, then stood undecided. She was exhausted, but not sleepy enough to go to bed. She went to the living-room area and sat down, thinking of Dr. Minnick and his trick with the hands. She put them out before her the way he had instructed, then shook her head. She had tried every technique suggested in the article she had read long ago, and nothing had worked. She still had moments of memory of what should be an epic story of her forgotten childhood. Flashes with no beginning, no ending and most often no meaning. Not her life, she reminded herself, that of her alter ego, Carolyn. It wasn't fair to be able to remember snapshots, fragments of an imaginary girl's life, and not her own.

She knew that if the back door of Darren's house had not been closed and locked, she would have run out in a mad, mindless flight until she was caught and stopped, or until she had fallen. Run away from what? She had no answer.

She continued to sit quietly for a time, and then got up and prepared for bed. It was no use trying to call the memories up. They never came when called.

She was drifting toward sleep when she glimpsed the other little girl, Carolyn. She held perfectly still for fear of banishing the image, then, moving very slowly she put her hands out before her and formed the box to hold the memory.

Carolyn often went through Mommy's purse, examining everything in it. She loved the little gold pen, and the compact with a seashell back. She pretended she was writing a check for a million dollars so she could buy a dog. She opened the lipstick and looked at the color, never real red, and it smelled good the way Mommy's clothes smelled. She was careful to put everything back exactly how it was, and she thought Mommy knew she did this and it was all right. She liked to look in Daddy's pockets, too. Sometimes she found bubble gum, and he said, how did that get in there? A reverse thief puts things in my pockets when I'm not looking. Once there were three tiny dolls, a mommy doll, daddy doll and little girl doll, and Daddy said the reverse thief followed him all the way home and slipped them in when he got a chance. Today nothing was in his pockets and Carolyn went to his dark suit on a hanger to check there, but Mommy said don't touch those, darling. Those are Daddy's work clothes.

Carrie sat straight up as the images blurred, but the memory did not fade away when the images did; even after she took her hands down she could still remember the room, the clothes, the suit on a hanger. Turning on the light did not make them vanish. She snatched up a pen she had been keeping on her bedside table with a notebook, so far without a mark in it. She wrote down the scene, everything she could remember, how the little girl had been dressed—in pale-blue pants with pink flowers down one leg, barefooted, a blue ribbon tying her long hair back…

It was a start, she thought when finally she could think of nothing more to add and put the pen and notebook down. She realized that she had not actually seen the father or mother, they had been presences only, voices, like dream people who were never quite seen, but whose identity was never in doubt. That was all right, she told herself. She had something to build on. She felt that if she could fill in the life of that other little girl, the one she had imagined so clearly, she would also find clues to her own early life.

25

Ray Manfried didn't mind pulling the night shift, easy work, sit drinking coffee for six hours or more, good pay, and nothing to do. He missed the old days, however, when he'd smoke a pack of cigarettes while keeping an eye out. Since he had given up smoking, there wasn't a thing to do with his hands. And when the fog moved in the way it always did that time of year, there wasn't much point in keeping an eye out from across the street, unless someone came in with a foglight, and he didn't think a night prowler would oblige. He shifted in his chair, emptied his thermos and finished the last sandwich he had packed. He should have brought peanuts in the shell, he decided, just for something to do with his hands. Then he stiffened in his chair.

He was in the coffee shop across the street from Holloway's office, and Bailey's orders were to call if anything happened out of ordinary. A black van pulling in and stopping seemed to be exactly what Bailey had had in mind. He hit the speed dial on his cell phone and Bailey answered in a sleep-thickened voice.

"Something's going on," Ray said. "Black van, maybe two guys. They're going in the shop under Holloway's office, and they turned off the lights."

"I'm on my way," Bailey said, and he hit the number for Herbert's phone. It was three-thirty in the morning. Herbert answered just about as quickly as Bailey had done. "You're closer," Bailey said. "Barbara's office. Something's going on."

Ray pulled on his leather jacket and cap, waited five minutes, then eased out the door and waited a bit longer. He couldn't see a thing happening across the street, just the van, and still no lights had come on. He pulled his revolver from the holster and put it in his pocket, keeping his hand on it. There were dim lights glowing through the fog at the upstairs offices, Holloway's offices. Maybe they had already gone up, using the inside stairs. Street lamps eerily glowed through fog, not providing much real light. He took his chances and darted across the street, froze in a shadow. The men had come out, had opened the sliding door of the van and were removing something big that looked heavy. He waited until they entered the shop with the thing to edge in closer.

He heard a sound from the van, but before he could turn something crashed against his head, and he fell to the sidewalk. He was aware of being dragged but was too groggy to struggle. A siren sounded, someone stepped on his hand and he passed out completely.

Herbert pulled to a screeching stop in the parking lot in

time to see the van rounding the corner, and right behind Herbert a police car stopped.

"After that," Herbert told Bailey when he arrived, "things got a mite confused. They claimed I was speeding, and they were pointing guns at me and everything. I told them my buddy called to say there was a robbery going on, and I mentioned that they might want to have a look around and see if a watchman was laid out somewhere."

By then there were several more police cars, and even two plainclothes detectives along with a forensic team. Ray was sitting on the floor cursing steadily, holding a wad of wet paper towels against his head, his other hand in his lap, already swelling and turning color. An ambulance arrived, the attendants helped Ray up and into it, and left with forensic specialists going along.

"What the hell is that thing?" a detective asked, eyeing the machine the men had dropped.

"It's a tankless water heater," Herbert said. "You plug it in a regular outlet, and the wires on that circuit get red-hot and there goes the building. Looks like them guys wanted to see if it would work and forgot it when they left in a hurry like. I wouldn't touch if I was you. You know, fingerprints or such."

At four-thirty Bailey called Frank.

"What the devil happened over here tonight?" Frank growled at Bailey in Barbara's office. She had made a swift check to make certain no one had entered. Nothing appeared disturbed.

Bailey was grim and he was sore. His man had been attacked and injured, and the case had become a personal affair.

He kept his report short. "Ray saw the van stop out front and a couple of guys get out and enter the decorator shop below here. He called me, and I called Herbert. The van was black, unmarked, with a film over the windows. He didn't see the third guy. They were inside eight to ten minutes. They were taking something into the shop. That's when he got bashed. They dragged him inside, and dropped everything and took off when they heard a siren. Herbert got here in time to see them going around the corner, and the cops were right behind him. They let Herbert go, and I sent him back to the house."

"What were they up to? They didn't come up here evidently," Frank said.

"Setting the stage," Bailey said dourly. "Back door's steel, it won't open from outside. They opened it, went out and rigged the circuit breaker. A nylon string on a piece of dowel, fasten it to the circuit breaker, close the box with the dowel on the outside, and the thing can't trip until the nylon melts. The dowel drops to the ground, the breaker trips, and it looks like just another one of those accidental fires. They opened a window or two for a good draft, and turned off the water to this side of the building, disabling the sprinkler system. Seems they knew exactly where everything was, and they were fast workers. That waterless heater takes forty or fifty amps. The arson guys will check the wiring, but I bet they'll find this office is on the same circuit as the shop below. The building would have gone up when those wires got hot."

"Don't those things have to be hardwired in or something?" Frank asked after a moment.

"This one's been modified. It has a regular plug. They knew what they were doing. Let the fire start, pack up the heater and beat it while the building burns from the walls out."

"The fire station's just a few blocks away. No fire would have gotten out of hand before they arrived," Frank said.

"Smoke and water damage," Barbara said. She felt as cold as ice. "Nothing would have been salvageable after the fire department did its work." She looked at Bailey. "What did Ray tell the police?"

"He was on a stakeout over at Johnny's coffee shop to see who was sneaking in at night and taking stuff. Johnny will back him up."

"How bad is Ray?" she asked.

"He'll have a headache, and he's got a broken hand or fingers or something. The forensic guys went to the hospital to see if they can get an impression of the shoe that stomped him." He winced at the idea of manipulating that swollen hand. "It'll be a Nike or Reebok or something that every other person in Eugene wears."

"Did he get a look at them?"

"Nope. Just their backs. That's what he wanted to do, get close enough to have a look. Now we've got to talk about security."

Barbara stood up and went to the window. The dense fog was brighter than when she arrived, but it was still heavy. And the police were still doing something down there. The detective had said he wanted to ask them a few questions before he left. No doubt, they'd stop everyone coming to work. Do you have any enemies who'd want to burn down your building? Nope, not me.

Frank got up to make coffee.

"Those guys tonight weren't playing around," Bailey said. "And you've got one guy at your house. Alan's the best, but he's one guy, and if three of them come rolling in, he's still just one guy."

Frank stopped in the doorway. "What do you suggest?"

"It's time to pull Herbert out of Darren's place and let him hang out at your house. If that means Carrie, too, then let her have the upstairs bedroom."

Frank nodded and continued to the reception room to make coffee. Bailey was right, but he'd have a houseful with Herbert, a dog, Alan, Carrie, Barbara. Maybe it was time to turn things over to the Feds, let them deal with the Wenzels. Too much and too little; the thought followed swiftly. They knew too much and had too little.

At the window in her office, Barbara was also considering Bailey's suggestion, as unhappy with it as Frank was. She hated the idea of being crowded like that. She needed privacy, room to pace and think without interruption. And what would they tell Carrie? They wouldn't be able to pretend any longer. They would have to tell her they were all under guard, and she would know that Herbert had been her protector for weeks now.

Barbara had kept her informed about her plans for the defense, to establish that Joe Wenzel had been blackmailing his brother, and the family or some of the family had put an end to it. So far Carrie had not pressed for the reason Larry had yielded to blackmail, but if she now realized that she had been guarded so long, it was certain to raise the question of what that family's secrets had to do with her.

Barbara and the prosecutor, Jason Mahoney, had had two pretrial meetings with the judge, and both sides had stipulated to a lot, with the hope of expediting the trial. Everyone wanted it over and done with before Christmas. Just one week ago, she had turned over most of her witness list. Had the Wenzels been told they were on it? Had one of Greg's friends told him that Bailey was asking questions about Greg? Had they tried to destroy that damning tape? She was deep in thought when Frank returned with the coffee.

"I think Bailey's right," she said, taking her chair again. "And I want to have Nora and Greg served with the subpoenas today if possible. They've made their move, it's our turn now. As soon as that's done, I'll inform the D.A.'s office. They know by now the direction I'm heading in, more or less, but it might come as a shock to the Wenzels to be hit with subpoenas. Let's keep them off balance."

"And maybe next time all four of them will come in a black van," Bailey said.

"If so, let Herbert prove he's as good a shot as you claim," Barbara said.

The cleaning crew came and were sent away again. The detective came up and asked the expected questions, got the expected answers and left, but not before saying this incident was being called an attempted burglary, at which everyone nodded, with the clear understanding that the arson squad was at work.

Before Shelley and Maria arrived, it had been decided that Bailey would see to security for the building. Frank would take care of the subpoenas, and Barbara would talk to Carrie and see to it that she got moved into Frank's house.

"Okay," she said to Shelley after Frank and Bailey had left. "They tried to burn us out, so I'm moving my operations to Dad's house, and today I have to pack up everything relating to the case and haul it over there. I want to be out of here by three, dump the stuff and go talk to Carrie."

"I'll finish correlating material, get things organized in the folders," Shelley said. "What else can I do?"

"I think that's going to be plenty. Let's get at it."

They worked on the stacks of papers and photographs together, filling file folders, labeling them, adding them to thick binders as they went, and by three it was mostly done. Barbara rolled up the maps and folded the easel, put them in her closet and locked it, and they loaded her car.

"Hold the fort," Barbara told Maria. "Keep the door locked and be on deck in case we need something. We'll be in and out for the next few weeks."

Maria looked woebegone.

It was ten minutes after four when Barbara arrived at Darren's house and found Carrie and Todd with Herbert in the basement rec room.

"Howdy," Herbert said. "We're pret' near done. Don't it look good?"

"It looks great," Barbara said after a swift glance around. To Carrie she said, "Can we talk a few minutes?"

Carrie said sure and they went up the stairs. When she paused in the kitchen, Barbara said, "Your apartment. Okay?"

Then, when they were both seated in Carrie's living room she said, "Last night someone tried to set a fire in my office building, and I'm moving everything to Dad's house. Since the trial starts on Monday, we think it's a good idea for you to move over there, too. It will make things easier."

Carrie paled at her words, then asked, "Why burn down the building? Were you in it?"

"No. It was at three-thirty in the morning. No one was there. But if they had succeeded, my papers would have been destroyed, if not by fire, then by water and smoke. That would have meant petitioning the court for a new trial date, and starting over from scratch. Six months more, maybe even longer. Maybe they figured we'd run out of money, or out of patience, or something."

Carrie moistened her lips. "That doesn't explain why I should move." She regarded Barbara with a level look. "Is Herbert going, too?"

Barbara nodded. "Yes. And Morgan."

"And Alan will be there?" It wasn't really a question. "A philosophy graduate who's afraid I'll want to talk about philosophy. A guard dog, Herbert. I heard him leave just after three-thirty, and I heard him come back nearly an hour later. He went over there, didn't he? Why, Barbara? Are you going to tell me why? What this is all about?"

"I hope you've come to trust us during the past few months," Barbara said. "I need your trust now. I promise you that after the trial is over I'll tell you everything I know, but for now we have to concentrate on the trial. You, too. We all have to keep our focus on every word said in court, watch every expression, note every nuance. We all have to concentrate on that alone for the next few weeks. Every scrap of information I've gathered has to be guarded, and Alan can't do it by himself. I need Herbert, too."

"Why do I have to be guarded?"

"If the defendant vanishes, or has a fatal accident, or anything else happens to her, the trial is canceled. Guilt is assumed, and the problem ends for the guilty person."

Carrie didn't move for a time, then she stood up. "I'll pack my things."

"Do you want me to help?"

"No. There isn't much."

"I'll go down and tell Darren," Barbara said.

She knew Darren had not been in the house long when she

entered the kitchen and saw how red his cheeks and nose were from the cold. It was insane to ride a bicycle to work in December, but he did. "Can we talk?" she asked.

"Sure. Herbert's having a talk with Todd, you want to talk to me. What's up?"

"You asked if Carrie would be safer somewhere else, and I said no. Now I'd have to say yes. Someone tried to light an arson fire in my building last night, and I'm moving all the trial material to Dad's house to keep it safe. We need Herbert over there. And I'll take Carrie over with me."

He studied her for a moment. "We'll miss her. Is there anything I can do?"

She heard Todd laughing and looked past Darren as Todd and Herbert entered the kitchen.

"He says he's going to be an undercover agent for Mr. Holloway," Todd said. "He's going to infiltrate a bunch of college radicals."

"Hey, boy, don't you go making fun of me. Wait till you see me in my school duds."

Todd laughed again.

Darren was still watching her, Barbara realized, and his question was still hanging. "You could bring Todd over to visit and play chess with Carrie over the weekend," she said. "I know she'll miss her games with him."

Todd looked stricken and Darren said, "With the trial coming up next week, it's a good idea to have her over at Mr. Holloway's house. But we'll go visit."

In her bedroom Carrie finished emptying her closet. As she had said, there wasn't much. Shelley had taken her shopping for clothes to wear in court, and those things along with her old clothes took only a few minutes to pack. She had made a habit of never accumulating more than her old car could hold easily. Two boxes, two suitcases, that was plenty.

And the only thing of any real importance was the box that didn't take up any space at all. Since Dr. Minnick had shown her the trick with her hands, she had turned the rectangle into a memory box. She had started to tell Barbara about it, then held back. In the beginning Barbara had tried hard to make her remember, then she had stopped, and Carrie had come to realize that Barbara no longer wanted her to remember her childhood. She had to remind herself that the memories she was storing away were not really of her own life, but that of her alter ego, but that was all right, as long as she kept it firmly in mind that she was reconstructing a phantom girl's childhood.

So far she had not been able to recall anything about her father and mother, living in a truck, traveling a lot, the crash that killed her parents and orphaned her. But she felt that if she kept adding memories to her memory box, one day the rest would start to come also. She believed that the other little girl would lead her to herself.

Part Two

26

Although Judge Henry Laughton had been on the bench for three years, Barbara had not had a trial in his court before. Shelley, who had tried two cases before him, pronounced him strict and fair enough. But Barbara kept in mind the fact that the judge had been a prosecutor for eight years, then a defense lawyer for three. He had worked both sides of the courtroom, as he had informed both her and the prosecutor, Jason Mahoney, and he would not stand for any shenanigans from either side. Also, he had told them sternly, he wanted this trial over with before the holidays started. No more than she did, she had added under her breath.

There were few observers in court that day: the usual court groupies, a reporter busily writing something in a notebook, and the older Wenzel son, Luther. Families generally preferred to stay away when the grisly details and photographs of murder were being presented.

Neither side dallied over jury selection. She used peremptory challenges three times, and Mahoney four, and by the end of the second day he had given his opening statement. Nothing he said had been unexpected: orphan, foster care, homeless drifter who spotted a rich and vulnerable man in Las Vegas, preceded him to Eugene where she maneuvered herself into a position in his lounge, and several weeks later into his motel bedroom where she killed and robbed him. Barbara deferred her opening statement until the defense presented its case.

Jason Mahoney was one of the younger prosecuting attorneys, thirty-one years old, without a history of many trials. He was slightly built with ginger-colored hair and very pink cheeks. Probably he was as overworked as everyone else in the district attorney's office due to budget cuts and loss of staff. Barbara suspected that he had been assigned this case because at the outset it had appeared cut and dried, but she remembered a warning Frank had given her years before, that the young ones could be the most zealous. In their determination to prove themselves they often overprepared, and they were more likely to take chances. They hadn't been slapped on the wrists often enough by magistrates to teach them manners.

Mahoney's first witness was the motel maid, Rosa Jiminez, who was twenty-six years old, thin, nervous and apprehensive. Her testimony was short and to the point. She had gone to work at seven-thirty, prepared her cart, saw the Maid Service card on room number 1, knocked, then entered. She had seen the body on the floor, had run out of the room and to the office to tell Mrs. Hall-Walling, the assistant manager. Together they had returned to the room to look, then had gone back to the office, called the police and waited there.

The policeman who had come told her to wait in the office, she said, and she did until the detective said she could go ahead and clean the rooms. He made a policeman go with her to open the doors and look around.

Mahoney placed a schematic of the motel on an easel and pointed to it as he said, "So you went all the way to the end of the hall here, then back looking inside the rooms. Did you look inside this one, room 3?"

She nodded, then said yes.

"Had it been used the night before?"

"No."

Mahoney returned to his table and nodded to Barbara. "Your witness."

"Good morning, Ms. Jiminez," Barbara said. "I have only a few details I'd like to clear up. You said you knocked at the door before you entered the room. Do you always do that when there is a Maid Service card on the door?"

She shook her head. "No."

"Why did you that morning?"

"I thought he might still be in there."

"Can you explain why you thought that?"

"I mean, he never went out so early. Usually not until noon or one o'clock."

"Had he ever put the Maid Service card on his door before that morning?"

"No. He mostly left the other side, the Don't Disturb side out."

Barbara pointed to the schematic. "He had two doors to the hall, the bedroom and the living-room doors. Which one did he usually hang the card on?"

"The living-room door. The chain was always on the other one."

"Was the living-room door the one that had the Maid Service card that morning?"

"No. It was the bedroom door."

Barbara pointed to the schematic. "You said this room across the hall had not been used the night before. How could you tell?"

"The towels and washcloths were folded, the soap was still wrapped up. The bed wasn't used."

"Are there opaque drapes on the windows? I mean drapes that don't let light in in the morning?"

"Yes. They were closed like we keep them."

"Ms. Jiminez, if I walked into a clean room like that and sat down in a chair, turned on the television and a light, if I didn't touch the soap or a towel, would you be able to tell the next day that I had been there?"

Rosa looked around the courtroom as if desperate to get out of it. She shook her head. "Not if you didn't use anything in it."

"Thank you, Ms. Jiminez. No more questions."

Mahoney stood up. "Ms. Jiminez, in your statement to the investigating officers, and again in court this morning you said no one had used that room. Is that a true statement, that no one used that room?" His tone, not quite openly rude, was brusque and impatient.

He should have let well enough alone, Barbara thought as Rosa looked at her beseechingly, then sent her gaze darting around the courtroom again. Two of the jurors, a black woman and a Hispanic man, clearly recognized intimidation when they heard it. They looked uncomfortable.

"Just answer the question, Ms. Jiminez."

"Nobody slept in the bed," she whispered. "Or took a shower or anything."

Mahoney looked disgusted, shook his head and sat down. "No more questions."

And he, Barbara thought, clearly recognized the significance of that empty room to which Gregory Wenzel had a key.

The next two witnesses came and went swiftly. Two uniformed officers had taken a look around, then secured the suite and waited for the homicide team to arrive. The first detective on the scene did little more than that. When they learned who the deceased was, he said, Lt. Curry was assigned the case, and he waited for him to arrive.

William Curry was a short heavyset man in his forties who had been in homicide for twelve years. He gave his background training and experience in a monotone, as if bored. He had been through this before and knew the routine. He gave his testimony with a minimum of prompting.

He described how his team had fingerprinted the doorknobs, had taken photographs of the deceased, then left the immediate crime scene until after the medical examiner did his work and the crime scene investigators had collected evidence. The forensics team had started in the kitchen, then the living room, bathroom, and only later the bedroom, he said.

Mahoney produced photographs of the dead man. He was sprawled on the floor with his robe open, the blood appeared black. Lt. Curry identified the gun as the murder weapon, registered to Joseph Wenzel. Then, telling what the forensic team had found, he identified two glasses from a coffee table in the living room, and several fibers he said had come from the sofa, black fibers similar to the cotton in the defendant's skirt, and white fibers similar to the cotton blouse she wore. He identified a skirt and blouse he said they had removed from the defendant's closet.

They recovered six long black hairs, two caught on a button in the deceased man's coat, one from the bathroom floor and three from the sofa, all identical to the defendant's hair. Her fingerprints were on the taller of the two glasses.

After the medical examiner finished, he went on, they had moved into the bedroom where they recovered more black fibers on the bedspread. A wallet had been found with no cash in it.

"When you questioned the defendant at the police station, did you search her purse?" Mahoney asked. Curry said yes. "What did you find?"

"She had seven hundred dollars in an envelope, forty-two dollars in her wallet, and a receipt for two new tires that cost a total of one hundred fifty-five dollars."

When Mahoney finished with Lt. Curry, he gave Carrie a long pained look and shook his head.

Barbara rose but before she could start her cross-examination Judge Laughton said, "The court will have a ten-minute recess at this time." He reminded the jury that they were not to discuss the case and walked out.

And that was the prosecutor in him taking sides, Barbara thought. Give the jury time to let the implications of the testimony sink in. She glanced at Carrie, who looked shaken. "Do you want to use the rest room, get a drink of water or anything?"

"No. I don't blame them for arresting me," Carrie whispered.

It was sixteen minutes before the bailiff led the jurors back in and another minute or two before the judge returned. Lieutenant Curry took his place on the witness stand again, and they resumed.

"Lieutenant," Barbara said, "when you discovered that much cash in Ms. Frederick's purse, did you note the denominations of the bills?"

He consulted a notebook and said yes. They were mostly twenties, one fifty-dollar bill, and the rest in tens and fives, with a few ones, all old bills.

"Lt. Curry," Barbara said, "when you tried to recover fingerprints from the various doorknobs, what were the results? Let's start with the door from the bedroom to the parking area outside."

"Just smudges inside and out," he said.

"And the door from the living room to outside?"

"The deceased's fingerprints on the inside and outside knob."

"Did you test the outside frame around either door?"

"Yes. There were no fingerprints recovered."

"All right, now the interior doors to the hall. What were the results?"

"Just smudges inside on the bedroom door. The outside knob had the maid's, the assistant manager's and the uniformed officer's. The living-room door had smudges on the hall side and the deceased fingerprints and the maid's on the inside knob."

"How do you account for recoverable fingerprints from some surfaces and only smudges for others?"

"If you're holding a cloth in your hand, you'd smudge the fingerprints already there, or if you had on gloves."

He said the gun had no fingerprints and no smudges.

"Did you recover Ms. Frederick's fingerprints anywhere in the suite besides on the glass?"

"No."

"Were there other fingerprints on the glass?"

"The bartender's, overlaid with hers."

"Did you find traces of hand lotion on the glass?"

"No."

She nodded. "You stated that the fibers you found were similar to the material in Ms. Frederick's garments. Exactly what do you mean by similar to?"

"The fibers we recovered had sizing on them, from the manufacturer. Her garments had since been washed."

"Your Honor, I ask that the lieutenant's last answer be stricken as prejudicial."

"Objection," Mahoney said. "The lieutenant answered the question she asked."

"Overruled. Strike the answer. Rephrase your answer, Lieutenant."

And that was the defense attorney in him, recognizing a misleading answer when he heard it, Barbara thought.

"In both cases the fibers we recovered had manufacturer's sizing in them. The defendant's garments had been washed. Otherwise they were the same." Curry's face remained impassive, and his voice was still the monotone he had assumed at the start.

And he knew exactly what his first answer had implied, Barbara thought. "Did you learn where Ms. Frederick had purchased her garments?"

"They came from Wal-Mart."

"You said you removed various objects from the rooms," she said. "Is this the inventory of those objects?" She handed him the inventory. He studied it, then compared it to his notebook before he said it was. "You took a tape recorder, but there is no mention of tapes. Did you find tapes in the room?"

"No."

"Did you find a key to a safe-deposit box?"

"No."

"Did you find a receipt for a cash withdrawal from the bank, or a deposit slip?"

"No."

"Did you find a wrist brace?"

He said no again, in that same flat tone.

"The inventory mentions a carry-on with wheels. Did you find any other luggage?"

"No."

"Did you examine the contents of Joe Wenzel's wallet?"

"Yes."

"Did you find his driver's license?"

"I don't recall if we looked for it."

"So is your answer no? You didn't find it?"

"I have no memory of it one way or the other."

"What was in the glasses you examined?"

"Bourbon and water, a residue in both glasses."

"When you removed clothes from Ms. Frederick's apartment, did you examine her shoes?"

"Yes."

"Did you find any fibers that matched the fibers in Mr. Wenzel's suite?"

"No. Not on the shoes we found."

"How many pairs of shoes were there, Lieutenant?" She was keeping her own tone easy, almost conversational, and in comparison his answers sounded more and more brusque.

"Two."

"Can you recall what kind of shoes they were?"

"Boots and black low-heeled leather shoes."

Barbara picked up a glossy magazine from her table and showed it to him. "Do you recognize this journal, Lieutenant?"

He said yes.

"It's the *Forensic Sciences Journal*," Barbara said. "Does your department subscribe to it?"

"Yes."

She worked at it, question by question, until he admitted that he read the journal regularly, and that the editors and the writers for it were all well established and respected authorities in the field of forensics, and the information contained in it was regarded as the standard for forensic investigators.

"Please turn to page forty-one," she said. "Did you read that article?"

"I don't recall," he said. "I read most of them."

"That article concerns identifying hair, Lieutenant. Will you please read to the court the italicized summary at the bottom of the page."

He looked it over, then read: "In conclusion, it can be stated that without positive DNA evidence, no two hairs can be considered identical. The most that can be said is that they share similar characteristics." He handed the journal back to her without a change of expression, still stolid and stoic.

"Did you have a DNA test conducted on those hairs?" When he said no, she asked, "Did you have any chemical tests conducted on those hairs?"

"No."

"Will you tell the court the difference between hairs that are pulled out and those that fall naturally?"

"If they're pulled, they often have the root and sometimes the follicle attached. If they fall out, the root is often withered or nonexistent."

She retrieved the photograph of the hairs. It was a sharp photograph with each hair full length against a white background. She pointed to the first hair in the series. "Please tell the court what we are viewing here," she said to Curry.

"That hair has the follicle attached."

"So it was pulled out?"

"Yes."

"And this one?"

"It has a partial follicle attached. It was pulled."

"Can you tell the court where those two hairs were found?"

"Wound around the button on the deceased's coat."

"When you say wound around it, does that mean twisted all the way around it at least once or possibly more times?"

"They weren't wrapped all the way around it."

"Could they have been caught in it in passing, something of that sort?"

"I don't know how they got there."

"Where did you find the coat?"

"In the closet."

"All right. Now this next hair, number three in the picture. What are we seeing this time?"

"It looks like it was broken by chemical or heat action or cut."

"Is there any sign of either chemical or heat action on the hair shaft?" She sharpened her tone for the first time. He said no. She went on to the next hairs, and each time he had the same answer: it appeared to have been broken or cut.

When Barbara finished with her cross-examination, Mahoney was ready for his redirect. "Lt. Curry, are there times when you have DNA tests conducted on hairs to ascertain the identity of the suspect?"

"Yes. If there are several persons with similar hair, I would. In this case there was only one person with long black hair. I saw no need for such a test."

27

A steady cold rain was falling when the luncheon recess was called, and Bailey was illegally parked at the curb with his new and roomy SUV. He handed Frank a ticket as he got in. "It's going to be at least one a day," he said gloomily.

Frank put it in his pocket.

At the house, Herbert called out a cheerful, "Howdy," and Morgan met them with a big dog grin and a wag of his tail. Thing One and Thing Two looked at them, then walked away with their tails rigidly upright. Ever since the shaggy dog had moved in, they treated everyone with equal disdain. Barbara headed straight upstairs.

"Soup's on," Herbert said. "Cream of broccoli soup and hot roast beef sandwiches in the dining room." They would eat all their meals in the dining room until the trial ended. Alan and Herbert were taking turns sleeping on a roll-away bed in the dinette.

Barbara paced back and forth in the upstairs hall, now and then paused to make a note, then walked some more. She was hardly aware when Herbert brought a tray with a sandwich and coffee. When she paused to make a note, if she remembered she took a bite or two, but what she really needed was not food, but exercise.

Then, back in court, it seemed to Barbara that the recess had been merely an eye blink. The first witness of the afternoon was the medical examiner, Dr. William Tillich. She had tried cases before at which he testified, and she sometimes thought he was the only state's witness she trusted thoroughly.

Mahoney had him give in painstaking detail the circumstances of the death of Joe Wenzel, and the probable time of his death. Dr. Tillich talked about lividity, the pooling of blood after the heart stops, the extent of drying of the lost blood, rigor mortis if present, body temperature, stomach contents and the degree of digestion that had taken place, ambient room temperature, the general condition of the deceased before death and how that might have affected timing the event.

Mahoney interrupted him only once to ask him to please use the numerical system more familiar to Americans instead of the metric system. Dr. Tillich bowed his head slightly toward the jury, and continued. He concluded by saying, "The time of death in this instance was from three to five hours at the most from the end of his last meal. Closer to three than to five."

"So, since we know that he had dinner starting at eight o'clock, ending by nine or a few minutes later, death would have occurred between twelve and two in the morning. Is that correct?"

"That is correct."

"And the fact that he drank alcoholic beverages after nine o'clock would not contradict that finding?"

"I have taken that into account," Dr. Tillich said.

The way Mahoney hammered away at how the time of death could be ascertained with such certainty made Barbara suspect that he believed she would try to put the death at three or later, in order to implicate Greg Wenzel and the empty room across the hall.

When she started her cross-examination, she said, "Good afternoon, Dr. Tillich."

He wished her a good afternoon as well. He was always polite.

"Doctor, is the length of time between death and when you examine the body a factor in determining the time of death?"

"Yes. We have charts that indicate how long it takes to lose body heat at different temperatures. The weight of the deceased is a factor, as well as the room temperature. In this case the deceased was twenty pounds overweight, for a total body weight of 195 pounds, and the room temperature was 74 degrees. Knowing how long it takes to lose one degree of body heat in ambient surroundings at 74 degrees allows us to add that to our calculations. The more correlation we can achieve between the various factors, the closer we can come to the timing of the event."

"And after the body reached room temperature, the stomach contents would no longer be sufficient to be so certain about the time of death?"

"That is correct. Each person's metabolism is different. We know approximately how long it takes on average to digest so many grams of steak, for example, but not with precision for any individual."

"If you had examined the body late in the afternoon, say at two or three o'clock instead of eight-thirty in the morning, would you have given a different estimate as to the time of death?"

"I would have extended the period. I would have estimated the time of death from between twelve and possibly four."

She nodded. "When you performed the autopsy, did you observe the various organs for disease or injury?"

"Yes. As I stated before, he had been in good health apparently. His heart was somewhat enlarged, suggesting he might have had moderately high blood pressure, but all the other organs were sound."

"Thank you, Doctor. No more questions."

The next witness Mahoney called was Mark Ormsby. Barbara could sense Carrie drawing herself in, stiffening, when Ormsby took the stand after being sworn in. He glanced in the direction of the defense table, then swiftly away. If he had been nervous talking to Barbara in his own office, it was nothing compared what he was like when he started his testimony. He squirmed and fidgeted, and looked everywhere but at the prosecutor, the jury, the defense table.

He told how he had come to hire Carrie with hesitation, pauses, backtracking and much clearing of his throat.

"Mr. Ormsby, when you interviewed the defendant did you ask for references?"

"Well, uh, I usually do that, but I, uh, I don't think so. I mean she was, uh, from out of state and there's the question of when I could have, uh, checked on them. And I just wanted her to play the, you know, play on weekends, not wait on tables or anything."

"Did she tell you why she left her previous job?"

"Well, she might have said something like not, uh, that a customer. I didn't think it mattered since, uh, playing the piano…"

It was painful, and Mahoney was losing his patience and showing it as his questions became more brusque. "Just yes or no, please, Mr. Ormsby. Did you know why she left her previous job?"

"Uh, I think… Yes."

"What was the reason?"

This time he managed to make a coherent statement to the effect that a customer had tried to embrace her, and she had pushed him away and was fired.

"So you hired her in spite of knowing she had assaulted a customer. Is that right?"

"Well, we don't have customers like, I mean, no one would try, and she was just playing the piano. I mean she wouldn't be interacting. And with business… I mean, I thought it would be all right."

It was not easy, but Mahoney got him to admit that Carrie had complained about Joe Wenzel and that he had called Larry Wenzel about it.

"Did the defendant complain a second time?"

"No. No. I mean—"

"The answer is no," Mahoney snapped. He finished with Ormsby soon after that and, scowling fiercely, nodded to Barbara.

When she said good afternoon to Ormsby, he looked as if he suspected a trap. "Mr. Ormsby, when Ms. Frederick took her complaint to you, what did she say?"

She waited out his lengthy reply and then summarized it. "She said he was harassing her, standing too close, brushing against her as she played the piano, watching her like a hawk. Is that right?"

He admitted that it was.

"When you related her complaint to Mr. Larry Wenzel, what did you tell him?"

It was harder to make sense of his tortured answer this time, but she waited him out again. "You told him only that Mr. Joe Wenzel was pestering her, and that you were afraid she might quit. Is that right?"

Bit by bit she had him testify that all of the Wenzels had gone to hear Carrie play and that business had improved after she started. Then she asked, "Did you tell the front desk clerk to inform Ms. Frederick that you were too busy to see her during the weeks that followed her complaint?"

He looked guilty enough to have murdered Joe Wenzel himself as he squirmed in his chair. "I was busy," he said. "I mean, I had duties… And I had taken care of it as much as I could. I mean, they owned the motel and lounge and everything."

"All right," she said. "Is your answer yes, you told the clerk not to let Ms. Frederick in to see you after that?"

He said yes in a miserable voice.

"So you don't have any way of knowing if she would have made a second complaint. Is that correct?"

"But she didn't. I mean, I didn't talk to her again."

"We know Joe Wenzel used the suite, but who used the other room reserved for the Wenzel family?"

"Objection," Mahoney called out. "That's improper cross and she knows it."

"He brought it up when he asked if they had some rooms

reserved for their own use," Barbara said, facing the judge. He looked as impatient as Mahoney.

"I meant the suite," Mahoney said.

"And I interpret it as some rooms, meaning the suite and possible other rooms," she said swiftly.

"So do I," Judge Laughton snapped. "Overruled." He turned his frown toward Ormsby. "Answer the question, and please be brief about it."

But he wasn't brief. Eventually Barbara dragged out of him the fact that he knew Gregory Wenzel used the room on occasion, and that he didn't check in at the desk when he used it. He didn't know how many of the Wenzels had keys for it.

When Barbara finished with him she felt as wrung-out as he looked, and by the time he left the courtroom, there was an almost audible sigh of relief all around. Some of the jurors had begun to regard him with the same kind of look they might have turned on a never-before-seen specimen found under a rock. One or two jury members appeared bemused, as if wondering how Ormsby ever became a manager of anything. Barbara wondered the same thing and chalked it up to his having an MBA. Or maybe he was good at ordering around subordinates. She saw Luther Wenzel scribbling in a notebook and suspected that Ormsby might not continue as manager very much longer.

Kristi Kagan was forty-six years old and handsome, with auburn hair streaked with gray. She had worked at the Valley Bank, she testified, for nine years as a teller.

"Do you recall the evening of August ninth when Joseph Wenzel made a deposit at your window?" Mahoney asked.

"Yes, I do."

"Please tell the court about that transaction."

She looked directly at the jury as she said, "He came in late, about ten minutes after five, close to our closing time. At that time of day on a Friday we usually are quite busy, and that day there was a line of customers. He had a deposit slip made out for a deposit of five thousand dollars, and he requested a thousand dollars as a cash withdrawal. The check was a Wenzel Corporation check, signed by Nora Wenzel. I asked him the usual security questions, he answered readily and I completed the transaction."

"Did you also ask for photo ID?"

"Yes, I did."

"Why was it necessary to ask more than one security question and also see photo ID?"

She glanced at him when he asked his questions, but addressed the jury when she answered like a good little witness, Barbara thought, one who had been coached.

"I did not recognize him. I had never met Mr. Joseph Wenzel. The Wenzel Corporation has an account at our bank, but that day Mr. Wenzel looked more like a construction worker than one of the management. It is our routine if we have any doubt at all to ask for photo ID for a large cash withdrawal."

"And were you satisfied with the photo ID?"

"Yes. It was an old photo. His license was due to expire soon, and I assumed the picture to be nearly ten years old. But I was satisfied. Also, he was holding a safe-deposit-box key, and I assumed that was the reason for his coming to the main branch instead of one of our neighborhood branches where he usually did his banking. The neighborhood branches don't have safe-deposit boxes."

Mahoney nodded to her as if well satisfied. "Thank you, Ms. Kagan. No more questions."

Barbara stood up and walked around her table. "Ms. Kagan, when you said he looked like a construction worker, what exactly did you mean?"

"He was dirty and unshaved, with a stubble of beard. He was wearing a dirty T-shirt and dirty chino pants. His hair was dirty and he had a streak of dirt on his arm, as if he had just come off a job."

"Was there anything else of note about him that day?"

"Yes. He was wearing a wrist brace, the kind you use for carpal tunnel. It was hard for him to sign the receipt and endorse the check."

"Was his signature recognizable?"

"It was a scribble, but I never saw another signature to compare it to so I don't know."

"All right. Now, you said that you were satisfied with his photo ID, and you also said you noticed that it was probably ten years old, or nearly that old. Does that mean his appearance had changed over that period?"

"Yes. He was neat and shaved in the photograph, and not as heavy. But it was the same person, just older and dirtier."

"Did you really study his features that day in the bank?"

For the first time Kristi Kagan hesitated. "No. I could smell alcohol on him, and I didn't keep looking at him."

"Would you recognize him now if he appeared?"

"Yes. I'm sure I would."

Barbara turned to her table and found a photograph, showed it briefly to Mahoney, then to the judge, and handed it to Kristi Kagan. "Are you certain that's the man in the bank that day?"

Kristi studied it for a moment, then said, "Yes. That's the same man."

Barbara took the photograph back and handed it to the clerk to be entered as an exhibit. He passed it to the jurors, and she waited until it had made the rounds before she asked, "What were the security questions you asked Mr. Wenzel?"

Kristi hesitated again, her mouth tightened, and she glanced at Judge Laughton. "I'm not supposed to reveal confidential information," she said.

"Come now, Ms. Kagan," Barbara said. "No one is going to try to access the closed bank account of a dead man, I'm sure. I'm not asking for the answers, only the questions you asked."

"Objection," Mahoney said. "Irrelevant, and she's badgering the witness."

Barbara shrugged and the judge said, "Overruled. Ms. Kagan, just answer the question." He looked as if he wanted to go home and have a beer or two.

Kristi looked pained when she answered, "His mother's maiden name and his birth date."

"Thank you," Barbara said. "Did you at any point make a note of the denomination of the bills you issued to Mr. Wenzel?"

"Yes."

"What were they?"

"Five one-hundred-dollar bills, six fifties and ten twenties."

"Thank you, Ms. Kagan," Barbara said. "No more questions."

Mahoney had her cover some of the same ground again in his redirect. Before he could call his next witness, Judge Laughton beckoned both attorneys to come forward.

"Who's up next?" he asked Mahoney.

"The bartender on duty the night of the murder."

The judge looked at Barbara and said, "And I suppose you have a thousand questions to put to the guy."

"I have a few," she said.

"I bet you do. I'm going to adjourn until morning."

When they walked out, Bailey was there. Silently he handed Frank another ticket and they all got in the SUV. After he started to drive, Frank chuckled. When Bailey glanced at him, he said, "She pulled a fast one. She had the witness identify Larry Wenzel as Joe."

Bailey looked at Barbara in the rearview mirror. "The fishing camp picture?"

She nodded. "Yep."

"They let you do that?"

Frank said, "Oh, there will be hell to pay when it comes out, but meanwhile, that's the picture they saw and heard a sworn witness identify it as Joe Wenzel."

At the house Shelley got into her red Porsche and, with Bailey following close behind, headed for home. When Barbara, Frank and Carrie went inside, Herbert greeted them jovially. "It came," he said to Frank.

"Let's have a look," Frank said, and they followed Herbert into the living room where a spinet piano now stood.

Carrie caught in her breath. "Thank you," she whispered. "Thank you."

28

On Thursday morning Mickey Truelove was like a fresh breeze blowing through the courtroom. He gave Carrie a big open grin, looked over the jury with interest and gave the judge an appraising glance before turning to Mahoney with a friendly gaze.

After his preliminary questions, Mahoney asked, "Mr. Truelove, were you tending bar at the Cascadia lounge last summer during the time the defendant played the piano there?"

"Yes, sir."

"Did you always take her a drink in a glass like this one when she played?" Mahoney retrieved the exhibit and showed it to Mickey.

"Yes, sir. It was water."

"All right," Mahoney said. "Exactly what was your routine on the nights after she finished playing?"

"I waited a few minutes, then I put a clean fishbowl on the piano, picked up the one with the tips, and the glass if it was there, and took them both back to the office. She usually was done tying up her hair and washing her hands by then, and she always gave me a five-dollar tip and put the rest in an envelope in her purse and she left. I took the glass to the kitchen, then I went back to the bar."

"Do you recall the night of August ninth?"

"The night of the murder? Yes, sir."

"What did you do with the glass on that night?"

"I guess I took it to the office with the fishbowl of tips."

"Do you recall if you took it to the office that night?"

"Since that's what I usually did, I probably did that night, but I didn't make a note to remind me later." His sincerity was apparent, also his bewilderment at these questions.

Barbara knew exactly where Mahoney was heading. Carrie's fingerprints had overlain Mickey's. She had handled the glass after he did.

Using the schematic of the motel, Mahoney said, "There are two doors, one to the hall with doors to the kitchen and the dressing room and passage to the front desk. This other door goes out to the lobby. Which way did she leave?"

"Through the lobby door."

"Did you always watch her leave?"

Mickey shook his head. "Usually I did. Sometimes, when we got real busy, I didn't stay that long."

"Do you recall if you watched her the night of August ninth?"

"I probably did."

"Were you busy on Saturday nights through the summer?"

"After she started playing we were."

"Your witness," Mahoney said to Barbara and sat down.

"Good morning, Mr. Truelove," she said. He grinned and said good morning.

"Mr. Truelove, where did you put the glass of water when you took it to Ms. Frederick?"

"On a little table by the side of the piano bench."

"On her left hand as she was sitting there, or her right?"

He thought a moment, then said, "Left, so a customer wouldn't knock it over passing by."

"Did you take her more than one glass of water each night she played?"

"Yes, ma'am. After she took a break and came back I took her a clean glass and took the other one back to the bar."

"Did she have more than one break on the nights she played?"

"Yes, ma'am, usually two, sometimes three."

"And you took her a clean glass of water each time?"

"Yes, ma'am."

"Was it always there for you to take back to the bar?"

"No. Sometimes one of the waitresses got to it first."

"Was that table with the glass on it always in your sight?"

He shook his head. "No. I mean, if customers were at the bar, or just standing around I couldn't even see it."

"After she finished playing, you said she washed her hands and tied up her hair. How do you know she washed her hands?"

"When she came out of the dressing room, she sometimes was still rubbing lotion on her hands. She said the soap in there was hard on the skin. And I could smell the lotion."

"Did you always take plain water to her?"

He told about the customer who ordered a drink for her. "She said she couldn't drink hard liquor because it made her sick."

"Did she keep her hair down when she played?"

"Yes, ma'am. She tied it like it is now before she left."

"Did she ever count her tips in your presence?"

"No, ma'am."

"Were you able to see what kinds of bills were in the fishbowl?"

"Mostly fives and tens, some twenties, and sometimes a few singles. I think once there was a fifty."

"You said she put the tips in an envelope, then in her purse. Do you recall what kind of purse she carried?"

"A big shoulder bag, sort of a print."

"Did you ever see her take her water glass with her when she left?"

He shook his head. "It would have been pretty warm by then and, besides, there's water and paper cups back in the dressing room. If she was thirsty, she could have had a drink back there. I never saw her leave with a glass."

"You said you put the glass on the table to her left in order to keep it out of the way when customers passed by. Did customers brush against her in passing?"

"No, ma'am, not the usual customers."

"Do you mean others might have brushed her in passing?"

"Objection," Mahoney said. "He already answered."

"He qualified his answer. I want to clarify it," she said.

Judge Laughton said "Overruled" and gave Mahoney a sharp look as if in rebuke. "You may answer the question," he said to Mickey.

"Well, Mr. Wenzel seemed to make a point of getting too close to her sometimes," Mickey said.

"Were you aware that she had complained to Mr. Ormsby about Mr. Wenzel?"

"Yes, ma'am. I told her to."

"Did she complain to you about it?"

"No, ma'am. I could see what was happening and I brought it up, that if he was bothering her to tell Ormsby."

"Did his behavior change after her complaint?"

"Not that I could see."

"Did Mr. Wenzel wear a coat when he was in the lounge?"

"Objection," Mahoney said. "Irrelevant."

"It isn't," Barbara said. "The detective found hairs on the coat. I would like to know if the coat was a usual garment when he brushed by her."

"Overruled."

"When he first started hanging out in the lounge he wore a coat a few times, but no one else did and he stopped."

"Did you ever see him wearing a wrist brace?"

He shook his head. "No, ma'am."

Barbara thanked him and nodded to Mahoney. "No further questions."

Mahoney's next witness was Staci Adelman, who spelled her name very clearly to make certain the court stenographer got it right.

Her testimony was straightforward and simple. "We left the lounge a few minutes after she stopped playing. Outside on the sidewalk, I happened to glance toward the far end of the parking lot and I saw her and a man. I told Bernie, my friend, and he looked, too. I said I thought the man was harassing her. He seemed to be a little behind her, then he caught up and put his hand on her arm, and she pulled away and walked faster. We were talking about it, Bernie and I, whether he should go down that way and make sure everything was all right. They reached the end of the building, and we couldn't see them any longer. Then Bernie said I should get in the car and lock the door and he'd just walk down that way and make sure the man hadn't forced his way into her car or anything. Before I got inside the car, the man appeared again, coming back our way alone, and we left."

Mahoney had a question or two, but nothing to alter her statement. She couldn't see the man's face, only a white shirt and dark pants, and he appeared to be heavy and had gray hair.

Then Barbara stood up and asked, "Was Ms. Frederick carrying anything?"

"She had her right hand on her shoulder bag. I couldn't see her other hand."

"When she pulled away from the man, did you get a look at her other hand?"

"No. The man was on that side of her."

"Was her hair up in a ponytail?"

"Yes."

Her companion of the night corroborated her story without adding anything to it. Then Mahoney called Mrs. Lorine Purdom, and she appeared to be five or six months pregnant and tired, with dark hollows beneath her eyes.

"We left a little before twelve-thirty. I had told the babysitter we'd be back by twelve-thirty, and I was keeping an eye on the time. Our car was across the lot, and about halfway to it, I heard a woman laugh and turned to look, and I saw Ms. Frederick standing by the door of the motel. She seemed to be talking to someone inside. Terry, my husband, turned to look, and we both paused a minute, then she pushed the door open wider and went inside and closed the door."

Mahoney walked closer to the jury box as if to draw Lorine's attention to them, perhaps to address them as she answered his questions. "Could you see the person she was talking to?"

"No. The door was open a few inches only."

"Was there a light in the room?"

"It was dim, as if a light was coming from the back of it or even from a different room, not that one."

"Did you hear anything besides the laughter you mentioned?"

"No. It wasn't like laughing at a joke. It was more like you might say 'Ha, ha.' Like you didn't believe what you just heard or something."

Mahoney looked at the jury, looked at Carrie, shook his head, then nodded to Barbara. "Your witness."

She smiled at Lorine Purdom. "I'll try not to keep you long, Mrs. Purdom," she said. "When you noticed the time were you still inside the lounge?"

"Yes. Terry was looking over the tab and getting money out to pay it. We left a minute later, probably."

"So it was a minute or two later than twelve-twenty-five when you actually were in the parking lot. Is that right?"

"Yes."

"Were many people leaving at that time?"

"A few. Some people were in the lobby talking, and we were behind another couple going out. They turned toward the front of the building, and we started across the lot."

"Was there much noise at that time of night?"

"There was some. I mean, there was traffic on Gateway."

"At which door did you see that person?" She pointed to the motel schematic. "Do you recall?"

"Yes. It was the first door."

"Was there a car parked in front of that door?"

"No. There was a black car in the next parking space, but not in the first one."

"When you first walked out, did you happen to glance that way, toward the rear of the building?"

"No. As I said, another couple was leaving ahead of us, and I watched them turn to the right."

"Was there any reason for you to pay particular attention to them?"

"Not really." She smiled slightly, then said almost apologetically, "The woman had on a very tight short skirt and spike heels. I thought it might be interesting to see how she managed to get in a car."

Someone in the sparse audience tittered and turned it into a cough, and several of the jurors smiled. Barbara smiled also and nodded. Then, pointing again to the schematic, she said, "And you were parked over here? Tell me when to stop."

She moved her hand along the row of parking spaces until Lorine said, "That's about where."

"That would be about fifty feet from that door, wouldn't it? And you were halfway there when you heard the laugh?" She moved her finger until Lorine said that was about it. "So you had a clear sight line to the door. No car blocking your vision, and you were twenty-five or thirty feet from it. Is that about right?"

"I think that's about how far."

"Were the drapes closed over the window near the first door?"

"Yes."

"So there was only the dim light from inside the room and the outside lighting along the walkway. Is that correct?"

She said yes, then added that the outside lighting was good.

"When you looked at the person at the door, could you see either hand?"

"One of them. I thought she might be holding the doorknob with one hand that was out of sight, and the other one, the one I could see, was on the door frame about shoulder high."

"Was that person wearing gloves?"

"I didn't see any gloves."

"Was her hair down, or up in a ponytail?"

"It was loose, down her back."

"Did you see a shoulder bag?"

"No."

"Did she turn so that you could see her face?"

"No."

Lorine had been watching Barbara and only incidentally the courtroom behind her. Something attracted her attention, and she appeared to focus on the back of the courtroom. Her eyes widened and she drew in a breath. Barbara turned to look. A figure with long black hair, wearing a black skirt and white blouse, stood at the door of the courtroom in the kind of pose that Lorine had just described.

"Does that look like the person you saw?" Barbara asked.

Lorine nodded and said yes at the same time that Mahoney yelled, "Objection!"

"Sustained. Counselors, come up here," Judge Laughton snapped.

The person at the door turned and pulled off the wig to reveal a young man of seventeen or eighteen. He grinned and slipped from the courtroom.

Judge Laughton's face was red with fury, his lips tight, when Barbara and Mahoney stood before him. He turned off his microphone and leaned forward. "Ms. Holloway, I warned you at the start that I won't tolerate any of your stunts. When I instruct the jury, I'll tell them they can't consider that charade. And if you cross that line again, I'll hold you in contempt of court. That little melodrama will cost you a hundred dollars. Do I make myself perfectly clear?"

"Yes, Your Honor."

He motioned them away angrily, and as Barbara turned she caught a glimpse of Frank. She could tell from his posture and the fixed expression on his face that he was laughing on the inside. She kept her own expression grave when she addressed the witness once more.

"Mrs. Purdom, will you describe the person you saw at the motel door?"

Lorine moistened her lips. She glanced at Carrie, away. "I saw the back of someone with long black hair, a white blouse and a black skirt."

"Can you positively identify that person?"

"No."

"No more questions," Barbara said and took her seat.

Mahoney hammered at Lorine but she stuck to her description: a person with long black hair, wearing a white blouse and a black skirt. She refused to say it had been Carrie at the door.

Terry Purdom was thirty-four, his hair was in a ponytail, and he had a small gold stud in one ear. He gave his occupation as a sound engineer. He seemed to weigh each question with deliberation before he answered.

After a few preliminary questions, he said in answer, "I heard her laugh, but I didn't look until my wife touched my arm and indicated that I should. I saw someone standing at the door, which was open a few inches, remain there for a minute, then enter and close the door."

"Who did you see at the door and then enter the room?" Mahoney asked brusquely.

"I don't know. I didn't see a face."

"In your original statement you said you saw the defendant at that door. Is that correct?"

"It is, but I was hasty and jumped to conclusions."

"Describe the woman you saw, if you will."

Barbara objected. "It has not been established that that person was a woman," she said.

The judge sustained the objection and Mahoney rephrased the question with heavy sarcasm. "Just describe the *person* you saw that night."

"I saw the back of someone with long black hair in a white blouse and a black skirt."

Mahoney frowned and leaned against his table as if preparing for a long ordeal. "Did you watch the defendant play the piano for over an hour in the lounge?" Purdom said he did. "Did you see her leave, walk away from the piano and go behind the bar and through a door?"

"Yes. I watched her leave."

"Will you describe how she looked walking away?"

"She was wearing a white blouse and a black skirt, and her hair was loose on her back."

"Is that the description of the *person* you saw at the motel door?"

"Yes."

"Would any reasonable person conclude that the *person* at the door was the same as the woman who played the piano?"

"I don't know," Purdom said. "I don't know what a reasonable person might conclude."

Mahoney kept at it, but Terry Purdom obviously had drawn a line that he was determined not to cross. He refused to identify the figure at the door as Carrie.

When Barbara stood up for her cross-examination, she asked, "Did you see the hands of the person at the motel door?"

"Not the left hand. The right hand was on the door frame."

"Did you see any gloves on that person?"

"No. I didn't notice any, but if there had been a flesh-colored glove, or a surgical glove, something of that sort, I wouldn't have been able to see it from that distance."

Barbara could have kissed him for his answer. Instead, she thanked him and said no more questions.

The judge called for the luncheon recess then, and when Barbara and her team went out, Bailey was there with his ticket and a sour expression. "I've been warned," he said. "I'm not supposed to stop there again."

Frank nodded. "We'll go through the tunnel. Meet us in the lot across the street from now on."

In the back seat Carrie huddled, drawing her jacket close. "Did you see the jury, the way they were looking at me? They think I went in the room. They think you're just playing tricks and that was me going in that room. I swear I never went in there, Barbara."

"I know you didn't," Barbara said. But she had seen the expressions on the faces of some of the jurors, and Carrie's assessment was accurate.

29

At one of the pretrial motion hearings Mahoney had argued successfully that the Wenzel Corporation had nothing to do with Joe Wenzel's private life, and that the defense must not be permitted to besmirch the reputation of one of the city's leading businessmen. No mention was to be allowed of whatever irregular arrangement had been reached with Joe Wenzel about his employment with the company, and since all the Wenzels had ironclad alibis for the night of the murder, they were not to be implicated by any suggestion or innuendo of any complicity in that murder.

Afterward, Barbara had said furiously, "But you better believe if he opens a forbidden door even a crack, I'll be in there like gangbusters."

That afternoon when Mahoney called Larry Wenzel to the stand, she was on full alert for a door left open a crack. Larry

Wenzel was as impeccably groomed as before, with a fine gray suit, tie, freshly shaved and coiffed. Nora and both sons were in the courtroom, and they all could have posed for a clothing ad for a glossy magazine. Luther, the older son, had inherited Nora's fair complexion and blond hair. Gregory looked very much like the photograph Barbara had seen of Larry and Joe when they were about his age, ruggedly handsome, with thick dark hair and a muscular build.

Mahoney led Larry Wenzel through a few opening statements: the company had been in Eugene since 1975; the Cascadia Motel restaurant and lounge were company property; Joe Wenzel had lived in the motel after a fire destroyed his house.

"Do you recall an occasion when the motel manager, Mr. Ormsby, spoke to you about your brother's behavior regarding the defendant?"

"Yes."

"And did you do anything about that?"

"I talked it over with my wife, and we agreed that Joe's personal life was none of our business, but I was curious about the lounge and restaurant receipts, which Mr. Ormsby said had improved considerably since she started playing the piano. We, my wife and I, visited the lounge to look over the books and saw that there was a vast improvement. Joe had a remarkable sense of business, and I knew appealing to the businessman in him would be effective. I suggested that he confine his attention to the piano player during her off-hours, not distract her when she was working."

"Did you hear of any more complaints following that talk?"

"No. I assumed he was following my advice. I never gave it another thought."

"Now, on Friday, August ninth, Mr. Joe Wenzel deposited

a check from the Wenzel Corporation for five thousand dollars, and withdrew one thousand in cash. Did you speak to your brother about that check?"

"Yes. He called on Thursday and said he needed an advance against his next paycheck. Since his checks were on an automatic electronic deposit schedule, it would have been a little hassle to do it that way, and I suggested that he could simply pick up a check. I asked him to meet Nora, my wife, at an auto repair shop and drive her home to meet me after she left her car there, because I wanted his advice about some property I was considering for possible development. I told him that if I was delayed Nora could sign the check, but I hoped to see him that late afternoon. I had a business trip scheduled, and had to leave on Saturday morning and didn't expect to return home until Wednesday of the following week. I wanted to talk to him before I left if possible. As it happened, I was delayed, and my wife signed the check and he was gone when I arrived home."

"Why didn't you have him drop by your office to pick up the check?"

"Nora was going to be tied up in meetings, and I was out on Friday. I had three properties to inspect, and it took all day to cover them."

"All right. Did your brother say why he needed the check?"

"Yes."

"What was his stated reason?"

"He reminded me of our talk about the piano player and said there wouldn't be any more complaints, that he was taking my advice and dealing with her in her off-hours. I'm afraid he used rather crude language." He turned an apologetic grimace toward the jury. "He said he planned to buy himself a piece of her ass that weekend, and there was nothing like cash to thaw a…" He shrugged. "Anyway, he had been drinking and his language tended to become vulgar at those times. I was a bit disgusted and cut the conversation short."

"Mr. Wenzel, did your brother specifically mention the defendant? Did he use her name?"

"Yes. He used her name, and he also referred to her with various street obscenities."

"When your brother was drinking, did he become physically abusive?"

"Sometimes, especially with women."

"Did he drink to excess?"

Wenzel shifted in his chair, then said in a low voice, "I'm afraid he was an alcoholic. He was cursed with an illness he couldn't control. Since our father died of alcoholism, I was concerned about it."

"Did you maintain a good relationship with him?"

"Yes. I didn't approve of his lifestyle, but he was the most astute businessman I've ever known and I had great respect for his advice. And he was my only living relative outside of my immediate family. I promised our mother years ago that I would always look after him and I did, always with the hope that he would seek help for his problems."

"Had he been married?"

"Yes. Three times."

"How long have you been married, Mr. Wenzel?"

He looked past Mahoney and smiled slightly at Nora. "Forty good years," he said.

"Thank you, Mr. Wenzel. Your witness," Mahoney said to Barbara.

Larry met her gaze with the same frank, open expression

he had shown to Mahoney, that of a man who wanted nothing more than to be helpful in a difficult situation.

"Mr. Wenzel," she began, "when your brother's house burned, did he lose all his possessions in the fire?"

"I believe he did, except for the few things he had taken along on a trip."

"He was out of town when the fire occurred?"

"Yes."

"Did he collect insurance on the house?"

"Objection," Mahoney said. "Irrelevant."

"I don't think it is," Barbara said. "A few weeks later he said he needed five thousand dollars. It's pertinent to learn how low in cash he might have been."

"Overruled," Judge Laughton said after a moment.

"The house was company property," Wenzel said. "The corporation collected insurance."

"I see. Did he have a lease arrangement, a rent arrangement, something of that sort?"

Mahoney objected again and this time was sustained.

"Whose idea was it to have him move into the motel after he returned home?"

"We discussed it, and he decided that would be best."

"Do you recall when the fire occurred?"

"I believe it was on July seventh."

"When did your brother return home?"

"The next day. I called him and he flew home the same day."

"Did you meet him at the airport?"

Mahoney objected. "Your Honor, this is irrelevant."

"It isn't," Barbara said. "I'm trying to learn how Mr. Wenzel's handgun escaped damage or destruction in a house fire that destroyed all of his possessions."

"Overruled," the judge said, but he sounded impatient, and he was frowning at Barbara as if in warning.

"Would you like for me to repeat the question?" she asked Wenzel then.

"No. I did not meet him. He had left his own car at the airport lot and he drove himself to the motel."

"He went straight there from the airport?"

"Yes."

"When did you discuss his living arrangements with him after the fire?"

"We talked on the phone about it when I called him," he said. "Later, I met him at the house site and we talked further."

"At that time did you discuss building a new house for his use?"

He hesitated a moment, then said yes.

"Did you know that he owned a handgun?"

"I knew he had owned one years ago. I wasn't aware that he still had it."

"Mr. Ormsby testified that he told you about Ms. Frederick's complaint on Tuesday, July 23, the day after she spoke with him. Is that your recollection?"

He shrugged. "I don't recall the date."

"How long after he notified you of possible trouble was it that you visited the lounge and inspected the books?"

"The following weekend," he said. "I believe it was on a Saturday night."

"That would have been on the twenty-seventh," she said. She went to her table and picked up a large calendar, placed it on an easel and moved it to where it would be visible to the jury. It already had a note by July 23, the day Ormsby had talked to Larry about Carrie's complaint. She made another note to indicate that Larry and Nora had visited the lounge on Saturday, July 27. "And how long after that was it when you spoke with your brother?"

"Not long. A day or two. I don't remember exactly."

"Isn't it true that you and Mrs. Wenzel flew to San Francisco on Sunday, July 28, for a week-long vacation?"

He narrowed his eyes slightly, and a new tightness appeared around his mouth, probably unnoticeable to anyone not looking for a reaction, she thought, watching him steadily.

When he hesitated, Mahoney called, "Objection. Improper cross. Irrelevant."

"No, it isn't," she said. "I'm trying to fix a chronology of when various events occurred that Mr. Wenzel referred to in his testimony."

The judge overruled, and Barbara repeated the question.

"I think that's about right," Wenzel said. "I just don't recall those dates offhand."

She added that note to the calendar. "So it was more than a day or two from the time Mr. Ormsby spoke to you that you spoke to your brother. Is that correct?"

"If you say so after consulting a calendar. I don't remember exactly."

"If you returned home on August third, a Saturday night, that would be eleven days," she said. "Did you speak with him on Sunday?"

"I may have done so," he said.

"Before or after you played golf?" she asked, keeping her gaze fixed on him.

"Not on Sunday," he said. "I think it was Monday, a working day. I met him at the house site."

"You spoke with him in person, not on the telephone?"

"Yes."

"That would have been on August fifth," she said, adding that to the calendar. "Almost two weeks from the time you learned about the complaint. Were you not concerned about the matter?"

"Not particularly," he said after a moment. "I was more interested in the increase in business than his private affairs. But I didn't put a high priority on it."

"All right. Did you leave work to go meet him at the house site?"

"Objection. Counsel is beating this into the ground, Your Honor. And to no purpose."

"I agree. Sustained. Please move on, Ms. Holloway."

She nodded. "Did you see Mr. Vincent at the house site that day?"

Wenzel hesitated, then shook his head. "No."

"You stated that your brother was planning to rebuild on the site. Would the new house have been company property the same as the one that burned?"

"Objection! This is all extraneous and has nothing to do with the trial we are hearing."

The judge sustained it, and then said, "At this time the court will have a ten-minute recess."

After the judge walked out and the bailiff was leading the jurors from the courtroom Barbara murmured to Frank, "I always suspect he wants a little nip of something to sustain life."

Frank grinned and nodded. And Carrie said, "Wenzel has the eyes of a snake, just like his brother. He's scary."

"Come now, he's a leading businessman," Barbara said. "Let's have a cup of coffee. We won't get back to it until about four, I'm afraid."

Shelley stood up, but Frank was already on his feet. "I want to stretch my legs," he said. "I'll bring coffee back."

Barbara was watching Wenzel and Mahoney having a conference at the prosecutor's table. She suspected, or perhaps simply hoped, that Wenzel was giving orders and Mahoney was explaining why he couldn't follow them.

When Frank returned, he said, "The press is out there waiting. They want to talk to the Wenzels, I suppose. I told Bailey to forget using the lot across the street. He can circle the block until we appear. I don't want us to wade through reporters, photographers and a video crew on the way out."

When court was in session once more, Mahoney stood up and asked permission to approach the bench. Judge Laughton motioned them both forward. "What now?" he snapped. Barbara caught a whiff of mint.

"Counsel for the defense is dragging this out through malice or spite or something to no purpose, Your Honor," Mahoney said indignantly. "Mr. Wenzel has an important meeting in the morning, and he doesn't want to be held here unnecessarily."

The judge looked at Barbara. She shrugged and said, "I'm doing the best I can. Of course, I can always try harder."

She thought she recognized a glint in the judge's eye that suggested that he knew exactly what she meant. He sighed, then said, "Do try harder to be brief."

"Mr. Wenzel," she said, when all the players were once again in place, "we've established that you finally spoke to your brother about Ms. Frederick's complaint on or about Monday, August fifth. Did you speak with him again that week before Thursday?"

"No."

"Did he call you on Thursday at work?"

"No. I was home when he called."

"Is that when he said he needed the five thousand dollars right away?"

"Yes."

"All right. Were you surprised that you had seen him only a few days before that and he had not mentioned it then?"

"Not really. He was unpredictable."

"On what days does your company make the electronic transfers of salaries?"

"The first working day of each month."

"That would have been on Thursday, August first. Is that correct?"

"If that was the first working day of the month, that's correct."

"Oh, I have the calendar here. We can refer to it—"

"Objection," Mahoney said a bit stridently. "We stipulate that it was the first working day."

"Thank you," Barbara said to him, smiling. She turned back to Wenzel. "So on the first of the month your brother received his regular monthly paycheck electronically. I assume he was well paid by the corporation for his invaluable advice."

Not a tinge of sarcasm colored her words, but Wenzel's mouth became tighter. "He was well paid," he said. His reasonable, measured tone was starting to become a bit frayed, the words more clipped.

"Yes. In fact, I have here his bank statement at the time of his death." She turned to Shelley, who had the sheet ready to hand her. She showed it to Mahoney, who looked it over with a frown, then to the judge, who barely glanced at it, and finally she handed it to Wenzel. "That statement shows that your brother's account had a fifteen-thousand-dollar deposit made electronically on the first of the month, that his balance was twenty-eight thousand dollars in checking, twenty-two thousand in savings, plus some CDs, and a money market account."

Wenzel took reading glasses from his pocket and put them on, then took a long time studying the statement. When he put it down, she said, "With that much money in the bank, accessible to him, can you account for his saying that he needed five thousand dollars right away?"

"I can't," Wenzel said. "As I stated earlier, I was disgusted and cut the conversation short. I didn't want to talk to him when he had been drinking."

"I see," she said. "What time did you arrange for him to meet your wife on Friday at the auto shop?"

"I told him she would leave work to take the car over at four, and it would take her a few minutes there. He said he would pick her up at about twenty minutes after four."

"It's about a twenty-minute drive from the shop to your house, isn't it? Possibly a little longer at the time of day on a Friday."

"I don't know," he said. "I don't time my trips to the minute."

"If he picked her up at four-twenty, and took twenty minutes at a minimum to arrive at your house, that would put him there at about twenty minutes before five. He was at the bank at ten minutes past five and the trip back to town to the bank would have been a bit longer than going to your house, probably twenty-five to thirty minutes. I would like to set up a map to confirm the distances and possible time involved," she said, glancing at the judge. He looked murderous. And Mahoney was livid.

"Objection! This is all irrelevant to the trial at hand!"

The judge beckoned them both to the bench. "What's your point?" he demanded of Barbara.

"Your Honor, there was not enough time allowed for a discussion between the brothers considering those times and distances to travel back and forth. Possibly Mr. Wenzel misspoke when he said he wanted to ask Joe Wenzel for advice."

"He said he was delayed. He meant to be there earlier," Mahoney said sharply.

"Would you like to take the stand and testify for him?" Barbara asked.

"Knock it off, both of you," Judge Laughton said. "Ms. Holloway, I'm warning you, don't continue to drag this out indefinitely." He motioned them away, then said, "Overruled."

Moving leisurely, Barbara placed the map on her easel and, referring to it, made the same points. Then she said, "So he couldn't have been at your house for more than five minutes. You stated that you knew he wanted to get to the bank to cash the check and might have assumed that he would want to start back to town before five. Had you left enough time for the discussion you said you wanted with him, the advice you were seeking?"

"I thought I'd be there earlier, and it would have taken only a few minutes. We had already talked the matter over."

"Why didn't you ask his advice on Monday when you met with him and had more time?"

"I didn't think of it then." He had started to snap off his answers, not quite rudely, but close.

"Where were you when you realized you would be delayed?"

"I don't know exactly."

"But at some point you must have realized it. Do you have a cell phone?"

"Yes."

"Does Mrs. Wenzel?"

"Yes."

"Why didn't you call her to say you would be late?"

"I didn't think of it."

"Did it occur to either of you that she could have handed your brother the check at the auto shop and have their courtesy car drive her home?"

"No."

A dark hue had come over his face, set in hard, furious lines. With his eyes narrowed as they were, he looked like the melodrama villain getting ready to drive the young widow and her infant out into the snowstorm. And that was exactly the face Barbara had been waiting for him to show the jury. She turned back to her table and lifted a paper. It was five minutes before five, and the judge's gavel tapping on the bench was not unexpected. It was time to adjourn for the day.

They were met with flashbulbs, a videographer or two and several reporters. "Why are you going after Wenzel? He was in Bellingham, wasn't he?"

"Move Carrie on out, Dad," she said in a low voice. "I'll catch up." She smiled for the cameramen. "There are a lot of questions to be asked and answered. Since my client, Carrie Frederick, is innocent, I intend to ask them all."

"Why him?"

"Will he be on the stand again tomorrow?"

"Is Carrie Frederick going to take the stand?"

She laughed and kept walking. "Too many, too fast. Carrie will take the stand in due time. Mr. Wenzel will be back tomorrow. I have more questions to ask him."

"Here they come," someone said. The videographer swung his camera around to catch the Wenzels as they walked out of the courtroom.

30

On the way home that evening Frank said, "She stirred the viper's nest with a stick today. And they're mad. Bailey, maybe from now on you should pick up Shelley and bring her to town, then drop her off on your way home."

Bailey nodded. "Easier that way than trying to follow in fog like this." It was already thick and would become thicker by the minute, the way it always happened this time of year. "No ticket today," he said then. "But the cop was keeping an eye out for me. Hated to disappoint him."

"Let's keep doing it that way," Frank said. He was uneasy, more so than usual, he realized. He had seen the look on Larry Wenzel's face and also on Nora's. Vipers, he thought again.

Herbert met them with his big Texas smile, his big Texas "Howdy!" and his big Texas belly, Frank thought when they entered the house. Morgan grinned his dog grin and wagged his tail in greeting. The house smelled spicy and fragrant with cloves and cinnamon, lamb and a lot of onions. Herbert motioned to Frank.

"Want to show you what I've been up to," he said genially. "Wine's on the dining-room table," he said to Barbara, and walked ahead of Frank to the kitchen.

Barbara grinned at Carrie. "Want a glass of wine?"

"No, thanks. I just want to stretch out for a few minutes. I don't know how you do what you do and stay on your feet. I'm wiped out."

"I'd be too if I had to sit still all day," Barbara said, going to the dining room.

In the kitchen, Herbert motioned Frank and went out the back door. "See, this package came today for Barbara, and Morgan here, he said, don't even touch it, partner. So I tossed it in your barrel. Sorry, Mr. Holloway. I'm afraid I ruined your rain barrel."

The barrel was in splinters, the remnants of a package strewn about, charred and twisted. Frank felt a rush of ice water surge through him and was grateful for Herbert's hand on his arm. "Christ on a mountain," he whispered. "Did you call the police?"

"Nope. It came about fifteen minutes ago. I figured I'd wait for y'all to get back and let you decide what to do about it."

"How in God's name did you detonate it?"

"Not hard. Morgan sniffed it out and told me explosives were wrapped up nice and neat, and I looked for a string, or a funny little bit of tape, or something like that, and found it. Just added my own nice long bit of string and tossed it in and ran like a jackrabbit."

"You could have been blown apart, you damn fool."

"Wasn't though." His grip tightened on Frank's arm. "Y'all

get the meanest fog I ever saw. Wants to dig in right to the bone." He turned Frank and they went back inside.

Barbara entered the kitchen just as they were coming in. "Hey, you two, what's— Dad! What happened?" She rushed to him.

"He'll tell you," Frank said, taking her glass of wine from her hand, then sitting down in the nearest chair. He watched Barbara and Herbert go back outside, and drank her wine. Gradually the ice that had claimed his veins warmed up, or retreated to wherever it kept itself, and he drew in a long breath. Herbert came in alone.

"She said she'll be in directly."

"Where's Alan?" he asked.

"He came out when the bomb went pop, looked things over and went back to bed."

Frank nodded, stood up and went to the wall phone to call Bailey on his cell phone. He kept his message short. After telling the bare facts about the bomb, he said, "Go in with Shelley and talk to your man out there. If his dog isn't trained in sniffing explosives, get one that is. Intercept all packages. You know the drill." He listened a moment, then said, "No, don't come back. This place will be crawling with police. We'll see you in the morning."

Barbara came in then, her face set in furious lines. She marched past Frank to the dining room and brought back the bottle of wine and another glass. "Hoggarth," she said. "Do you have a number where I can reach him without going through a bunch of troglodytes first?"

"I'll call him," Frank said. He took the wine from her and poured for them both. She seemed to have forgotten to take that next step. "You're too mad to talk to anyone."

"And a bomb squad," she said. "No flashing lights, no sirens, and for God's sake no reporters!" She practically snatched the glass from his hand and drank as if it contained water. "I have to warn Carrie," she said, setting the glass down hard. "My God, I want to go shoot that goddamn bastard!"

"I'd better make us up some snacks," Herbert said, watching Barbara stride out with an awed expression. "She knows the words and she knows the tune, if you get what I mean. And she used them all out there. Anyways, dinner's going to get on the table a little bit late, I reckon."

Frank went to his study to look up Lt. Hoggarth's cell phone number and make the call. Milt Hoggarth was in homicide, but if Barbara had been the one to open that package, that was exactly the investigative squad who would now be on the scene.

Later, the lead detective in the bomb unit talked to Herbert in the living room while the technicians set up bright lights and went to work at the site of the shattered barrel, and Hoggarth sat with Frank and Barbara in the study. Morgan set up a din when the men all arrived, and subsided when Herbert gestured to him. Herbert did not introduce any of the detectives, and Morgan watched and quivered from time to time, but he didn't bark again.

"Frank, give me something to go on," Hoggarth was saying in the study. "You can't stonewall something like this." He was red-faced, with a red scalp, and previously red hair fading to gray in a tonsure. He kept rubbing his hand over his head as if he couldn't believe it was bare.

"Milt, if you were freelance I'd probably want to hire your services now and then, but you aren't. There are people over you with people over them, and I don't trust any of them worth a damn."

Hoggarth looked from him to Barbara. He was as grim as she had ever seen him, and increasingly furious with them both. "And that's it," he said. "An unknown enemy sent you a bomb. Goddamn fucking period."

"After the trial's over," she said coldly, "I'll make you a captain yet, Lieutenant. It's worth waiting for."

"Right. That's what I'll put in my report."

"Hoggarth," Barbara said softly, "I can offer a suggestion. It doesn't have to go into a report. Have someone keep an eye on the Wenzel crew. It wouldn't hurt a thing to let them spot someone, and of course you'd deny it come hell or high water if they complained."

His expression changed from furious to a bleak, remote mask.

At the same time Frank said, "Barbara!" That tiger had already been baited and didn't need any additional teasing.

"It's all right," she said. "He won't do it, and I won't say another word."

In her room upstairs Carrie stood at the window watching the men working under the bright lights. She had turned off her own light. Barbara had said she should not leave her drapes open even a second when the lights were on in the room.

The room was warm, but she couldn't stop shivering. She was remembering the boys with cap guns, running, falling. Not cap guns, she thought suddenly, louder. Like a bomb would sound.

She closed her eyes, but nothing else followed the flash of memory. Instead, she saw the other little girl sitting at a table on a terrace, playing with Tookey, talking to him in a low voice about a parade. She would ride on his back and they would lead the parade with a million people watching and a million people marching and singing.

"How's the little June bug?" Uncle Silly said, coming out to the terrace.

"I'm not a bug."

"Sure you are. You hatched out of your egg in the month of June, and that makes you a June bug. You know what your sign is? Gemini, that's what. The sign of the twins."

"I don't have a twin."

"Yes, you do. She's invisible. So she can go places you can't go, she can see things you can't see and hear things you can't hear. She knows things that you don't know, but sometimes she'll whisper to you and tell you if you listen hard."

"I don't have a twin and I'm not a bug."

"Cyrus, stop teasing her," Aunt Loony said. "Come on, Carolyn, time to wash your hands for dinner."

Carrie didn't move or open her eyes when the memory stopped as abruptly as it had started. She summoned her special memory box and carefully stowed the memory inside. "Cyrus," she whispered. That was his name. Uncle Cyrus.

Then, keeping her eyes closed, she said under her breath, "Carolyn, please tell me more. You know things I don't know. I'll listen hard if you'll please just tell me more."

31

Friday morning Shelley invited everyone out to her house for Saturday afternoon and then dinner. "We can hike up in the woods and cut Christmas trees," she said. "Unless it's pouring rain, I mean."

Or even if it was, Barbara thought, yearning suddenly for a long hike in the forested hills above Shelley's house.

"Dr. Minnick said he would make dinner, and if we have some work to do, I have my office there," Shelley went on.

"I'll help him with dinner," Frank said. "Bobby, you need to move some. Let's do it."

"If it's all right with you, I thought I would ask Darren and Todd," Shelley said. "Todd loved it out there before. And Darren probably saw that article about the bomb. He must be anxious."

In spite of her warning not to break the story to reporters, someone had leaked it, and the article, while brief, had appeared in the morning newspaper.

Barbara drew in a breath, then nodded. "Fine with me. I intend to hike for hours, rain or no rain."

"I'll pick you up," Bailey said. "But I don't hike in cold wet muddy steep woods."

When they left for court, they went out into the cold wet fog that had settled in over the city and looked as if it might persist for days. Bailey drove them to the courthouse and stopped only long enough for everyone to get out. They were met instantly with a bevy of reporters and a video team, all firing questions.

"A houseguest got suspicious and tossed it into a rain barrel," Frank said as Barbara hurried on ahead with Carrie and Shelley. "That's all we know about it. Ask the bomb squad what they found. I haven't heard a thing." He had a way of appearing to be accommodating while actually walking steadily forward, and they made their way to the courtroom where the media crew was stopped at the door.

Inside the courtroom Barbara was told by the bailiff that the judge wanted her in chambers. Mahoney had already gone back, he said.

"To recess or not to recess," Barbara murmured to Shelley. "That's the question. Wanna bet?"

And it was the question. "Are you all right?" Judge Laughton asked, putting a football on a shelf. His room was more like a locker room than a judge's sanctum: photographs of him in his football days, a trophy or two, uncomfortable rugged furniture... He was not yet in his robes, and she was not surprised to see that he wore a green-and-yellow university T-shirt with a fighting duck.

"I'm fine," she said. "Thank you. No harm was done."

"If you want a recess, it's understandable," he said. When she assured him that she wanted to continue with the trial, he nodded. "There's a problem about the jury," he said. "We all know that they see the newspapers or television, or people tell them things. They'll know a bomb was sent to you and might speculate that it has something to do with the trial. I intend to talk to them and say that it is not related to this trial. Do you object to that?"

"I don't know what else you could tell them," she said. "I have no objection."

"May I make a suggestion?" Mahoney said then. "If you will instruct Ms. Holloway to stop pounding on Wenzel, just to take it a little easier, that would put an end to such speculation."

She gave him a derisive look. "In your dreams."

"Knock it off," Judge Laughton said. "One other matter. Mr. Mahoney says he has another witness to call, one not on his witness list, Tricia Symington, the safe-deposit-box attendant at the bank. Do you need time to review her statement before she's called to the stand?"

"Since I have her on my list, she's okay by me," Barbara said. She added to Mahoney, "You planning to put the gun in the safe-deposit box?" She grinned at the flush that colored his face.

"I have a request," Barbara said then. "When Symington's up to bat, I get to ask her the questions I'd like answered. There's no need to bring her back a second time in that case."

Judge Laughton looked at Mahoney. "Any objection?"

"No. Let's just get all this over with as fast as we can."

Back at her table Barbara asked Shelley to find Tricia Symington's statement. "It's going to be a few minutes before we start," she told Carrie. "The judge is telling the jury to disregard the bomb incident. For all the good that will do."

Shelley found the statement and they both scanned it in the next few minutes before the jurors were led back in and the judge, now properly clothed in judicial robes, took his place. Wenzel was recalled to the witness stand and reminded that he was still under oath and the day really started.

Barbara stood up and wished the jurors a good morning and was given a few smiles, some nods, and looks of curiosity in response. She turned to Wenzel.

"Mr. Wenzel, you stated that you didn't approve of your brother's lifestyle. Can you be specific about your meaning?"

"I don't approve of overindulging in alcohol," he said.

"Is that all you meant? Not his work habits or anything else other than that he drank too much?"

"Basically that's it."

"Did your brother share family festivities? Holidays, birthdays, social events, things of that sort?"

"Rarely. He preferred not to."

"I see. So your dealings with him were primarily about business? Is that correct?"

"Yes."

"You stated that when he was drinking he could become physically abusive and that he used vulgar language, and you indicated that you didn't want to be around him at those times. Is that correct?"

He was eyeing her warily. "I said I didn't like to talk to him at those times."

"So when he was giving you valuable advice he was not drinking?"

"Yes. When he was sober he was a good businessman."

She nodded. "You also said that when he was drinking, he became physically abusive with women. Is that correct?"

"Yes."

"Did you witness such abuse?"

"Sometimes I did."

"When?"

"I don't recall just when," he said. "I don't keep a diary of such incidents."

"Well, did you see an incident during the past year?"

He hesitated, then said no. "I think it was longer ago than that."

"All right. You said sometimes you saw such abuse, indicating more than one incident. Did you mean more than one incident?"

"I think it was often." He was sounding more defensive, less sure of himself with each answer, as if he suspected that she was trying to trap him and he was trying to avoid entrapment.

"Mr. Wenzel, can you give us one specific example of such abuse? When it was and where?"

"A few years ago," he said after a moment. "At his house. He was slapping a woman around."

"Did you intervene?"

"Yes. I made him stop. She ran out and left."

"Who was the woman?"

"I don't know. I had never seen her before."

"And the other incidents you mentioned? Where did they occur?"

"Usually at his house."

"Did any of those women ever press charges against him?"

"No. I don't think so."

"How many such incidents did you happen to witness?" she asked, not bothering to conceal her disbelief.

His eyes narrowed and his words came out more clipped. "I said several times. I can't be more specific."

"Did these incidents occur during the day, or at night?"

Mahoney finally objected. "Your Honor, this is all irrelevant to the trial at hand."

"He brought it up in previous testimony," Barbara said. "I'm just trying to get some specific details. We can't leave it as a simple generality."

Judge Laughton looked disgusted, but he overruled the objection.

"Daytime or at night," she reminded Wenzel.

"I think late afternoon," he said icily.

"On those occasions were you calling on him to seek advice?"

"Usually."

"When you wanted his advice did you call ahead of time to make certain you could find him at home?"

"Most often I did. Not always."

"Mr. Wenzel, you've stated that when your brother was sober he was a good businessman, and also that you did not like to talk with him when he was not sober. Are you now saying that you happened to drop in on him more than once when he had been drinking heavily, just in time to see him abusing a woman?"

"Yes, I am," he snapped.

"When you visited him to seek advice did you take various documents to review, like cost estimates, appraisals, EPA statements, photographs, blueprints of what you had in mind and other materials?"

Mahoney called out his objection almost before she finished.

"Sustained," Judge Laughton said without hesitation.

She smiled slightly and turned away from Wenzel, but not before he saw it. His face was a shade darker when she turned toward him again. "Mr. Wenzel, when did you promise your mother that you would look after your brother?"

He blinked at the change in subject. "Just before she died."

"Do you mean days before, or weeks? How long before her death?"

"Weeks, I believe."

"And when was that?"

"In 1960."

"How old were you and your brother at the time?"

He hesitated, then said, "I was nineteen. Joe was seventeen."

"Were you living at home at the time of her death?"

"Yes, I was."

"I see," she said. "I have copies of two clippings, one from the monthly newsletter published by the First Methodist Church of lower San Diego, and the other from a county newspaper, *The Bugler*." She showed them both to Mahoney, then to the judge, and finally handed them to Wenzel. "Will you read through them, please," she said. "Then I'd like to ask a few questions about the accuracy of the reports."

He took out his reading glasses, put them on and read the two articles slowly.

When he put the articles down and took off his glasses, Barbara asked, "Are the articles accurate?" He said they were. "Then you weren't living at home at the time of the accident that claimed your mother's life. Were you rooming with another apprentice carpenter near the construction site at the waterfront?"

"Yes. I had forgotten that."

"According to both articles, your mother was killed in a boating accident while attending a church picnic. Is that accurate?"

He said yes again, and she went through the articles item by item, stopping frequently to ask if that was correct. His father had been a department-store deliveryman, he had taught a Sunday School class and led prayer meetings on Wednesday nights. Both boys had made good grades in school, worked part-time after school and were active in sports. Joe was already planning on following his brother into the construction trade.

She summed it up then. "Your family was close, active in church, in good health all around. Your mother was forty-two years old at the time of her tragic death. She would have had a life expectancy of another thirty years at least. Your father was active in the church, hardly an alcoholic at that time. Why would she have told you to look after your brother?"

Mahoney objected angrily. "Counsel is making speeches."

"Sustained. Just ask your questions," the judge said to Barbara.

She asked the same question.

"I don't know why. Maybe just because I was older."

She regarded him for a moment, then turned away. "Did you ever see your brother using a wrist brace?"

"Yes. Now and then he used one."

"Do you know what was wrong with his wrist?"

"Years ago he fell and hurt it. He said it was just a sprain, but it flared up painfully now and then, and he used the brace."

"You stated that the house he planned to build would be company property. Was he responsible for the design of the house?"

"Yes."

"Was there a monetary limit to what he could build?"

"We assumed it would be kept within reason. There were no real plans yet, just ideas and sketches."

"Was one of your company architects working with him on the plans?"

"Yes."

"Was he keeping you informed of the progress being made on the design of the house?"

"No. I told him that after there was something on the boards, something on paper, the three of us would discuss it."

"So, in effect, the architect and your brother had carte blanche for the preliminary plans. Is that correct?"

"Within reason," Wenzel said after a moment.

"And if the final plans had come in for over a million dollars, would you have had veto power, forced a cut back in the design?"

"We would have discussed it," he said stiffly.

"Would work have continued on the project without your approval?"

"I think our discussion would have led to a mutually satisfactory outcome."

"Mr. Wenzel, is it customary for your company to let plans go forward to a final design before you determine a price range of the project?"

"Objection!" Mahoney called out. "This is totally irrelevant!"

"Sustained."

"No more questions," Barbara said.

Mahoney was brief in his redirect. All he wanted Wenzel to repeat was that Joe Wenzel had been an alcoholic, that when drinking he was often abusive to women, and that he had wanted cash in order to buy a piece of the defendant. He didn't specify again which piece he had in mind.

After the usual midmorning recess, Mahoney called his last witness, Tricia Symington. She was a thin, middle-aged woman with dyed blond hair that looked as dry as straw, and reading glasses that she kept putting on and taking off. When off, they dangled from a black silk cord around her neck.

She told her history at the bank, and what she was responsible for, and then Mahoney had her describe her encounter with Joe Wenzel.

"Well, he was dirty and he smelled of alcohol, so I asked the security questions we use. He answered them and he had the key to the box, and his photo ID seemed all right even if his signature was unreadable. But, of course, he was wearing the wrist brace and that makes a difference. I took him to the vault, we opened the box and I left him alone in there."

"Was he carrying a briefcase or something similar?"

"Yes. A briefcase."

There was very little more to her testimony and then Barbara stood up. "Ms. Symington, had you ever seen Joe Wenzel before that day?"

"I don't think so," she said. "Not that I recall. I mean, he might have come into the bank on occasion and I could have seen him, but it didn't stick in my memory if I did. If he had ever come in looking like he did that day, I'm sure I would remember."

"Do you have a record of his transactions regarding the safe-deposit box?"

"Yes. I brought it with me." She put on her glasses again and looked for the paper in her purse, found it and started to hand it to Barbara.

"No, you keep it. Just tell us when he made use of the box."

"Well, he started using it in August, 1978. He visited it in October of that year, 1978. And in the spring of the following year, March, 1979, and January of 1980. He didn't visit it again until January of 1986, and then not again until May, 1997. That was the last time until August."

"Were you employed by the bank in 1997?"

"No. I started in April, 1998." She took off the glasses and held out her record in a tentative sort of way. This time Barbara took it and handed it to Mahoney to look over.

"Did you compare all those signatures with the one from August this year?"

"Yes. I looked them over," she admitted. "It was quite different, but he answered the questions, and he had a driver's license, and a deposit slip in his hand, and with the wrist brace…" She put her glasses on, took them off, and looked miserable.

"Did you pay particular attention to his face, if he looked like his photo ID?"

"Not a lot," she said nervously. "I mean he was dirty and unshaved, and the picture wasn't like that. It was hard to compare the two."

"Would you recognize him if you saw him again?"

"I just don't know," she said. "I mean, I followed our protocol and he seemed all right."

Barbara nodded sympathetically. She thanked her and said no more questions.

When the witness was excused, Mahoney rested the state's case. He looked disgruntled, and Barbara didn't think it inappropriate. He had expected to end his case with the damaging statements from Wenzel, and instead had to retrace his steps to try to account for the gun and ended on a sinking note. Not a good way to end a case.

Judge Laughton beckoned them and asked Barbara, "Are you prepared to present your opening statement at this time? Or do you want to wait until after lunch?"

It was eleven-thirty. "I'll do it now," she said. "It will be brief."

"Good. And will your first witness be available after lunch? I'd like to move this along today as much as possible. I want us out of here in time to do some Christmas shopping."

"So do I," Barbara said honestly. "We'll be ready with at least our first witness."

Her opening remarks were as brief as she had promised. She recounted Carrie's history, the accident that robbed her of her memory and left her an orphan, and her long odyssey after graduating from high school. "Carrie Frederick is not on trial for being homeless. Or for being an orphan. Or for being poor. She has no expensive habits. She doesn't smoke or drink and has never used drugs. When she repulsed the unwanted advances of a drunken customer in Las Vegas she was accused of assault and fired, another sad case of the victim being accused of the crime.

"Carrie had no motive for murder. She was making more money in tips than she had ever made in her life, and she was saving her money to put tires on her car and get a tune-up. That is not a motive for murder, ladies and gentlemen. She could have left her job and gotten another one readily, as her history demonstrates. She is a gifted pianist and that alone assured her of a livelihood. When Joe Wenzel harassed her, she properly complained to the manager. She did not want his attentions pressed upon her and sought to avoid him."

She was watching the jurors' faces carefully. A few were openly sympathetic; they understood victimhood. There were the impassive ones who revealed little or nothing. One woman, who had appeared hostile from the start, continued to gaze coldly back at Barbara as she spoke.

"Murder is a heinous crime, ladies and gentlemen, but perhaps even more heinous is the attempt of the guilty to shift the blame to the innocent. As the defense presents its case in the days to come, you will hear testimony that is contradictory to what has already been stated, and you will see an alternative case developed that indicates that Carrie was chosen to bear the stigma of guilt undeservedly, and that this attempt was very deliberate…."

Lunch was a blip in Barbara's awareness. She couldn't have said afterward what she had eaten, and then they were back in court, and Delia Rosen was called to the stand.

The only thing she added to what she had already told Barbara was that the first thing Carrie did after buying three white blouses and two black skirts was to wash them all.

"I thought it was weird to wash brand-new clothes, but she said she always did. She didn't like the way they felt or smelled until they had been washed. Then she ironed everything and was ready to start work on Friday."

"Was there anything in the want ad you answered to indicate that the Cascadia lounge was a Wenzel Corporation property?" Barbara asked.

"No. I mean, it just said cocktail waitresses and when to apply in person. That's what we did, applied in person on

Monday morning. I didn't know about the Wenzel Corporation until Mr. Joe Wenzel started hanging out there and one of the other gals told me he was part owner."

"Were you aware of the attention he was showing in Carrie Frederick?"

"Yes. We all were. He watched her all the time."

"Did she ever give any sign of friendliness toward him, smile back, or flirt, anything at all?"

"She never did. She tried to keep out of his way, you know, take a break when he got there, pull away if he got too close. Mostly she just ignored him."

Mahoney got her to admit that she hadn't known Carrie outside of the casino where they both had worked in Las Vegas and that she couldn't say if Carrie had met Joe Wenzel there or not. Also, she had been out the night of the murder and she had no way of knowing when Carrie got back to their apartment.

At three that afternoon Barbara called her next witness, Dr. Takenoshin Makino. He was a dapper, slightly built man in his fifties with flowing black hair over his ears and down to his collar, rather like Prince Valiant's hair. After he was sworn in Barbara asked him to recite his credentials—doctor of biology, professor at Stanford, consultant to the FBI forensics unit, author of numerous articles dealing with biology and/or forensics, author of three books on biology... It was an impressive resume.

"Dr. Makino, are you a coauthor of this article in *Forensic Sciences* concerning the identification of hair?" She showed him the journal, and he said he was. "When did you begin to specialize in the study of hair?"

"Roughly nine years ago."

"Will you please tell the court what characteristics you consider when you are called upon to make a match of hairs, or disprove such a match as the case may be."

He gave a lengthy lecture on the structure of human hairs, their growth patterns, how they could be affected by illness, stress or chemical processes.

"Human hair color is genetically determined, as is the length of human hair. Other factors such as dyes or heat, illness and such are inflicted upon it and leave their own characteristic marks." He paused as if waiting for her to signal that was enough. When she made no such sign, he continued. "Normally a human being loses from fifty to one hundred fifty hairs a day. They are shed naturally, most often in brushing the hair or in shampooing, and they are constantly being replaced so the effect is not noticeable. Often the hair that is no longer being nourished and is ready to fall is dislodged by brushing and falls at a later time."

This time when he paused Barbara nodded and he waited for her question.

"Can you tell if a hair has been shed through the process of naturally aging as contrasted with one that is pulled out?"

"It is readily distinguishable. In the first instance the root is released with the hair and it shows signs of atrophism. It is withered and aged, no longer providing nourishment to the hair shaft. In the case of one that has been pulled prematurely, that is not the case. That root is intact and healthy. Often if it is a violent enough pull the follicle is detached along with a healthy root mass."

"Have you had the opportunity to study the hairs under question in the present case?" She passed him the plastic envelope with the hairs.

"Yes."

"Will you please describe your findings?"

"Yes. May I use my own photographs? I made photographs and enlarged them so that the hairs are more easily identified." He was already reaching into his briefcase to bring out a folder with his photographs. Barbara put them on an easel and Dr. Makino moved from the witness chair to stand by the easel and point at the hairs as he talked about them.

"Number one has the intact follicle," he said. "And number two has the partial follicle. They were both pulled out violently. None of the others have any root or follicle." He talked about the similarities first, then said, "You can clearly see the effects of weather and aging on the first two hairs, at the end here. A little bit frayed and this one is a little dry from wind or sun likely. Also they are both thinner toward the end than at the upper section. The other hairs show no sign of similar wear. They were cut at the bottom, as well as at the upper end. Presumably they all came from longer lengths of hair and were cut for uniformity."

"They were cut at both ends?" Barbara asked. "Not pulled or broken?"

"Definitely not. Normal hair does not break cleanly like that. An acute onset of illness might weaken the hair but then the shaft would become thinner and dryer. All these hairs were in a healthy state without any trace of the thinning caused by illness. And since there are no root cells, they clearly were not pulled out prematurely."

"Is there any way you can prove or disprove that all those hairs came from the same person?"

"There are several tests that can be done. You could look for trace elements, for example, to ascertain if it was present in all the hairs. That is a simple test that a high-school student in chemistry could perform."

"Did you do such a test?"

"Yes. I obtained hairs from Ms. Frederick's head and tested them and found traces of arsenic. Most Americans have such traces. The cut hairs have no such traces."

"Would that be sufficient to prove that the cut hairs were not from her?"

"In my opinion it would be. The definitive test is always the DNA test, but that was not possible since the cut hairs have no root or follicle to yield DNA."

"You stated that human hair length is determined genetically, and these two hairs apparently are intact and have reached their natural length. Is it also true that the other hairs had a longer natural length?"

"Yes. They were cut at both ends and now are approximately the same length as the first two. It is impossible to say how much was cut from those hairs and what their natural length might have been."

"Dr. Makino, in your opinion, would you say all those hairs came from the same person?"

"No."

When Barbara finished with Dr. Makino, Mahoney struggled to find a weakness in his testimony and ended up stressing the similarities of the hairs, they were all black, straight, not dyed. Dr. Makino was imperturbable and agreed that the outward similarities might lead one to assume the hairs all came from the same person, but all he could say was that they were similar, but not identical. They had not all come from the same person.

32

Saturday was perfect, misty and not very cold, with fog wreathing the Coburg hills and the buttes that were the north and south landmarks of Eugene. Bailey came promptly at one

o'clock, and they all loaded up and headed out to Shelley and Alex's house where they met Bailey's guard, Carl Zimmerman, and his dog Jackie, a huge German shepherd that took his duties seriously, snarling and showing fangs until proper introductions were made. They hiked in the wet woods and found three perfect Christmas trees. Darren said no when Todd pointed to a cedar that was twelve to fifteen feet tall. No tree in the house taller than he was, Darren said firmly. After the trees were safely deposited near the house, Barbara eyed the hills again.

"Now I'll take my hike," she said.

"You mean that wasn't enough?" Carrie asked. She had asked earlier if there were bears, and her apprehension about the woods and forest was apparent.

"Nope," Barbara said. "That was warm-up time."

"Mind if I tag along?" Darren asked.

"Think you can keep up?"

"I can try."

"And promise not to talk?"

"I'll try that too."

"Okay then. Let's do it before it gets too rainy."

The mist might more properly have been called rain or at least drizzle by then, and she didn't care. The woods smelled mossy and green and vibrant. The ground was spongy, not too muddy, and the trails Alex and Shelley had made were ideal. She set a brisk pace until the path got steeper.

Darren didn't say a word until they stopped at an outcropping of lichen- and moss-covered boulders. "Is it all right if I worry about you?" he asked then.

"Only if you don't mention it," she said.

"Deal. But I do."

She looked out over the valley below them, the sprawling house with lights haloed by mist and fog, everything indistinct and without edges, one thing merging with another. "Isn't it beautiful," she said softly.

"All it needs is a pagoda," he said.

She looked at him in surprise. She had been thinking of Japanese paintings. "I'd put a stream in front of the house, not way over there."

He laughed. "You're a creature of the forest, aren't you? Did you notice that it's raining?"

"So it is. It's also going to get dark very soon. Time to head back. Did you bring dry clothes? I did."

"I'll stand by the fire and steam," he said. Then he laughed. "Actually I brought other clothes and made Todd bring some along, but I bet he hasn't changed yet."

Frank and Dr. Minnick were busy in the kitchen when they got back to the house. Bailey looked them over with disgust and shook his head. "You guys are crazy," he said.

They had a bountiful meal of ham with sweet potatoes and baked apples, green beans, salad and corn bread. Not a gourmet haute cuisine meal, Dr. Minnick said, but filling. It was wonderful, they all protested, almost simultaneously. Then Shelley stood up and tapped her spoon on her wineglass.

"You might wonder why I gathered you here together," she said, blushing furiously. "We have an announcement to make, Alex and I. We're engaged. We're getting married in April."

Dr. Minnick brought out champagne and there were toasts and a lot of laughter, but Barbara could not help the pang of regret she felt. Something of it showed, and Alex said, "She will keep working, you understand. One of us has to." No one had told Darren and Carrie that Alex was the mysterious, anonymous X whose cartoons appeared in national magazines and whose comic strip was syndicated in hundreds of newspapers. There was more laughter.

They didn't stay late; Barbara pleaded work to do, and they were all tired from the trek through woods in the rain. When they got back to Frank's house, Barbara went straight up to her office, Frank to his study, and Carrie went to the piano and played softly.

She never had felt the lack of family so much. She had been an outsider all her life, always looking in, never really a part of any family. She could share their meals, join in with their laughter, but always with the awareness that they shared secrets, things no outsider could ever fathom. She yearned for Carolyn to come and whisper secrets to her.

She had come to think of that other little girl as her invisible twin who knew things she wouldn't divulge, and who stayed away most of the time, returning with tantalizing hints only to vanish again. Even as she yearned for her return, she feared it. She had to keep reminding herself that none of those memories in her magic box were real, they were make-believe, fantasies, part of her delusional bout with insanity.

She realized she had been playing faster and louder variations on her song to Carolyn Frye and she stopped abruptly.

Sunday afternoon Frank and Barbara spent several hours preparing Carrie for the ordeal she would face testifying in her own behalf.

"I hope to finish my witnesses this week," Barbara said when they finished. "You'll be the last witness, and if all goes well that should be on Friday. We'll have closing statements on Monday, and then it's up to the jury."

Carrie nodded mutely. She looked exhausted. Frank had taken the role of prosecutor and had proved to be a tough one, possibly tougher than Mahoney would be.

"Are you sleeping okay?" Barbara asked. "If you want to see a doctor, get a mild sedative, or a tranquilizer, we can arrange it."

"No!" Carrie said, shaking her head.

Belatedly, with regret for her hasty words, Barbara remembered Carrie's phobia about doctors. "You wouldn't even need to see anyone, in fact, if you want something to ease the tension."

"I'm all right," Carrie said.

"Well, if you change your mind, whistle. Another week, Carrie. Hang in there."

On Monday morning the wind changed, the fog dispersed and the sun even came out for a short time. It was a good omen, Barbara thought. Luther Wenzel was the only one of the family in court that morning, apparently their own personal court recorder.

Barbara's first witness was Mrs. Alexis O'Reilly, who had been married to Joe Wenzel from late 1975 to 1980. She was fifty-two, probably a little heavier than she had been when married to Joe, but pleasant-looking with big brown eyes and pretty brown hair that curled around her face.

After her brief history had been given, Barbara asked, "When you married Joe Wenzel, were you both working?"

"Yes. He was very busy and I had a new job at Sacred Heart Hospital."

"At that time was he drinking a great deal?"

"No. A social drink now and then, maybe a drink before dinner, not much more than that."

"Would you describe your marriage with Joe Wenzel as a good one?"

"For the first year or two it was very good. We were building a house and picking out furniture and curtains, things like that. We were having a good time with it all."

"Then what happened?"

"I don't know for sure. In the summer of 1978 things just changed. I never did understand why. He stopped working, for one thing, and for several weeks he drank very heavily. When I tried to get him to pull himself together and go back to work, he said he had retired, that he never intended to work again. In early September he wanted to go to a rock concert up in Seattle, but I couldn't get off work, so he went alone. He had never done that before. After that he went off alone a lot, to Las Vegas, or a rock concert somewhere, or Miami. He began to follow the horses and go to wherever they were racing. I couldn't take off to go with him, so he went alone."

"Was he still drinking heavily?"

Mahoney objected. "This is irrelevant, Your Honor. Joe Wenzel is not on trial."

"Mr. Larry Wenzel brought up his lifestyle," Barbara said. "I'm trying to find out what that lifestyle really was."

Laughton overruled.

"Did Joe Wenzel continue to drink heavily?" she asked again.

"No. After a few weeks that ended. He drank more than he had early on, but not really heavily."

"Would you call him an alcoholic?"

"Not after a few weeks. He never drank enough to black out or anything like that."

"When he was drinking was he ever abusive to you, physically abusive?"

Alexis looked shocked at the idea and shook her head vigorously. "Never. What he did when he had too much to drink was use gutter talk, really vulgar talk, but he never got physical."

"Do you know if he had a handgun when you were married to him?"

"Yes. It made me nervous and he kept it locked up in a desk drawer."

"When he said he didn't intend to return to work, did money become an issue? Were you concerned?"

"Yes. I told him he had to work because I didn't make enough money to pay our mortgage, and he laughed. A few weeks later he had me sign papers that meant the house was to become property of the corporation. He said we'd never have to worry about the mortgage. We had more money than ever without the mortgage payment, insurance and taxes and all."

"Did you try to get him to seek help of any kind after he changed so drastically?"

"Yes. I wanted him to see a doctor, but he wouldn't do it. I talked to his brother Larry about it and he said to be patient, that Joe had been through times like that before and he would snap out of it."

"Did he snap out of it?"

"No. If anything it got worse, and he was gone more and more."

"How long did that go on, Mrs. O'Reilly?"

"Like I said, it started in the summer of 1978, and in January of 1980 I had to leave him. I couldn't take it any longer."

"During the time you were married to Joe Wenzel, did you ever see him wear a wrist brace, or did he complain about wrist pain?"

"No. He was as healthy as a horse when I knew him."

When Mahoney did his cross-examination, he asked, "Did it occur to you at the time that your marriage might have been the cause of his change in behavior?"

"Of course," she said. "That was the first thing I thought of, that something had gone wrong between us. But I decided that was not true. Whatever happened to him had nothing to do with me."

Mahoney asked if she agreed that a bad marriage could change people, and she said yes, but she was adamant about her own marriage not being at fault in this instance.

Tiffany Olstead was five feet ten, languorous and heavily made up, as if she hated being forty years old and wanted to cling to thirty forever. Her story echoed Alexis O'Reilly's. Joe had told her he was retired, and he would take her around to see the world, but all she ever saw were horses, roulette wheels and blackjack tables.

"When he was drinking or at any other time, was he ever physically abusive to you?" Barbara asked.

"No. He would slouch down in a chair and talk dirty, that's all."

"Was he an alcoholic?"

"I don't think so. He drank a lot, but it didn't seem to have much effect. He didn't pass out or anything like that. He didn't drink when he gambled."

"Did he ever complain about a bad wrist, or wear a brace on his wrist?" She said no.

"Did you ever see a handgun when you were with him?"

"He had one that he kept in a desk drawer. I asked him what for and he said varmints."

"Did he ever work when you were together?"

"No, he was retired. When he wasn't traveling or something, he played with his music tapes or read racing newspapers. No work."

"Did you and Joe socialize with his brother and his wife?"

"I never even met them," she said.

When Mahoney asked if her marriage to Joe had worked out, she said with a shrug that neither of them got what they had bargained for. She had left him after eighteen months.

Over vehement objections from Mahoney Barbara called a travel agent who had arranged Joe's trips for the past five years. He furnished a record of Joe's various trips. There were a lot of them and they were all for first-class flights and four- or five-star hotels.

Before Barbara could call her next witness, Mahoney asked the judge for a conference in chambers. In the sparsely furnished room a few minutes later, he said he would move that the testimony of the travel agent be stricken. "We know there was an irregularity in the relationship of the brothers," he said. "We stipulated that there was no call to go into it at this trial. Joe Wenzel is not on trial, and his brother and brother's family are not on trial. All of this is extraneous. She's throwing out not just a red herring, but a whole school of red herrings in an effort to confuse the jury. Hints and innuendoes, that's all she's showing, not a shred of proof of anything."

"Why don't you bone up on the law?" Barbara said coldly. "Your job is to prove my client is guilty, and my job is to show reason enough to question what you offer as proof. I don't have to prove diddly. Everything I've done to date is relevant to my showing there is more than enough doubt that you and your investigators have done your job. You see that pattern as well as I do. Joe Wenzel was into blackmail, pure and simple."

"Whatever he was or wasn't into has nothing to do with this trial," Mahoney said furiously. His face was very red. "If he was a serial killer, it wouldn't have anything to do with this trial. Next thing, you'll suggest that a cross-dressing hit man was hired. Another red herring."

"That's an idea," Barbara said.

"Both of you, cut it out now," Judge Laughton said, regarding them with bitterness. "Ms. Holloway, as you say, a pattern has emerged. I see no need to draw it out further unless you can make a direct link with the trial we are hearing. Mr. Mahoney, I will take your motion under advisement."

"Judge," Mahoney said then, "her next witness is the architect, who has nothing to add except that Joe Wenzel was going to build an expensive house. Just more of the same kind of innuendo she's been presenting. She's trying a case against Larry Wenzel and he was in Bellingham, with more than enough eyewitnesses to prove it."

"Mr. Vincent has a little more than that to add," Barbara said, possibly angrier than he was. "Do you want to take over my case for me? Don't you have enough to do on your side of the aisle?"

"I said to stop this bickering," Laughton said sharply. "Ms. Holloway, what will your witness testify to beyond the fact that Joe Wenzel was planning to build a house?"

"He met with Joe Wenzel every day until Friday of the week of the murder. Larry Wenzel never showed up. He never talked to Joe about Carrie or anything else that week."

Mahoney threw up his hands in disgust. "So he made a mistake. What possible difference does that make?"

"Maybe we should let the jury decide if it makes a difference," Barbara snapped. "Now you want their job, too?"

Judge Laughton stood up. "Beat it, you two. I'm going to call for the lunch recess, and I advise you to cool off and cool it when you get back this afternoon. Ms. Holloway, if you stray beyond that fact, and if he objects, no doubt I'll sustain. You've made the point, and there's little to be gained in extending it further."

During the lunch break Barbara went up and down the stairs at Frank's house endlessly. When Herbert asked if he should tell her lunch was ready, Frank shook his head. "She'll get a bite when she's ready," he said.

Then, back in court, Barbara called James Vincent to the stand. He was a good-looking young man of twenty-eight, fair-haired, blue-eyed and very earnest. He gave his occupation: architect for a firm in town.

"Were you formerly employed by the Wenzel Corporation?" she asked. He said yes. "Were you assigned to do the preliminary planning for the house Joe Wenzel wanted to build?" He said yes again, and she said, "Will you tell the court something about the working arrangements you had with Mr. Wenzel?"

"Well, at first, for a few meetings we met at a brew pub. Later we met at the house site. It had been bulldozed level, and he wanted me to see the surrounding area. He liked to step off where the old rooms had been and where he wanted the new rooms. Then, after I began to make some sketches, we met at a café a lot, the Xenon, or the Ambrosia, or someplace like that, usually at an outdoor table, and I'd show him what I had so far and we talked about it. Then we'd go back to the site, and he would begin changing things."

"Did you ever meet at your office?"

"No."

"How did you get in touch to arrange to meet?"

"He had my cell phone number and he'd call, usually

around noon and say meet him in an hour or two, and he'd say where. Or at the end of a meeting he'd say to draw up what we'd been talking about and meet him the next day and he'd say where."

"Did he ever fail to keep an appointment he made with you?"

"A lot of times he'd be late. You know, he'd say meet him at two at the site and he wouldn't get there until three or even later sometimes. And one time he didn't show up at all."

"When was that, do you recall?"

"Yes, it was the Friday before he was killed."

"That would have been on August ninth. Is that correct?"

"Yes. He said he'd be there at about one, but he never showed up. I waited until five and left."

"Had you been meeting with him regularly before that day?"

"Every day that week. He had come up with a couple of new ideas he wanted me to draw, and we met at the site every day. He wanted a climate-controlled wine cellar and an acoustic room. So there were a lot of changes to make. He told me on Thursday, tomorrow, same time, same place."

"So on August fifth through the eighth you met with him every day at the house site, and on the ninth, Friday he didn't show up. Is that correct?"

"Yes, it is."

"What time of day were you meeting with him that week?"

"Well, I'd do drawings all morning, and then go to the site after lunch, about one-thirty, and wait for him there. Usually we left at the same time, around four or five."

"On any day of that week did his brother Larry Wenzel join you?"

"No. He never came to the site when I was there."

"On any of those days did you leave before Joe Wenzel did?"

"No. I never left first. I mean, he'd get a new idea of something and he'd want to tell me on the spot, not wait until the next day."

"When you met with him was he drinking heavily?"

"The first few times when we met in a bar or something like that he had some drinks, quite a few the first two or three times, but after I began bringing sketches to show him and when we went to the site later on, he wasn't drinking. At first it was all just talk, about the biggest house in the county, with no definite plans in mind, I think, but when it began to take shape, he hardly drank at all."

"Did he get dirty when you went to the house site?"

"Yes. He liked to walk through the site and pace off where he wanted things, and it was dirty. They had leveled it, but there was still ash, and blackened shrubs and things like that. He got pretty dirty a lot of times."

"Did you ever see him wearing a wrist brace?"

"No."

"On Friday when he failed to show up, did he call you to say he wouldn't be there?"

"No."

"You said you waited for him until five. Did you have your cell phone with you?"

"Yes, but he didn't call. I just sat in my car and read a book. I kept thinking he'd turn up, but he didn't."

She thanked him and said no more questions. When Mahoney said he had no questions, she suspected that his game plan was to simply discount this testimony as irrelevant. So Larry had made a mistake about when he talked to his brother. It didn't make any difference when that talk occurred.

* * *

That afternoon when Barbara called Mattie Thorne to the stand, Mahoney objected. "May I approach?" he asked, already advancing toward the bench. Judge Laughton motioned both attorneys forward.

"Now what?" he asked.

"Your Honor, we stipulated that Gregory Wenzel was in the company of six to eight other people from about eleven until about three in the morning on the night of the murder. There's no reason to drag his name into this trial at this time. Counsel is just going after the Wenzel family for her own ulterior purposes. Will she want to bring six or seven of those young people up to cast doubt on his alibi? Will she go after Larry Wenzel's business associates in Bellingham next? We'll be here until after the first of the year."

"And I object to having Mr. Mahoney try my case," Barbara said hotly. "I have no intention of trying to break Greg Wenzel's alibi."

Impatiently Judge Laughton said overruled. "Let's just get on with it," he said to Mahoney. "I'm calling it quits early today," he said. "Around four. I have an appointment, so don't dally."

Mattie Thorne was twenty-six and looked younger, as if she still carried a bit of baby fat on her face. She also looked nervous, but a lot of people did when they were called as witnesses.

Barbara had her give a little background and then asked, "Do you recall the events of the night of August tenth?"

Mattie nodded, then said yes.

"Will you describe what you did that night to the court, please?"

"I, that is we, my girlfriend and I, went to the Bijou that

night and met some friends there. Then we all went to the Steelhead, the minibrew pub, and had nachos and things. We all went to a couple of other places and danced and listened to music until the last place closed at two in the morning. Then Greg Wenzel took me and my girlfriend home."

"All right. Now at two, when it was closing time at the last place you were, how did it happen that Gregory Wenzel took you and your friend home? Do you remember how that came about?"

"Yes. Bobby Brainard took us to the movie earlier, but he had been drinking beer and we decided he shouldn't drive, or that we didn't want to ride with him if he drove. We were just going to walk home. It wasn't far, six or seven blocks. And Greg said we couldn't do that, not at that hour. He said it wasn't really out of his way, and he hadn't been drinking because he had an upset stomach that night. He said he'd drive us home. Tina lives about a block from me, and that's what we did. He dropped her off and then took me to my apartment building."

"Do you recall what time it was when you reached your apartment?"

"It was about fifteen after two by then."

"And did he leave as soon as you arrived home?"

"No. He had said earlier that he missed the movie because he was feeling sick that evening, and when we got to my place, he asked if he could come in and use the bathroom because he wasn't feeling good, and I said yes. So he went in with me."

"Had you been dating him before that night?"

"No. I never had a date with him."

"How long did he remain in your apartment that night?"

"A few minutes, not even five probably. I asked him if he was okay and he said he was a little shaky, but okay. It's only about ten minutes from my place to his house, so I thought he'd be home in a few minutes and if he was feeling sick he'd be better off at home. I didn't really encourage him to stay. I was tired."

"How do you know how far it is to his house?"

Mattie looked puzzled, then said quickly, "I never was at his house, but I know where it is, in the Crescent Estates, just a minute or two away from LCC. I went to LCC for two years, and it only took ten minutes to get there, so I knew."

"Where is your apartment?" Barbara asked then. "Not the specific address, just an idea of where it is."

"Off Franklin on Villard. Just a minute or two from the interstate once you get on Franklin, and then LCC in less than ten minutes. At that time of night even less than that."

"Do you know what time he left your apartment that night?"

"Before two-thirty. I know that at two-thirty I turned off the lights and was ready for bed."

Mahoney seemed at a loss about what to ask her since she had simply confirmed Greg's alibi. "Had you been drinking that night, Ms. Thorne?"

"A glass of beer at the Steelhead, then I switched to lemonade because I just wanted to dance later."

"How can you be so sure about the time Mr. Wenzel left your apartment?"

She looked puzzled again, then said, "I looked at the clock when I went to bed. It was two-thirty. And it took me a few minutes to brush my teeth and put on my nightshirt and things like that."

He let it go at that and she was excused.

Barbara had one more witness to call that day, Matthew Shiveley, who worked security two nights a week at the Crescent Estates. He was in his sixties, heavily built, and with a slight limp. He said he had retired, but needed a little extra so he took on the part-time security job. He worked from midnight until six in the morning on Saturday and Sunday nights.

"Were you on duty on the night of August tenth?" Barbara asked.

"Yes, ma'am."

"Exactly what were your duties as a security guard?"

"Not much. I sat in a little gatehouse and read most of the time. I checked in cars that got there after midnight, made sure they belonged there, and that's about all. There isn't a gate, but there's a speed bump so they have to slow down. A couple of times I'd drive through the subdivision and check things out, you know, for fires or something. It was a quiet job. Nothing ever happened."

"When you checked cars arriving after midnight, did you keep a log, a record, anything like that?"

"Only if they didn't belong there. Then I was supposed to stop them and ask for ID and escort them to wherever they intended to go, or turn them around and see to it they left. You know, if the folks up there had company that got in late and I didn't know the cars, I'd stop them. No one else ever came in when I was working, just the folks who lived there, and once or twice visitors they had."

"On the night of August tenth did you see Gregory Wenzel arrive home late?"

"Yes, ma'am. At ten after three."

"If you didn't keep a log, how can you be sure of the time?"

"On Sunday when I read about the murder of his uncle I said to my wife that he got home late that night and I said it was at ten after three. It was real fresh in my memory, and then saying it to my wife like that made me remember. That's what I told the police."

"Did you actually see him, or just his car?"

"Well, I know the car, all right, and he sort of waved when he drove by. I knew who it was, all right."

She thanked him and said no more questions, and Mahoney shook his head. He had no questions.

Things were so peaceful, Barbara thought, when Judge Laughton called for a recess until the following morning. And in the morning, she knew, things would start popping all over the place.

33

Those nights Shelley was staying to work with Barbara until ten or later, then Bailey drove her home, and Barbara continued for several more hours. That night soon after Shelley left, Barbara started downstairs for a drink of water. Halfway down she paused and realized she had been listening to Carrie playing for quite a long time. She frowned and went down the rest of the way. Frank's light in the study was still on, his door ajar, and she went there instead of to the kitchen.

"You're up late," she said at his doorway.

He lowered the book he had been reading, another law book, and nodded. Both cats were with him, one on his lap, the other on his feet. As long as the monster dog stayed outside, they were willing to pretend an armistice had been declared.

"Have you been listening to Carrie?" Barbara asked at the door.

"Yes. Variations, but the same thing over and over."

"I'm worried about her," Barbara said in a low voice. She was thinking of Janey Lipscomb's warning, that an abreaction could bring about totally unpredictable behavior.

"And there's not a damn thing we can do about it," he said. "Just a few more days, that's all we can hope for. Let's just pray she hangs in there until next week."

Barbara got her water, found coffee in the carafe and poured a cup. Frank didn't let her make coffee in his house any more than Maria did at the office. She went back upstairs, back to work. Later, she heard Carrie come up and go into her room. The house felt eerily quiet after the piano music stopped.

Carrie was in a state between wakefulness and sleep, with dream images running through her mind, aware that they were dream images. Lucid dreaming, she thought sleepily. Carolyn flitted across her mental landscape.

Carolyn couldn't sleep, she was too excited and, besides, it wasn't even really dark yet. "Tomorrow," she whispered to Tookey, "we'll go to a ranch and I can ride a horse, a real horse. Daddy said so. And we'll get a baby sister and a house, a whole house all for us." She tossed and turned but sleep wouldn't come and she got out of bed, thinking about Daddy's briefcase. He said he had the king in there, she heard him, and maybe he had a toy for her or candy. She slipped across the hall to Mommy and Daddy's room where the briefcase was on the bed. She looked in the briefcase, but there wasn't a toy or candy either. She saw some pictures and pulled one out, just a bunch of men and a truck. There was a funny circle around one man's head, and she drew in her breath. It was like a crown, she thought. It wasn't a very good crown, she could draw a better one, but Daddy probably was in a hurry when he made it. She studied the king, and thought the men with him were all his warriors, and his castle was somewhere else. She wished Daddy had a picture of the castle. Tomorrow she'd tell Ramon the queen wouldn't have to be lonesome anymore because Daddy was going to bring her a king. She put the picture back.

Carrie sat straight up in bed as the images faded and full wakefulness came to her. She didn't turn on a light yet. That always made dream imagery fade away before she could grasp it. Instead, she went over the dream again and again to fix it in her mind. Dreams, she had learned, were not like the waking memories Carolyn sometimes gave her. Dreams were more elusive, harder to catch and put in her memory box. She had to write them down. When she was certain she had everything firmly in mind, she turned on the light and reached for her notebook.

Finished, she lay in the dark, thinking of the dream, the other memories she had collected. "Even if it's a sign of insanity," she said to herself, "they're all I have. I can't let them go anymore." It was like gathering puzzle pieces, and when she had enough of them maybe she could piece them together to tell herself a story with a beginning, a middle and an end.

Except for a brief flurry of interest when Larry Wenzel testified, the case had not caught the public's imagination. It had become no more than a rather sordid story of a barroom piano player who had shot and robbed a drunken lecher. Barbara had offered to bet Frank that things would change after that day. He had snorted.

Barbara called her first witness, Zoe Corelli, and Mahoney objected. At the bench he voiced the same complaint he had made previously. "This has nothing to do with the trial. It's another red herring."

"Are you going to object to everyone I call?" Barbara asked mildly. "Why not just make it a blanket objection and be done with it?"

Judge Laughton glowered at her. "I've heard all I want to hear of cross talk between you two. Are you going to link this witness to this trial?"

"Yes, I am."

"Overruled. Let's get on with it." He appeared to be as impatient with her as Mahoney was.

Zoe Corelli was sixty-something, as thin as a stick, with fuchsia-colored hair that matched her blouse, her lipstick and nail polish. She wore a lime-green suit with a very short skirt.

"Mrs. Corelli," Barbara said, "will you please tell the court your occupation and where you practice it?"

"I own a wig shop in San Francisco, Hair Galoreous. Isn't that a delightful name for it? I chose it myself."

Barbara smiled. "It is. How long have you been in that business, Mrs. Corelli?"

"Oh, dear, let me think. Sometimes I believe I must have invented wigs myself it's been so long. Forty years? Forty-five years? Something like that."

"So you must know a great deal about wigs, how they are made, how they are fitted, things of that sort?"

"Dear, what I don't know about wigs is something that neither man nor woman is meant to know. Ask me anything."

Some of the jurors smiled, and someone among the sparse spectators laughed. Judge Laughton tapped his gavel, then said, "Mrs. Corelli, will you please just answer the questions?"

"But that's what I'm doing," she said. She smiled at him. "Yes, sir, Your Honor."

"I have a receipt here," Barbara said, showing it to Mahoney, then the judge. "Can you identify it for the court?" She handed it to Zoe.

She held it at arm's length, then said, "You have to wait a minute, dear, while I find my glasses." She groped in an enormous tote bag and brought out eyeglasses, sky-blue cat-eye frames studded with rhinestones. Wearing them, she looked over the receipt and nodded. "Yes, that's mine. See? Hair Galoreous, and my name right here. What a lovely wig that was."

Barbara turned to Shelley, who handed her the wig. She held it up for Mahoney and the judge to see, then handed it to Zoe. "Is that receipt for this wig?"

Zoe examined the inside of the wig, then nodded. "It certainly is. But how on earth did it end up here?"

"Mrs. Corelli, please explain to the court how you can tell if that is a wig from your shop?"

"Well, I know my merchandise," she said, then smiled. "But there's a serial number, too. You can see it right here. If your eyes are pretty good, I mean. Personally, I need my glasses. It's little. Number 97351, see? Right here? And that's the number on the receipt. I always put that on the receipt in case there's a problem. I mean I guarantee everything I sell. Well, maybe not everything, because some of my wigs are quite inexpensive, you know, and you don't expect them to—"

"Mrs. Corelli, limit your answers to the questions, if you will," Judge Laughton said.

Zoe looked at Barbara. "What was the question again, dear?"

Gravely, Barbara said, "I believe you answered it. When the wig is expensive you make a note of the serial number on the receipt. Is that correct?"

"Yes, that's exactly what I do, because—"

"The answer is yes," Barbara said. "Do you keep a record of the serial number and the sale?"

"The answer is yes," Zoe said and smiled again at the judge.

Barbara retrieved the receipt and the wig and handed both to the clerk to be entered as exhibits. "That wig cost two thousand five hundred dollars. Is that correct?"

"Yes, that's what the customer paid, but she didn't dicker at all. I mean if they object to the price I always come down—" She stopped and said, "The answer is yes, dear."

Barbara was biting her cheek to keep from laughing, and she didn't dare look at Frank. "Did you have more than one wig like that one?" she said, motioning toward the exhibit table.

"Oh, yes. I had three. I called them The Three Furies and had them on alabaster forms. They were so striking, the contrast of jet-black and stark white."

"Did you sell the other two?"

"Well, I sold one of them and I still have one. It's a real bargain now. I've reduced the price, you see, but I have platinum hair next to it, and that's stunning, too. I couldn't very well call it the One Fury, you see, and now—"

"Mrs. Corelli!" Judge Laughton rapped his gavel sharply. "Just answer the questions, if you can."

"Well, I can, but you don't get much information with just a yes or no, you see, and I thought. I'm sorry, sir, Your Honor. I can do that."

"Do you have with you a record of the other sale of a wig

like that one?" Barbara asked, and Zoe said brightly that she did and groped in her big bag for a sales book.

"See? Here it is. That's why I brought this great big bag, so I could bring things like this. The ledger is so big, you see. One of these day I have to start using a computer, but—"

The judge banged his gavel and she gave him a quick smile, then said, "It was a cash sale. I remember she said she didn't want to use a credit card because it was maxed, and I didn't believe that, but when you're dealing with retail, you just go along with whatever the customer says and let it go at that." She looked at the judge again and said, "I'm sorry."

"What is the serial number of that wig?" Barbara asked.

Zoe put on her glasses and read the number.

"Do you know the customer's name?"

"No. She said it was Blondie, and I wrote that down, but that wasn't her name, I could tell. And she had dyed hair. It was blond so I guess she thought the name was suitable."

"What was the date of that sale?" Barbara asked.

"July 30. I had to make an adjustment in the wig, and she came back for it on August 2. She made a five-hundred-dollar deposit because that was all the cash she had with her, and she paid the rest when she came back. Two thousand two hundred dollars total. See, she objected to the price and I lowered it for her. I'm always willing to do that for the expensive ones."

Judge Laughton raised the gavel, then put it down and leaned back in his chair and closed his eyes for a moment. Barbara added the two dates to her calendar.

She had a series of questions to ask, and by the time she finished, Judge Laughton's face had taken on a dark reddish-purple hue, and Mahoney looked apoplectic. Zoe said the wigs could be washed, set, permed, anything that human hair could undergo without causing any harm because, of course, the wigs were real hair from Polynesian girls who sold it for quite good money, although the middlemen were the ones who really made a profit from them. They should be kept on forms, she said, to maintain the shape. The hairs were hand tied in, and they couldn't be pulled out without tearing the lining. And she said no she probably would not recognize the customer again because she didn't pay a lot of attention to faces, they all had eyes, a nose and a mouth, like that, but she never forgot hair, unless it was dyed and then it could be changed so easily that even that wasn't for certain. Barbara let her ramble without interruption until Judge Laughton more or less told her to shut up.

When Mahoney got up to cross-examine her he asked brusquely, "Mrs. Corelli, just yes or no, do you know who bought that other wig?"

"I already said she said her name was Blondie and I—"

"Yes or no!"

"Well, if— No!"

"No more questions." He sat down, scowling at her.

Barbara had no more questions and Zoe was excused. She was still in the courtroom when Barbara said to the judge. "Your Honor, I would like a short recess at this time in order to make a photocopy of that entry in her records."

"Oh, dear," Zoe said from near the door. She turned and approached the front of the courtroom again. "I can't let you do that. You wouldn't believe how many people wear wigs, and it's all confidential information. They can be so sensitive about it."

Judge Laughton pounded the gavel vigorously and said there would be a short recess. He fled.

"Shelley, will you go with her?" Barbara said. "Tell her to cover everything except that one entry, and try to get back today. Get her to sign and date the copy."

Shelley, smiling widely, went out with Zoe, and Barbara turned toward Frank, who was no longer suppressing his laughter. "I'm going to follow her to San Francisco and ask her to marry me," he said.

"She's married, Dad," Barbara said.

"I doubt she'd let a detail like that stand in the way."

After the recess Barbara called Gloria Love to the stand. She was in her thirties, with a pixie face and masses of dark curly hair down over her shoulders that tended to make her face seem even smaller. She owned and operated a beauty salon in south Eugene.

"Ms. Love, do you ever arrange wigs for your customers?" Barbara asked after Gloria had given preliminary information about herself.

"Yes, often."

"Did you ever arrange hair on a wig similar to this one?" Barbara retrieved the wig from the exhibit table and handed it to her.

"Yes. It looked just like this one."

"Did it have a serial number in it the way that one does?"

Gloria examined the wig again and found the number. "I couldn't see a number in the other one," she said. "It had been covered over with a permanent laundry marker or something."

"It wasn't cut out?"

"No. You can't cut them out without damaging the lining. It was just blacked out."

Barbara took the wig back, then asked, "Will you please tell the court about that incident?"

"Well, this customer brought it in with a picture of how she wanted it to look, and I washed it and styled it for her. That's all."

"I see," Barbara said. "Do you recall when that occurred?"

"Yes. In September, the last day or two of the month. I forget the exact date."

"Did you happen to take pictures of the wig you styled?"

"Yes."

Barbara returned to her table and Shelley handed her two photographs. The wig was positioned on a closely woven wire mesh frame, a front and back view of the Cleopatra hairstyle. "Are those your photographs?"

She looked them over, then said yes.

"Did you take any pictures before you styled the wig?"

"No. Later I wished I had, but I didn't think of it in time."

The photographs were entered as exhibits.

"Are you certain the wig you styled was like this one?" Barbara asked then. She held up the wig and Gloria said yes, exactly like that.

"What was the name of the customer?"

"Mrs. Nora Wenzel," Gloria said without hesitation.

"Is she a regular customer?"

"Yes, she comes in once a week."

Barbara turned to Mahoney. "Your witness." Several rows behind him Luther Wenzel was writing furiously in a notebook. And behind him a reporter slipped from the courtroom.

"Ms. Love," Mahoney said, "if you had ten wigs that all had black human hair could you positively say which two were identical?"

"You mean if they all were alike?" she asked.

Barbara suppressed a smile. Good question, she thought.

"Let me rephrase," Mahoney said. "How can you, months

later, say that a wig you saw then is identical to one you're seeing today?"

"If I were just seeing it, probably I couldn't. But if I handled it, I probably could."

"All you can say is that both wigs had black straight hair. Isn't that correct?"

"Objection," Barbara said. "Leading question."

"Sustained."

Mahoney kept at it until he got her to admit that without having both wigs side by side to examine she was relying on her memory of one to say they were the same.

When she did her redirect examination Barbara asked, "What else do you rely on to compare two wigs, besides their outward appearance?"

"The quality of the hair, the workmanship of the wig, the quality of the lining."

"Do you remember those characteristics of the wig you styled in September?"

"Yes."

"What made them stick in your memory?"

"I never worked on a wig of such high quality before. It was the most expensive wig I ever handled."

"Is the wig we have here in court comparable in those respects to the one you styled?"

"Yes, in every way."

Barbara called Simon Ulrich next. He was fifty, stockily built, a freelance photographer whose photo essays so̶ times appeared in local, state and even national p̶u̶b̶

"Mr. Ulrich, on Halloween night this year ̶
engagement to make photographs?"

"Yes, I did."

"Please tell the court what that occasion was."

"I was hired to do a photo shoot at a masquerade party."

He gave the details of Sylvia's party and its purpose to raise money for the homeless. Barbara brought out the pictures of Nora Wenzel in her Cleopatra outfit with the wig on, and he identified them as his work.

"Did you ever photograph any other member of the Wenzel family?"

"Yes."

"Please describe that occasion," she said, expecting Mahoney to object, which he did. She assured the judge that she would connect it to the case and the objection was overruled.

"I was out on the Rogue River doing a photo shoot," Ulrich said. "I heard about a group of businessmen who were out there fishing, and I decided to get some shots. I had an idea for a photo essay about how high-pressured businesspeople relax and I thought that would work in. So I took a couple dozen shots of the men, and the group included Mr. Larry Wenzel."

Barbara showed him two pictures of the men, some of them holding fish. They were all wearing slickers and several faces were indistinct, or shadowed by rain hats. Ulrich identified the pictures as his, and explained how his stamp and numbers on the backs of them helped keep the sequence in order. He iden-
~~d a release form the men had signed allowing permission
tereo use the pictures. Larry Wenzel's name was on the
that series half a dozen other prominent local men.

hit of Larry Wenzel that had been en-
to Ulrich. "Is that a picture from

He said it was. "That was number nine of the series," he said.

Mahoney was on his feet yelling, "Objection!"

Laughton motioned him and Barbara forward.

"She's been deceiving the court, lying to a witness, deceiving the jury," Mahoney said, almost incoherently. "I move that that picture and everything connected to it be stricken."

"I haven't lied to anyone," Barbara said.

"We'll talk about this in chambers," Laughton said, tight-lipped, and clearly as angry as Mahoney.

When Barbara returned to her table she mouthed to Frank: "Chambers," and he winked at her. A recess was called, the judge stalked from the room and the jurors were led out. Instantly the bailiff collected Barbara and Mahoney to take them back to Judge Laughton's inner sanctum.

"Explain this fiasco," the judge ordered as Barbara and Mahoney stood before his desk.

"She misled the jury, pretending that picture was Joe Wenzel when she knew damn well it wasn't. That's cause for a hearing, for sanctions, maybe disbarment."

As Mahoney's anger mounted, his voice became shriller. Barbara crossed her arms and did not try to interrupt as he continued, but gazed at the wall behind the judge.

"She's been playing tricks on this court from the start. She knows Wenzel is out of it and she keeps trying to drag him in—"

"Jason, zip it!" Laughton snapped.

He looked at Barbara. "Well?"

"Neither of those women really saw the man they waited on that day," she said calmly. "Both of them doubted his signature, and both of them said he didn't look like his photo ID. What they saw was a filthy, disreputable-looking man who

was unshaved and smelled of alcohol. I never said that picture was Joe Wenzel. I asked the teller if that was the man she
saw that day and she said yes." She turned to Mahoney. "You
saw the picture and didn't raise a question. Unshaven, dirty,
messed-up hair, the description of Joe Wenzel all the way.

"Your Honor," she said, "no one else ever saw Joe Wenzel
wear a wrist brace, he wasn't at the house site drinking and
getting filthy that day, and I can't believe Larry Wenzel would
ask a drunken blackmailer to drive his wife home and wait because he wanted his advice. That whole scene was a setup from
the git-go."

"He was in Bellingham!" Mahoney yelled.

"I told you to zip it," Laughton said.

"I know he was," Barbara said. "I thought we were discussing Friday, not Saturday night. On Friday he was masquerad-
ing as his brother."

"You're the one who's been setting things up," Mahoney
muttered.

Laughton glared at him and he stopped. "I'm going to
think about this and review that bit of testimony," he said. "Are
you through with your witness, the photographer?"

"I am," Barbara said.

"I want him out of there as fast as we can move him along.
It's about time for the lunch recess and at two I want you both
back in here and meanwhile, in fact, for the duration of this
trial, no talk outside of court. No press interviews, not a word.
Do you understand? A complete and total gag order's in effect. So help me, if either of you crosses that line, I'll toss you
in jail."

34

After meeting with the judge and Mahoney at two, Barbara told Frank, "He's waffling. He hasn't decided yet, but he will before closing statements. I think he's leaning toward striking the picture." She didn't add that Judge Laughton had also said that one more such stunt from her, and she would sit the rest of the trial out in jail for contempt of court.

Frank had expected as much, but the jury had seen it and they would remember, no matter what the judge told them to consider in their deliberations.

Nora Wenzel was called to the stand. The whole family was in court again, all neat and clean and sober-faced. Elena Wenzel, Luther's wife, attended that afternoon. She was tall and slender with hair the color of ripe wheat and blue eyes, and a minimum of makeup. She looked like the perfect wife for a rising young executive. Barbara thought fleetingly that they had missed a bet, they should have brought their two-year-old toddler with them to round out the picture of a wholesome family.

Nora's pale raw silk suit with a matching blouse, and a single strand of pearls, seemed to whisper good taste and money, but she still had on too much makeup. She was sworn in and gave some brief background. She had been with the company from its start and was a corporate director along with her husband. Her voice, not as sultry as it had been in Barbara's office, sounded refined, elegant and cool. She looked Barbara over when she stood up and did not look directly at her again as she testified. She looked and sounded a little bored.

"So you were aware of the various Wenzel Corporation enterprises. Is that correct?" Barbara asked.

"Yes, I was and still am."

"Were you aware that the Cascadia Motel, restaurant and lounge had been having financial difficulties in the past few years?"

"I was."

"Were you aware of the complaint lodged by Ms. Frederick about the behavior of Mr. Joe Wenzel?"

"Yes. My husband and I talked about it, certainly."

Barbara asked her to relate what they did subsequently, and she repeated Larry's story almost word for word.

"How long did you stay in the lounge that night and listen to Ms. Frederick play?"

"We left when she took her break. We had seen quite enough. Just another showgirl who had caught Joe's eye."

"You both decided your interest in the matter was solely a business concern. Is that correct?"

"Yes. Joe's romantic affairs were none of our business."

"Do you know if your husband talked to his brother about the matter?"

"Yes. He told me he had talked to Joe."

"When did he talk to his brother?"

"I don't remember."

"When did he tell you he had done so?"

"I don't remember. That was not a pressing issue."

"Were you in San Francisco the week of July twenty-ninth to August third?"

"Probably about then."

"On July thirty did you visit a wig shop?"

"No."

"Did you buy a wig while you were in San Francisco?"

"No."

"When did you buy a wig, Mrs. Wenzel?"

"In September, right after Labor Day."

"Where did you buy it?"

"A shop in Portland. I don't recall the name of it."

"Did you retain a receipt?"

"No."

Barbara picked up the wig from the exhibit table. "Was the wig you bought like this one?"

"It looked like that."

"Did you have a fitting, need an adjustment made to the one you bought?"

"No. I just tried it on and bought it."

Barbara regarded her for a moment, then asked, "How much did you pay for the wig you bought?"

"Four hundred dollars. I paid cash."

"I see. How much after Labor Day would you say it was when you bought your wig?"

"Just a day or two. I don't remember exactly."

"How did it happen that you bought a wig at that time, Mrs. Wenzel?"

Nora had not for a moment lacked self-confidence, but she looked almost triumphant when she said, "I was on a planning committee to stage a Halloween masquerade party to raise money for the homeless. I saw the wig in the shop window and decided on the spur of the moment to buy it and dress as Cleopatra for the party."

Barbara returned to her table, leaned over and whispered to Frank, "Get Sylvia." He stood up and walked out. She turned back to Nora.

"Did you already have a picture of how you wanted the hair to be arranged when you bought the wig?"

"No. I had to hunt for a suitable picture. I hadn't thought of it before."

"Did you obliterate the serial number in the wig you bought?"

"No. I never saw a number in it. The previous owner might have done so. I don't know."

The triumphant gleam had come back to her eyes. Another gotcha, Barbara thought. "Do you mean that the wig you bought was a used wig?" She looked Nora over and raised her eyebrows.

"Yes. For my purposes it didn't matter."

"Where is that wig now?"

"I threw it in the trash after the party."

Barbara looked from Nora to the jurors, who were remaining impassive, and shrugged slightly. Not a person on that jury could have bought such a wig and then just tossed it.

"Were you on friendly terms with your brother-in-law?" she asked Nora, keeping her voice noncommittal.

"Relatively friendly."

"Did you meet him for lunch, or have him to dinner, invite him to parties, things of that sort?"

"No. It was a friendly business relationship."

"On Friday, August ninth, who arranged for Joe Wenzel to meet you at the garage and drive you home?"

"My husband suggested it."

"Does the garage provide a courtesy car for its customers?"

"I don't know."

"Do both of your sons work at the same office complex where you have an office?"

"Yes."

"Why didn't you ask one of your sons to drive you home that day?"

"My son Luther was out with a prospective client all afternoon and my other son was at a meeting." She seemed bored again.

"Did you know that your husband would be out all day?"

"We thought he would be home by the time I got there."

"Did Joe Wenzel come into the garage when he met you there?"

"No. He drove to the curb and blew the horn. I was ready to leave and went out to the car."

"What kind of car was he driving?"

"A black Lexus."

"And you had no trouble recognizing it?"

"No."

"Was that a company car?"

"Yes."

"Does your husband drive a black Lexus also?"

"Sometimes he does on company business."

"When you got to the car did you notice that Joe Wenzel had been drinking?"

"Not until I got inside."

"Did that alarm you? To be driving with someone who had been drinking enough for it to be noticeable?"

She hesitated a moment, then said, "Yes. But I was already in and he was already driving."

"Was he using vulgar language that day?"

"Yes. He always did when he was drinking."

"Why didn't you sign the check and hand it to him and take a taxi home?"

"I didn't think of it. And Larry wanted to talk to him."

"Mrs. Wenzel, your husband testified that he didn't talk to his brother when he had been drinking. Are you saying now that he would have talked to him that day?"

She hesitated again, longer this time. "I didn't know he had been drinking until I got in the car. We didn't expect him to start drinking so early in the day."

Barbara had been aware that Frank had returned, and now she went to the table to ask if he had reached Sylvia. "Another half hour," he said. "She'll be here with her engagement book." It was three-thirty.

Then, addressing Nora again, she asked, "Did you ever use the room at the motel reserved for your family?"

"No. I never was in it."

"Do you have a key for it?"

Mahoney objected and was sustained. Judge Laughton looked impatient, as if he wanted a bit of refreshment.

"Did you call your brother-in-law on Saturday?" Barbara asked. Nora's eyes narrowed and her mouth tightened. Bull's-eye, Barbara thought.

"No. I didn't."

"Did you know that Joe Wenzel owned a handgun?" she asked.

"I know he used to. I didn't know he still did."

"Were your sons on friendly terms with their uncle?"

Her eyes narrowed again. "Yes, they were."

"They didn't object or resent it that he was on a large salary and did little or no work for the company?"

"Objection!" Mahoney yelled.

"Sustained. Move on, Counselor," Judge Laughton said to Barbara.

She shrugged. "No further questions at this time."

When she sat down, Shelley showed her a note that had just one word: Botox. She grinned, then looked up to see Nora watching her the way a snake might watch a mouse. She smiled at Nora who turned away quickly. Barbara wrote her own note and passed it to Frank. *Bailey, where was Luther that day?*

Mahoney's questions were harmless. He had Nora repeat some of her statements and go into a few more details about the committee that had organized the masquerade party.

When Nora was excused, she looked as if she had won a fierce competition, and Barbara asked permission to approach the bench.

"Your Honor," she said, "I would like a short recess at this time. I have one more witness for today, one not on my witness list. She should be here any minute."

"I object," Mahoney said. "It's too late in the game to be bringing in undisclosed witnesses without time to examine their statements."

"It's Mrs. Sylvia Fenton," Barbara said. "Just to clarify some facts about the committee for that masquerade party."

"Will she be brief?" the judge asked.

"Yes. Just that one point about the committee and the timing." She looked at Mahoney. "Fair's fair," she said. "You brought in an undisclosed witness earlier. Remember?"

Laughton shook his head at her. "Enough. We'll have a recess and then call her."

Sylvia could enter her magic closet and emerge as a scrub-woman, Peter Pan, a can-can dancer, Florence Nightingale, or whatever else was demanded. She was older than sixty and probably younger than eighty, but where she fitted in between Frank had never been able to guess. He had seen her in jeans and a plaid flannel shirt, as well as a slinky black evening gown, and she wore whatever it was with a certain elan. That day she appeared to be either the queen mother, or else the grandmother on her way to church with a turkey in the oven and pumpkin pie cooling on the counter. She wore a shapeless gray suit, a gray hat with a pink flower, fawn gray gloves, sensible low black shoes and black hose. What hair showed from under the hat was snow-white, although without the wig she might reveal lime-green hair, or sky-blue, or even be bald.

When she took the witness stand, she inclined her head respectfully toward the judge, bowed slightly more toward the jury and nodded at Mahoney, then folded her hands before her and regarded Barbara with interest. She did not acknowledge Frank with so much as a glance.

"Mrs. Fenton," Barbara said, "will you please tell the court some of the charitable committees and causes you have been involved with over the past few years."

It was an impressive list: Food for Lane County, Women-space, Friends of the Library, Literacy Forum, Oasis for the

Elderly, the Red Cross… She served either as a committee member, a director or the chair. Her voice was clear and the words articulated in a way that suggested her past as an actress at one time. She had presence, Frank thought, listening.

"This past fall, for Halloween, did you organize a new fund-raising endeavor?" Barbara asked.

"Yes, I did. It was to raise money for the homeless."

"Please tell the court how that came about."

"In mid-September it occurred to me that with so many ongoing projects to raise money for the neediest among us, there was a certain lassitude setting in, a certain reluctance to subscribe to yet another cause. There are so many requests that one becomes weary of being asked over and over. Yet, with winter approaching, I worried about the homeless whose needs are so very great. I began to think of a way to interest others with the thought that once one becomes involved, that involvement often is continuing. And I thought of a masquerade party, an event that would provide entertainment and also raise money. I wanted a steering committee to help organize it, and since time was running short, I knew I could not delay. In the following few days I began calling on others to contribute time and effort, and I invited seven women to a luncheon at which time we put together the final plans."

"When did you have the luncheon meeting?" Barbara asked.

Sylvia reached into her purse and brought out a red-leather bound notebook. "I have it noted in my engagement calendar," she said, and flipped through it. "Yes. Here it is. Our first meeting was on September 23, a Monday."

"Was Mrs. Nora Wenzel among the women at that luncheon?"

"Yes, she was."

"Did you make a note of when you contacted her about it?"

Sylvia looked at the notebook again, then nodded. "Yes. I called on her at her office on Friday, September 20, at four in the afternoon."

"At that time did you tell her that you were planning the masquerade party?"

"No. I wanted to save that for the luncheon when I could get comments from everyone. I said I was organizing a fund-raiser to help the homeless, and I promised that it would not involve biweekly or monthly meetings, that it was to be a one-time event. Later, after we realized how successful it was, we decided to make it an annual affair."

"At that luncheon was the idea of the masquerade received with enthusiasm?"

"My goodness, yes. Everyone loved the idea."

"Did the women discuss how they would dress for it?"

"Some of us did. One woman said she had always wanted to be Marie Antoinette and this was her chance. I said I would be Medusa. Everyone was enjoying thinking of costumes and talking about them."

"Did Nora Wenzel mention her costume?"

"Yes. She said she would be Cleopatra. I remember that Alice Bernhan said if the rains started early she could arrive by boat."

"Thank you, Mrs. Fenton," Barbara said. "No further questions." Sylvia inclined her head in a little bow and turned her bright gaze toward Mahoney.

"Mrs. Fenton," he asked, "did you talk about this idea with anyone when you first thought of it?"

"Yes. I talked with my husband. He thought it a splendid idea."

"Do you know if he discussed it with anyone else?"

She smiled slightly. "My husband never discusses anything with anyone," she said. One or two of the jurors smiled as if they knew all about such husbands.

"Do you have a secretary?" Mahoney asked.

"Yes."

"Did you discuss the party idea with her?"

"Of course I did. She helped with the names and telephone numbers, and she saw to the invitations."

"Did you talk it over with her before mid-September?"

"Before I even thought of it? Of course not."

"Is it possible that with such a novel party idea, she might have mentioned it to others?"

"Absolutely not. She is my confidential secretary. She has been with me for twenty-seven years."

"Since the party was not going to be a secret, isn't it possible that she might have spoken of it without breaking a confidence?"

"Sir," Sylvia said, drawing herself up straighter, "a confidential secretary *never* discusses an employer's business. She would cut out her tongue before she would mention a thing that is said between us."

And that was the queen mother asserting herself, Frank thought, and doing a damn fine job of it, too. She looked haughty and as regal as hell.

Mahoney shook his head and made a slight waving of the hand gesture, as if to say he knew better, but he sat down with no more questions.

When they left the courtroom, the Wenzels were being photographed and asked questions by half a dozen reporters. One of them broke away and approached Barbara. "What are you suggesting with that business about the wig?" He motioned to a photographer who began to snap their pictures. Carrie ducked her head.

"Sorry," Barbara said, and drew her finger across her lips as she stepped between the photographer and Carrie. "No comment. Judge's orders."

"They're giving a regular press conference. Don't you want to answer them?"

"Can't," she said and moved on. None of the Wenzels paid any attention to her group as they headed for the stairs.

35

Day after day Barbara had watched the hollows under Carrie's eyes darken and deepen and her appetite decrease almost to the vanishing point. Dr. Minnick had written a prescription for sleeping pills and Carrie had accepted the small container silently, but Barbara was certain she had not used any of the pills yet. After dinner that night she said, "Tomorrow it will be Greg Wenzel's turn on the stand, and very likely by afternoon I'll call you. Are you up for it?"

Carrie nodded. "I just want to get it over with." She sounded as dispirited as she looked.

Barbara told Shelley to go on home early that night. The ducks were in a row and she had to prepare her closing remarks, but that was solitary work and, when done, she would try it out on Frank, the way he had always tried out his closing remarks on Barbara's mother. He was a good listener, and a very good critic. Another late night was coming up, she knew, and got to it. But when she finally left the upstairs office for her bedroom, there was a tracery of light under Carrie's door.

Carrie was writing feverishly. Disjointed memories of Carolyn's: an elevator with Mommy and Daddy holding her hands, an airplane ride, a special cushion she could use on the piano bench so she could reach better, Mommy playing on a stage with a lot of people clapping… It seemed to Carrie that by admitting that Carolyn could be her elusive, mostly invisible, twin, she had breached a dam, first allowing few memories through, then more and more until it had become a torrent of Carolyn's memories, given to her in dream states, in flashes, in brief scenes without beginnings.

Try as hard as she might she could not dredge up a memory of riding in a truck with her father and mother, of seeing him paint houses, of camping out, sleeping in a tent.

Now and then a nightmare brought her wide awake, shaking, freezing cold and sweating at the same time. The nightmares were always about fires and hospitals, doctors, loud noises and pain. In the past, when the nightmares bedeviled her she could get in her car and go somewhere else and put them to rest with new scenery and a new job. Now all she could do was sit up in bed shaking, waiting for daylight, waiting for the trial to end, for something new to start, either prison or freedom. She yearned to get in her car and drive forever.

When Greg Wenzel took the stand the next morning, Carrie stared at him fixedly. He was very handsome, with thick dark hair, and apparently a great body. But it wasn't his good looks that held her gaze. She had seen him before, she thought, a long time ago. Barbara led him through preliminary questions: he lived with his parents in their home, and he was employed by the Wenzel Corporation, and he had gone to the Cascadia lounge with his brother to look over the piano player. That was it, Carrie thought. She must have seen him there briefly.

"When did you go watch her play?"

"I don't remember. A week after my folks did, probably."

"Was it while they were in San Francisco?"

"I think they had returned. My brother and I went on a Sunday night and they were home by then."

"How long did you stay at the lounge that night?"

"Not long, just until her break. It would have been rude to walk out while she was playing."

"So she took her break and left and that's when you got up and left also?"

"Something like that." He paused, then said, "Actually, I think it was when she finished playing for the night. Twelve, something like that."

"Had your parents talked to you about the complaint she made to Mr. Ormsby?"

"They mentioned it. That's why I wanted to see her for myself."

"Was your brother present when they discussed it with you?"

"I think so."

"Was it in the nature of a family problem, something you all felt you should deal with?"

Mahoney objected and was overruled.

"We were all concerned about the business," Greg said.

"Did your father mention that he had talked to his brother about the complaint?"

"I don't remember if he did."

"Do you recall when you had the family discussion about it?"

"I don't remember what day it was. Before they went to San Francisco. That's all I remember about it." He glanced toward Carrie, then hurriedly looked away and squirmed in the witness chair as if he were finding it uncomfortable.

"Mr. Wenzel, do you have a key to the room at the motel that is reserved for your family?" Barbara asked.

"Yes, I do."

"When was the last time you made use of that room?"

Mahoney objected and was sustained.

"Did you ever lend your key to anyone else?" Barbara asked.

Mahoney objected again, and Barbara said quickly, "I believe it is of interest to know if that room was entered on the night Joe Wenzel was murdered."

The judge overruled and Greg said no, he never loaned the key to anyone. "I keep it in my possession all the time," he said.

Barbara saw one of the jurors writing a note, then pass it to the foreman of the jury. He motioned the bailiff and handed him the note, and the bailiff took it to the judge. Barbara waited.

Judge Laughton read the note, nodded to the foreman, then said, "Ms. Holloway, Mr. Mahoney, the court will have a brief recess. Please, don't leave the courtroom." He walked out and the bailiff led the jurors out.

Barbara looked toward Mahoney, who shrugged and held out his hands in an *I don't know* gesture. She returned to her table.

It was a very brief recess. Everyone filed in again, the judge sat down and motioned Barbara and Mahoney forward. "One of the jurors has lost a crown," he said. "She has to see a dentist today, and I'm going to recess until tomorrow morning. We don't want a juror with a throbbing toothache, or one filled with novocaine." He looked resigned.

That afternoon Barbara and Frank worked in his study while Shelley worked in the upstairs office on the files. Carrie wandered through the house, now and then stopping to gaze at a steady rain. She picked up the newspaper to work the crossword puzzle, put it down, then picked it up again to read about the Wenzel family. She glanced at the picture of all of them posed in the courthouse, started to turn to the continuation, then looked again at the photograph and caught in her breath sharply. She was holding the pencil she had been using for the puzzle, and slowly she drew a circle around the head of Gregory Wenzel. Crowned, she thought distantly, as the world seemed to fall from around her.

She dropped the pencil and the newspaper and clutched the edge of the table, taking one long breath after another until the world settled once more. Then, moving like a somnambulist, she stood up and walked upstairs to her bedroom.

In her mind's eye she was seeing another photograph, the king and his warriors standing by a truck, the king with a crude crown drawn around his head. This was what crazy meant, she thought then. Schizophrenia. You can't tell what's real and what isn't. That couldn't have been Greg Wenzel in that old picture, yet in her mind they were the same, now and then all the same.

She sat on the side of her bed for minutes, seeing that old picture from her father's briefcase, and she drew in another sharp breath. Not her father, Carolyn's father. Real, fantasy, real...

Pain in her hands brought her back from a swirling maelstrom of images and thoughts, and she looked at her palms.

Her nails had dug in, there were droplets of blood. She stood up and pressed a tissue in her hand, then, holding it tight, she went to the closet and took out the box that held the folder Barbara had put her papers in after photocopying them—birth certificate, school records, medical records, the newspaper article about the deaths of her parents, their death certificates...

She returned to the bed and examined the picture of her mother and father, tracing their faces with her forefinger. She had worn a white blouse and a long black skirt when she played on the stage. Carrie shook her head violently. After a moment she looked at the birth certificate, then the death certificates, and she whispered, "It's a lie. All of it. It's a lie!"

Moving again like a sleepwalker she got up and found her manicure scissors in her makeup bag, and carefully she cut the picture of her parents from the article, then put the article and everything but the picture back inside the folder. Holding the picture, she lay down, overcome by an exhaustion deeper than any she had ever known.

Carolyn couldn't sleep. There was too much to think about and morning wouldn't come. She got up again to look out the window for a sign of daylight, and she saw someone fixing Daddy's car even though it was still dark with only a dim outside light. She moved the curtain aside for a better look, and he looked up at the window. The king, she thought with excitement. Then he closed the car and ran out the driveway to another car that sped away with him. She'd have to tell Daddy the king came and fixed his car while everyone was sleeping. But it was still dark and she went back to bed, thinking about a little sister, and riding a horse, and seeing the king....

* * *

Carrie rolled over and plunged the rest of the way into a profound, dreamless sleep. Her hand relaxed and the picture fell to the floor. There was a drop of blood on it.

When Barbara went to bed that night at two, there was a tracery of light under Carrie's door.

The Wenzels were in court again, and there were several reporters present in expectation of seeing Carrie testify. Greg returned to the stand and was reminded that he was still under oath, and they started.

"Mr. Wenzel, where were you on the night your uncle was killed?" Barbara asked, curious to see if Mahoney would object. He didn't. He had no objection to Greg stating his alibi apparently.

"I left the house at about eleven to join friends in town," Greg said confidently. His whole statement was said in the same confident way. "I met them at the Steelhead and we had a little to eat, and then went on to a couple of other places. At about two I drove Mattie Thorne and Tina Jacoby home. Mattie asked me in and I went in with her and stayed until about three, and then I went home and got there at around ten minutes after three."

"Are you certain of those times, Mr. Wenzel?"

"Yes. I waved to the security guy at our place and happened to notice that it was ten after three. It's about a ten-minute drive."

"Are you certain you left Ms. Thorne's apartment at three, not at two twenty-five?"

He smiled slightly and nodded. "I'm sure. She wanted me to stay longer, but I wasn't feeling too good and said I had to take off. I noticed the time because I was hoping my mother would be asleep when I got home. She would have been upset if she knew what time I got there since I'd been feeling bad earlier."

"Did you have the key to the room in the Cascadia Motel with you all that evening and night?"

"Sure. I always kept it in my wallet with me."

"Did you ever see the wig your mother bought last summer?"

"Yes. I thought it was neat."

"Do you recall when you saw it?"

"I think late in September."

She regarded him for another moment, then turned away. "No further questions."

Go for it, Mahoney, she thought as she sat down.

He did. "Mr. Wenzel, you say you saw that wig late in the month of September. Is that right?"

"Yes, sir. She had just bought it."

"Can you be more specific about the date?"

Greg frowned in thought, then said, "Well, it must have been around the twenty-fourth or twenty-fifth."

"What makes you recall the date?" Mahoney asked.

"I was out of town that weekend. I left on Friday the twenty-seventh, and I saw it a day or two before I left."

Mahoney nodded. "No further questions," he said, well satisfied.

Barbara stood up again, frowning at a clipping in her hand. "Mr. Wenzel, are you certain about those dates?" she asked, holding the clipping.

"Yes, I am."

"I have a newspaper clipping here from Ashland, Oregon," she said, showing it to Mahoney, then to the judge. "It states that Mr. and Mrs. Larry Wenzel were in Ashland from September 24 to September 26 to celebrate the opening of a theater complex the Wenzel Corporation built." She handed it to Greg, and he read it slowly. He looked at the spectators, at his family, then away quickly. "Is that article correct?" she asked.

"I think the dates must be wrong," he said. "Articles get the dates wrong a lot of times."

"Or is it possible that they drove back from Ashland and raced up to Portland in time to buy a wig for you to see before you left town?" She didn't try to hide the sarcasm, and Mahoney objected and was sustained.

She took back the clipping and handed it to the clerk, then started to return to her chair. As if an afterthought had struck her, she faced Greg Wenzel once more. "Mr. Wenzel, on the night of August 10, after you left Ms. Thorne's apartment, did you make a detour before driving home? Did you drive to the Cascadia Motel?"

"Objection!" Mahoney yelled. "Irrelevant!"

He was overruled.

Greg had appeared frozen at the question. His confident smile vanished and for a moment he looked very young and frightened. He shook his head after a quick glance at the spectators. "No. I told you I went straight home and got there at ten minutes after three."

"No more questions," she said. She looked at Greg again and shrugged slightly.

After Greg was excused she called Carrie. She had been worried about Carrie for days, and the previous night her concern had grown considerably. Carrie had appeared remote, pale and withdrawn, had hardly said a word and had eaten only a few bites. The same mood had persisted that morning at breakfast, and now she looked even more remote, almost catatonic.

She was sworn in and took the witness chair, then asked to state her name and spell it.

"Carolyn Frye. *C-A-R*—"

"Objection!" Mahoney called out, enraged.

Barbara felt almost as if she had been socked in the mid-section, and she heard Frank make a grunting sound. There was an eerie silence in the courtroom for a moment, then a reporter left as the judge motioned Barbara and Mahoney forward. "The court will be in recess," he said brusquely. "Chambers, immediately," he snapped at Barbara.

36

When furious, Mahoney turned red. Enraged as he was that day in the judge's chambers, his face looked ablaze. Judge Laughton, in contrast, was icy cold. Fixing Barbara with what looked like a prosecutor's going-in-for-the-kill penetrating gaze, he demanded, "Just what the hell are you pulling?"

"She's been manipulating the court from day one," Mahoney said bitterly, "manipulating the evidence, the jury, and now her own client. You can't change horses in the last hour of the last day—"

"Mahoney, I advise you to speak when I ask for a comment and to be quiet until I do," Laughton said. "Ms. Holloway, I warned you that one more stunt would be the last. You're in contempt of court. Do you have an explanation?"

"Yes, I do. I didn't know Carrie would say that. As of yesterday she still didn't know she was born Carolyn Frye. I hoped her amnesia would last until the trial was over."

"You knew she was here under an assumed name?"

"Your Honor, I met her as Carol Frederick, known as Carrie. I saw documents to that effect, her birth certificate, parents' death certificates, medical records, school records, her driver's license, everything. All issued or made out to Carol Frederick. In the course of my investigation I learned that her birth name was Carolyn Frye, but she had amnesia for the first years of her life and she believed her name was Carol Frederick. I don't know when she came to know the truth. I haven't had a chance to talk to her."

"Bah!" Mahoney muttered. "Why didn't you inform the prosecution or the court?"

"Mahoney, I'll throw you out if you butt in again," Laughton said.

To Barbara he said, still icily, "You came into court knowing that? Why didn't you inform the court?"

"I feared for her life," Barbara said.

Mahoney made a strangled, inarticulate sound and she turned on him. "I had cause to fear for her. Her parents were killed by a car bomb when Carrie was a child. There was an attempted arson fire at my office building, and I was sent a bomb. There was reason to be afraid for her. I've had her under twenty-four-hour guard ever since I learned her true identity."

Laughton drew in a long breath. "Both of you, sit down, and Ms. Holloway, you'd better start back further. Who is Carolyn Frye?"

They drew two straight chairs closer to the desk and sat down. Then Barbara said, "She is the daughter of Robert and Judith Frye. Her father was a staff assistant for our former senator, Jerome Atherton. Her mother was a concert pianist. Robert Frye was on a fact-finding mission for the senator and due to deliver materials to him on a Saturday at his ranch near Pendleton. But on Saturday morning a bomb exploded in his car, here in Eugene, killing him and his wife instantly, and critically injuring their seven-year-old daughter, Carolyn. When she woke up, she was in a Boston hospital with a new identity and a new set of parents. Her surviving relatives were told she had died from her injuries. They were given a death certificate and an urn of ashes identified as Carolyn's."

Laughton's face never changed its expression, but he leaned back in his chair and held up his hand for her to stop. "Jesus Christ," he said. "Are you saying she was put in a witness protection plan?"

"Yes. That's what it looks like."

"None of that has anything to do with this trial," Mahoney said. "If any of that is even true."

Laughton didn't look at him. After another moment or two, he leaned forward again and said, "You know that's going to be spread in every newspaper in the state, maybe beyond, by tomorrow morning. I'll have to sequester the damn jury." His expression was baleful when he said to Barbara, "I have to make arrangements for the jury, and I have to talk to them, tell them something— God knows what. Then I want you back here with that documentary proof of her identity, and I want a complete report of what you learned and an explanation about why you didn't disclose it sooner. Half an hour. Back here in half an hour."

"Your Honor," Mahoney said stiffly, rising as he spoke, "I believe we have cause here for a mistrial."

"I don't know if we do or don't yet," Laughton said. "We'll discuss it in half an hour. I will recess until Monday morning, give us time to sort this out."

* * *

Back at her table, Barbara said, "After the judge calls for the recess, I want Bailey to take Carrie to a safe place. Don't go to the house first, just get to a safe house. Stay with her, Shelley, and when we're done here, I'll call your cell phone and find out where you are. And you have to get in touch with Louise Braniff. They'll mob her as soon as word gets out."

"Can she go to wherever Bailey takes Carrie?" Shelley asked.

Barbara looked at Carrie who was unmoving, as remote as a statue, and nodded. "Why not? Bailey can pick her up, too. But after he hides Carrie. Carrie, are you all right? Do you need something? A drink of water, anything?"

"No." She sounded as remote as she looked.

"As soon as I'm done here, I'll pack some of your things and come to where Bailey takes you and we'll have a long talk. Will you do what Bailey and Shelley say? Cooperate with them?"

"Yes."

"Okay, that's it, then. Alan can come pick me up when this is over."

"And me," Frank said. "I'll stick with you for this next interview with the judge."

At his table, Mahoney was having his own spirited talk with his assistants, two of them now, and a reporter in the rear of the courtroom was speaking on a cell phone. He hurried out.

It was closer to forty-five minutes than half an hour before they were escorted back to Laughton's chambers. He had removed his robes and today he wore a blue chambray shirt with the sleeves rolled up partway and Dockers pants with a stain on one knee. Barbara introduced Frank, and he pulled a chair in closer to the desk between hers and Mahoney's.

"Now," Laughton said to Barbara. "Start from the beginning, if you will."

She started with Louise Braniff's visit and being retained. She took various photocopies of certificates and the newspaper article from her briefcase and handed them to Laughton. He studied them all carefully, then put them aside.

"Didn't she make an effort to tell people who she really was?" Laughton asked.

"She did. She had multiple surgeries and therapy that included a lot of anesthesia. Months were spent in that state when she was incapable of saying much of anything. The hospital personnel believed she was Carol Frederick, age eight and a half, and diagnosed amnesia caused by post-traumatic stress. They discounted whatever she said about a different life as a childish fantasy. Her foster parents believed the same thing. All those adults, plus paper proof, were more than she could counter. Her foster mother told her she was crazy and that crazy people were put in hospitals, and she had developed a phobia about hospitals. The memories of her former life had to be denied. Since she couldn't remember a truck or a painter father, an itinerant life and, according to the birth certificate and what everyone kept telling her, a whole year and a half were a blank, she had to accept amnesia. She was only seven, even if everyone thought she was eight and a half. She had no defenses."

"And overnight she made a miraculous recovery," Mahoney muttered. "Right."

Barbara ignored him and said to the judge. "I don't know yet how much she remembers. Today she looked like someone in a state of shock. I believe the FBI created the new identity for her, and that they must have had reason to think she was in danger. Her aunt believes that, and I've come to believe it also. I didn't want to get into any of that while the trial was underway. I was told by a psychologist that she should be under a doctor's care if her memory started to come back, that whatever she remembers now may be as traumatic as the explosion she experienced. It could be that the stress of the trial itself was a trigger for her memory, but I don't know."

She was choosing her words carefully, confining them to Carrie and excluding any mention of what she had learned about the Wenzels. That was for a different set of investigators.

"So who's on trial here?" Laughton said. "The woman named Carol Frederick, or Carolyn Frye?"

Frank had been listening without a word, but now he said, "Judge, I've been doing a bit of research into case law for a book I'm planning to write, and I've come across other instances where a person on trial was found to have more than one name and identity. I have numerous cites. Ten or twelve, I believe. They cover a range of procedures that were followed." He extracted a folder from his briefcase and put it on the desk. "The preference seems to be to follow through with the name the accused was using when arrested unless that name was taken to avoid prosecution or for some other ulterior purpose."

For a moment Barbara thought Laughton looked grateful, but the moment passed swiftly and he nodded to Frank. "I'll look them over during the weekend," he said. "Meanwhile, nothing that was said here today is to be repeated outside. God knows the media will have a circus, and I don't want to add to their sideshow." He was looking fixedly at Mahoney as he said this. Mahoney nodded.

"Do you require police protection for yourself or for your client?" he asked Barbara then, surprising her.

"Thank you, Your Honor. I believe the security we've been providing is sufficient."

"The gag order is in effect until further notice," he said. "I don't know yet how we'll proceed, but I will know by Monday morning. We'll discuss it at eight on Monday. And you all know as well as I do that the courtroom is going to be a madhouse by then." He sighed. "Anything else for now?"

Mahoney said stiffly, "If the case can move ahead exactly as it started, with Carol Frederick accused of murdering Joe Wenzel, I don't see that any of this other matter is an issue for this court. There's no reason to bring it up at this time."

"I agree," Barbara said. "I had no intention of bringing it up before this court." She couldn't have stated the truth more clearly.

In the judge's outer office Barbara hit the speed-dial number for Alan's cell phone. "Where are you?" she asked when he answered on the first ring.

"Circling the courthouse, on Eighth at the moment."

"Okay. We'll be at the Seventh Avenue entrance in two minutes. See you there."

She hit the number for Shelley, who was just as fast to answer.

"Where are you?"

"Sylvia's house."

Barbara blinked in surprise, but it was a good place to hide someone, with more security than Fort Knox. "Okay. Where's Bailey?"

"He's meeting Louise Braniff at three, then heading out here with her."

"Good. I'll have him pick me up, too. How's Carrie?"

"I just don't know," Shelley said in a worried tone. "She's sitting down and not doing a thing, just sitting there."

Barbara bit her lip. "Okay. We may have to get her to a doctor, but hang on until I get there."

Frank nudged Barbara's arm and motioned toward the door. Time to leave. She hit Bailey's number as they walked.

"Where are you?" she asked him when he answered. He said a coffee shop in the university area.

"Okay. After you get Louise Braniff come by the house for me. I'll be waiting."

"There are reporters at Braniff's place," he said. "There'll be others at your old man's house."

"We'll deal with them there," she said. "I'll tell Herbert to sic the dog on them or something."

The rain was hard and steady when they reached the door to Seventh, where a reporter hurried to Barbara's side. "Hey, what's going on? How did Carolyn Frye turn up all at once? Where's she been? She was supposed to be dead."

She shook her head. "No comment. Sorry. There's our ride."

Drenched in the short sprint to Alan's car, she brushed rain from her hair and wiped her hands on her coat. "Dad, I really owe you this time. A hug and a kiss and even a box of chocolates when I have time to get it. Thanks. I didn't dream she'd do that."

He squeezed her arm. "Neither did I, but it's good to be prepared, just in case."

She told him the plan, then asked, "Are you going out to Sylvia's with us?"

"Nope. I'm going to stay home and guard my castle with Herbert and Alan." He sounded grim, and she knew he wasn't thinking of bombs or arson fires. He was thinking of the reporters.

* * *

By the time Bailey arrived with Louise Braniff, Barbara had packed enough clothes for Carrie for the next few days, and was ready to leave. "Reporters," she said to Bailey. He nodded glumly, then slouched away to talk to Herbert.

"Ms. Braniff," Barbara said then, "apparently Carrie has recovered enough memory to know her name. I don't know how much more yet, not until I talk to her. But as you saw, the press is hot on the trail. She's in hiding, and I want to take you to her and keep you away from the media for the next few days, if you agree."

"With her?" Louise asked. She was pale and anxious. "Is she all right? Not in danger?"

"Not where she is, but we have to keep her out of sight until this is all over."

"Of course. I don't have anything with me," she said hesitantly.

"I'm sure your hostess will be able to provide whatever you need." She looked past Louise to Bailey, who nodded.

"We'll wait five minutes, then take off," he said. Morgan began to bark, and Bailey nodded. "Right now, bet Herbert's saying that if anyone gets out of a car on the property that dog will take off a leg or head." He nodded again when they heard Herbert's truck start in the driveway and leave. Bailey looked at his watch.

Minutes later they were in Bailey's SUV heading first toward downtown, then he turned onto Fourth Avenue, a street barely wide enough for two cars. At the Lincoln Street stop sign he said, "Two of them. Thought there might be more. Here we go." He made a left turn, and Herbert's truck pulled up to the narrow entrance to Fourth and came to a stop, blocking it. Bailey drove to Sixth, turned, then made several more turns, and finally got on the Jefferson Street bridge. The rain was heavy and steady, traffic was slow, but he seemed unconcerned as he headed toward Springfield, then made another turn and was on the interstate. "Home free," he said.

Half an hour later he stopped at the gate to Sylvia's estate south of Mt. Pisgah, told the man on duty his name, waited for the gate to swing open and drove through. It was an awesome estate, thousands of acres of forested hills, then a manicured lawn, a swimming pool covered for the season, many gardens, all meticulously maintained, and finally a big house with several levels, and a portico out front.

Outside, the grounds were all professionally maintained and could have been exhibited on the cover of *Horticulture,* but inside the house was all Sylvia's doing. Picasso and Miró cheek by jowl with calendar art, a few stark portraits of grim-faced bearded men, and God alone knew who they were, side by side with photographs by Ansel Adams or Weston, priceless Ming vases and depression glass bowls. Every wall was covered, and every flat surface held surprising objects, some very fine art, or kistch that might have been won at a state fair midway.

Sylvia met them at the door and seized Barbara in an embrace. "I can't tell you thanks enough," she said. "You are an angel. My very own angel. Where is Frank? Don't tell me he didn't come. Bailey, I did well, didn't I? I did good work. You'll have to call me more often, you foolish man. I work cheap and I do a good job for you."

Barbara extracted herself and introduced Louise Braniff, who was looking awestruck at the clutter all around, or possibly at the sight of Sylvia. Her hair was canary-yellow that day and she wore black silk pajamas with a scarlet sash.

A young woman in black pants and a white sweatshirt was standing patiently behind Sylvia. "Tanya will take your coats and put them somewhere to drip," Sylvia said. Smiling, Tanya stepped forward to take the coats. Over the years that Barbara had known Sylvia and visited in her house, she had come to realize that without exception all of her servants adored her.

"Now, do you want refreshment first, or to go directly to Carrie and Shelley?" Sylvia said then.

"Carrie," Barbara said. "I'd like to talk to you a minute after I see her, of course."

"Well, of course," Sylvia said. "And you'll want some lunch. All of you." She looked at Tanya. "Dear, will you tell Dorothy we'd all like a little snack soon." She started to walk down the wide hallway, motioning for Barbara and Louise to follow. "I thought she might be comfortable in the music room," she said. "But the poor child, I don't think she'd be comfortable anywhere right now. Come along."

They passed other rooms, all showing the same kind of clutter. Then Sylvia stopped at a door and tapped lightly before opening it. Inside, on a green velvet-covered sofa Carrie was sitting with her hands in her lap. She didn't look up. Shelley stood up when they entered, and she looked very relieved to see them.

"Carrie," Barbara said softly. "You have company."

Carrie turned toward them, and for a moment she didn't move. Then she jumped up and held out a hand. "Gramma!" Her face underwent a change into that of a child afraid that Santa would take back the new toy, then changed again to disbelief. Louise dropped her purse and ran across the room and took Carrie in her arms. Carrie leaned into her and started to weep as Louise stroked her hair.

Barbara backed up a step, another, turned and almost pushed Sylvia ahead of her out the door. Shelley came after them and closed the door behind her.

37

Barbara said she would give them an hour and while she waited she picked at the sumptuous spread that Sylvia's cook had provided, and assured Sylvia that her performance in court was first-rate, Academy Award stuff. Sylvia beamed.

"But where on earth did you get that outfit?" Barbara asked.

"Oh, I keep a few things on hand so that when Bailey lets me work I'm ready to go. Tell him to let me work more often, Barbara. There must be a lot of things I could do."

"I'm sure there are," Barbara said. Sylvia's husband had joined them, and he beamed even broader than Sylvia. Frank often said that Joseph Fenton was the happiest man in the state, as well as being one of the richest. "Do you mind if she does detective work?" Barbara asked him.

He shook his head. "It makes her happy," he said, as if no more needed saying.

Barbara glanced at her watch again. Ten more minutes. "Sylvia, over the next day or two would you mind getting some pictures of Carrie, something suitable for a passport. They need to be a certain size, I forget just what."

"Done," Sylvia said.

When the time was up, Barbara and Shelley returned to the music room. Sylvia wanted to tag along, and Barbara shook her head. "Lawyer business."

Carrie and Louise were sitting side by side on the green sofa, Louise holding Carrie's hand. Their faces were both tear-streaked.

"We have to talk a few minutes," Barbara said.

Louise started to stand up and Carrie held her hand tighter. "You can stay," she said.

Barbara nodded, and she and Shelley sat down in chairs near them. "Can you talk about it? What happened to make you remember?" Barbara asked.

"It was seeing Greg Wenzel on the stand. I kept thinking I'd seen him before," Carrie said. "Then I saw his picture in the newspaper and it looked like a picture from a long time ago." She told about it haltingly, seeing the picture, seeing the man at her father's car.

She ducked her head. "It hit me that that's who I am, their child, their daughter, and I didn't tell him someone tampered with his car. It's as if that's what the whole trial is really about. I didn't tell him. It, whatever happened, was my fault because I didn't tell him. I've been running away from it all my life and I had to stop running."

Louise put her arm around Carrie's shoulders and drew her close. "You were only a baby," she said.

"Everything people told me was a lie," Carrie mumbled. "I don't know why they did that. Why didn't they let me go back to Aunt Louise and my grandmother? Why did they lie to me and act as if I was crazy all those years?"

Barbara leaned in closer. "They thought you overheard something or saw something that put you in danger. They did it to protect you. The people in the hospital, Adrienne and Stuart Colbert, they all were lied to as well. They thought you were Carol Frederick." She drew in a breath. "Did you see something or hear something that might have been incriminating to anyone?"

"A picture," Carrie said after a moment. "From my father's briefcase. Men around a truck with a circle around the head of one of them. I thought he was the king. I heard my father say he had the king, and I thought that's who he meant."

"Did you recognize that man, then or later?"

"I don't know," Carrie said. "When I saw Greg Wenzel's picture in the newspaper, I thought he was the king, and I thought I really was crazy because he's too young."

"Okay," Barbara said. "We don't know what the judge is going to do on Monday. We hope he'll let the trial go on with you continuing as Carrie Frederick. If he does, can you go through with it knowing what you know now?"

Carrie looked at her in dismay. "You mean I have to pretend my past doesn't exist, doesn't matter?"

"I mean that no one will mention anything to do with the time before you were on an airplane heading for Terre Haute. Just as we would have done if you hadn't remembered. We can't mix up that past with the present trial or we could end up with a mistrial and you'd have to go through it all again."

A long shudder rippled through Carrie. She hesitated, then nodded. "I'll do whatever you tell me to. I just want it over."

"Good girl," Barbara said. She turned to Louise. "There are Robert Frye's relatives in Los Angeles. They'll hear the news or read about it. Can you get in touch with them and let them know what's happening? They'll be besieged by reporters just as everyone here will be."

Louise nodded. "Of course. I'll call."

Driving home again, Barbara said they might as well take Shelley home first, while they had the reporters at bay. "Have you had a chance to find out where Luther Wenzel was on Friday before Joe got himself killed?" she asked Bailey.

He gave her a mean look. "I think Sylvia had a point," he said. "She wants to be my partner, help with all my cases. She could disguise herself as a secretary, learn a little shorthand, work her way into the corporation, make a play for Luther, and get him to tell all. It's an idea."

"Okay, okay," she said, scowling at the rain. "When this is over, I'm going to take my gear out to the coast and walk for a hundred miles, rain or no rain."

"I could stop and let you get started now," Bailey said.

"Don't tempt me," she muttered. "This is going to be a weekend out of hell."

That night she found the newspaper picture with Greg Wenzel's head circled and showed it to Frank. "That reminded her of a picture her father was going to take to Atherton," she said. "She thought she recognized the man with the crown, but it's Greg, who looks remarkably like his father at that age."

"Not enough," Frank said. "The word of someone who had

amnesia many years, and was only seven when she saw it. They'd crucify her."

"I know," Barbara said. "We still know too much and don't have enough."

The weekend was as hellish as she had predicted. They turned the ringer off the telephone, but reporters came and Morgan barked and, according to Herbert, bit two reporters and one photographer. "Good old dog," he said. "I warned them."

The story of Robert and Judith Frye's deaths was spread out in the newspaper on Saturday, along with photographs of Carrie and Barbara's team, and more pictures of the Wenzels, with a fuller account of the trial than had appeared before. They had found old pictures of Judith and Robert, and Carrie as a child. There was no mistaking it, Carrie Frederick was really Carolyn Frye. There was the long black hair even then, and the bold horizontal eyebrows. She had been a beautiful child. The attempted arson at Barbara's office and the bomb stories were replayed, and there was much speculation about what it all meant.

One article even suggested that terrorists might be involved. The sordid little trial in a backwater town had become the media circus that Judge Laughton had foreseen.

It was worse on Sunday with headlines asking who had kidnapped the seven-year-old Carolyn Frye. A tabloid had picked up the story and had stringers in the area. Bread-and-butter item for them, they reveled in stories about little girls missing, abused, or killed. They had already interviewed Adrienne and Stuart Colbert. That headline: "Foster mother always suspected a conspiracy."

Barbara talked to Louise, who had been in touch with

Robert Frye's relatives, and who said the story was in the Los
Angeles papers. Robert's brother planned to arrive in Eugene
later that day. Darren called on her cell phone and asked if
there was anything he could do, and Barbara said, "Stay away
or they'll invade your house and rampage through the clinic
with questions."

On Monday Bailey collected Shelley and Carrie and they
all headed for the courthouse. Barbara had pleaded with Louise not to attend or risk being mobbed, and Carrie had urged
the same thing. Reluctantly she had agreed.

Barbara's group was instantly surrounded when they got
out of Bailey's SUV. Flashbulbs, questions, a dozen microphones, hordes of media people, curious bystanders made it
almost impossible to work their way through to the upper-
level courtroom, which was filled to capacity already. Shelley and Carrie took their places at the defense table, and
Barbara and Frank went to the judge's outer office. Mahoney
was already there waiting. He was wearing what looked like
a new suit, and his previously unruly ginger hair was neatly
cut and styled.

Judge Laughton was brusque that morning. He nodded to
Frank. "Your cites proved very useful. Thank you. The trial
will proceed as it started. I will explain to the jury that people often take pseudonyms for legitimate reasons, particularly
performers, and that your client—" he nodded to Barbara
"—misunderstood the question and believed she was required
to give her birth name when sworn in. For the duration of the
trial she will be addressed as Carol Frederick, and no mention is to be made of her previous existence before she was
placed in foster care." He went on to say that he wanted the

trial to proceed with all due speed, no grandstanding, no histrionics, no stunts. He kept his sharp gaze on Barbara as he said that. Also, he said, he would strike the photograph of Larry Wenzel and it could not be referred to again. That was a case of misleading a witness, and as such was inadmissible.

"Do either of you have anything to say?" he demanded then.

Neither of them did. "Then we will get on with it and, again, I'm telling you both, I want this trial concluded with all speed. Ms. Holloway, I am providing an escort for your client as she enters and leaves the courthouse. I don't want a bloodied or maimed defendant in my court. Do you require police protection for her overnight until this is finished?"

"Thank you, Your Honor," Barbara said. "I appreciate help in getting her in and out of the courthouse, but I believe we can manage afterward."

Barbara had a brief talk with Carrie, and then the jury returned, Judge Laughton took the bench and Carrie was called to testify. When asked her name she said in a clear voice, "Carol Frederick."

She had lost that zombielike appearance, and was composed and attentive. She answered Barbara's questions without hesitation, and gradually her life with foster parents, and then of roaming from city to city, state to state was revealed. She described some of the jobs she held along the way: waitressing, housecleaning, flipping hamburgers… She had no credit cards, had no debts, had never been arrested or stopped by the police, never had a traffic ticket… She owned a fourteen-and-a-half-year-old car, a few books and clothes, nothing else.

She told how she had lost her job in Las Vegas, about talking with Delia Rosen and deciding to drive to Eugene with her.

"When you were in Las Vegas, where did you work?" Barbara asked.

"Circus Circus, in the family restaurant."

"Is that the kind of restaurant where dinners are under ten dollars, where children are allowed?"

"Yes. Most dinners were about seven or eight dollars, some were less."

"What were your hours there?"

"From three until eleven, six days a week."

"Did you ever see Joe Wenzel in Las Vegas?"

"No."

Gradually Barbara led her up to the time she had complained about Joe Wenzel. "Did you make an effort to complain more than once?"

"I tried," Carrie said. "I was told two times that the manager was unavailable and couldn't see me."

Barbara had her describe her tips and what she was doing with the money she made, and finally asked her to tell what happened the night Joe was killed. It was straightforward, exactly what she had told Barbara months earlier.

"You say he was talking crazy when he accosted you as you were going to your car. What did he say?"

Carrie looked at her hands on the stand before her and said in a low voice, "He called me a bitch and a slut. He said I would learn that it didn't pay to play games with him, to fuck around with him."

"Then what did you do?"

"I hurried on to my car and got inside and locked the door. He was holding the handle when I started the car, then he let go, and I drove to my apartment and got ready for bed and went to bed."

Barbara asked her several more questions: Had she ever talked to Joe Wenzel, encouraged him? Had she ever called him on the telephone? Had she ever carried her own glass away from the piano? Did she always tie up her hair after playing? Did she always put on hand lotion when she was through for the night?

"Why didn't you use the lotion when you took a break?" she asked.

"It would have left lotion, or traces of lotion, on the piano keys, then dust or dirt would have collected on them. I wouldn't have done that."

Two and a half hours after calling her, Barbara said, "Thank you, Ms. Frederick. No further questions."

The judge called for the luncheon recess after Barbara sat down. Two uniformed police officers escorted the group through the mob of media people out to Bailey's SUV, and they went home, followed by several cars. None of the photographers or reporters ventured out of their own cars at the house. Morgan was on duty.

Neither Barbara nor Carrie ate much lunch. Carrie lay down for an hour, and Barbara walked up and down stairs, back and forth in the upper hall, then up and down stairs some more.

When Carrie rejoined them, they all told her she had done a wonderful job on the witness stand, and she smiled faintly. "Now comes the real test," she said.

"Honey," Frank said, "I doubt Mahoney will be as rough on you as I was."

Actually, they agreed later, Frank's words had been well chosen. Mahoney was brutal in some of his questions, but Carrie maintained her composure and answered steadily. Frank had prepared her well.

38

Once, years before, Frank had said to Barbara, "You have to wonder if you've done enough, if you should have called another witness, asked another question or two, cleared up a point that might be ambiguous today. And you will wonder that in ten years, or twenty, or however long you practice law. But you have to remind yourself that the other side is probably having the same doubts. And the answer is always yes, you might have done more, but this is where you are and you have to go with it."

And that was where she was, on the last day, prepared to make her closing statement.

The media was swarming like flies at a dead fish, she thought, when the police escort parted a path for her group the next morning. The courtroom was filled to capacity again, and she spotted Luther in the back row. Scribble, scribble, she thought at him. The jury filed in, the judge took his place and they began.

Mahoney started in a low, almost mournful key. "Ladies and gentlemen, this is not a complicated case, no matter how many complications the defense has tried to introduce. We can't know what lies in anyone's heart, all we can judge by is the factual evidence before us, and the facts of this case prove that Carol Frederick is guilty of the crime for which she stands trial."

He made the same case the newspapers had made months earlier. Carrie was homeless, a drifter, penniless and she saw a chance to enrich herself by a thousand dollars and seized it. Something went wrong, and Joe Wenzel ended up shot to death and the money gone.

"We know why Joe Wenzel wanted cash that weekend. He told his brother he intended to buy the defendant's favors. This was in keeping with all that we know about Joe Wenzel. Is this what he told the defendant when he followed her to her car? We don't know. We can only surmise. She got inside her car and he walked away. Did she then sit in her car thinking about a thousand dollars and what it meant to her? Her old car needed tires, and it needed major work. A thousand dollars could have been the difference between repairing her car and continuing her wandering life, or working for many more weeks weighing every penny. Minutes later she was seen entering his motel room. What happened inside that room is something else we don't know and can only surmise. He was known to be abusive to women when he was drinking, and he had been drinking that night….

"We know she was in the room. Fibers that matched her clothing were found there. Her hair was found there. And her glass was found in the room with her fingerprints on top of the bartender's fingerprints. She was the last person to handle that glass and she took it with her when she entered Joe Wenzel's room that night, and she left it there."

He talked about her assault on a customer in Las Vegas. "There's nothing in the police records about that incident," he said. "No one pressed charges, and that often is the case, but it demonstrates that she could turn violent. She did become violent at that time."

He said that she could have seen Joe Wenzel in Las Vegas, that she might have come to Eugene with the purpose of finding Joe Wenzel. That was more likely, he said, than believing that it was all a coincidence, their being in Las Vegas at the same time, her finding a job at a motel he owned jointly with his brother and attracting his attention there. But even without that background, the facts of the murder itself more than satisfied the requirement of the law to find her guilty as charged.

He dwelt on the matter of the cash she had when arrested, and the facts that she had put two new tires on her car, and that her rent was paid through the month, and he claimed that her tips alone could not account for her expenditures.

He talked for an hour and a half and concluded by saying, "This is a simple case of murder, committed for one of the oldest motives—greed."

After a short recess Barbara stood up. "Ladies and gentlemen, any case can appear simple if two conditions are met. The first is a rush to judgment, and the second is that if no hard questions are asked and answers demanded. In this case both conditions have been met. One week after Joe Wenzel was murdered, Carrie Frederick was arrested and assumed guilty.

There was a rush to judgment. The second condition has also been met. Once guilt is assumed the questions stop, and that is exactly where they should have started in earnest. Since the prosecution did not ask the questions and demand answers, it will be up to the defense to pose them and up to you, the jury, to determine if truthful answers have been forthcoming.

"Let us consider the question of the thousand dollars," she said in a conversational tone. "Joe Wenzel had more than fifty thousand dollars in the bank, he had received an electronic transfer of fifteen thousand dollars on the first of the month. There was no need for a check, for a drive to his brother's house to take Nora Wenzel home, and then a dash back to the bank to cash the check and withdraw the cash. The only statement we have heard concerning the request for that money and the reason came from his brother.

"Both employees of the bank questioned his signature, and it was excused on the basis of a wrist brace that made writing difficult. No one else ever saw him wear a wrist brace, not his former wives, no one at the motel or lounge, not Mr. Vincent, the architect who had been with him on a daily basis for weeks. His brother's statement that he sometimes used such a brace is the only testimony relating to it.

"And where did the wrist brace go after that visit to the bank? It was not among his possessions in his room inventoried by the police following his death.

"When he visited the safe-deposit box, he had the key to it but, like the wrist brace, the key vanished afterward. It was not among the possessions inventoried in his room.

"Both bank employees questioned his appearance, which they said was unlike his photo ID, and that was excused on the basis of being an old photo in which he had been neat and clean, and they testified that the man they saw was disheveled, dirty, unshaved, ten years older than the man in the photo, and that he smelled of alcohol. His driver's license was not in the inventory the police made following his death.

"Where would Joe Wenzel have accumulated so much dirt that Friday? He had not been to the house site where Mr. Vincent waited for him all day.

"The security questions they asked Joe Wenzel were of the sort that anyone who knew him well could have answered."

She referred to the calendar she had been filling in and, pointing to it, she went over the dates. "There is the question of when Mr. Larry Wenzel could have talked to his brother about the complaint Carrie made."

She gazed for a moment at the jurors, all intent, all impassive, and said slowly, "You have heard a great deal of conflicting testimony during the past two weeks, sometimes so contradictory that answers have been on the order of black *and* white, or yes *and* no. In each instance you will be required to ask yourself which answer to accept, which witness to believe when both can't be right. That will be your task."

She moved to the night of the murder then. "Carrie was never known to have taken her glass with her when she had a break, or when she finished playing for the night. When she was seen walking toward her car, the witnesses saw her shoulder bag with her right hand on it, and they saw that her hair was up in a ponytail. They did not see a glass. The two witnesses who saw someone enter Joe Wenzel's room did not see a shoulder bag, and that person's hair was loose. The right hand was on the door frame, the other one presumably on the doorknob and they did not see a glass. They could not identify that person as Carrie Frederick. All they saw was long black hair, a white blouse, and a black skirt, and they would not have seen that much if that person had not made a noise loud enough to attract attention."

She paused a moment. "After being hired to play the piano at the lounge, Carrie bought three white blouses and two black skirts at Wal-Mart, inexpensive garments available from most discount stores. She took them home and immediately washed and ironed them. The fabric fibers found in the motel room still had the manufacturer's sizing, the finishing they put on all new garments, which is removed when the clothing is laundered. The fibers could not have come from her clothing."

She talked about the hairs on Joe Wenzel's coat. "I ask you, ladies and gentlemen, to consider the hairs on the coat. Is it plausible to think that Carrie would have entered that room, would have gone to that closet and pulled hairs from her own head violently enough to damage or pull out the follicles on a coat hanging there? Of course not. They were pulled out when Joe Wenzel got too close to her as she played the piano, and she jerked violently away. He wore that coat on his early visits to the lounge, and then stopped wearing it, and it hung in the closet from then on with the hairs caught on the button.

"And consider the other hairs in that room. You heard the foremost expert talk about those hairs. They were cut from a human head, or else from a wig made of human hair. They were not pulled out or broken off. They did not have traces of arsenic, and Carrie's hairs do have traces of arsenic. Those cut hairs were not from Carrie's head. He also said that the only way to state positively whether hairs that look similar are actually the same is to do a DNA test. No chemistry test was conducted, no DNA test was ordered."

She looked at the calendar again. "There was a wig, you'll

recall. First, a wig of long black human hair was bought in San Francisco on July 30 by a woman who called herself Blondie, and paid two thousand two hundred dollars. The wig had a serial number sewn into it. According to testimony, Mrs. Nora Wenzel spent the week of July 29 to August 3 in San Francisco. Again, according to testimony, Mrs. Wenzel bought a similar wig in Portland a day or two after Labor Day for four hundred dollars and paid cash for it, but she no longer remembers where she bought it and she did not keep a receipt. That wig had a serial number obliterated by a permanent ink laundry marker. It was delivered to a hairdresser toward the end of September. Ms. Love stated that it was of exceptionally high quality, in all respects like the wig purchased for two thousand five hundred dollars which you have seen in court. Looking at the calendar, we are faced with several questions. Mrs. Wenzel learned about the masquerade party on September 23, and before that date she had no need for such a wig. On the following day she and her husband drove to Ashland where they remained until Thursday evening, September 26. Their son, Gregory Wenzel, saw the wig before he left town for the weekend on the morning of Friday, September 27. The question is when did Mrs. Wenzel have time to go to Portland and purchase the wig? Not after Gregory Wenzel returned home, not if he saw it before he left and said it was neat, but also by then it was in the hands of the hairdresser."

She paced back and forth for a time then as she talked about fingerprints. "There are a number of puzzling things about where fingerprints were found and where they weren't found," she said. "Carrie's fingerprints were on a glass that had a residue of bourbon in it. No one ever saw Carrie drink alcohol at the lounge and, as she testified and also told the bartender, she can't drink alcohol because it makes her sick, except for a very little wine with a meal. Her glass was left on the table by the piano three times at least each night she played, after her two breaks and when she finished for the night. It was not in the bartender's sight constantly. At any of those times it could have been removed by anyone. You have to ask yourselves if it makes any sense for her to have carried it out, to have taken it to her car, and then to have taken it back to Joe Wenzel's room and to have left it for the police to find. But someone put it there, and that person was careful not to smudge her fingerprints. And the fact is that not a single fingerprint of hers was found anywhere else in the room.

"Also, consider that Carrie always put on hand lotion when she finished playing for the night, not before then since she did not want to leave traces of lotion on the piano keys. There were no traces of lotion on the glass with her fingerprints on it. There would have been if she had handled it after she finished playing that night.

"But there are other puzzling details. The person seen entering the room had one hand on the door frame, where no fingerprints were found, although the fingerprints on the doorknob were smudged, not wiped clean. That suggests that that person was wearing gloves that smudged the fingerprints on the doorknob and left none on the door frame. Since gloves were not seen from twenty-five or thirty feet away, they must have been clear or flesh-colored latex gloves or something of that sort. Or else you have to assume that someone carefully cleaned the fingerprints from the door frame and simply smudged the ones on the doorknob.

"Also, the gun was wiped clean of all fingerprints. Why, if the killer was wearing gloves? That suggests that there were other fingerprints on the gun that had to be removed. The briefcase was wiped clean. Why? If Joe Wenzel had taken it to the bank, his fingerprints logically would have been on it, but if someone else had handled it there might have been other fingerprints on it.

"And where was the gun when Joe Wenzel went to Las Vegas? He couldn't have taken it with him in a carry-on. His house burned and his belongings were all consumed by the fire. No gun was found at the site. His two ex-wives testified that he kept the gun locked in a desk at home. How did it turn up in his motel room?"

She talked about the Maid Service card on the door. "Joe Wenzel had never put the card on his door. He had never left his room before twelve or later. Why put the card up that night? If the usual routine had been followed, and the room not entered until one or later, the time of his death would have been reckoned as between midnight and 4:00 a.m. or later in the morning."

She went on to Greg Wenzel's testimony. "On the night of the murder, Gregory Wenzel joined friends shortly after eleven and remained with them until two in the morning. After that time he drove Ms. Thorne and her friend to their apartments. Then he entered Ms. Thorne's apartment with her, arriving there at about fifteen minutes past two. So far their two stories, Ms. Thorne's and Mr. Wenzel's, coincide. Then they deviate. According to Ms. Thorne, Greg Wenzel left before two-thirty, and she was ready for bed and turned off her light at two-thirty. According to Mr. Wenzel, he left her apartment at about three in the morning and drove straight home, arriving there at three-ten. Both stories can't be correct. Black is not white. Yes is not no. He either left before two-thirty and arrived home forty-five minutes later, or else he left at about three and arrived home ten minutes later."

She examined their faces one by one, then said, "If you can see no reason for Ms. Thorne to have misspoken or misread her clock, then you have to ask where Greg Wenzel was during those forty-five minutes."

She turned away and walked a few steps, then faced the jury once more and said briskly, "From testimony we know that Gregory Wenzel had a key to an empty room across the hallway from Joe Wenzel's suite. The maid couldn't tell if anyone had entered and spent time in it. We know there was a wig bought by Mrs. Nora Wenzel, and that Gregory Wenzel saw it before the hairdresser arranged it and he pronounced it 'neat.' We know that hairs were cut from a human head or from a wig made of human hair and left in the room where Joe Wenzel was killed. We know that Joe Wenzel lived high, that he lived in a company house, drove a company car, and for the last weeks of his life lived in a company-owned suite at the motel. He traveled first-class and stayed in first-class hotels for months each year. If you see a pattern of misstatements, events or dates that cannot be recalled exactly, conflicting testimony, you have to ask in each and every instance which person testifying might have had cause to be evasive or claim a faulty memory."

She paused again, then said more slowly. "Also you have to ask yourselves if a mother would charge one son with looking after the other when they were both healthy and robust, starting out in life with no signs of alcoholism and with no signs of such a problem in their family history. The father of Larry and Joe Wenzel was a workingman, devoted to his church, with no drinking problem when a tragic accident took the life of the boys' mother. When would she have made such a demand? Why would she?

"And ask if Joe Wenzel was an alcoholic. No one ever saw him pass out from drink or lose control of himself. The medical examiner said his organs were healthy with no sign of disease such as cirrhosis of the liver, which afflicts alcoholics. The medical examiner testified that Joe Wenzel had been a healthy man with a slightly oversized heart and a bit overweight. Obviously he was not a man who needed looking after.

"Two of his ex-wives testified that when he was drinking he resorted to vulgar language, but also that he had never been physically abusive.

"Why would his brother paint such a contradictory picture, label him an alcoholic who needed looking after, and one who abused women?

"These are not insignificant questions, ladies and gentlemen. These are all questions that should have been asked and answered long before an arrest was made."

She turned to regard Carrie for a moment, smiled slightly at her, then faced the jury again.

"Carrie Frederick is not on trial because she is homeless, or because of her lifestyle. We would grant a young man the right to roam all over the country, to see as much of it as possible, and we have to grant the same right to a young woman. She has been self-reliant and independent ever since she graduated from high school with honors. She has never asked for government help in any form. An accomplished pianist, she could have settled down anywhere she chose, but she chose to see the country first.

"You heard her testify about the night of the murder, and there's nothing more she can add to it. She did not enter that room. She did not murder Joe Wenzel, and she had no motive to do so. She has no expensive habits, she doesn't drink alcohol or smoke cigarettes, and she does not do drugs. Everything she owns fits into her car...

"When she repulsed a drunken customer's unwanted embrace, that was not an assault. That was a woman protecting herself, and when Joe Wenzel made unwanted advances, she lodged a complaint with the management."

Barbara looked at each juror in turn finally and said, "Carrie did not murder Joe Wenzel, but someone went to great lengths to cast the blame on her. The fibers that were not from her clothing, the hairs that were not from her head, the glass with her fingerprints, all placed in the room where murder was done were acts of deliberation intended to incriminate her. After hearing the testimony presented these two weeks, if you have any doubt about her guilt, you must find her not guilty. Any reasonable doubt is sufficient to find an accused person not guilty. And in this case there is overwhelming doubt.

"Did the investigators satisfy the requirements of their task to put to an end all such doubt? I say they did not, ladies and gentlemen. She is not on trial because she is homeless, a stranger in this city, friendless and penniless, but those facts played a part in her arrest. And they played a part in the superficial investigation that was conducted. A deeper and more thorough investigation would have exonerated her because she is innocent. Thank you."

39

That night, after turning off the light, Barbara stood at the kitchen window gazing at fog, thinking about patterns. The winter weather had a pattern: a front moved in from the Pacific Ocean bringing storms to the coast, torrential rain to the Coast Range, rain to the valley, snow to the Cascades, and when the rain ceased, fog followed. A day or two of some sun, some clouds, then another front blew in to repeat the pattern. Indoors, warm and snug, it was easy to admire the fog, softening every sharp edge, blurring every object, shrouding every light, but she always felt chilled by it, no matter how warm the room, and she always felt threatened by it. A result, she suspected, of early conditioning through the books of Conan Doyle, or other British writers who hid menaces in the fog of moors or London.

She was thinking of the pattern trials took as well as

weather. The prosecution presented a case, the defense answered, both sides made a plea to the jury to understand and agree with their arguments, the judge instructed the jury, and then everything stopped while the jurors did whatever they did in seclusion.

They had entered the foggy period, she thought, when things were obscure and concealed and all she could do was wait, chilled and apprehensive.

For her this was one case of many that she would try, winning some, losing some, but always free to move on to the next. For Carrie it was the difference between exoneration and freedom, or many years in prison with a future forever clouded by what happened in the next day or two. It was an unsettling thought, that if she had not done enough, if she had failed, another person's life would be destroyed. She wondered if that burden was not too much to take on over and over, if gambling with another person's life was not too big a risk for one's own peace of mind.

She heard footsteps and turned to see Frank in the doorway. He came to her side. "It's hard," he said. "You do your best but you always have to ask if it was enough, if you were up to it."

She nodded.

"You did your best, Bobby. You did a damn fine job, and I'm very proud of you." He put his arm around her shoulders, drew her close and kissed her cheek. "Go on to bed. Get some rest. You've earned it."

"If we get a hung jury, I don't think any of us can stand this kind of siege for six more months waiting for a new trial," she said.

He knew which two jurors she suspected would not agree

to acquittal. Sometimes they made up their minds almost as soon as the trial began and never budged. Sometimes there was the attitude that innocent people did not end up in a courtroom accused of criminal acts. "Let it go for the night, Bobby. You've done what you could do. No one can ask for more than that." Except the one who stood worrying about not doing enough, he added to himself. That one could always question if he or she had done enough.

She had warned Carrie about how it would go: they would have to appear in court, the judge would ask the jury if they had reached a verdict, they would say no, and everyone would leave, then return at closing time to be dismissed for the day, or else be called back if the jury signaled that they were ready to deliver their verdict. A waiting game, she had said lightly. Routine.

"I talked to Sylvia last night," she told Carrie, "and we agreed that your aunt should come and help you wait. Sylvia will send a car with her to the mall and she'll take a taxi from there to her house to pick up a few things, and then come over. We don't want anyone to connect Sylvia with our secret hideaway if we can help it."

Carrie's face brightened. "She can have the other bed in my room. I'm so glad, Barbara. Thanks."

Everything followed the routine Barbara had described that morning, to a point. When they left the courtroom, Frank detoured for a minute to speak to Lt. Hoggarth, who had been waiting, then rejoined them and the police escort to Bailey's SUV. Inside, underway, he said, "There are a few things for Barbara and me to attend to at the office so we'll go there, and Shelley and Carrie can go on to the house."

"Your office or hers?" Bailey asked.

"Mine," Frank said.

Barbara gave him a sharp look, but asked no questions. He would have told more if had wanted to.

"What's up?" she asked after Bailey deposited them at Frank's office building and they were in the elevator.

"Hoggarth," he said. "I don't know why, but he wants to talk to you. I said I'd deliver you to neutral ground."

"Your office? Neutral? He must be desperate if he went for that."

Lt. Hoggarth was in the waiting room already when they entered the outer office. He stood up and followed them down the corridor toward Frank's office. When they passed the receptionist, she looked startled to see Frank, and a moment later Patsy, his secretary, stuck her head out of her own office and looked overjoyed to see him, then cast a reproachful glance at Barbara, and a disapproving look at the lieutenant. Frank waved to her, and motioned Barbara and Hoggarth to enter his own office with him.

It was an impressive office, big, with windows on two walls, another wall of glass-fronted bookshelves, comfortable seating around a coffee table on one side and his spacious desk, as clean and polished as metal, on the other. He nodded toward the coffee table and chairs, then said, "What can I do for you, Milt?"

"Not you," Hoggarth said. "Her." He eyed Barbara curiously, and shook his head. "Have you seen today's paper yet?"

She sat down in an upholstered chair. "Nope. What's Doonesbury up to these days?"

"You'll think Doonesbury when you get a look. The Wenzels plan to sue you to hell and gone. Slander, besmirching their reputation, malicious lies, false accusations, God knows what all."

Barbara grinned. "I got me a mouthpiece, dude. Let them sue."

"Way it plays back in the office is that you practically came out and accused the kid of conspiring to kill his uncle, hiring a gun, furnishing the key to the room, the wig, everything."

She laughed outright. "Is that right? Is that what you came to tell me, a summing up of my case and that I'm going to get sued?"

He shook his head, then sat down opposite her. "A different mission."

"First," she said, "tell me something. I mentioned a while back that you might want to put that bunch under surveillance. Ever get around to it?"

"You know how shorthanded we are?" he said bitterly.

"Okay. Just asking. What's your mission?"

He was poker-faced when he said, "Two guys are in town who want to talk to your client. The D.A. said he couldn't produce her, that she's under your wraps until the trial is over. He got in touch with my captain and he said that since we have a good relationship, I should approach you and arrange a meeting."

"They want to talk to Carrie? Why? Who are they?"

"They want to talk to Carolyn Frye," he said, still expressionless. "One's from the Mexican Federales, the other one's a homicide captain from California State Special Investigations. And I don't know a damn thing about why they want her." He looked at Frank. "For God's sake, what's going on? I feel like a messenger running around with a stick of dynamite and I don't know why, or if the fuse is lit. How did Carolyn Frye come back to life after all those years?"

Barbara and Frank exchanged a glance and she shook her head slightly. He shrugged. "It's her show."

"I thought it might be," Hoggarth said, frowning at her. "What are you up to?"

She held up her hand, then stood up and walked across the office and stood with her back to Hoggarth and Frank. When she turned around again, she said, "Lieutenant, let's make a deal."

He groaned.

She sat down again and leaned forward. "It's simple enough. Quid pro quo. Tit for tat. You want something, I want something."

"What do you want?"

"I want Carl Laudermilch. In my office today. You can come along if you want."

"You're nuts," he said. "I can't get Laudermilch to come at my beck and call. FBI, remember? They're got other things to do these days."

"No," she said. "You're wrong. I can't get him, but you can. Just tell him what you told me and tell him it's in his interest to come see me. And as I said, you can tag along and listen in."

His eyes were narrowed as he watched her closely, shaking his head. "What do I get except a visit to your place?"

"After I talk to Laudermilch, bring along your new friends and we'll have a long talk. You can sit in on that one, too. Otherwise, I'll see them in private. In any event, they can't see Carrie."

"We have ways to get her," he said.

"And we have ways of fighting you. She doesn't have to talk to anyone she doesn't want to see, and I will defend her right to refuse an interview."

"Jesus Christ!" he said after a moment. "You want too much. No deal."

"Then beat it. I have things to do."

He glowered at her, looked at Frank and got no help there, and glowered at her some more. "Supposing Laudermilch is in the area, and God knows he could be in Washington, or Kuwait, or on the moon, but supposing he's around, when?"

"I don't expect the jury will bring in a verdict today, but you never can tell. Any time, the sooner the better, just so I'm free to get back to court by four-thirty or five without interrupting a conversation. Maybe Laudermilch early, that talk won't take long, and the other two right after him. You have my cell phone number. That's the only phone I'm answering these days."

Hoggarth stood up and went to the door where he turned and said, "You keep walking back and forth across that line, but one day you're going to go too far across and find yourself without a way to get back." He left.

"Just what the devil are you planning?" Frank asked as soon as the door closed.

"I want a passport for Carrie, and Laudermilch's going to get it for her."

Frank shook his head. "Like the man said, you'll go too far on the wrong side of that line one of these days."

She was already on the phone calling Bailey for a ride home.

They stopped at her bank where she retrieved the tape of Nora and Joe talking, just in case, she said to Frank. At the house she examined the photographs of Carrie that Sylvia had made and added them to her briefcase with two of the tape recorders and an extra cassette, and then she waited.

Hoggarth called at eleven-thirty. "Your office, twelve-thirty," he said brusquely. "It's his lunch hour."

"And mine," she said. "We'll be there."

* * *

Carl Laudermilch was the most elegant man Barbara had ever met. That day, wearing a gray worsted suit, discreet maroon tie, mirror-polished shoes, with his gray hair neatly trimmed, his fingernails buffed, he looked more like a high-level banker than an FBI district chief. His manners were as impeccable as his clothing. He shook hands with her and Frank, inquired about their health very politely, then sat down and crossed his legs.

"I'm afraid I don't have very much time," he said. "As you know we are quite busy these days."

Barbara nodded. "I understand. Sometimes, Mr. Laudermilch, with the pressure of national and even international catastrophes piling up one on another, it is too easy to overlook single individuals. But I have to call your attention to just such an individual and her particular needs at this time, and hope you can alleviate a severe problem."

He smiled slightly, an ironic smile that acknowledged that she was playing his game along with him. "And those needs are?"

"I want a passport for Carolyn Frye, and I don't want her to have to wait for many weeks or months for it to work its way through the maze."

"I see," he said. "I'm afraid that's not really in my job description."

"Mr. Laudermilch," she said, smiling, "make it your job. Okay? You can understand my dilemma, I'm sure. If she isn't free to leave immediately after the trial, I'm very afraid that the tabloids will get to her, and maybe Larry King or someone like that. A desperately injured little girl kidnapped by the FBI, hidden away, denied access to her loving relatives, labeled insane when she insisted her name was Carolyn Frye and not the name assigned to her by a government agency. An ugly story, but a heartbreaking one, you'll agree. Pictures of her at the age of seven. A few tears when she talks about her pain and loneliness, never knowing what happened to her parents or why she was being so cruelly punished." She shook her head. "The FBI has come under such fire recently, such a story could only fan the flames."

He regarded her with the same ironic smile. "The alternative?"

"She has a passport, off she goes to a distant land without giving any interviews. In time the story fades into oblivion. Fifteen minutes of fame, isn't that about the limit of the public attention span?" She stood up and found the pictures of Carrie in her briefcase and held them out toward him.

He made no motion to take them. "I'm not sure that anyone could do what you want these days."

"Come now. You have people who can fake birth certificates, death certificates, send ashes to a grieving family. This would seem very minor in comparison." She tossed the pictures on the table and sat facing him again. "If I go the other route, Mr. Laudermilch, I'll go all the way. Articles, interviews, a publicist, maybe a book contract, bodyguards. It won't be for just fifteen minutes."

After a moment he reached for the photographs and studied them. "What name is the young lady using these days?"

"Her real name. Carolyn Frye."

He slipped the photographs into his pocket and stood up. "Ms. Holloway, it's always a pleasure to see you. Frank, Lieutenant, I'll be off now. I'll be in touch." Frank walked out with him.

"Jesus," Hoggarth said. "Blackmailing the FBI in front of a police officer. That's going too far."

"So turn me in." She looked at her watch. "What time are the other two guys going to show up?"

"One-thirty."

Frank rejoined them and she asked if Bailey was still there. "Let's send him out for something to eat," she said. "It's going to be a long day."

"Herbert was making a carload of sandwiches. That would be fastest," Frank said. "He can go round up some for us. I'll put on coffee."

"What makes you think she'll be free to go anywhere?" Hoggarth asked.

"They aren't going to convict her," Barbara said. "It's either acquit or a hung jury. If it's hung, the D.A. won't push for a new trial."

"Ha! So you think."

"No. They won't. You're going to see to that."

He stood up, then sat down. "First the FBI, now a cop. What's the threat and or the bait this time?"

"You'll see before the day's over."

40

Frank called Herbert and told him to get enough sandwiches for five ready for Bailey to pick up, he was on the way. Barbara unlocked her closet, brought out the easel with the Georgia O'Keeffe poppy and replaced the maps on the other side. Milt Hoggarth sat silently, his face a study in suspicion.

When Bailey returned and put a box of sandwiches on the table, Barbara picked up her briefcase and motioned to him and they went out to the reception room.

"Take whatever you want to eat into Shelley's office," she said. "I want you to make a copy of this." She brought the tape from her briefcase, the tape recorder and the blank tape. "But wait until we're all in my office with both doors closed. No noise. Okay?"

He shrugged. "It's going to be a lousy copy," he said, eyeing the tape recorder.

"I'm not after high quality," she said, "just so it's audible. We'll keep the original."

"I thought you weren't going after that gang until the trial was over," he said. It wasn't really a question, but it was close enough.

"That could still be the plan. It depends on what those two guys want to talk about and how much they already have." She turned to Maria, who had been as happy to see her as Frank's secretary had been to see him. "Have something to eat," Barbara said. "After two men come, no calls, no interruptions unless it's Shelley. She'll call if we have to go back to court early."

Then she went into her own office, sat down and ate her lunch.

The two investigators were prompt, arriving almost exactly at one-thirty. Captain Jon Diebold was a massive man of about sixty, over six feet tall, broad, with white hair, a deeply weathered and tanned face, and blue eyes that seemed too small for such a large face. His companion Carlos Romero stood inches shorter and was stocky, with thick black hair and limpid big brown eyes.

Hoggarth made the introductions and after they were all seated at the round table, Barbara said, "What can I do for you?"

Diebold took the lead. "Ms. Holloway, my colleague and I are conducting a joint investigation and we have reason to believe that Ms. Frye could be of help. We are here to ask permission to interview her."

Barbara shook her head. "You know we are awaiting a jury verdict at this time. I'm afraid your request is not possible."

"Look, if she can't help us, two minutes are all we need. If she can, twenty minutes. We're not here in an adversarial posture. Simple questions and either she has answers or she doesn't."

"I'm really very sorry, but this is not a good time. Ask me your questions. Maybe I can help."

He drew back as if she had offered to bite him. "I'm afraid not," he said.

Romero leaned forward then. He had been watching the exchange intently, and she suspected his big brown eyes saw things that eluded the little blue eyes of the captain. Softly Romero said, "Perhaps you can help, Ms. Holloway." His English was flawless with an attractive accent. "We are conducting an investigation into the death of her father, and her mother, of course. But primarily into her father's death. We believe that Ms. Frye, as a small child, may have seen something or heard something that would help in our investigation."

Slowly, choosing her words with care, Barbara said, "In 1978 Robert Frye was on the staff of Senator Jerome Atherton. He was assigned to look into a letter the senator had received concerning possible cross-border slave labor. Or perhaps something else entirely. Before Robert Frye could deliver the results of his investigation he was murdered. Carolyn Frye was seven at the time. Of what assistance could she be now, gentlemen?"

Romero nodded. "Your senator has never admitted to such an investigation, Ms. Holloway."

"I know. And he is still denying any knowledge of it, but you know and I know that what I said is true."

"Yes. It is true. Perhaps if I tell you a story, you will be so kind as to reciprocate and tell me another?"

"I think that would be a fair exchange," she said.

"Many years ago," Romero said, "in one of our small villages near your border there lived a widow, her seventeen-year-old son Juan, and her eleven-year-old daughter Martica. They were poor, but Juan had found a source of income. Two, three times he had gone north to work, sometimes for a week or two, or perhaps months. He sent money home, or brought it when he returned, and he brought his little sister small gifts. One was a Polaroid camera. She was very proud of it. One morning she set out with him to bid him goodbye, as he was leaving again for more work. She asked him this time to please bring her back a certain doll. He promised that he would. She took a Polaroid picture of him at the pickup place, along with others in front of a truck, then she stood and waved until the truck was out of sight. He never returned.

"When her mother saw the picture, she was very afraid and she took it away from Martica. The person who arranged for the workers to find jobs was gone, the police were corrupt, there was no one to ask for help, and the mother took her daughter and moved from that place after many months passed and Juan had not come back. None of those workers who left with him ever came back.

"In time, six years later, the mother died and Martica found the picture in her Bible. She had learned enough English that she could write letters, and she wrote for help, not from her own police because she knew that evil things happened to people who suspected how corrupt they were. She wrote to some of your senators and to a governor. One senator sent an investigator who found Martica and won her confidence. She gave him the picture which he found exciting because it had a license plate that was partially visible. She circled the head of the man who drove the truck. There was also a woman, but in the picture she was turned away and her face was not photographed."

No one moved or made a sound as he talked. Now he spread his hands and shrugged expressively. "She never heard from the American again. He, of course, was Robert Frye. In her village they did not get American newspapers. She knew nothing of his death. She came to believe that he was as corrupt as her own police, and her fear grew. She fled that part of the country and settled in Puerto Vallarte where she found work, married, had a family and tried to forget. Many North Americans travel to that part of the country and their newspapers follow. She saw the story about Robert Frye on Sunday, and this time she went to the police. I am the result. It was decided that I should try to interview Ms. Frye immediately before she vanishes once more."

"Thank you, señor," Barbara said. She stood up and crossed the office to the easel with the poppy and turned it to reveal the map of Southern California. Romero sucked in his breath and stood up and Diebold jumped to his feet. Both men hurried to her side to look, with Hoggarth close behind.

"How did you get that?" Diebold demanded.

"Let's sit down and I'll tell you," Barbara said, returning to her own chair. She told them about her interview with Inez, then the investigation her own team had made. When she finished there was a prolonged silence until she broke it. "If you will excuse me a moment, I'll see if we have coffee." She saw that Maria had anticipated her, as usual, and looked past her to Bailey.

"Did you make a copy that's audible?"

"Not great, but you can hear it and understand," he said, handing her the tape.

She took it and the tape player, asked Maria to bring in the coffee and returned to her office, holding the door for Maria following closely behind her.

Then, as they sipped coffee, she played the tape. Hoggarth's face turned redder and redder as he listened. When the voices stopped, and Jerry Garcia was strumming the guitar again, she turned the tape player off and Hoggarth exploded.

"Jesus Christ! You've been sitting on that? How long? How did you get it?"

"Lieutenant, you're an observer, remember? You don't have a role to play here yet."

"I believe we have much to talk over," Romero said softly.

She nodded. "I believe we do."

Later, with the picture Inez had given her of the Wenzel brothers and their wives with their truck, and the newspaper picture with Greg Wenzel's head circled on the table, she said, "That picture of Greg is what made her remember the rest of it. She thought that was the man in the picture from her father's briefcase, a man she thought was a king, and then realized it couldn't be. She saw him, the man who looks like Greg, doing something to her father's car during the night. And that's all she knows. She can't be a witness. A defense attorney would rip her to shreds. Post-traumatic stress, possible juvenile schizophrenia, amnesia. She would not be a credible witness."

"But may we take a statement from her, even if no one ever calls her to testify?" Romero asked. "Perhaps she can recall a number from the license plate. Martica, alas, cannot."

"She has not mentioned such a number. She was interested in the man she thought was a king, and she was only seven. I believe she is in grave danger. The man at the car that night knows she saw him, and he knows she overheard a conversation. All these years he believed her to be dead, now he knows she's alive. My duty is to protect her."

"I'll put her under police protection," Hoggarth said.

After a moment Barbara nodded. "After the trial, and only if she agrees. She will need a few nights of rest first."

Romero bowed his head slightly. "Thank you. You had a piece, I had a piece, now we have a picture."

"Yes," Barbara said. She looked at Diebold. "And your part? How did you, a captain, get involved?"

He was looking at the map, and kept looking at it when he said, "I was a rookie in the group sent to investigate that. I found one of the bodies. They had been there for weeks, months maybe, nothing human about them, nothing recognizable. When I heard the Mexican authorities were making inquiries and had the right date, that it might be reopened, I wouldn't send anyone else. I had to take it myself." His voice dropped lower. "None of them had a hat or even a cap."

In her mind Barbara heard Joe Wenzel's mocking question: "What did you do with their hats?"

Frank had been quietly listening, but now he spoke. "I believe, as my daughter does, that Carrie is in danger, but I also believe my daughter is, too, and that she will be until that whole crew is locked up. That tape isn't conclusive, as we all know. It's corroborative at the most. Your investigation is going to be involved and it will take a long time." He looked at Hoggarth. "I suggest you get them for a more immediate crime while the investigation proceeds."

"You mean Joe Wenzel, don't you? Frank, they all have airtight alibis. That was the first thing homicide looked into. Give me something to go on, for Christ's sake."

Barbara responded before Frank had a chance. "They decided to kill him last summer. He was a healthy man and could have lived another twenty years or longer, and he was not going to ease up on his demands. Meanwhile, two sons were coming along also wanting corporate executive paychecks. They had to get rid of him. First they burned the house. They had to make sure that whatever tapes he had in the house were destroyed. Also, they got the key to his safe-deposit box and probably the gun at the same time before they set the fire. They knew they would be suspected of his murder, and they planned alibis right down the line. Then Carrie came along and must have seemed a godsend, someone easily framed. Nora bought the wig. Find out where Luther was on Friday before the murder. I suspect it was his job to keep Joe out of the way long enough for Larry to impersonate him and get to his safe-deposit box for any other tapes. I don't know how they got his driver's license, maybe Luther swiped it. The cash wasn't important, just another bit to add to the frame-up of Carrie. Greg's job was to have a good alibi for the pertinent times, and then get to the motel to pick up the killer. A few hairs in the motel room, a few white and black fibers, her fingerprints on a glass, make sure someone saw a person dressed like her and wearing the wig enter the motel room. They were all set. It would have been a snap for any one of them to pick up the glass ahead of time. They thought of everything."

"And where the hell did the killer hang out waiting for Greg? Walking up and down the parking lot?"

She shook her head impatiently. "In the empty room that Greg has a key for. Go in there, get dressed, ring Joe Wenzel's doorbell and get admitted. Joe was already dead by the time that person was seen standing at the open door. Plant the incriminating evidence, then go back to that empty room and wait for a ride."

Hoggarth looked disbelieving.

"Look," she said, "review Carrie's statement about what Joe said to her as she was walking to her car. It sounds as though he fully expected her to go along with him, and he was sore because she wouldn't. I suspect Nora called him earlier, pretending to be Carrie. If she whispered something to make him believe Carrie would play along later, he would have opened the door. Look out the peephole, see a white blouse, face turned away but with long black hair showing, that's all it would have taken."

"A family conspiracy," Hoggarth said in disgust. "Without a shred of proof. Right, I'll haul them all in."

"So get the proof," she said with a shrug. "Fingerprint the whole gang and see if you get any matches from that tankless heater they put in my building." Then she added, "Hoggarth, Greg's the weak link. And he's frightened. Start asking Mattie Thorne's neighbors if they saw a car leaving at around two-thirty in the morning." She looked at her watch. "I'm afraid I have to excuse myself at this point, gentlemen. I'm due back in court very soon."

"The three of us can continue in my office," Hoggarth said. "And I'll want to talk to you a little later," he said to Barbara. His voice was not friendly.

They shook hands all around and when they left, Diebold had the map and Romero had the copy of the tape. Frank turned to Barbara as soon as they were alone. "What the devil are you up to now?"

"A hunch, Dad. Just a hunch. You don't want to know." She stretched. "Let's send Bailey for Shelley and Carrie, and let him swing by here for us. No point in wading through reporters at the house if we don't have to. We'll go to court, the jury will say they don't have a verdict yet, and we'll go home again. I'd just as soon stay here a bit longer."

"That judge won't let them go more than another day," Frank said. "Too close to Christmas. Tomorrow we'll know one way or the other."

"Hung," she said. "That's what we'll know."

41

It happened exactly the way Barbara had predicted, and back in the house again, she sipped wine and grinned as Herbert related how Morgan had ripped the pants nearly all the way off a photographer who had tried to come over the back fence. "He's a good old dog, that Morgan," Herbert said. "And them photographers don't have the sense of a flea. I told them and told them, but they don't hear, and if they hear they don't believe."

Carrie was more strained than ever, and Louise was showing the same signs of tension. Waiting was the hard part, Barbara reassured them both, but it would soon be over.

"And then a new trial," Carrie said. "We're planning an escape, Aunt Louise and I. We have it all worked out." She attempted a smile but it was a poor effort.

The next morning the judge beckoned Barbara and Mahoney to the bench. "If they can't decide by three," he said,

"I'm releasing them. They know something's up, all this crowd in the courtroom every day, and shopping to do, it's making them nervous and sore. They're snapping at one another like a bunch of turtles. Be back at three."

He looked and sounded as sore as he said the jurors were. As they walked back to their tables, Mahoney glanced at Barbara and started to say something, then clamped his lips, and they both took their places and listened to the judge announce that court would be in recess.

They made their way through the reporters and photographers on the way out, and a few minutes before three did it again on their way in.

The jury filed in, the judge took his seat, and he asked the foreman if they had arrived at a verdict and was told no.

"Will the jurors be able to reconcile their differences?" he asked, and the foreman said no. He dismissed them and declared the trial a mistrial.

Barbara had asked Shelley to be watchful, to hang on to Carrie when the verdict came in, just in case, and Shelley was there, but Carrie couldn't repress a low moan, and she turned as white as a living person could get. She clung to the edge of the defense table. Run away, no matter what Barbara had said. Run. Hide. Kill herself. Anything except six more months of fear, another trial, imprisonment for six more months. She swayed, then steadied as Shelley grasped her arm and she felt Mr. Holloway's hand, warm and firm, on her shoulder.

Barbara felt a cold dread surge through her. Even anticipating it did not lessen the reality of a hung jury, another trial, a failed defense, a client at more risk than ever since now the prosecution knew what path her defense would take....

Judge Laughton nodded toward her table, toward Carrie, and said stiffly, "Ms. Frederick, you are free to go." He rose and left the bench as if the aftermath of his words were of no concern to him, as if he didn't know that his was a meaningless statement, since the prosecution could immediately rearrest Carrie and call for a new trial.

The courtroom erupted as the jurors left the jury box; some of them headed for the defense table, others fled; reporters surged into the courtroom with flashbulbs popping, bright lights flashing.

Carrie's stomach spasmed when she saw Mahoney pushing his way through a crowd toward her and Barbara. She clutched Barbara's arm.

"Good job, Counselor," Mahoney said, shaking Barbara's hand. "The district attorney's office is dropping all charges against your client." He nodded to Carrie, turned and elbowed his way through even more people. "We'll take questions in the corridor," he kept saying.

Carrie looked stunned, her hand on Barbara's arm shook violently, and color flared on her cheeks, drained away. "Does that mean they aren't going to try me again?" she whispered, disbelieving.

"Sure does," Barbara said and embraced her. Carrie was shaking as if with a seizure.

Some of the jurors were drawing near them, and some reporters who had rushed into the courtroom were cornering any juror they could get near, in spite of the bailiff who was trying to restrain them. Most of them, some with microphones, were pushing their way toward Barbara's table intent at getting to Carrie, the mystery child who had been resurrected. Then Hoggarth was at Barbara's side.

"We'll go out through the back way," he said, motioning a uniformed officer to come along. The bailiff led them out through the maze of halls to a rear exit. "I'm sending you home in a police car," Hoggarth said. "I'll flag down Bailey and come with him in a few minutes. We have some arrangements to make."

Carrie held her tears until they entered the house and she saw Louise, then she wept. "I'm sorry," she said, laughing and weeping. "I'm free, but I can't seem to stop crying."

"They aren't going to try her again," Barbara told Louise. "All charges are being dropped." Louise looked as near tears as Carrie was, and they both went into the living room. "Lt. Hoggarth's coming along with Bailey," Barbara said to Herbert. "Don't let Morgan tear off his pants, okay?"

He grinned his big grin. "Now wouldn't that be a sight. A homicide detective getting chewed up by a guard dog."

When Hoggarth arrived and was introduced to Morgan, he shook his head. "Mountain lions and a dragon. You keep funny pets."

They went into Frank's study, and this time Shelley was with them.

"Thank you, Lieutenant," Barbara said when they were seated. She had wine, the others were drinking coffee. She felt that she had earned wine, and she had been drinking so much coffee she was afloat. "I said you'd be the one to see to it that no new trial will happen."

He grimaced. "We had a conference, Diebold, Romero, the district attorney, a couple of others. It's a can of worms."

"Box," Barbara said and took a sip. "Box of worms."

He gave her a suspicious look and Frank grinned and

leaned back in his chair. Frank's little composting worms were kept in a box on the back porch.

"It's a mixed bag," Hoggarth said. "Mexican nationals killed in California, three murders in Oregon." He was eyeing the wine longingly. "What will Ms. Frye do now? Where is she going? I'll make sure police protection is in place before she leaves here."

"I imagine she'll want to go to her aunt's house. And in a few days I hope she'll have a passport and then take off for distant shores."

"After she gives us a statement," he said quickly.

She nodded. "If she's willing, and after she gets a little rest."

He watched her take another sip of wine, sighed, and drank more of his coffee. "The two uniforms who brought you home will take her wherever she wants to go and they'll hang around until we get a plainclothes man on her. And we want the original of that tape."

"When I know Carrie's on an airplane heading out," she said. "I'll hold on to it until then."

His lips tightened, but he held whatever comment he wanted to make. "You'll call us when we can talk to her? Soon, I hope. Our Mexican friend doesn't like our weather. He wants to go back south."

"A couple of days," she said.

He put his cup down and stood up. "That's it for now. Funny thing, though. The word's out that all charges have been dropped and the case is being reinvestigated. And someone let it slip that we're asking questions about Greg Wenzel's timetable for the night of the murder. Reporters got wind of it, asking questions. You can't keep a secret in this town." He shook his head. "I'll be in touch."

Frank went out with him and Barbara finished her wine. "You want to go on home, or sit in on my talk with Carrie?" she asked Shelley. "I have to tell her all about it."

"I'll hang out with you," Shelley said.

"Okay. Let's do it. They're in the living room."

After she told Carrie all she knew about the deaths of her parents, and the death of Joe Wenzel, she said, "You're free to do whatever you want now. The police want a statement, and it's your decision. Also, you can talk to the reporters, or keep them away." Carrie shook her head. No reporters. "You'll have police protection around the clock, and in a few days I expect you'll have a passport, and then the world's wide open for you."

"Hamburg," Louise said. "We'll both go. I'll see to the tickets."

"Good. You're welcome to stay here, of course, or you can go to your aunt's house, whatever you want to do."

"The house with a thousand rooms," Carrie said. She looked at Louise. "Can we go there?"

"I can't think of a better place."

"I'll be in touch," Barbara said, "and you have my number if you want me for anything. Call me when you decide about giving the statement to the investigators. If you do, I'll be there. Did you see a license number?"

"No. I was just looking at the man I thought was a king."

"Carrie, there's something else that needs saying. You said you've been running away from it all your life, but you have to ask yourself if you were running away from it, or searching for a way back to it in order to right a terrible wrong. You have nothing to feel guilty about. You were such a small child, and now you and another brave woman in Mexico have both come forward, and you'll be the ones who will bring them down. Two brave women who had to tell the truth. Remember that when you start blaming yourself again."

They stood up and Carrie gave Barbara a long, searching look. "I'll never forget you," she said. "I can't repay you in any way, I know that. But I'll never forget you."

They packed their things from the upstairs bedroom, and Herbert walked out to the police car with them. When the car left, the media cars and vans followed.

It was five o'clock and already dark and foggy again. Another typical December night, Barbara thought, watching the vanishing taillights. "You might as well take off, too," she said to Shelley when Herbert came in.

"I'm ready when you are," Bailey said to Shelley. "Do you want me to call off my guy at her house?" he asked Barbara.

"After tonight," she said. "And Alan too."

"Do I get my walking papers now?" Herbert asked in a mournful tone.

"A couple more days," Barbara said. "Why, do you have a big date or something coming up?"

He grinned. "Nope. A new recipe I want to try out on your dad. But it takes time. A couple of days will do it."

She went to the kitchen and poured another glass of wine and in a moment Frank joined her. "You still look keyed up," he said. "Usually along about now the adrenaline's gone, the system says is that all, and you sort of poop out."

"I don't think it's quite over yet," she said. "We'll see."

At the stove Herbert was stirring something in a pot. Without looking at her he said, "Barbara, my old pal Darren's been calling every day, just to see how you are, like that. He didn't want me to mention it and, dang, there it slipped out. He asked me to call him when the coast is clear. Reckon I can give him a call?"

"No," she said. "Don't you dare." She walked from the kitchen.

Frank scowled at Herbert. "You're going to wear out that spoon or the pot." He went to his study and gazed at the wine-glass Barbara had left there earlier, and he cursed under his breath.

At seven-thirty, as Herbert was setting the table, Morgan barked once, and a moment later the doorbell rang. Herbert opened the door and Hoggarth stormed in.

"Where is she? And muzzle that monster dog."

Barbara came down the stairs as Frank emerged from his study. "What happened?" Frank asked.

Hoggarth was looking at Barbara with a mean and bitter gaze. "You were playing them off against each other. You've been talking to them from the start, not the fucking jury. You knew something like this would happen, didn't you? Larry Wenzel's been shot dead, and Nora Wenzel said a stranger did it."

"For God's sake," Frank said. "Tell us something."

"I am. She says a guy came to the house and Larry Wenzel took him to his study, and they began yelling at each other about more money. Then she heard a shot and went running to see what was going on and the guy slugged her in passing and took off."

"Did you happen to have anyone watching the house?" Barbara asked from the bottom of the stairs.

"Happens I did," he snapped. "No strange car drove in and left in a hurry. She came to and called the cops and they found her husband dead."

"And no doubt Luther was home with his wife and a few other people, while Greg happened to be somewhere else with a bunch of other people," she said. "How about that?"

He looked at her with murder in his eyes. "You planned it all. You knew she'd turn on him, didn't you?"

"She killed Joe," Barbara said. "Greg took her to the motel and she called her daughter-in-law from that room at eleven, and then waited until she reasoned that Joe was alone. She knocked on his door, went in and shot him. She stood outside his door laughing with a dead man until she was sure someone saw her enter. He was already dead by then. Then she waited for Greg to pick her up again at three. I told you he was the weak link. He'll break and tell you all about it. No hit man. No stranger. Just another little bit of family business."

"Why her husband now all of a sudden?"

"Not all of a sudden. She's crazy about her sons, and she once said sincerely that she wished Larry would fall into the river and never surface again. She'll try to lay it all on him now that he's gone. She probably has a neat story all prepared. She's protecting her child, Hoggarth. You were going after him. Mother love. Something like that."

He narrowed his eyes and said, "You're going to cross that line and wander too far from it to get back, and so help me, I want to be there when it happens." He wheeled about and left.

Frank faced her with a distant, bleak expression, and she said, "Now it's over. Two down, the others will fall." Her own expression, as bleak as his, was implacable. She started back up the stairs, paused, and looked at Herbert in the doorway. "Now you can call Darren and tell him the coast is clear."

Turn the page to read an excerpt from
THE PRICE OF SILENCE
the exciting new thriller from Kate Wilhelm, *available now in hardcover from* MIRA Books.

Todd drove into the parking lot behind her town-house apartment building that sweltering afternoon in August and braced herself for the next few minutes. She knew Barney was already home; she had spotted his truck parked back in the separate section reserved for oversize vehicles. He would greet her, hope lightening his face, and she would shake her head. Then he would try to cheer her up. They spent a great deal of time trying to cheer each other up these days, and that was about as futile as her going out for yet another job interview.

Overqualified, today's idiot had said; they could start her at nine dollars an hour at best. But, he had added with the perfected personnel director's smile she had come to loathe, they would keep her résumé on file for a possible future opening.

She pulled away from the back of the seat, where her blouse was plastered to the leather. Neither of them was using air-conditioning, not in the car and truck, not in the apartment. Trudging up the flight of stairs to their apartment, she drew in a deep breath and straightened her back, ready to smile and wave away the disappointing interview as inconsequential, just like the others.

The apartment was as hot as outside, the only sound was that of a whirring fan. She took off her shoes and, carrying them, walked to the door of the second bedroom, Barney's studio. He had fallen asleep in a chair, his notebook and pen on the floor, a book on his chest. With his curly hair stuck to his forehead with sweat, he looked like a little boy worn out from softball practice.

"It isn't fair," she whispered, backing away from the door. Barney had worked his way through college, taking summer jobs, odd jobs, whatever he could find, and now, with his dissertation to write in the next two years, they were two weeks away from real desperation. In two weeks her unemployment would run out, and they couldn't survive on Barney's job in a book distributor's warehouse—exhausting work that paid very little and left him too tired to work on the dissertation when he came home.

It wasn't fair, she thought again, as she went through the spacious and beautiful apartment to the master bedroom. There were scant furnishings, not because they had been unwilling or unable to buy furniture, but because neither of them had wanted to take the time to shop. A bed, a chest of drawers, a few other pieces from Goodwill that they had bought when they first married three years earlier. Now she was more than grateful that they were such poor shoppers. What few new pieces they had acquired had gone on credit cards—an overpriced sofa, a good chair, Barney's desk.... She could admit that they had been like kids in a candy store with a dollar to spend, buying on impulse with no thought of tomorrow.

When they rented the town house, sixteen months earlier, they had given little heed to the price. Her job had paid too well to consider cost. They had bought her Acura and his truck, and now owed more on both than they could realize by selling them. In February her company had been taken over, and she had not worked since.

But they had a great view of Mount Hood, she thought, eyeing it out the bedroom window as she stripped off her sodden interview clothes, and put on shorts and a tank top. Silent with feet bare, she wandered out to the kitchen to make iced tea. Barney had brought in the mail and she glanced at it listlessly as she waited for the water to boil. Bills, pleas for money, offers for credit cards... She picked up an envelope addressed to G. Todd Fielding, the name she used on her résumés, and frowned at the return address: *The Brindle Times*. From Brindle, Oregon.

"Where the hell is Brindle, Oregon?" she muttered, opening the envelope. She had sent her last résumé to a box number. She sat down at the kitchen table and read the enclosed letter, then read it again.

"The person we are looking for must have editorial skills, computer skills and the ability to lay out a newspaper as well as periodicals. From your résumé and the journal you submitted it appears that you have the necessary skills. You would have to relocate, however. If you are interested, call any afternoon and we can arrange for a telephone interview."

The letter practically quoted her own résumé, she thought in wonder. That was exactly the kind of work she had done for nearly three years. Her hand was shaking as she reached for the telephone, but she drew back. *Where the hell was Brindle?*

She located the town on the state road map, and had to fight back tears. On the other side of the mountains, south of Bend. Barney had to teach two classes during the coming year. It was bad enough to have to drive from Portland to Corvallis, as he had been doing this past year, but across the mountains?

She finished making tea, then sat and read the letter one more time. It *was* her job, she thought, exactly right for her, made to order for her.

She considered the alternatives. She could not support them on the kind of money she had been offered in her job search. If Barney had to work even part-time while teaching his classes, he would not be able to finish the dissertation in the next two years. His adviser would retire, and, university politics being what they were, he might be stranded.

They had already cut frills, everything that could be cut, and were still left with car payments, student loans, health insurance, rent, utilities, food. They could not afford the town house, but neither could they afford to move with first and last months' rent payable in advance, plus a cleaning deposit. She knew to the penny how much they had to have each month, and even if both of them worked at entry-level jobs they probably couldn't make it.

All right, she thought angrily, don't go down that road again. She had traveled it so often, she could do it sound asleep, and frequently did. No more recriminations about past stupidity, she and Barney had agreed, think alternatives instead.

If Barney could arrange his two classes for consecutive days, go over one day, come back the next… One long commute a week… He could stay in a motel one night a week… Have the rest of the week free… What he needed was access to a library—their apartment was crammed with the library books he needed for his research—and time. A lot of time without exhaustion from menial labor and, more important, without worry about money.

She picked up the letter and went to the bedroom, closed the door softly, then sat on the edge of the bed and dialed.

* * *

In the office of *The Brindle Times*, Johnny Colonna was glaring at his mother, who was holding the weekly edition of the newspaper and shaking it furiously.

"It's a shambles, a mess, a loathsome unholy mess!" she said again. "I won't have it, Johnny. I'm telling you, I won't have it! I'll shut down before I let a mess like this go out again!"

He looked relieved when the phone rang. "Yes," he snapped. "Who?" He held his hand over the mouthpiece. "It's that woman, Fielding, the one who sent her résumé last week."

"Tell her we'll call back in five minutes. And I'll do the talking."

He repeated the message and hung up. "Mother, I thought we decided on Stan Beacham. Why bother talking to this one?"

"I haven't decided on anyone," she said. "That man's a twit. He'd stay just as long as it took to find something better. And he doesn't know any more about computers than you do. I'll get her résumé and make the call in here."

Ignoring the sullen look that crossed her son's face, Ruth Ann marched from his office, crossed the outer office to her own and picked up Todd Fielding's folder. None of the three women in the outer office dared glance at her on her first trip across their space, nor on her return. When Ruth Ann was in a snit, it was best to look very busy.

Ruth Ann was eighty, and from the time of her father's death when she was twenty-one, she had published, edited and, for much of the time, written every word in the newspaper. And, she had decided that morning, reading the latest edition, she would be damned if she would see it become a piece of crap. *Crap,* she repeated to herself. That was what it was turning into. Ungrammatical, words misspelled, one story cut off in midsection, strings of gibberish… Crap!

She placed the call herself, seated at Johnny's desk, while he took up a stance of martyrdom at the window. He blamed it all on the computer system he had installed the previous year. They would get the hang of it, he had said more than once. It just took time. Everyone knew it took time. Well, time had just run out, she thought as Todd Fielding answered the phone on the first ring.

"Ms. Fielding, my name is Ruth Ann Colonna and I'm the publisher of *The Brindle Times*. I was quite impressed by your résumé. And by the quality of the trade journal you provided. I have to tell you up front that we could not pay you the kind of salary you were receiving previously, however, there is a house available rent-free through another party, therefore not to be considered part of your pay package. You would be responsible for property taxes and insurance, roughly a thousand or a little more annually. We offer excellent health benefits."

Ruth Ann watched Johnny stiffen, wheel about and shake his head. She ignored him. "I'd like to ask you a few questions about the journal," she said.

It was a long interview. Ruth Ann asked questions, and Todd answered in a straightforward way. When Ruth Ann asked what Barney's dissertation was, Todd said, "The Cultural, Political and Religious Movements that Account for the Fluctuations in the Ascendancy of Rationalistic Belief Systems."

Ruth Ann laughed. "My God! That's a mouthful. A philosopher, for goodness sake! I didn't know anyone studied philosophy these days."

When Ruth Ann finally hung up, she regarded Johnny thoughtfully. "She'll do," she said.

"Mother, be reasonable. You can't hire someone you never

even met on the basis of a phone call. And whose house are you offering a stranger?"

"As for the first part, I believe I just did," Ruth Ann said. "And the house is Mattie and Hal Tilden's. Mattie begged me to put someone in it. Their insurance has quadrupled since it's been empty, and she knows an empty house invites trouble. But you're right about strangers. The Fieldings will come over on Friday to meet in person. And, Johnny, I suppose you haven't even glanced at that journal, or paid much attention to her résumé. I suggest you look them over carefully. She's had art training, and studied all sorts of computer technology, software and hardware, whatever that means. You don't know a pixel from a pixie, and neither do I, but she does. She can edit, and she's a good writer. She has excellent recommendations. If you take the press in the direction you're thinking of, you'll need someone just like her."

She walked to the door, paused and said, "I want to see every word, every paragraph, every ad on paper before you go to press next week. Every goddamn word."

In her bedroom Todd disconnected and carefully put the phone down on the bed. She stood up, flung her hands in the air and screamed a Tarzan yell of triumph, then raced from the room, only to meet Barney in the hall. He looked sleep-dazed and bewildered.

"What's wrong? Are you okay?"

"It's going to work! I've got a job! Oh, God, you're wearing too many clothes!" She began to pull at his shirt. "We need to celebrate! Right now!" Giving up on his shirt, she yanked off her tank top, and started to wriggle out of her shorts.